'An extraordinary work of sustained intensity ...'

Ian McFarlane, *Canberra Times*

'... a brilliant achievement ... As this rich and credible exploration into the psyche of a "battered woman" unfolds, the author's considerable powers become increasingly apparent. Indeed, *The Bone Flute* is almost flawless ... This achingly sad book glimmers with Bourke's deep empathy. Her capacity to write provocatively, even beautifully, about pain is reminiscent of Jeanette Winterson.'

Ceridwen Spark, *Sydney Morning Herald*

'A poetic and poignant novel which draws the reader into the psychological maelstrom caused by domestic abuse.'

The Gold Coast Bulletin

'Thanks to Bourke's beautifully crafted prose the novel reads as a sobering story of survival in spite of the disturbing nature of much of the subject matter ... In its delicate treatment of distressing themes combined with its lyrical statement on the power of music and memory *The Bone Flute* is an impressive debut novel.'

Wendy Davis, *Idiom 23*

'The lyrical prose balances the dark subject matter of incest, abuse and dysfunctional family love, and compels the reader to lift the carpet of the mind and think about the sad dust of contemporary Australian life.'

Jill Watkinson, author of *The Architect*

'Bourke has dealt sensitively with powerful subject matter ... the contrasting softness and harshness of her writing coalesce to form a promising talent.'

Bronwyn Rivers, *Australian Book Review*

The Bone Flute

Nike Sulway (née Bourke) won the Queensland Premier's Award for *The Bone Flute* in 2000. Since then she has published the novels *The True Green of Hope* (UQP, 2005), *Rupetta* (Tartarus Press, 2013), and *Dying in the First Person* (Transit Lounge, 2016), as well as the children's picture book *What The Sky Knows* (illustrated by Stella Danalis) (UQP, 2009). Her works have won or been shortlisted for a range of national and international awards, including the Queensland Premier's Literary Award, the Commonwealth Writers Prize, the Children's Book Council of Australia's Book of the Year Award, the IAFA Crawford Award, an Aurealis Award, the Norma K. Hemming Award, and the James Tiptree Jr. Literary Award.

n. a. bourke

The
Bone
Flute

UQP

First published 2001 by University of Queensland Press
Box 6042, St Lucia, Queensland 4067 Australia
New edition 2004
Reprinted 2017

www.uqp.uq.edu.au

Typeset by University of Queensland Press
Printed in Australia by McPherson's Printing Group

 This project has been assisted by
the Commonwealth Government through
the Australia Council, its arts funding
and advisory body.

 Sponsored by the Queensland Office
of Arts and Cultural Development.

Cataloguing in Publication Data
National Library of Australia

Bourke, Nicole A.
  The bone flute.

  1. Family violence — Fiction. 2. Women — Violence against —
  Fiction. 3. Drug abuse — Fiction. 4. Incest — Fiction.
  5. Death — Fiction. I. Title.

A823.4

ISBN 978 0 7022 3446 0

For my mother

The link of music with cannibalism is a sublime paradox.
When the music of the bone flute opens the doors, absences
   flow in.

— Wilson Harris

Inside the van the rusted roof is perforated by sunlight. The annexe is also riddled with tiny holes, the canvas mildewed and dusty, sometimes puckered and sometimes flat, pierced with light. The fabric is stretched tight where the poles lean out; it curves down between them in lazy scallops. The sun spreads strange constellations on my palm, they bounce and shudder; spill on my dress, on my thighs, on the flattened ground. My dirt-black feet are decorated with freckles of light as I sit on the step of the van. I turn up my palm and reach to catch them. I watch them collect like tiny stars. The metal is warm, almost burning behind my knees as I look out at the blistered day. I squint. The horizon wavers, irresolute.

I bring the flute to my chin. It is heavy with the memory of Sara's scent; when I begin to blow across the mouth-hole my breath is tangled in the perfume of her. She always fought me — in my body, in my dreams, in my past. My throat aches with the strain of breathing into her *just so*. This much and no more. I never understood how to love carefully, gently. She resisted me. Still resists me. It is as if she wants to remain silent. I move my lips against her slippery curve and blow gently, feeling my breath swell in her hollows.

I cannot feel her breathing. Her empty bones reproach me. Her silence mocks me, taunts me with what we cannot speak, cannot say. I am not God. I am not the fairy queen. I cannot change the world and everything in it. Instead, I sit here breathing into her. Sounds to hollow out the world.

It is an alto flute with a deeply resonant sound, a kind of soft complaint. The first flute I owned was a handmade thing — not elegant and thin. Like this one its pipes were thick, its hollows roughly bored. This is not a gossipy soprano, or a serious and self-indulgent bass. It is a simple transverse flute constructed of four pieces: the head, two central pieces and the foot. The head extends almost two-fifths of the length of the whole instrument. The second piece carries the mouth-hole. The third piece has three finger holes and the foot carries four, each pitched a fifth apart. The foot terminates in an elongated egg shape. A single silver key is the one thing I saved from my mother's flute. It is laid against the end, carried by a slot cut into a small ring.

She produces a simple order of music, although with the use of forked fingering she will produce just over two octaves in the beautiful, if mournful, scale of D. She is not constructed of bold shining metal but almost translucent bone, so new that it has not yet started to yellow. My daughter's flesh has been pared away to reveal the shining bones beneath. When the notes come, when they slide through her spare cylinders, her voice is plaintive. I feel the blood turn in my veins and have difficulty holding my breath steady as her notes slip together and scale the burning air.

The longer I play the warmer the hollows become. Looser somehow, as if through use her throat learns the structures of sound. I start to feel the breath gesturing, drawing my fingers, sending long threads of air through holes and tunnels. As I close my eyes I feel the timbre shift and I begin to rock with remembrance. I have played these notes before and each one brings back the scent of hours spent in other places. Of weeks and years spent pushing my shoulders against the skin of the world.

I begin to sweat. The sticky indecisive sweat that comes from remembering when I do not want to. When I sleep the memories creep in next to me, wrinkle the sheets, remind me of things long gone that should have been forgotten. Things I am trying to forget. I wake with light burning through the thin curtains, through my skin, through my dreams. I wake and listen to my heart beating in every vein. Feel my fists clenched tight. I drive and drive and drive and drive. Just to have something to do. Somewhere to be. Not to be sitting here with nothing to do but remember.

I used to pity old people; those shuffling unsure strangers who had lost their memories and spent hours checking behind bureaus and in empty cupboards trying to remember just what it was they had lost. Now I can imagine nothing sweeter. I want to forget — to speak with an innocent tongue. If I spoke, my voice would shimmer in my mouth. My words would waver and grow indiscreet, wrinkling the air like heat. If I speak, I can only speak against the faces, the people, I remember. I can only speak against memory. Better to let the notes drift. Better to have memories suspended in hollow sounds that stretch and fade. Better to forget altogether that I have nothing to give and nothing to be taken away.

But still, the fates will leave me my voice,
And by my voice I shall be known

— Ovid, *Metamorphosis*

This is the sound of what cannot be remembered, what cannot be sung. This is the sound of the first house I lived in. It sits wrapped in screens and porches. A few trees, a tangle of brush along one side, dark stairs leading down into a bowl of dust and scorched grass. Pots of flowering geraniums along the verandah. A pale curtain bulging from my bedroom window. In my memories there is always a man and a woman standing at the bottom of the stairs. His firmly knuckled fist curled over hers. This is the house of their secret life. The public secret of their life before mine. The insincere memories I have been taught and which I can recite like storybook poetry.

This is the sound of morning, with its indecision and promise. The heat breaking like yolk over the soil, cracking the tin roof until I wake in my mother's bed. In my father's arms. The sound of his breathing, heavy with grief and alcohol, and his rough skin catching on the linen sheets.

This is the sound of the morning after my mother's funeral when I woke early, ashamed that I had slept at all. My mother was dead. My father lay sleeping beside me, his face crumpled and soft, grey in the uncertain light. His arm lay over my stomach, his hand curled around my ribs. I could feel his breath on my cheek. I crunched my toes together and wriggled them around in circles. I put one hand on his and tried to lift his arm. He half-turned his head and smiled, nuzzling closer, his mouth half-open against my shoulder. I held my breath. I don't remember if it was then or later that it began. I remember that he held me, and that I wanted him to; that I desperately wanted to feel warm and safe, loved and needed.

The morning of the funeral I fought viciously with my father. He was sitting in my mother's chair and pulled me up onto his lap and put his arms around me. He cried into my clean dress, his sobs shaking me as his hands moved over me. I sat still and stiff as long as I could, my own hands fisted in my skirts, but in the end I darted from his lap. He blindly clutched for me, slipping to the floor; calling me by her name. He half-crawled towards me, grabbed at the hem of my dress, trying to pull me down into his arms. I hurled my glass of cordial at him. It spun through the air and bounced onto Mother's chair, the colour spreading deeply into the cream upholstery.

I ran to my room and lay on the floor under my bed until the guests arrived. They came at different times all through the day, until our yard was filled with their cars and the house echoed with the sound of them whispering discreetly to each other. Even a funeral was a chance to catch up, a chance to exchange gossip and recipes. How I hated them, those small people who had eyed my mother like some exotic creature in a travelling circus. They seemed to relish the chance to see inside her home, to wipe their fingers over her dusty shelves and picture frames, to take liberties they would never have taken had she been there.

We held the ceremony late in the afternoon, when it was cooler, and everyone had gathered at the house. We buried her beneath a tree not far from the house. Afterwards, at the wake, my father was silent. People whispered to him. Our counters and tables creaked beneath the weight of casseroles in Corning Ware dishes. Plump scones lay steaming on a yellow plate. I sat on my mother's chair. My skirt spread wide to cover the stain. People moved around me, they frowned and fretted over his silence and my peculiarities. They decided it was only to be expected. She had been such a strange creature, no aprons in the kitchen, no gossip, always barefoot, always humming or singing, too young. Too wet. It was indecent — to see her raising a young girl with no understanding of the ways the country demanded, of the practicalities. She would never have lasted out here for long.

'It's for the best,' someone said.

'She would have left him to go back to the city sooner or later.'

'It would have been better for him if she had.'

The women stood with teacups balanced on their palms. One of them was near my mother's music stand. She reached down and turned the pages, her fingertips trailing cake crumbs. No one ever touched my mother's music. Not even Father. I itched to stand and walk across the room and grab the woman's hand and tell her to stop. *That*, I would say as carefully and clearly as possible, *is my mother's and I will thank you not to touch*. I fidgeted in my seat, my thighs sticky and sweet with sweat and cordial. I watched her fat hands grubbing at the music.

I curled my fists as tight as I could, twisting them into my skirts. I could feel the springs beneath me, the thin layer of wadding and fabric moulded to each circle. I closed my eyes and willed the woman to stop. *Stay still*, I said to myself. Over and over and over. I stayed where I was, glued to my mother's chair by the fear that my tantrum would be discovered. That they would see the stain and it would prove somehow that they were right about my mother. I was determined that they would never be right about us. I spent four hours with my fist twisted into my skirt so that it would not fall away and reveal me, feeling the sticky dampness spread across the backs of my legs. The stain seeping deeply into the cloth.

That night I lay in my bed crying and when he came in I'm sure that it was out of simple fatherly concern. I sat up and reached to put my arms around him. I could smell his clean skin, the half-buried scent of soil beneath his after-shave, his surprisingly soft hair. When he began to cry I felt his tears soak through my nightgown onto my chest. It felt oddly powerful to be comforting my father, to be holding him. I don't remember being afraid as he put his arms around me and pulled me down beside him. Looking back, I guess I should have been. I know that as the years passed I understood it was wrong, that it was a secret no one wanted to hear. My father, my brother and I were all careful not to admit anything was going on. Callum is only a year older than I am so I guess that at first, like me, he didn't really know what was happening.

The flying doctor service came to our town when I was about eight — maybe nine. They set up a makeshift surgery in a room at the back of the pub and people came all day to see them; the young men who worked on the properties, some of the local Aboriginal people, a family who had driven all night to get there from their home. Dr Paul nearly fell out of the plane when it landed. I had only seen him once or twice before and each time he was drunk. By mid-morning he was snoring in a day bed on the verandah while the young nurse attended to all the patients. I stayed to help her, handing her needles and swabs and bandages, making tea, showing each patient into the room. Tommy Bowls had an ulcer on the back of his leg that she cut open with a scalpel and drained into a metal dish. Melly Trap had cut her hand. All the Swale children needed immunisations. They sat wide-eyed and silent in a row on the trestle table as Carol, the nurse, jabbed each of their skinny, brown arms. By the end of the day we were all tired. I made tea and Carol and I went to sit on the verandah to drink it. She shook her head as we passed Dr Paul still sleeping open-mouthed with a hand on his chest. 'Useless old bastard,' she muttered, 'I don't know why he bothers coming.' She smiled down at me. 'About time I checked you over.' I nodded sheepishly as I sat down. 'We'll finish this wonderful tea first, eh?'

When we went inside she lifted me up onto the table and looked into my eyes. She listened to my heart and banged on my scabbed knees with a rubber hammer. 'No problems?' I shook my head. 'You look all right to me,' she said.

'I'm a princess,' I said.

'Are you now?'

'Yes. Just like in all the stories. My real mother is dead and now I just have to wait and he'll come and rescue me.'

'He will, will he?'

'Do you think it matters that I don't have a wicked stepmother for him to save me from?'

'I'm sure he'll understand.'

'Callum says there's no such thing as being rescued any more. He says Mother just died for no reason.'

Carol didn't say anything. I realise now that she, like most adults, was largely silent in the face of death. That despite what I thought then she was probably only young, in her early twenties, and didn't know what to say to a little girl with a dead mother. For a long time I don't think anyone knew what to say, except Father. His grief was so deep and horrifying that, as he curled around me at night, I was more afraid of his tears than I was of her death.

'It doesn't matter,' I said, 'I'm going to marry Daddy when I grow up anyway.'

She laughed, 'Are you now?'

'Yes, and we'll move our bed into the big room and I'll cook pancakes for dinner every night.' Carol looked at me strangely and I began to squirm.

'Whose bed?'

'Mine and Daddy's. We sleep in my room now, but when we're married we'll move into the big room. He promised.'

She frowned. I smiled uncertainly, not knowing what it was she had heard or seen. I was anxious. She was one of the only young women I knew and I wanted her to like me. I wanted her to see that I was not a country girl like those women who had gossiped about my mother, that I was as smart as a city girl underneath. Sophisticated, intelligent, special. She looked at me oddly and I bit my lip, worried that I'd said something wrong, but I didn't know what it was I'd said or how to take it back. As I looked towards the door I saw Callum loitering outside. 'Can I go now?' I said. 'My brother's here.'

She nodded and I jumped down from the table, pushing past her to run after Callum, skidding on the wooden floors. When I caught up to him he punched me in the arm and I wrestled him to the floor.

'Did she give you any needles?' he asked.

I shook my head. 'I think I said something wrong, though.'

'It's a checkup not a maths test, stupid.'

I shrugged and he wriggled away from me, dashing out into the street. I ran after him, my bare feet sending up little clouds of red dust. I couldn't find him anywhere, then I spun around just in time to see his thin legs disappear under the verandah. He turned back and waved at me to follow him. He was hunched down in the dirt, panting and grinning. As I reached him he put a finger to his mouth and pointed to the floor above us. 'Dad,' he mouthed at me and grabbed my hand, pulling me down out of sight. As I hunkered down beside him I could hear my father's boots and Carol's soft-soled shoes.

'Does she sleep with you all the time?' I heard Carol saying.

'It's been hard on her since her mother died.'

'How often?' she insisted.

'I don't know. A lot, I guess.'

'It's been years since her mother died. She can't just keep sleeping in your bed. She's a young girl.'

'What do you want me to do? Just kick the kid out?'

'You have to do something, Jack.'

I shifted on my heels and tried to look up through the thin cracks between the verandah boards. It was hard to see. I could just make out the edge of an old chair. I could see my father's boots and the worn hems of his jeans.

'Do you know what she told me?' Carol said. 'That you had promised to marry her.'

'All little girls say that.'

'When they're four. Five maybe. Not at this age.'

They fell silent again and I looked at Callum, who was glaring at me. 'It's not my fault,' I whispered.

'Shut up,' he said. 'They'll hear you.'

'Well, it's not.'

Callum didn't answer me, but lay back in the soil with his eyes closed. I reached over and kicked him. As he swung away I heard my father sigh and move towards the stairs. I half-knelt in the dust to press my eye to a gap in the floorboards.

'Alright,' he said, 'I'll make sure she sleeps in her own bed from now on.'

'If you don't I'll have to tell Paul. You don't want that.'

They stood quietly for a moment. I could hear my heart beating and put my hand over it, trying to stop the sound from going up through the cracks. When my father took another step a pale stream of dirt drifted down onto my leg. I wanted him to say something, to tell her to shut up, even to strike her as surely and irrevocably as he sometimes struck Cal and me. I wanted him to defend himself, defend us, against her oddly reticent threat of disclosure. I didn't want to sleep alone in that wide bed with its cool white sheets and the soft dip where my mother once slept. The scooping embrace that I rolled into night after night before he caught me and held me.

He glanced over his shoulder toward the day bed at the other end of the verandah, where Dr Paul still lay sleeping. I couldn't see their faces, but I saw Carol turn her back on Father as he walked away, and I felt Callum's hand wrap around my wrist. He yanked me closer to him.

'Maybe he'll stop now,' he said.

'Maybe.'

'It's because you look like her, isn't it.'

'I don't know.'

'It is. I know it is.'

'How would you know?'

'I hear things, stupid. I hear what he says to you. *Oh sweetie. Oh baby.*'

'Shut up.' I put my hands over my ears and screwed my eyes shut.

Callum moved closer and pulled my hands down, pinning them against my sides. '*Come on, sweetie, it's alright. Jack loves you. Tell Jack that you love him.*'

'Stop it, Cal.' Callum laughed and started making kissing noises. I felt his hands on my hips and twisted away from him. My eyes were screwed shut and my hands were over my ears. I tried to focus on something other than Cal, tried to listen to the echoey noise, like an empty telephone line, of my hands pressed hard against my eardrums. Callum leaned in closer to my face and touched my cheek. He stared at me and I shook my hair out of my face, glaring at him to show I didn't care, he hadn't hurt me. When he opened his mouth I closed my eyes and pulled my shoulders in, took a deep breath and screamed at him. 'Shut up. Shutupshutupshutup.'

I heard my father above me and realised, too late, that he had heard us talking. I looked at Cal, wanting to know what to do, what to say, but he glared back at me. I heard Father getting closer, heard his boots thudding angrily into the soft dust. My body felt thin and small and it trembled the way it had when I had gastro months before. I tried to scurry backwards, thinking about nothing but hiding. Not wanting to think about how much he had heard. I felt Cal's knees sticking into my back and his hand holding onto mine. 'It'll be okay,' he whispered and when I turned to look at him his face looked pale and terrified but also, somehow, more determined.

'You're never going to do anything,' I said, and then I heard Father's voice beside us, the calm voice he used when we had pushed him too far, when there was no longer anything to do except wait for the cold anger to crack.

'Germaine. Callum. Get in the truck,' he said.

Cal and I sat scrunched together in the passenger's seat but I refused to look at him the whole drive home. I stared out the front windscreen, watching the road twist and buckle in the afternoon heat. At one point Cal tried to push his hand in under mine and squeeze it gently but I pulled away, folding my hands together in my lap. As soon as we arrived home I clambered out of the van and ran for the shed. I could hear Father calling out after me, but I knew he wouldn't follow. After a whole day away there were things he had to do before dark.

I closed the door and hunched down on the cool concrete floor in the middle of the slaughter shed, my knees pulled up to my chin. I stared and stared at the blue slice of sky above the door, at the soft shine of the chain and hook that hung from the ceiling. I didn't hear Cal until he pulled the door open slightly and crept in beside me. He put his thin arm around my shoulders and I tipped my head towards him.

'You're crying,' he said.

I shuffled away from him and wrenched the hem of my shirt up to wipe my face. 'I am not,' I said, glaring at him. He dropped his gaze and I saw him shake his head slightly. I crossed my arms and held my head high as I watched him.

'I'm sorry, Germaine. I was just kidding.'

'I don't care. You're just jealous. You just want Dad to love you best, but he doesn't, he loves me.'

'I'll make him stop,' Cal said quietly.

I looked up at him, at his soft boy's face and his thin neck sticking up out of his dirty collar. Dad would snap him in half like a twig. Just pick him up and toss him aside. I didn't think there was anyone in the whole world who could make our father stop doing something if he didn't want them to. No one in the whole world.

'It's alright, Cal. It doesn't hurt that much.'

'But you don't like it.'

I turned away, watching the shining chain now glowing warmly in the half-dark. 'I promise I'll make it stop. I will. As soon as I can, I will,' he said.

I stopped and turned to look at him. His earnest face was caught in a line of light. 'Promise?'

'Promise,' he said.

Callum took his pocket knife out of his jeans and grabbed my hand. I watched him place the tip against my palm and push, but as soon as the blood welled up he flinched and pulled it away. I took the blade from him and did it myself, pushing the tip into the fleshy bump at the base of my palm and dragging it across. Callum held out his hand. White-faced but determined. I felt him flinch as I made the incision and when I looked up his pale face was turned away, his eyes squeezed shut. I smiled. When I'd finished making the cut I folded the knife and passed it back to him, then we pressed our bleeding palms together.

'Should we say something?' he asked.

'Like what?'

'I dunno. Something important so we know it's for real.'

I racked my mind, thinking of all the rhymes our mother used to tell us, all the sayings in fairytales that opened doors and sealed promises. 'Blood is thicker than water,' I said.

'What does that mean?'

'It means you're my brother and that's stronger than anything else. You have to protect me from him forever because we have the same blood.'

Callum nodded and we said it again, together. It was the most sacred way we could think of to seal a promise.

For several years Callum and I laid plans to make him stop, but it didn't work straight away. I guess the promises we made, and the whispered deals I made with the universe, were not powerful enough back then. I kept thinking someone, anyone, would hear me. I remembered the fairytale about the silent princess who told tales to the kitchen pipes and was eventually overheard and saved. I always believed I would be rescued some day, I just didn't know when. Or by whom. Callum and I struggled to understand how to make our father stop. We would lock the door, or sleep together under the house. He would leave me alone for a while, sometimes weeks at a time, but eventually he would find me in the bath, or swimming at the river, and follow me back to my room.

We felt helpless in the face of his persistence. He was the only adult we knew, the only adult we saw every day of our lives. We didn't go to school, except by radio, and when we did go into town Father was always with us. I stopped eating, at first because I could not face food when he watched me so carefully from the other side of the table, waiting for me to finish, to leave the table, to go to my room or the bath. Later it was because I'd forgotten how to be a little girl, how to eat just for the sheer pleasure of food. I was desperate. *We* were desperate. Cal and I decided to run away together, we hid cans of food under the house, but neither of us knew where we could go. We got an atlas delivered with our schoolbooks but when we opened it to the map of Australia it was so big we couldn't even find ourselves. For all we knew it would take days to reach the nearest highway and hitch a ride, and then what?

After I read *Huckleberry Finn* I decided we would build a raft and head off down the river. We spent weeks building it from fallen logs and old forty-four-gallon drums. Finally, we hauled it out into the muddy river and climbed on board. It didn't move. The water was only a foot or so deep and with our weight added to the load of clothes and food our raft sank until it settled on the bottom. Cal jumped off and began swearing as he tried to pull the raft out of the mud but I just sat there, water shifting warmly around my thighs, feeling the timbers shift apart beneath me.

'Get up and help,' he yelled at me.

I stared at him quietly as he gave another yank to the rope in his hands. One of the drums slipped out from under the raft, dragging two planks with it. I stood up and clambered to the edge of the water, watching the raft slowly break apart. Cal was swearing and sweating and crying as he lunged after the pieces, yelling at me to grab whatever I could before it sank into the mud.

'It's not going to work,' I said.

Cal stopped and glared at me. 'It was your idea,' he said, and turned away. He moved more slowly this time, stubbornly retrieving the broken pieces and piling them up on the dry riverbed. 'I'll make it work.'

When I was twelve my father went away. The night before he left he lay beside me weeping uncontrollably. *It has to stop*, he said, but his hands were fumbling with my nightgown as he said it. He cried like a child, like Callum when he was little, shrinking from the thunderstorms that rattled the timber walls. Afraid of something he had no power to change. *Please*, he begged me. But what could I do? What did he want me to do? I placed a hand on the side of his face and tried to turn him to look at me but he pulled away, his whole body tensed against itself. The next morning he was gone. Callum and I didn't talk about it much. We were quiet and waiting. We weren't sure what it meant. Where he had gone. Whether he would come back.

When he returned he brought Emma with him. They sat at the kitchen table together, not touching, and he told us they'd gotten married a week ago. She'd been a schoolteacher and would take over our lessons. When he had finished talking he stood and walked out of the house, leaving the three of us sitting in silence at the table. Emma smiled uncertainly. Callum reached out and took my hand and we stared at her.

'You're not my mother,' Callum insisted.

She didn't say anything. She simply stood and walked over to the kitchen bench. 'Would you like some cake?' she asked. 'Perhaps some tea?' We didn't answer her and by the time she turned around we were both gone.

At the time I believed she had saved me although, listening at their bedroom door, I pitied her. The worst part, the part I could never admit to Cal, was that at first I resented her. My father didn't come into my room at night any more. He didn't sneak in and watch me in the bath, or swimming in the dam. It's not that I wanted him to, just that I felt rejected. I'd lost what I'd had with him — the connection with my mother, the sense of being special, of being so special that even my own father could not resist me. Unlike the fairytale princess I had not escaped or been rescued. I had merely been replaced.

As I got to know Emma, however, I lost the feeling of being displaced. Emma was never a rival. She was too thin and sad. She was used to property life before she married Father — worn in to the drudgery of it, used to the soil that lived and breathed in us. She slipped quietly into our lives and we, quietly, moved aside to make room. She was like someone long lost and suddenly found — an aunt or cousin — oddly familiar and yet unknowable. She smiled, but only sparingly. I never saw father lean into her the way he had with my mother. I never saw him hold his breath when she walked into a room. I used to think that he didn't love her, that love was something magnificent and desperate and reserved for people like my mother who had herself been magnificent, and desperately out of place. Gradually I learned that the love he felt for Emma was something different. Something precise measured out in practicalities. As precise as the creases she pressed into his pants, or the turned seams that ran down the centre of our sheets. As pure and neatly kept as her manicured gardens and the pressed cloths she spread over our table. Her clarity, her careful life, reassured him. His life had fallen apart because of a woman whose eccentricity left him hollow and hum-ming with grief. He needed Emma. He needed a woman who was quiet and careful and didn't demand of him that his life be grand. If my mother had been too much for him, too much for us all, then Emma was supposed to be the cure for her excesses. A pure and almost ascetic wife and mother. She taught us practical things. She saved the bath water for the vegetables and the flowers she grew in pots along the verandah. She always set an extra place at the table for strangers. She made preserves. She set a saucer of milk on the doorstep every night for her unborn babies, and smiled every morning to see the saucer emptied. She told us that in India they buried the stillborn beneath the doorstone in order that the baby's spirit might rise into the womb of another woman as she passed.

Even her eccentricities seemed careful and harmless.

I would not say that I didn't love her. She was safety and security and the luxury of clean sheets, warm meals. She never frightened me with her love as my mother had. She never threatened to tear me out of childhood before I was ready, never demanded that I comfort her, be there for her, live for her. I felt reassured by her presence, although it took me a long time to recognise how much I needed her. Once she came I slowly learned to sleep through the night, with the door unlocked.

When her son Erin was born it was the middle of winter. He came too soon and too fast. His fist curled at his cheeks. His hair thick and black. After the false beginnings, the months of fear, of walking like a woman made of glass, the tide of birth left Emma blushing and triumphant. She pressed her cheek to his and breathed in hard, gulping at the vigorous live smell of him. When my father came into the room he saw her sitting upright, the light dim, the child bundled warmly in her arms. He saw her face flushed with pride and expectation. She had done it. She didn't see what he saw.

There had been a storm the night my mother died. Dust-clouds beating at the windows like red ghosts. My mother's skin was shiny and pulled thin over her bones. A nurse moved in the room quietly. My mouth was dry. Father stood behind me and rested his hand on my head, but there was no weight in him. His feet were silent on the floor.

There must have been a moment when she slipped, when her keel tipped. I used to believe that I could have caught and righted her. If I had held on, just a little tighter, to her bone-white fingers. If I had said the right thing. If I hadn't been so afraid. If I hadn't turned to him, instead of her, for comfort. Whatever it was, the secret thing I should have done — the thing that would have kept her alive — I didn't do it. When she finally went I heard my father cry out. He pressed himself into the edges of the room. His shoulders catching on the timber. His hands clutching at me. His wet mouth opening and closing like a fish hooked and left to die in a basket.

So when Erin was born and Father walked into the room and saw Emma and his new son, he did not really see them. He saw instead the shadow behind them. That other mother who threatened to engulf us all. Emma had wanted to give him something precious and unnameable, something magical, but he was too afraid. The fear made his hands shake. He did not know how to love his sons bravely. Or with hope.

'Fine boy,' he said, as he leant over and kissed her forehead. 'Well done.'

Erin died a week later, and when she laid him in the ground Emma

21

didn't cry. He was the only living child she ever bore and she set her heart aside when we buried him. She grew thinner every year, and more determined. She paved over the doorstep and took to drinking a cup of pennyroyal tea every day.

My father would snap his fingers in front of her face. 'Where are you?' he'd say. She would look at him slowly, as if she didn't quite know, and open her mouth to speak, but there was no answer to give. Or none that she knew. Only a dry moth that fluttered on her tongue. I dreamt of her body splitting open, the fat worm of death sitting in her gut. I dreamt that she was thinner than a post-rail, than a broomstick, and that death slipped from her mouth like a fat white worm, leaving nothing but a brittle skin clutching at the eaves of my mother's house.

He will chant impiety
From a table in the front of his house;
All his people will answer:
'Be it thus. Be it thus.'

— Anon. *Adze-Head*

My mother's house was full of echoes. Each sound we made was caught or bent or grown in the splintered timber until it seemed that the beams themselves might crack open and wail. When she was alive you could hear her in the house all the time, humming or singing or laughing or playing her flute. But when she died the house fell silent. Turned in on itself and folded up. The hallways swelled with absolute quiet until just the sound of my feet in shoes was too loud and I was careful to always walk barefoot inside. At night I would lay my cheek against the floor and try to hear her echoes, slowly fading. At times I would play my flute like a weapon. Striding down the long hallways and blasting the notes as harsh and loud as I could. I dreamed of Jericho. Of the walls falling to the sound of trumpets. To the sounds of the righteous. I dreamed of my father, caught in the rubble of his own ridiculous dream as it fell around him, and Callum and I walked away.

My father built this house for my mother. Each room was planned to be as large as possible. The sound of her voice was carried from room to room in long, wide hallways. The floors were sanded and polished and polished again until they gleamed like water and felt soft beneath her bare feet. Every room emptied onto the verandah through tall thin doors with glass panes. The sound of her flute spun in the huge rooms and over the polished floorboards. Her laughter glanced like sunlight off the blue glass she had him place in the full-length window of the dining room.

The day the house was finished he brought her here and they laid out their wedding china on the boards of the unfurnished dining room. It was the first Sunday evening meal. Since then it has changed only slightly. Gradually. The table is laid with the finest china; a bottle of wine is brought from the cellar. As a small child I was allowed a tiny dribble of sweet wine in a glass of water. The hot elaborate meal is served with condiments in tiny bowls. The complex arrangements of forks and knives and plates and bowls are set early in the afternoon, making sure each utensil is straight, each napkin clean and crisply folded. My father sits at the head of the table, and Mother at the other end.

One Sunday she was in the kitchen struggling with a roast too large to fit into the oven. I was sitting beneath the table, inexpertly carving faces into the half dozen potatoes that had rolled onto the floor. It was hot, as always. It had been a long time since the last rainfall. Not long enough for it to be officially declared a drought, but long enough that the tanks were hot and hollow. My father came in and knelt at her feet, burying his face in her skirts. He was shaking. Her fingers were in his hair like white snakes and her chin was lifted. The wind blew in through the window. She drew one hand up over his skull towards the sink and scooped up a handful of water, which she sprinkled over his head. He looked up at her as water dropped on his forehead, on his cheek, on his mouth. He smiled. Water poured from her hand. Water skimmed his surface and made him shine. It ran down his face onto his chest, it wet her skirts and dripped from her hem. The timber darkened. Her feet were wet. I crouched in the puddle spreading beneath the table. She moved her hand in a circle and water sprayed over the room. It flew out the window and the water seemed suddenly to come from everywhere. In the home paddock the men cried out as rain cracked like bullets on the tin sheds. Their faint voices were laughing. Someone was singing.

Inside the house it was so hot that the sunlight pushing through the window was heavy, almost translucent. My bare feet slid over the floorboards as I moved down the side of the long table, leaning over the chairs to place a bowl of flowers in the centre.

'Don't put them there. You know she'll just move them.'

'I like them.'

Callum looked away from me, turning a knife over so the blade faced away from the plate. I moved down another seat, carefully placing each utensil, measuring the space between them by the width of two fingers, the napkin on the bread plate folded like a hollow pyramid with one face gone. I moved the glass at the head of the knives a little closer. Scratched one calf with the other foot. Callum picked up a carefully folded napkin from his side of the table and replaced it with another.

'What's wrong with that one?' I asked.

'It's dirty — look.' He flung it across the table at me, toppling two glasses that stood between us. I reached out quickly to catch them. One of the glasses glanced off the tips of my fingers and rolled towards the edge of the table. Callum caught it in his cupped hand and placed it back at the head of a place setting. 'I don't see why we can't eat outside, or have cold food occasionally.'

He knew why, or at least he knew that the Sunday evening meal would never change. As long as I could remember we had all come in for the Sunday evening meal dressed and showered, our fingernails scrubbed and wet hair combed neatly. When my mother was alive we would all sit in the living room before dinner while she played the flute. I would be sweating uncomfortably in my starched white dress. Father would lean forward in his chair and watch her as she closed her eyes and leaned into the rhythms of the music. He would watch her carefully, her chest rising quickly and falling slowly, her mouth pressed thinly against the warming metal. He would be intent and concentrated.

At some point he would stand and take the instrument from her hands and we would all walk quietly into the dining room. After she died the meal was quieter, even after my father remarried and the work of the meal became Emma's work, the conversation never flashed over the warm food as it had with Mother, the food was never exotic or adventurous, but neither was it burned or undercooked.

The ritual of the meal was something my mother struggled with, something she never seemed to understand the way Emma did. She tried. She would spend hours in the kitchen with food piled up on the table and benches, the stove shimmering with heat, her legs bent at the knees, her arms akimbo. She would pour tea one-handed from a metre above the table as she ran the index finger of her other hand over the pages of a cookbook. When I came in to show her a lizard I had found beneath the house, or to tell her some child's story, she would crouch down, cross her arms and rest her chin on the table to listen to me. She told me about Ricdin and Ricdon, about the fabulous underground kitchens they discovered that spread for miles and miles. About the princess who demanded feasts every day; quail and pheasant, honey cakes and wine, delicate pastries and sugar-frosted rose petals, turkish delight, mint julep, sashimi, sugar plums and bitter lemons, borscht, collops, huge timber barrels of cider and beer, haggis, buttered snails, ambrosia and warm spiced wine. *How she loved to eat*, my mother would say. The two brothers were drawn by the scent of those kitchens, by the cacophony of nutmeg, mustard, cinnamon, cayenne and saffron. *The princess was as luscious and sweet as the puddings she devoured*, my mother would say, *how could they help but love her?*

Are you a princess? I would ask, and she would gather me up in her long brown arms and stride out onto the verandah. She would throw her free arm wide and gaze triumphantly out over the burnt red ground. *My kingdom*, she'd declare.

My father would stand leaning against the wall, watching her. He would say she was *just too much*, and laugh.

I heard Emma in the kitchen, her thin voice rising above the steam. She was singing an old folk song. Something about Mary Hamilton who cast the king's child out to sea. I bent to take a pressed and starched white cloth out of the drawer and spread it over the polished buffet. Callum placed four large platters along the top and two polished silver candleholders at the back. When the meal was ready we would bring in the lidded bowls which sit on top of these — the two oval ones to hold side dishes, the pumpkin-shaped tureen with the splayed foot for soup, and the flatter one with the domed lid for meat.

With Mother gone and Emma in her place the meal was no longer preceded by music. For a while we tried. I would fumble with my childish fingers while Father stared out the window of the sitting room. In the face of my ineptitude and Father's indifference it seemed that the pre-dinner gathering would be abandoned completely. It was awkward without Mother. Without the energy of her enthusiasm to draw us together we would drift into the room and just stand around. That last day we sat quietly. Emma wandered in from the kitchen every now and then, wiping her hands on the apron tied at her waist, to place her hand on Callum's shoulder or ask me to come and help her with something. I felt guilty about her tentativeness at times, as if we had forced her out; as if by some collective and imperceptible will we had made her an outsider.

I heard father pull up in his ute, the motor straining and rumbling. Years ago there would have been a handful of men with him; quiet strangers who came for a few weeks or months and then drifted away. But in those last years, with the drought, with the poverty that haunted us despite the wealth of land that stretched further than I could see from the house, there was no money for water or feed, let alone wages. Even the meal — with its extravagances of bought foods and fresh-picked, water-fed vegetables — was a little thinner, a little *meaner*, each week.

'You should go and shower. Get ready,' Callum said. I looked up at him and away again, towards the window where I could hear, just faintly, my father's boots as they fell through the dust. 'What are you worried about?' he said. 'Just lock the goddamn door.'

I lifted the hem of my shirt to polish the knife in my hand before placing it carefully on the table.

'You can't just let it start again,' he said.

'I don't know what you mean.' I looked away from Cal, down at my hands. I could feel his eyes on me.

'Germaine,' he said, half whispering, 'we can just leave. Both of us.'

'Where would we go? There's nowhere for us to go.'

'It doesn't matter where. We could get out of *here*, that's the point.'

He was leaning over the table towards me, the edges of his hair hazed with the blue light that fell from the window. I bit my lip. I thought about just leaving. I pictured us in Cal's van, driving through acres and acres of dry red landscapes until we reached the green strip of the coast. Miles of highways and towns we didn't know. People we had never met. A future with nothing old in it. Nothing to remind me of my father. I thought about us sitting on a beach miles from here, warm from the sun, our feet in the ocean. I pictured my father, as tall and wide as a giant, striding along the beach towards us. His huge hands fisted at his sides. I felt him wrench us away. There were tears in my eyes and I shook my head. I thought about us miles away, standing together in a garden where we could see the water reaching out towards the curve of the world's end. I saw him coming. His huge hands rattling the fences, ruffling the surface of the ocean, pulling up weeds and trees and roads and rivers to find us. To bring us home. We couldn't leave. There really was nowhere to go. Nowhere we would be safe. Nowhere he wouldn't find us.

'Fucking hell!' Cal shouted, slamming one fist down onto the buffet. The glasses and candlesticks clattered against each other. One candle fell from its holder and I heard Emma's footsteps at the door.

'What's going on in here? Callum? Germaine?' She walked between us and picked up the fallen candle, twisting it firmly into the small cup of the candleholder and wiping some tiny flakes of wax into her cupped palm. She glanced at Callum as he ducked his head, then at me as I turned towards the window. She walked to the table and quickly looked it over, straightening and tidying. 'You're one place short,' she said. Callum turned and looked at the table, counting again as if unsure.

'There are enough places set,' he said sullenly.

'Always set an extra place for strangers.'

'Who's going to turn up out here? We're in the middle of nowhere.'

Emma looked at Cal, her face bare; she looked like a child who had been spoken to in another language. Completely lost. She shook her head and waved a hand at Cal, brushing away his protest as she walked over to the buffet and took out an extra set of silverware. She polished each piece with a serviette before placing it on the table. Her movements were slow and careful. I envied the precision of her actions, the way everything she did seemed simple and clean. She always knew what needed to be done and did it.

As she walked away I felt Cal come and stand close behind me, his hand resting on my arm. 'I know how to get away,' he said, his voice almost a whisper. 'I've found someone to help, but we have to go now.' I turned towards him and looked into his face, at the desperate way he leaned towards me. I could feel him pulling me closer to him, pulling me away from everything I knew, everything I understood. He seemed so sure that he was right and I wanted to believe him, I wanted to be the person he still believed I could be, his innocent little sister.

I showered with a chair wedged in under the locked door and dressed quickly, plaiting my still-damp hair. I walked past Callum, who was sitting in the wing-backed chair that was once my mother's. The chair was covered by a blue throw. Beneath the throw was the stain that had been there since the day of my mother's funeral, despite Emma's efforts to remove it with bleaches and detergents. One night I found her kneeling on the floor with a bucket of warm water at her elbow, scrubbing away at it with tears in her eyes. I never offered to help. I stood in the shadows watching her scrub and scrub until her knuckles were red and raw.

Callum looked up as I walked past him, glaring at me and then looking pointedly at Father. The chessboard with the game we started last week sat on the windowsill. The heavy rippled glass of the window made the room seem washed and watery, belying the heat and lack of moisture outside. Father was sitting in his chair, a book in his hands, his legs thrust out before him, his ankles crossed. His clean 'good' boots (identical to his ordinary boots but never worn for work) shone dimly from freshly applied polish. His hands were scrubbed, although the taint of red soil still lingered beneath his nails and in the creases of his skin. 'Evening, Germaine,' he said, without lowering his book. I walked over to the windowseat and began to play out the unfinished game alone. When Emma came into the room no one looked up until she turned to walk away, calling me out to the kitchen.

She was flushed and steaming, the windows of the kitchen were thrown open to catch what little breeze there was. She filled my hands with serving dishes, which I carried through to the dining room and placed on the buffet. She followed me through with the last dish and adjusted each one using a damp cloth to wipe any spilled food from their rims. She walked once more around the table, a slight frown on her forehead. Finally she picked up the bowl of flowers from the table's centre and placed them instead on the windowsill. I stood behind my chair, waiting, as she went to the sitting room to get Father and Callum.

Father said grace, as he has always done, his deep voice rumbling over the words in a soft but meaningless intonation, more habit than faith. Emma picked up one dish at a time from the buffet and moved around the table serving food onto each plate. Father waited until she had finished before beginning to eat.

No one spoke until after Father had first tasted the food and congratulated Emma. She blushed girlishly and thanked him. We passed the compliments around the table, each as dry and passionless as the last. Accepting and not noticing the gifts she gave us. I stumbled over mine, my eyes focused instead on Callum's dusty knuckles as his hand curled over his fork in a rough fist.

'I beg your pardon, Germaine?' said Father.

'I said thank you, Emma. It's lovely.'

'That's all?'

'The meat is especially tender. Emma.'

'Thank you. That's better.' He glanced at Emma.

'Thank you, Germaine,' said Emma. Callum knuckled his fork up to his mouth and I tipped my head to stare at the steaming food on my plate.

I watched Emma sitting upright in her seat, as careful as someone barefoot in a room full of broken glass. She looked up at Callum and Father, whose knife I heard calmly slicing into the food on his plate.

'You can come out with me tomorrow, Germaine,' said Father. 'I need some help getting feed out to the bottom paddocks.'

I nodded my head. I heard Callum grunt beside me. 'I'll go, Dad,' he said. 'She can stay and help Em in the house.'

We fell silent. I felt Callum tensed beside me, watching father. I opened my mouth to speak but couldn't think of anything to say. I could have said it was okay, that I'd go with Father, but Callum would have known what that meant. I could have said I wanted to stay with Emma, but Father would have been angry, he might have insisted and that could have been worse. If Callum hadn't said anything, if we had all just pretended it was nothing, perhaps I could have slipped away early. I could have found somewhere to hide, something to do, until he left without me.

'No,' Father said, 'I need her with me tomorrow.'

I felt Callum hesitate beside me before his voice came, shocking me with its steadiness, its surety. He sounded just like a man. 'You need to leave her alone,' he said.

I glanced up to see Emma's face shifting; the skin flickering, unsure of where to settle, how to understand this moment, how to feel. She flushed warmly, almost violet in the blue light of the dining room.

'She's coming with me tomorrow, Callum,' Father said, 'and that's the end of it.'

Callum pushed his chair back from the table. I struggled not to flinch, not to curl away from him. I closed my eyes, not wanting to see him strike out. In those long seconds I pictured him driving his fists at my father and being thrown to the ground, being humiliated, but as I opened my eyes I saw him still standing beside me, his fists at his sides, his face red and hard. I heard his disgust and frustration come out in a wordless and amazed grunt just before I felt the chair at his feet rise in his hands and swing out over my head towards the window. I turned to see it fly elegantly through the air. The curved legs like frozen wings as it burst through the windows which were not so watery after all, though the sound of broken glass scattering on the cracked earth outside, on the timber floors inside, was a little like that of water. Falling.

I closed my eyes and pressed my fists into my thighs, gripping the edge of my shirt. I walked through my room, brushing my hands over familiar objects, and found something strange, something unexpected. I bashed my shins against my bed and almost fell across it. I found papers strewn over the floor and didn't know what they were. I picked up a book and put it down again — I sat on the floor. Even sounds assaulted me. I heard my father's footsteps as he walked through the house, felt them reverberating slightly through my thighs. I heard Emma's lullaby-soft voice following him from room to room. Outside the sheds cracked, the tree limbs rattled at my window. I could even hear the curtain shifting against the first evening breeze.

'I'm not going after him, Emma,' Father insisted, 'he's not welcome in my house any longer.' Then his footsteps again, closer this time. He banged on my door. I willed myself not to hear it. I pulled my hair forward and began to unravel my plait. My fingers slipped between the cool, still-damp shanks. 'I'll be back later,' he said.

I worked the knots loose, listening to him wend his way back through the house to the screen door, which screeched open and slammed closed. Emma slipped away into the kitchen where I could hear the soapy dishes chink.

I screwed my eyes shut and sat as still as possible, listening carefully to the sounds outside, to the trees and buildings and soil that stretched endlessly out around us. Could I hear Callum? The tense thread of his absence, the toneless shunt of the van's engine as he stopped at each gate, leaving them open behind him in protest. He drove for hours through the quiet paddocks, the road packed and dense beneath him before there was a change of tone — the tyres crunching — as he turned onto the paved road and drove the last two hundred metres to the pub.

Inside the hotel the warm hum of men's voices ran like a bass-line against the chink of glasses, the watery hush of beer on tap, the rising contralto of the sports channel beaming from above the bar. Cal played pool with Jason that night. He and Cal were the only men in the bar under forty. They had met before, when Cal spent a few days helping out on the Bowls' property. Jason had been quiet and watchful, listening to Cal and the other workers as they watched the cattle shuffle out of his truck. Jason told them about Sydney, where he came from, and the road trains he'd been driving. They talked a lot about opportunities for a young guy to make money, to be independent. Jason had asked Cal if he would be interested in coming with him to the city, investing in some deal he had going, and Cal had said maybe — if things were different, but right now the old man wouldn't go for it. That night in the bar he listened more carefully, eager to hear about a life of possibilities, of movement. Perhaps he was just ready to go. Perhaps he knew that it was time for us to leave and Jason was our ticket out.

They rested their beers on the damp baize of the table. 'So,' Cal said, 'did you get the money together yet?'

Jason leaned over the table, his chin barely an inch above the cue, as he shook his head and gently knocked the ball home.

'Thought you weren't interested.'

Callum hesitated, taking a long drink from his beer and walking around to the other side of the table. 'Maybe.'

Jason watched Callum over the rim of his glass as he stood and rested the cue against his shoulder. 'Maybe nothing. Either you're coming or you're not.'

'I can't go without Germaine, and she says she won't come.' Callum leant down beside him, his elbow close to his body as he lined up his shot.

'Fuck her,' Jason said. The two of them stood, watching the ball roll slowly over the felt and gently knock another into the pocket.

'When are you going?' Callum asked.

'Tomorrow. Maybe the next day. I have to wait to get the call from Wayne. And get some wheels organised.'

'Are you staying here?'

'At the pub? I suppose.'

'Why don't you come back with me? Maybe you could talk some sense into her. If you can get her to agree to it we'll come — we can take my van.'

'What about your old man?'

'What about him?'

'He won't like it, will he?'

'He doesn't have to.'

During the night I had heard my father leave the house. I got up from my bed and watched him walk naked across the home paddock to the trees where she was buried. The wind seemed to push him, to carry him across those few hundred metres. I felt sure that he was asleep, or had become a ghost. I watched him for an hour. He barely moved, but something seemed to rise in him. He stood taller. I watched him stretch his body till his head tipped back and the stars settled on his throat. A sound came over the paddock. At first it was quiet, almost shy, and I thought perhaps it was the wind, or a lost calf, or the horses on the other side of the house. Soon it swelled like a sail and I knew it was his voice. It trembled then seemed to put on flesh. It moved in his body like a drumbeat. Then he was dancing. His arms curled, his body stark and ridiculous. He was laughing. I hardly dared to breathe. My father was singing. My father was dancing. I curled up in my bed and fell asleep to the sound of his voice and his bare feet beating a tattoo on her grave.

Early the next morning I crept barefoot out of the house, skirting the circle of broken glass that glinted in the half-light. It was still dark and cold, the soil crumbling and icy beneath my feet. I walked quickly across and searched the ground where he had danced. I found his footprints, the bare impression of his feet, and the remains of my mother's flute. It was lying in the middle of a small charred circle. One single key survived undamaged.

I held it in the palm of my hand. It was small and cool, but also solid. I put it in my mouth, rolling it over until it rested beneath my tongue, and listened. Nothing. A pure metallic silence. I pushed the key upwards with my tongue, holding it against the roof of my mouth. I could taste soil and charcoal. My father's sacrilege still warming the surface. I sucked the key clean, polishing it with my own spit. I crouched in the soil and listened, my fists against my ears to drown out the wind, the bright air, the humming distance. I could feel a knot in my body, high up beneath my ribcage. Something dense and heavy that refused to move. As I tipped my head down onto my knees and closed my eyes I could hear, just faintly, something. My mother's voice, only not her voice, something even smaller than that, even harder to hear or remember. A soft empty sound exhaled from a small space. As a whole my mother's flute had contained her memory, but this key could barely hold a note. It could only tremble against my tongue. Memories need space just as a voice or music requires air to breathe. Something to resonate. My mother once told me a Japanese fairy tale about a flute haunted by a murdered child's voice. She said that the sound was that of the soul which had simply moved from the empty body — from the lung — to the empty instrument. She said that to play, to really play, was to almost die. You had to allow your soul to be borne out of the body with each breath, knowing it might never return. A little death each time.

In this story a man left his only daughter in the care of her stepmother while he went away on business. His daughter begged him not to leave, but when he insisted she gave him a small bamboo flute to take with him. When the father had been away for a long time he remembered his daughter and took out her flute to play it. As he blew across the mouthpiece a terrible scream sounded and the father was filled with dread. He rushed home. As he scrambled through the garden he called out his daughter's name many times but there was no reply. Eventually he took out the little flute from his sleeve and began to play. No music came — only the sound of his daughter's voice telling him of her death at the hands of his second wife and of her bones that lay buried beneath his feet.

The story ends when the father cuts off the head of the wicked stepmother with his sword. But his child is still dead.

Mother said that her true voice was in her flute rather than her body but I could never hear it while she was alive. I was distracted by the beat of her heart, the warmth of her hand on me, the scent of her breath. After her death it haunted me. Left alone and unadorned it become more fine and pure than any other sound. The sound of her music drowned out everything else; the sound of Callum and Father at dinner, the awful sound of Father's voice which became quiet when he was angry, until he was almost whispering, and Callum's which rose and became unstable, quivering with rage until he fell silent and they stood facing each other across the table. My mother's silence was the loudest thing of all, drowning out everything in a rush of wordlessness.

It was late. The house was settled and quiet. I heard my father's feet in the hallway, each step slow and careful. My mother's flute was silent. I took the key out of my mouth and placed it carefully back in its box, sliding it under the bed. I held my breath as I heard him turn the door handle only to find it locked, a slight hesitation before he started working at the lock with something metallic. I crawled in under the bed, watching the door. In the end he broke it open with a sudden sharp crack and pulled me out from under the bed. I hunched my back and sat as still and small as I could on the floor. He stood behind me, a rough hand sliding down over my shoulder. I felt the night sky rushing towards me, threatening to crush me in its monstrous grasp. My father curved around me and his voice, as he whispered against my skin, drowned out the sound of the burning stars.

Now, in the courtyard in front of their house stood an almond tree; and one day in winter the wife was standing beneath it, and paring an apple, and as she pared it she cut her finger, and the blood fell upon the snow.

— Brothers Grimm, *The Almond Tree*

Cal's voice is deep and comforting. It is the kind of voice I always imagined he would have as a man, quiet and somehow meditative. Even during those days in the van as we drove to Sydney, when he was smiling and eager, jubilant that he — that we — had finally succeeded, his voice was soft and even. As we were growing up we used to make up stories about what we would do when we escaped. Stories about how we would travel and where we would travel. Many of Callum's stories had us journeying endlessly. We became stars floating in an unfixed sky, or ravens or unicorns. We became mystical beasts. Sometimes he settled down to a life as a wise old man of the woods, quiet and still, but I was always journeying.

Once upon a time there was a brother and sister named Callum and Germaine who lived in a stone tower in a small town in the middle of a desert. It had not rained for centuries and the people who lived in the kingdom were as dry and thin as paper. One day grey clouds began to cluster around the turrets, full of the heavy promise of water. The brother and sister went up onto the roof with an old tin drum, which was the closest thing they owned to a boat, and waited.

It began to rain.

It rained and rained and rained. First they could hear the rain crack as it hit the ground, and then a breathy sigh as the cracked earth grew soft and melted. Steam rose from the earth as it took its first drink in over five hundred years. Then the water began to run, forming thin creeks and rivers that ran like opened veins over the earth. The two sat and watched for hours as the world they had known began to beat and pulse like a body. They thought it rather grotesque.

They tipped back their heads and stuck out their tongues to catch the rain. It ran down their throats and flooded their bodies and they dreamed that they too began to run and beat like the earth beneath them. When the water had laid itself out over the whole world in a dirty pink swathe the two took their tin drum down to the second storey and climbed out the window into it.

They had no sail or oars or rudder, but dandled their hands in the water (so heavy and thick) and pushed it behind them until they were paddling over the drowned landscape of their childhood.

They grew tired and drifted. Like all adventurous children in these kinds of stories they were not afraid or joyful or hopeful, they merely travelled where the world took them. By the time they reached the sea they were ravenous.

They pulled their rusted boat onto the sand. A few metres away was a man selling fish and chips from a small booth. Beside him was a bucket of fish that flipped against its plastic sides. They built a shelter and woke every morning to see the sun rise over the ocean, to smell the water and the wet salt, to hear the waves creep and crash against the continents. The man cooked them fish fresh from the ocean each day, and when he passed away the boy received his rod and bucket, his small box of sinkers and hooks and lures. And what became of the girl? She took to swimming in the ocean every day, grew scales and gills and fins. Her hair and teeth fell out, as did her finger and toe nails. When her skin finally fell away, in one thin pinkish sheet, her brother wrapped it in paper and buried it beneath the sand. She never needed it again.

The real story of our escape was less fabulous, but it was one Cal loved to tell, over and over again. It wasn't as if it had a point, but I think it made him feel hopeful and excited just to talk about the fact that we had done it finally, that we had left. He would talk about him and Jason coming to get me — like two knights on a crusade — but he never mentioned the dragon, or the night between when they arrived and when we left together. In those first few days after our 'escape' we were never alone, and even when we were he found it hard to look into my face. I think he was frightened by what he had seen that morning, but what scared him more was the look he didn't want to see in my eyes. He wanted me to be afraid and ashamed and as terrified as he was. I guess the fact that I wasn't was hard for him to understand.

It was hot as they drove back from town the next morning. The road had turned to dust several miles back and even with the windows wound up Jason could hardly breathe. The air conditioner in the van didn't work. The windscreen was a fleshy, dusty pink. His skin was slick with sweat and sleeplessness. An empty coke bottle rolled on the floor with a plastic rattle. The fence rode up beside him, the squashed landscape slid beneath him. His feet were cramped.

'You're sure your old man won't be there?' Jason asked.

Callum gazed through the windscreen at the familiar stretch of flat redness and shook his head. 'He'll be out on the west run today.'

'Did you call Germaine?'

Callum shook his head again. He said he didn't want anyone to know they were coming. He wanted to sneak in and out quickly. He never said why it didn't happen that way. He never really said why Jason came with him at all. According to his version of the story, it's hard to imagine why he needed someone else, especially someone like Jason.

Jason slowed the van to a stop for the last gate and looked over at Cal. 'Open the gate,' he said, but Cal was leaning against the window, his shoulders hunched around himself and his eyes closed. Jason shook his head and climbed out of the van. It was the first time Jason saw our house and I guess to him it looked ordinary enough. A house sitting in its flat circle of dust and dead grass. A few trees clustering around the tanks. Some buildings and stables and a series of long, low sheds sitting at right angles to each other. The once-white house a dusty ochre. It hovered a couple of metres off the ground on spindly, tin-capped legs. Emma, who had been sitting on the stairs, stood and walked towards them as they parked and clambered out of the van. She stopped walking and stood with one hand on her hip and one over her eyes to shade her face from the dust and sunlight.

Callum gestured towards Jason and muttered his name as Emma put her arm around Callum's waist. 'Where have you been? I was so worried.' Callum was silent. His mouth was dry, his head thick with heat and alcohol. Jason looked away. He took off his sunglasses and rubbed them on his shirt.

'I'm sorry. I just needed to get away for a while. I had to do something.' Emma stood silently, watching Cal shift beneath her gaze. He stared at the ground, at the red blush that coloured her bare feet.

She nodded her head and looked at him carefully before turning to Jason. 'Jason, isn't it? Thanks for bringing him home.'

Jason glanced over her shoulder towards the house and she, too, turned. Jack was coming towards them. Emma looked down and put a hand on Callum's arm.

Jack's face was still. His body firm but hollow, something scoured out. He looked at them all carefully, measuring them one by one before finally settling on Callum. 'What did you bring him back here for?' he said. Jason looked away, out across the paddocks.

'Big place you got here. Is it good land?'

'You looking for work, is that it?'

Jason's gaze crossed the paddocks slowly, the dusty sheds and thin-armed trees, the three blister-grey tanks against the side of the house. In a tiny shed with a concrete floor he could see me. A small calf was slung by its ankles from a hook and chain in the centre of the roof. It was squirming and crying out as I took a knife and ran smoothly across its throat. I made a long deep cut from groin to chin. Blood spilled from the wound and the animal fell silent. Long slippery cords of intestines and other organs fell into a large tin bucket positioned beneath the animal. I reached inside, between the furred curtains of flesh, to pull the rest of the internal organs from the cavity suspended above the ribs. I separated several of them and placed them in a large baking dish sitting on a bench beside me. My face was still and somewhat distracted. I worked in a smooth rhythm — lifting, wielding the knife or holding a container to catch something as my other hand cut it away. I was humming to myself, as if sipping at a cup of tea or bent over a quilt, some ordinary housewifely chore. Jason turned away from the image of my long arms shining whitely beneath my rolled up sleeves, my hands warm and red with blood. When he looked towards Jack he was slightly pale.

'Are you looking for work or not, son?' Jason didn't answer him, letting Jack's voice hang in the dry air as his gaze was drawn back to the neatly framed image of his daughter moving inside the little shed.

I was calmly working a thin-bladed knife between fur and flesh, removing the skin.

Emma lifted a hand to Jack's shoulder and he turned towards her. 'Come inside,' she said, 'have some tea. It's hot in the sun.'

'There's work to be done,' said Jack.

'There's always work to be done, and always time to do it. Now come inside.'

As the others moved to go inside Jason came to the door of the shed. He saw me stand up and brush the hair from my eyes with the back of my forearm. I pressed my wet hands into the small of my back and stretched. As I turned I saw his shadow outlined in the sunlight and raised a hand to my brow so I could see him more clearly. He didn't wave or smile and neither did I, but we stood watching each other. Eventually, I dropped my hand to my side. There was a smear of blood across my cheek which he later told me he had felt an odd desire to wipe away. To make me pure and clean. I wiped my hands across my thighs, picked up the bucket at my feet and stepped out of the shed. The bucket was heavy and I stooped slightly as I walked. Jason came over to me and I placed the bucket on the ground to stand straight and look into his face.

If I could have thought of something to say then I would have said it, but it was a strangely silent moment and there were no words between us. Perhaps he just wanted to see what I looked like, if whatever Cal had told him about me was true. Perhaps he just wanted to help. He seemed oddly curious, intrigued. His face bore the same distracted intensity I had seen on young boys pulling the legs off lizards, just to see what they would do, whether they would survive. I'll never know what he was thinking. What he thinks. I suppose it was just his way, something I would never understand. I think that moment was the beginning of something simple and unspeakable between us. That moment made us what we were to each other.

Cal and Jason took off on the bikes in the early afternoon. Father insisted that they go out to the west run as he had intended to do that day. The dams had been drying out slowly and he wanted to know whether he needed to buy water, how the stock were going, whether any of the fences needed repairs. We had lost a day's work, Jack said, and it was Cal's responsibilty to see that the work got done somehow. Jason and I sat on the verandah as Cal and Father argued inside. I don't remember anymore what he said. I remember the sound of his voice that afternoon, how it slipped in underneath everything else and made my skin hum with expectation. I remember the intimacy of his smile as he stood to follow Cal out to the sheds. How he bent towards me as he stood and I felt his breath burn my shoulder.

Late that afternoon I sat on the verandah. There were spiders in the eaves of the house, hanging in clusters against the beams. I sat sipping at my tea, watching their thin legs as they spun across the timber joists. Three or four of them were busy at their new webs as the day slipped out of sight; they knew no rain would come, that the seeds would lie burning and hollow in the dry soil. I tipped the cup to my mouth and looked at the brittle grass in the yard, the stone-coloured earth. It had been three weeks since Emma and I had planted a fresh crop of seedlings in the vegetable garden and we would lean on the fences like the farmers, watching the sky. Watching the soil. Breathing hope into the dry air. The cattle stood pale and resolute beneath whatever shade they could find, their thin hides already leathery. My cup rattled in the saucer, the leaves forming the shape of a crescent moon, a new moon.

I could hear my father inside the house. His boots fell rhythmically against the floorboards as he came down the hallway to stand behind me. His hand rested on the back of my chair. His knuckles firm against my shoulder.

'Stan's going out tomorrow to start thinning his livestock. We should be doing the same.' He turned his head and looked across the front paddock. His quiet voice hummed against my skin. 'Being a farmer,' he said, 'is the only thing that still makes sense to me.'

I watched the road leading away from the gate, the cracked earth, the lazy rise and fall of land, looking for the secret he believed was there. He moved a hand across the back of my neck, lifting my hair to run his hard-skinned fingertips over my skin. I looked into the teacup in my hand, at the dark crescent starting to shift. He ran his thumb along my collarbone and traced the edge of my shirt against my breast. 'You're just like your mother, you know,' he said. The edge of his thumb scratched my skin as his hand slipped forward over my ribs, under the faded cotton of my shirt to the bare skin of my belly and the warmth of my breast. 'Beautiful.'

I shifted forward and spilled the dregs of my tea down the front of my jeans.

The spiders continued spinning, their webs catching the last of the light.

When I walked into my room my father was sitting on the bed, his hands dark and thin-fingered against the cloth. The bed was my mother's. I was born in it. When my father married Emma he bought a new bed. He said he couldn't ask his new wife to sleep in the bed my mother had died in. I remember the first time I climbed into it, how I believed I could still smell her, still feel the weight of her body beside mine.

My father's face was still. He turned to look out the window and I watched the thin stripe of a vein swell and beat in his temple. He was watching the moon through the trees. He was watching the dust buck and settle around the buildings. I was watching his face and his uncertain hands that pulled at the sheets. I put my hand on his shoulder and felt him flinch before he turned towards me. I leant forward and placed my mouth against the vein that jumped in his throat.

I stood in the middle of the room with my hands open. I wanted to tell him something, anything, which would melt into his seamless skin. I wanted to give him a gift that would penetrate him in the way that the sound of the stars' imperfect music penetrated me. I told him about the flashing and burning. I told him how the rhythms of the sun's boiling surface beat in me. How I felt that I could sense somehow when the next flare would erupt. I traced burning arcs with my fingernail on the sheets and I wanted him to see, to really see, how the incredible burning arcs switched like snakes, stalking hydrogen across that furious globe. He lay watching my face and when I looked at him I could feel the sudden bursts of heat in my own skin. I pressed my cheek to his belly, to his porcelain-smooth cool belly, and fell silent. I could hear him beating. His pulse a seashell echoing against my ear. I imagined my head like a burning sun laid against the soft black night. My hair spooled like flares under his fingers.

He was gentle with me. Loving. He didn't hurt me, although I knew, in that moment when he shuddered and fell weeping and apologising against my shoulder, that I would leave now. His voice drifted against the beat of his belly. His hands moved over me. I lay beside him listening, held by his voice as I was once by my mother's.

I remember vividly this moment of hers, of mine. Of her hand lifting up the sheet so the light fell through and spread a linen-stained halo across her hip. Her breasts tipped softly from her chest and her hand was flat on the sheet, marking out the space for me. I remember her naked body curled against my back. Her skin smooth and cool. I remember the density of her arm wrapped around me, as if our bodies still beat to one pulse, her voice like a heavy drum. I remember the sheet like a skin — our skin — as if she'd never noticed when I tunnelled out of her. As if I never had. The two of us lying, body against body. The texture of her voice as it stirred beneath the sheets. I remember listening to her voice, to his voice, shifting inside me.

I was riding beside him, across the blood-soaked paddocks where the bones of cattle and women lay half-buried in the soil. This is the land of death where snakes lie shining in the earth. Their skins whispering against the grass, glistening between the cracks of soil, beneath the horses' feet.

I'll tell you a secret, they whispered, and as I leant down from the saddle one of them looped around herself and twisted along my arm. *There is nothing here but death*, she said. I shook her down from my shoulder but she twisted into my shirt, sliding against my skin. The feel of her was cool and smooth and it made me want to scream. She coiled around my belly as I rode, pressing me like a whip until her skin had become my own shingled gut.

So I rode and rode. Further into the paddocks than I had intended. Past the dam with its cracked bowl. Through the grass that was silver and dry, that flashed against my skin and left my shins laced with tiny cuts. I rode into the silence that waited like a lover and woke with my face pressed against the floor.

The timber was cool and my father was gone. The house was quiet. Everyone was sleeping and I wished that I could dream again, as carelessly and hopefully as I had when I was a child. My mother's house, my mother's bed, were once places of coolness and comfort but the sheets had turned feverish and fecund. After all the years of planning and plotting, of poring over maps and reading about journeys made over oceans, rivers and roads, after all the years of failing to get away it was, finally, a simple thing. It was time to leave.

A wish for all people when they lie down in bed —
Smooth linen, cool cotton, the fragrance and stir of herbs
And the faint but perceptible scent of sweet clear water.

— Rosemary Dobson, *Folding the Sheets*

If you lie in bed as quiet as a mouse, as still as a stone, you can hear the day breaking. It doesn't break like glass, all glittery and tinkling, falling and smashing open. Or like china which cracks open and falls into neat pieces. Nor does it break like an egg, sticky and almost silent. Day breaks the way an ocean does, or a wave, rushing at the shore in tiny increments, spilling over itself, swallowing itself. First the approach, a breathy exhalation, then the half retreat into night again — a susurrus heard over the rasp of soil or sand rolling in her embrace. It is not regular or precise, but it is as rhythmic as a broken heart.

In my mother's house the morning light was tidal and uncertain. It was the colour of oceans and it spilled into my room — into my bed. In the night I would wake and see my father sleeping uncomfortably, one arm thrust against the sheet towards me. Later, when I woke again, he would be gone. I would hear him moving through the house. When I buried my face in my pillow and breathed deeply, I could inhale the woody scent of him. I would slip out of bed and kneel on the floor, lay my cheek against the timber.

Since my mother's death, since the first night my father came to my bed, I had struggled to remember her. I lay there, on the timber floor, feeling the flat polish and the rippled grain of the wood, registering the slight tremor from people moving in other rooms, trying to hear her. Each year, each minute, the memory of her voice burrowed deeper into the walls, disappearing into them. I listened as hard as I could. I squeezed my eyes shut and laid both palms against the floor trying to feel her, but all there was was him — his footsteps on the timber, his hand at the door, his smell, his mouth, his stubborn hands. He hoarded her in this house. Alive she had always hovered just beyond his reach, spilling out of his hands like water, between his fingers. Dead she haunted him, not because she wouldn't let go, but because he refused to allow her to slip away. He kept her in that house, in those walls. *Peter Peter, pumpkin eater. Had a wife and couldn't keep her. Put her in a pumpkin shell and there he kept her very well.* He hoarded everything, every memory, every scent, every particle of breath she had once breathed he boarded up inside himself. He had stolen the scent of her from the sheets where we lay, the sound of her breathing. He was a bottomless well. A hole in the world. If he could, he would have taken everything into his hollow, starving gut. His hundred-year-old bones. But I was her daughter, and something of her belonged to me. Something was mine and I would take it back from him. I would strip the skin from his bones and take her in my arms.

The open windows of my room let in a slight breeze, but also the dust. A thin film of it lay over the timber floor, the curtain hems were a faint red. I sat on the bed and pulled my braid forward, twisting my fingers between the ropes, unbinding my hair. I went to the cupboard and took out a dress, slipping it over my head. It fell loosely around my ankles. I took the key from my mother's flute and placed it under my tongue. I bundled the stained sheets up off the bed and stuffed them into a basket. Without water in the tanks we were careful, each litre was as precious as blood. We did not waste it on washing things too often, or with too much water. Emma often drained our bath-water into the cement laundry basins to scrub and soak our clothes before watering the plants with it. We did have a machine, but the motor had died a year ago and never been fixed; it was too expensive and it used too much water.

Outside again the grass was sharp, the dirt dry and cracked beneath my feet. It was warm — the earth, the air, my skin. I walked slowly, my eyes straight ahead, my head high, my dress shifting and brushing the soil. The morning air glanced across my shoulders as my hair was lifted by the first faint breeze of the day. My dress curled like a thin white shell. I shifted the basket, pulling it higher onto my jutting hip. The dust collected between my toes. I moved like a cloud with red-soled feet. I turned off the road and headed down the thin dog-track to the creek. Here the grass was longer; but still singed, still silver. It hushed me. It cut at my ankles like paper. I shifted the basket to the other hip and brushed the hair back from my face.

The creek was nearly dry, barely a foot of water licked at the cracked banks. It had never run dry, although what was once a river had become a muddy creek, running fitfully through a deep split in the earth. I had to climb slowly down the embankment, using roots and half-buried rocks to steady myself. At the bottom I put the basket down and hitched up my dress, tucking it in bunches at my hips. My brown legs shone. As I bent and pulled a sheet from the basket the wind caught it, snapping it like a sail before I plunged it into the water. My hair spilt forward over my shoulders. My bare arms were wet and smooth. I held one sheet down with a foot as I floated the other. Spiralled it. Caught the rush of water. I pulled the sheet up and twisted it so the water slid down over my wet thighs and shins. The water slipped. Rushed. I twisted and curled the cotton. The water spilled. I waded back out to the cracked bank and placed the sheets in the basket. They slapped and licked at the wicker. I pulled the basket onto my hip and moved further up the bank to a large, flat rock. I put my basket down and knelt on its surface, staining it darker with my wet shins, my wet dress. My feet curled like pink commas beneath me. Water dripped from the basket.

I looked up through the angled branches, the sparse leaves. The sky seemed thin. Stretched. The last morning stars were fading. The air curved around me. I took one of the sheets between my hands. My polished knuckles gripped as I beat the cloth on the rock.

Water sprayed up in swinging arcs, it circled and crowned me. Drops spat and spilt on my skin, in my hair. The sheet snapped. Spat. The rock turned slowly darker. My shoulders shifted beneath my dress, the cloth stretched and sank. My arms whipped the sheets. They clung to the rock, coming away with a wet lick, curving up and slapping heavily. The sheets shed water like tears, like diamonds, like stars. Water that spun and rattled on the dry ground. The wind picked up, clicked the tree limbs together. The sky bent. I arched my back like an earth-bound moon and whacked the sheet across the rock. The sound echoed and was whipped away by the wind. The drops arced out, were caught. I whipped again. The sheets heavy and chafing my hands. My palms red. A wisp of cloud formed a pale shade over the fading moon. The morning star was caught in her veil. The drops arced. Slid. Fell. The wind sang.

When I looked up the sky was pale, the stars indistinct. I bunched the sheets into the basket, swung it up onto my hip, and strode across the rock. I struggled up the embankment to the track and through the hushed silver grass. The dirt clung to my wet feet. The basket was heavy. When I reached the main track a drop of rain fell on my cheek. A drop fell on my shoulder, on my thigh as I swung my leg forward, on the sheets lying curled and ruddy in my basket. I walked slowly, head high.

Walking towards my father's house I felt the rain on my shoulders. The warm light slipping between drops of water. The red earth was suddenly rich with rain and early morning light. The rain-washed buildings looked fresh, their tilted dimensions quaint and picturesque. Even the horizon was a scrub-faced stranger, the sun bleeding colour into the sky.

I heard someone come up the stairs behind me and could not turn. A house full of people and I couldn't remember how to feel when they came. Should I turn and smile? Walk away? Would my silence be an invitation? I listened carefully — for the breath, the step, that would reveal them.

His hand beneath my rib was warm and the tension in my belly shifted. I leant backwards and inhaled the pale almost watery scent of his skin. I felt his breath above me, his face against my hair, his unshaven chin grazing my scalp. Scalding me with a kiss, my mother's key warming beneath my tongue. His fist was nestled in my gut, the hairs on his arm bristling against my dress. The skin of his forearm was sun-fresh and firm. He bent down over my shoulder and I turned my face — my mouth — to catch his kiss.

As I turned, I saw Callum and Jason walking towards us. Their faces uncertain. I looked back at my father. In the middle of the sudden rain, I saw his face. The taste of the kiss turned sour, my mouth suddenly awkward on his. The weight of his hand in my hair seemed somehow more than the weight of the world, pressing me down. I felt the red soil wet in my lungs and could not breathe, could not catch hold of the uncertain air.

My father's face, already still, turned cold and he moved away from me. He pushed me out of the way. I reached my hand to touch him but even the rain, the rain he had prayed for, could not touch him now. He was swift and burning. I stood watching his back, how the rain made his shirt cling to his skin, as Jason moved to block his way.

My father held his shoulders taut. The two men stood face to face at the top of the stairs. Their eyes were steady and filled with the peculiar fury of men. That strange still anger I have never understood. A hollow silence grew between them, the tension held in their shoulders like huge cats ready to pounce. When I opened my mouth to speak, Jason reached past my father and took my hand, leading me down the stairs as he glanced over at Callum, who was standing, white-faced, beside the van door. As I shuffled past my silent father, Jason put a hand in the small of my back and gently pushed me towards Callum and the van.

'Where do you think you're going?' Jack called after me and I hesitated.

I stood with my back turned, feeling the weight of the house stretching towards me. Reaching to hold me again. The floorboards that shrank and cracked in the heat. The empty rooms full of wet light. I felt every breath in my father's body, every grain of dirt blown against the windows. Silence fell on my father's face and in the house and in the paddocks that stretched their endless palms beneath us. Silence fell and was caught in my hair, in my hands, in my teeth. I took another step away. Each one easier than the last, until I was almost running through the rain. At the last minute I turned and saw him standing there, his hands fallen open at his sides.

'You're mine,' he said.

I almost spoke but silence clutched at my tongue and as I turned away I heard it rattle in my father's throat, stealing the weight of his words, stealing their power, stealing his name.

Jason followed close behind me as I walked away. Slowly now, more certain that my father would not try to stop us. Sure that there was nothing he could do. Nothing either of us could do anymore. My bare feet were red with wet soil, the basket of clean sheets still riding on my hip. I held my head high and watched the sky spill its wet stars towards me. I watched Callum come forward and speak but I didn't hear him — I was listening to my father's breathing. I saw Callum hold his hand against my arm and slide it into my elbow. I watched Cal's face as he looked back at the house, as he screamed out, his mouth open and wet with disaster. I felt the soil sucking at the soles of my feet. The oily warmth of the van's door, the resistance as I yanked it open and climbed in, carefully balancing the basket of wet pink sheets on my knees. The warmth of Callum's thigh as he climbed up next to me. The tremor as Jason started the engine and we turned out of the yard. I saw my father turn back to the house as we pulled across the yard and I watched him tip his head back to taste the rain, saw it slipping into the cracks of his skin.

The wet sun caught me. Spun sugar melting against the windscreen. Pulling my skin tight against the bone. My mouth half-open and sour. My elbows resting among the damp sheets. I felt my skin flushed red and sweat-shiny as I tipped forward and caught my head in my hands. My round, heavy head.

The young man did not know where the tree of life was to be found, but he set out and went on and on, as long as his legs could carry him, but he had no hope of finding it.

— Brothers Grimm, *The White Snake*

Sleeping crushed and thinly. I woke to the change in tone as we pulled off a dirt road onto a paved one. I kept my eyes closed and heard rather than saw the trees reaching over us, the quietness of shade, the tunnelled sound of the van's engine pushed down upon itself after years of hearing motors whose sounds were lost in empty paddocks. I heard Cal's dry cough and the half-grunted question of Jason's reply. The soft creak as one of them shifted in his seat. Radio static blurred everything. It had been hours since we lost the signal from the last station and neither of them had bothered to retune it. I wriggled to make my stiff body more comfortable and drifted back into sleep. I woke and slept. Woke and slept. It was all confused and the same. There were long roads and oddly unnatural stops when we sipped silently at styrofoam cups of weak, bitter coffee and stared out the windows. Our bodies still thrummed to the endless vibration of the van. Cold toast. Warmed over eggs. Chipped plates and dog-eared magazines. The same dry town repeating itself over and over again.

Mostly we just drove.

Callum's dry cough bothered me more and more each hour. The sight of his thin arms, his lank hair. His stained red feet that dangled from the end of the bed as though abandoned. The firm freckled back of his neck as he sat up front in the van with Jason. The two of them laughing and smoking, the radio static buzzing between them.

The fetid smell of two men in an old van, half a carton of beer and a carton of cigarettes, a leak in the roof and piles of dirty clothes festering on the metal floor. I was rusted and irritable with exhaustion.

'I need a drink, and something to eat.'

'Yeah.'

'Well?'

'Well what?'

'Are you going to stop or do I have to jump out the fucking door?'

'We'll stop when I'm ready to stop,' Jason snapped and I fell back onto the foam mattress, staring sullenly at the roof. He's tired, I thought. We're all tired and we have a long way to go. I rolled my head to the side so I could see him, the side of his head and the jut of his elbow, his hand on the gearstick. His fingers were clenched tightly on the stick, the knuckles white. I was tired and thirsty and I felt faintly claustrophobic and nauseous, the gritty ugly nausea of carsickness. I thought about asking Cal to swap places but worried that Jason would snap at us again. He made me nervous with his intense staring and cockiness. I wondered how it was that both Cal and I were already deferring to him — how he had become the leader of our trek — and what it was about him that made this seem logical, inevitable. I studied the back of his head, his strong tanned neck and the line of his jaw, the way his mouth was so definitely closed when he didn't speak. The way he held his body like a dam holding back the threat of a thundering river. He seemed so taut, so volatile and it was this, more than anything else, which made me want to hold him. I watched his throat and imagined what it would be like to place my mouth against it — to feel his pulse beat hard and fast on my tongue — to feel his quiet desperation focused on me. When he half-turned and caught me watching him in the rear-view mirror I blushed. He didn't smile. His eyes stayed on me until the blush spread deeper — into my gut — and I could barely breathe.

It was hours before we stopped for the night in a small town whose name I no longer remember. At the first corner was a service station, the price of fuel scrawled in third-grade chalk lettering on a sign that had fallen over. The counter inside swayed beneath its load of lighters and chocolate. The cigarettes were locked behind greasy glass. The cock-eyed boy behind the counter was reading Stephen King. He carefully marked his page and put the book face-down on the counter before him so that we could see the back cover. He tilted his head and thumbed our change sullenly into my hand. He had a tattoo between his thumb and finger. A swastika done in high school with a compass and ink.

At the second corner stood a hotel with rusting fretwork and timber floors. There was a strong smell of cheese on toast and stale beer. The bored barman watched cricket, only half-turning away from the wall-mounted set to pull beers. I was left alone to shower in a communal bathroom where someone's teeth sat soaking in an old glass. Down the hall were our two rooms, separated by thin timber walls, with beds sunk in the middle and covered in puckered chenille bedspreads of orange and green. I lay on the bed listening to the faint rumble of men's gossip downstairs — small-town politics, crops, subsidies, prices, rainfall.

We ordered a meal of overcooked roast and warmed-over vegetables in the bar downstairs. There was nowhere else to eat. Callum was silent over dinner. Sulking, shovelling his food into his mouth he looked not at me, nor at Jason, but at the unsteady table beneath us. Jason was also quiet, but not tense. His hand as it grazed my knee was warm and reassuring.

After dinner I went outside and walked along the edge of the river behind the pub, leaving the men to their beer and stilted conversation. It felt good to stretch my legs. To undo the knots and cramps from endless sitting in the van. My belly felt heavy and full, my breasts throbbed and my back ached. I tried vaguely to remember when my last period had been, when the next one might be due. Soon, I thought. Today, maybe tomorrow, sometime this week surely. As I circled back towards the hotel I walked up to the street where a few stores were still open. At the late night chemist the woman behind the counter told me the river flooded nearly every year. She showed me the blue line painted six feet up the wall where the floodwaters had reached in 1978. That year a woman had drowned while trying to save an old rocker from her home. She had been dragging it down the hall when the water just reached in and pulled her away.

'I was about five years old,' she said. 'My mother had us all sitting on the roof, even though the water barely reached the third step of our house, and I saw Mrs Oliver float past. She was still holding onto that rocker.'

As I left the chemist I walked down to the park and lay on the grass near the edge of the river, listening to it lumber quietly along. The night air was empty and comforting. It was several hours before I returned to our room.

When I walked in Callum was reading on one of the beds. He only half looked up. I walked over to the window, looking down into the street where we had parked the van. I could see Jason standing near it, a cigarette in his hand. As I watched he glanced up and saw me. He smiled and waved.

'Where's he going?' I asked. Callum didn't answer me. He rolled over on the bed, pulling his knees up toward his chest. I turned around and leaned back on the windowsill. Callum looked at me over the top of his book.

'I think I'll go with him,' I said.

'Whatever.'

I shook my head and turned away.

Downstairs Jason was already in the van, his hands resting lightly on the wheel as he took one last drag on his cigarette. The engine had been running for a few minutes, warming up. I climbed in beside him without catching his eye, and pulled the seat belt down over my lap. He didn't say anything, but as we pulled away from the hotel I saw him smile.

At the house I followed him inside uncertainly. It was a small, ugly brick box in a row of almost identical buildings. An old car was parked in the driveway, with a bumper sticker that read *I shoot and I vote.* Inside a group of men were sitting around a coffee table, the room stank. They were all thin and desperate looking. One of them glanced up from his seat as we walked in, his face alert and suspicious until he saw Jason.

'Mate,' he said, 'about time you got here.'

'This is Germaine.'

The man nodded at me without meeting my eyes. 'I'm Wayne.' He gestured at the two men sitting at the table. 'This is Pecker and Steggles.' They did not look up, intent as they were on measuring the white powder on the table into small packets. Jason and Wayne exchanged a few blunt words before going off into another room.

Jason looked back at me once and winked. 'I'll be back in a sec.'

I sat down on the lounge and watched the two silent men as they got to the end of their work. The taller one — Pecker — leant back in his chair and stretched. 'I'll put this lot away,' he said to his friend, 'you get that ready.'

As Pecker walked away with the tray full of drugs in neat packages, Steggles quickly prepared a syringe. By the time Pecker got back he had his arm tied and the needle sliding into a vein. Pecker leant over and took the empty syringe from his open hand. He sat down and tied the band around his arm, holding it tight with his teeth. When he leant back into his chair he caught my eye and hesitated. He took the band out of his mouth. 'Want some?'

I looked at the needle in his hand, then at his friend lying back with an idiot smile on his face. 'I don't know.'

'It's good stuff. No sugar.'

I stared at the needle he was holding out to me, wondering how it felt to have the drug slide into a vein. The only needles I'd ever had had been the sudden jab and sting of immunisations, or the slow throb of blood being taken. I bit my bottom lip and leant forward. 'What does it feel like?'

Pecker laughed, 'Better than fucking, baby. Better than anything.'

I heard Jason come back into the room. From the corner of my eye I saw his legs, and those of Wayne beside him. They were still talking like old mates, their voices soft and friendly.

'Come on. Do you want it or not?'

I shifted in my seat, trying not to catch Jason's attention. I wasn't sure what he knew about me, but I didn't want him to think I was a naive little girl. I didn't want him to see me as nervous or afraid. I shook my head and lowered my eyes, hoping Pecker would let it go.

'What's wrong with her?' Pecker said to Jason.

I felt Jason's attention switch from Wayne to Pecker and me. I heard him walk over and as I looked up I saw him watching me in an odd, questioning way. I smiled nervously.

'Time to go,' he said.

'Come on, Jase. Aren't you going to stay and party? It's been a while, mate.'

Jason shook his head and rattled the keys in his pocket. 'I don't use the shit anymore, mate, it's bad for business.'

'I know what you mean,' said Wayne. 'These blokes shoot up as much as they sell.'

'Never make any money that way,' said Jason.

'Lay off,' said Pecker, as he slid along closer to me. 'What about you?' He placed a hand on my thigh.

I blushed and pulled away, but his hand rose up insistently until it was resting near my groin. I tried to pull away but he reached over with his other hand and grabbed my breast. I could hear what I presumed was Jason laughing to himself. I tried to say something, but the only thing that came out was a half-mumbled cry of shock. I felt a deep and wordless shame, but also a sense that this was right, that this was who I was. Unable to move, I was frightened by how small and voided I was in this house full of strangers. I looked down at the floor, staring at the tile pattern beneath my feet, thinking abstract geometric thoughts of shape and colour and design. I felt tears in my eyes and quickly blinked them back, biting the tip of my tongue and thinking about the squares, studying how they were laid out first this way and then that.

Jason reached down and grabbed Pecker by the shirt, pulling him away. 'Leave her alone,' he said. Tears of shame and fright spilled from my eyes. Jason knelt down in front of me and gently wiped them away. 'It's okay,' he said, 'we're going now.'

As he pulled me up beside him his arm slipped around my waist and I felt the warmth of his body beside mine. It was a warmth which seeped into me where our bodies touched. I felt safe. Protected. Still looking at the floor I concentrated on his arm gently looped around me. He turned back to Pecker as we headed for the door. 'She's not that kind of girl,' he said and placed a light kiss on my temple, 'not like the drugged-out sluts you hang with.'

Early morning in a strange bed. The light crept in under the curtains at an unfamiliar angle. Outside it was quiet, but a different quiet from what I was used to. The silence of an almost urban place. The quiet of a paved street instead of red earth, instead of distant cattle. The sound of a river slipping by. The miracle of too much water outside my window and my brother sleeping in the next room. It was too early to wake up, and I was too awake to sleep. In the hall outside I heard a man's footsteps and then his hands fumbling with keys before he dropped them and knelt down in a drunken fog, running his hands over the timber floor.

I rolled over and looked at Jason lying beside me. Asleep he was as soft and unrestrained as a child. His unlikely feet turned out like a dancer's, his hair tufted in ridiculous beaten-egg-white peaks. When I unlaced his boots he shifted slightly, curling into me like a child.

I brushed the hair off his face. His skin was warm. He frowned and shook his head. I leant closer, close enough to smell the traces of pot on his breath. I kissed the polished knob of his cheekbone. *Touch me*, I thought, and perhaps it was this that made him open his eyes and stare at me in that astonishing and insistent manner. I was shocked by his looking, by the bare scientific scrutiny of his gaze. He gazed at me so strangely, as if he could see not who I was, but who he was. I felt pinned and curious; a blush began in my stomach and spread over my skin. I opened my mouth to speak but when he frowned slightly I decided against it.

He turned his head and caught my mouth; his lips warm against my own. As his arm slid up to circle me I smiled and moved closer. This, at least, was something I understood. This movement of two bodies together. Unlike Jack he was not urgent or insistent. When I tensed against him he moved away slightly, became almost still until I moved towards him again. He did not grope blindly and desperately at my body. He touched me gently, slowly, sliding the flat of his palms over my skin. I had to tell myself to breathe. Although I gritted my teeth and had to turn away, I think he believed it was because I'd never been with a man before, and it made him even more tender. More careful. For hours afterwards I could feel the warmth where his fingertips had pressed into me. He held me as if I was something pure, as if although I moved against him he knew that I was fragile and could well break apart in his hands. At the last, when he was moving inside me, I glanced up to find him scrutinising me with his startled blue eyes wide open and intent. I felt the shock of recognition in my gut. *I know this man*, I thought, although it was in most ways untrue. But there, in that bed, in that moment, I recognised something that I knew I needed. Something I could not live without.

As we fell asleep he was still inside me, my legs wrapped around his thighs and his hand holding the back of my head. When I woke later he was curled against me and I felt the sudden kick in my gut at seeing his skin, his body so startling in its careless nakedness. So willing to be revealed.

Are there charms against love? Is that what the apple held? Is that what the snake had to say? Poison your heart, it will only destroy you.

Eve was sleeping when he came. The house was silent. Lilith had gone away for a conference somewhere in the Mediterranean, Eve imagined lemons and wine and bitter coffee. He pushed open the door, which was not locked, and walked into the bedroom. 'Get up,' he said, 'it is four in the afternoon. There are things to be done.'

'She isn't here,' Eve moaned. 'What is there to get up for?'

He frowned and pulled back the sheets, took her by the wrist and yanked her from her bed. He took her out into the garden and Eve leant against a tree, twisting an unripe apple from its branch. Lilith had grown this tree — grafted it in the shed at the back of the garden and nurtured it in a pot for months before planting it in the ground. She had promised to return home in time to harvest the fruit. Eve thought about the sun-ripened bodies of women in the Mediterranean, of the white houses perched on cliffs, of the blue ocean. 'She's not coming back, is she?'

She was polishing the apple against her thigh when he leant over and kissed her. It was a sudden thing and she didn't have time to turn away. She was still thinking of Lilith's skin growing warm in the sun, how her hair would begin to lighten and her cheeks to glow, how she would sit and drink glasses of water and peel oranges in the afternoons, spitting the pips out into the street. She felt him pressing her against the bark of the tree. His hands were clenched around her wrists as he pushed her to the ground. She lay beneath him, watching the apples shudder on their branches.

'I love you,' he said.

'Yes,' she replied.

I eased off the bed and sat on the floor watching the sunlight beginning to seep across the carpet. Soon we would be in the city.

Sydney. Unlike my mother I had never been to a city. Never lived in one. Our local town had no more than three thousand people, and that was when swelled by the influx of tourists and other strangers from outlying properties during the annual Show. Even our own house used to be full of people during that one week of the year. Suddenly children whose voices I heard every day on the school radio took on skin. Ordinary, freckled or brown-bellied skin. The town had only one street — everything huddled together in a single row facing the pub. I could only imagine Venice, London, New York. The strange and huddled existence of people on the television news, the shunt and shift of murder, big business, high rise and high heels. Precariousness. My mother lived in cities most of her life before she married Jack. She lived in London for five years, Sydney for ten, studying music, teaching, playing. She owned a music shop in some dusty arcade in the city before it was demolished to make way for a new department store. A city girl. All swank and glitter and sexuality. Surety and dangerousness.

She played music on the harbour on weekends, busking near the ferries and train stations just to be there, just to watch the music settle on people as they huddled over coffee and newspapers.

I fingered her tiny silver key in my pocket, the smooth dent that cupped my fingertip. She met my father after the shop failed and she took to the road. She took gigs wherever she could and travelled, looking for a new place to settle down, to start again. She wanted peace and quiet, she said. She had dreams about the country life, visions of herself calm and smiling in a postcard farm. When she first met my father he seemed like the kind of man who could give her that. They met when he was in town trying to refinance a mortgage on the property. Things were not going well and he was sitting in a pub late at night when she walked up and asked him to buy her a beer. He shook his head and she laughed, throwing her hair over her shoulder and placing her flute on the bar in front of him. *What is it you want?* she said. When he turned to look at her his face was smoothed open with surprise and she laughed again, placing her cool hand on his forearm. *I'll trade you*, she said, *a beer for a song*, and she pulled her flute out of its case and twisted it together. *What do you want to hear?* My father shook his head and watched her flick her hair out of the way, she took a few steps away from him and lifted the flute to her lips, caught his gaze with her own, and began to play. My father had never been much of a music lover. Of course, he listened to the radio occasionally and there was a dusty and eclectic collection of records in his parents' house, but that night when she played he finally understood something. The whole bar fell silent listening to her, and when she finished they erupted in a raucous round of applause. She continued to hold my father's gaze the whole time, as she played, as the crowd applauded and several people congratulated her, as she crossed the room to stand before him again. When she reached him she took his hand and placed it on her chest. He could feel her heart beating beneath her sweat-slippery skin, hammering at her ribs, and as he looked at her she smiled. Damnedest smile he ever saw, he said. What else was there to do with a woman like that but marry her?

Sometimes I would catch them, leaning against the side of the house, her hand on his wrist. He would speak quietly and she would smile from behind an escaped lick of hair. He would lean towards her and breathe in, just to be closer, just to smell her. He would cup her elbow in his palm and hold her like water that threatened to spill through his fingers. His hand lingered awkwardly, never really getting a hold on her.

For myself, I remember the sound of her music that scaled the walls of my room. I remember her arms that sprouted like brown weeds, smooth and dusty, always shining with sweat. Her voice was quiet but it filled up a room. It filled my head. When she tucked me in my bed at night her hands would brush over my shoulders and down my arms. She would hold my hands and look at my face. She was looking for something and I never knew what it was. Her eyes were huge. I would look back. I would bite my tongue and hold my breath. Hoping she would find it, whatever it was. I could not imagine what she wanted — something outside the thinness of my child's life. Something more than I could imagine in that ordinary room. She told me stories, but they were huge and shapeless. I didn't understand them. I could only listen to her music as it filled my room with light and rhythm and colour.

Her energy, her resilience, resided in her hands, which were like creatures wholly unto themselves. I watched her carve mountains and angels and stars out of the indifferent darkness. I lay quietly in the safe world of my bed, fingering the edge of my sheet. I curled my toes over each other anxiously. I folded my hands neatly over my belly. The bed would slide; would scrape on the timber. The window would fly open at her touch and she would stand there with her flute at her chin and the faint evening light glowing around her. The wind would pick at her hair and she would blow. The notes were cool and heavy; something of water and green leaves hung in them. She would say, *Magic is something ordinary, like a child. Or rain.*

The stars had a rhythm, and my mother knew their meter. She would tilt her head and listen, her eyes wide, to the metronomic tick of the universe. To the planets sliding. She would weave long tuneless melodies. She would hold my hand and lean close to my face and whisper. Her eyes would shine. Her skin was luminous. In the dark she was like a mountain leaning precariously over my pillow. Always threatening to fall. She was too much woman in such a small room, such a small country.

She would take her flute to her mouth and blow. Gently at first and then quickly, faster and faster until I lay breathless beneath her. She leaned closer to my face. Her hair spilling into mine. Her eyes wide and full of secrets. *Can you hear?* She would say. *I can hear you. Your blood, your heart, your lungs. You are like a song on a flute and a drum and a star. Here and here and here.* She kissed my cheek, my throat, the soft crease of my belly. Her skin was warm, her lips soft. I lay silent. Listening. My head tipped sideways, watching the curtain slide over the floorboards and drift upwards.

Jason's jacket was lying on the floor where he'd dumped it; when I picked it up it unrolled and one of the fat packages from last night fell out. A solid mass wrapped in brown paper and tied with string, but underneath I could feel cellophane, or plastic wrap, and beneath that the densely packed substance. I turned it over in my hands, weighing it. Amazed at the ordinariness of brown paper and blue nylon string and cling wrap. I felt a weight in my stomach, something heavy and round, at the thought of what the package meant. For a moment, perhaps, I doubted what we were doing. What we were getting ourselves into. For just a moment I wondered what kind of man dealt in brown paper packages.

Downstairs there was only a handful of people. Some men gathered together at one end of the bar. An old man was sitting nodding absently to himself at a table. I wondered if they were his teeth in the bathroom upstairs. A middle-aged woman was serving behind the counter. I introduced myself, asked about the possibility of coffee or tea and she laughed silently. 'How 'bout a beer, love?' As she placed the beer on the counter before me a man came to the bar and stood silently beside me.

'Mornin', Pierce,' she said. 'This here's Germaine.' He tipped his head at me slightly and took the two glasses of Scotch Dolly poured for him to a chair outside the front door. Dolly pointed after him with her chin. 'Odd one, that. Comes in here every week. Been coming here for at least the ten years me and Des have had the place. Doesn't talk much. Reads roads, though. Like a clairvoyant, you know? Might read yours if you ask.' She smiled again, that strange open mouth, the cramped and broken teeth. 'Left his family twenty-one years ago, never says why, didn't have anywhere to go. No family or friends he felt particularly close to. He just intended to drive into the next town, to a motel. But there were no motels, or they were closed, so he kept going. Been driving for twenty-one years. I guess he doesn't know how to stop any more. That's his home out there, the old heap.'

I turned to see him sitting on the edge of the verandah with one foot resting gently on the road beneath a dusty old car. The air inside the bar was cloying. The men at the end, not as old as I had first thought, were starting to look towards me. Laughing and smirking. I decided to take my beer outside and try my luck with the Reader of Roads.

At first I thought I had made a mistake. He sat watching his car, his hands fidgeting in his pockets and along the seam of his jeans. He drank from his glasses of Scotch — first one glass and then the other. Back and forth. Rattling the keys at his waistband, running his finger along the jagged edge of one. Watching the road and the wheels of his car. When he spoke to me it was almost a shock. 'Well,' he said, 'well then,' and I had the feeling he was not talking to me at all, but starting again halfway through a conversation he had been having with somebody else, with his car perhaps.

'Hi,' I said, 'I'm Germaine.'

He glanced over at me without meeting my eyes, nodded his head slightly and went back to watching the road.

'Dolly tells me you come here a lot.'

This time he didn't even turn, but his eyes moved away from me, looking in the opposite direction. I shifted uncomfortably on my seat, watching his hands that were two different colours, the left pale and thin-skinned, the right tanned to a deep honey.

'I'm sorry,' I muttered. 'I just thought — I mean I wanted to know — to say — I'm not sure what — something. I'll go,' I said, defeated.

He looked over at me, weighing me up in some way, and I smiled uncertainly. 'It's alright, girl. I just don't like unnecessary talk. Enough words in the world already, I reckon, without adding more of the same.'

I nodded my head in agreement. 'A different language, you mean?' He seemed disappointed. I wished I could think of something interesting to say.

'It's not like that. It's more like … like a road been driven so many times you can't hear her anymore. Can't hear the branch that snaps as you push past 'cause it's already been done. Already been there too many times.'

'Like old books?'

'Maybe.'

'Ones read too many times, by too many people. Books in libraries that have gone yellow and are stained with old coffee cups — sometimes even a hair falls out, or flakes of skin — and handwriting all over the margins till you can't see anymore what it was that was there in the first place.'

'No such thing. No stories that don't already belong to other stories. Nothing that ain't already been said.'

'What about secrets? Secrets are kept in your gut. Secrets are unspoken, but you can still hear them.'

'Have to listen between what's said and what's not. Have to pay attention to hands half-raised and people leaving rooms and such like.

Like a road. Got to pay attention to where she don't go. Got to listen to the road, but also to where the road ain't carved. Country has its secrets, people falling through the cracks like fish through a net. Falling right off the edge of the world.'

He stopped to drink again. I looked at him more carefully, watching his hands and the thin line of his legs. He looked naked, an unlikely knight shucked of his armour — almost blue — and his hands were like my father's hands. He said, 'This whole country is covered in roads. Whole earth, actually. Some roads you can see. Some roads tar, some dirt, some concrete. Some hardly there at all, just tracks in the soil which shift every time it rains, or the wind blows. Some made of rocks, but they shift too — slowly maybe — but still they shift. Rolling over each other when they think no-one is there to see. Thing is, those roads, they know where you're going. They carry you.'

He cocked his head to one side and I saw the ring of dirt around the top of his blue-brown collar, the pearl-white skin beneath. He said, 'Do you want to know which road to take?'

At first he frowned with concentration and then he closed his eyes and I could see him listening to the road speak to him, his hands spread out on the tarmac, his fingers twitching impatiently. He was quiet for a while. Occasionally grunting in agreement, or shaking his head to disagree, with the map that travelled beneath his hands. When he finally opened his mouth to speak, his eyes flicked open.

I sat and listened to him keening, to the strangled sound of his voice trying to squeeze itself between his teeth and tongue. But the words wouldn't come and the longer he tried the more startled his eyes became. In the end I grabbed his hands to pull them from the road and he looked away. He seemed stunned. He stared into the palms of his hands as if he had never seen them before, as if they had betrayed him. I stood and walked back past the men leaning against the bar and Dolly absently polishing glasses, up the stairs to my room. From the window I saw his car pull out from the front of the hotel and drive north.

With my eyes I traced our route on the map laid out on my lap. The highway flowed down the coast in a thin vein-blue line but I had not seen the ocean for hours. It was a stagnant, ugly afternoon. The line of the highway veered inland where a coffee stain rumpled the paper — around Gosford — distorting the town names for miles around. One milky finger even spread as far north as Taree. The radio hissed as we passed out of the range of yet another radio station. Callum fumbled in the glove compartment for a tape but there were none, only lolly wrappers and an empty tissue box. I threw the map on the floor and lay down on the mattress. Through the rear window I could see the tops of the trees that flashed past, and the watered-down colour of the sky. I closed my eyes. I could hear the boys talking, but not what they were saying, just a low hum that blended with the sound of the motor beneath me.

I fell into a light sleep and woke hours later. Outside the window the pale sky had been replaced by the shadowy glare of streetlights. I heard Jason's raised voice over the sound of the engine and realised that this was what had woken me. 'Just admit it, you wouldn't have done shit without me there.'

'Fuck off.'

I heard Jason laugh. 'I'm just saying, you're the kind of guy who needs other people. That's not me.' We must have passed through another town. I turned my head slightly until I could see the moon following us. She was almost full.

'You needed my wheels,' Callum said.

'I would have found another way.'

It must have been a small town, already the light had fallen away and the stars seemed bright again. It was cold in the back of the van. The breeze that flew in through Jason's window smelled of exhaust fumes. I heard him light a cigarette and offer Callum one. A long truck rushed past us in a tunnel of wind, lights and music blaring. The van shuddered.

'Was that your stepmother back there?'

Callum didn't answer. I could feel his anger bristling.

'Emma,' I said.

'How long has she been around?'

'A few years.'

'Since your mother left?'

'She didn't leave. She died,' I said.

'She wanted to die,' Callum said.

I sat up and leaned forward between the seats. 'That's not true. She just died. People just die sometimes.'

'Not her. She wanted to go, she left us.'

'Shut up,' I said, my hand reaching around to grab at Cal's wrist.

'Come on,' said Jason, 'it doesn't matter anymore. That was then, you know.' I leant my head against the back of his seat and closed my eyes. Jason reached his hand back and caught mine, squeezing gently. 'Everything's gunna be different now. I promise.'

I didn't answer him, but I squeezed his hand gently in reply, leaning down to kiss the side of his palm. I heard Callum make a noise beside me and turned to see him glaring down at our hands.

'How long before you get rid of the stuff?' Callum asked.

'You'll get your money.'

'Okay, but how long will it take?'

'Don't worry about it. You can stay with me until the money comes through.'

'What about Germaine?'

'She'll be fine,' Jason said. 'I'll look after her.'

Girls who run away from their amorous fathers are pursued. They clothe themselves in ashes or donkey's skins or become trees. Their toes grow long and burrow into the ground, their skin thickens and their arms split into a hundred — even a thousand — branches, growing thinner and thinner. Leaves sprout from their fingertips and the beat of their blood slows until it is almost imperceptible. Their hearts grow hard. Become wooden.

Wandering my father's property I would come across trees whose crusts had been damaged. They were thin-limbed and twisted and tall. Blood would seep from their wounds and I would press my ear to their trunks to hear them breathing, I would whisper secrets to them, trying to get them to whisper back. What secrets they kept! As I listened I would prise their blood tears from their trunks and place them in my pocket. At home I kept them in a jar, as glassy and precious as rubies.

I wondered where they had come from. At night when my father wandered the hallways, seeming old and inescapable as fathers do, I imagined that the trees were my sisters and that I was the One — the younger sister who would not only escape our father's unnatural desires but free my sisters as well.

I lay in the back of the van reading and dozing, listening to the drone of the radio, watching the trees and telegraph poles through the rear window, listening to the boys' conversation that grew more and more antagonistic as we approached the city. Callum asked about the money and the drugs, and Jason answered without answering — evading the details of when, where, and how. He made it clear it was his deal and that, despite our investment, he wasn't going to allow Cal to intrude on it. The more he avoided giving Callum straight answers the more nervous and inquisitive Callum became. Eventually they were barely speaking to each other, their hostility as palpable as the heat.

By the time we stopped for lunch at a roadhouse they hadn't exchanged a word in several hours. Callum ordered food at the counter and went outside to eat while Jason and I sat at a booth in the empty restaurant. The linoleum-topped tables were yellowing, the plates chipped and the heavy cutlery mismatched and worn. The waitress shuffled up to the counter in old shoes. As she took our order she kept glancing back to the booth where she'd been sitting — a *New Idea* crossword lay on her table beside a cup of coffee. She barely spoke to us and there was no radio playing, no sound at all except the traffic on the highway outside. We ate silently and quickly. Before we left, Jason went to the counter for cigarettes and some hot chips to take with him, while I went to the bathroom.

For days I had felt something pushing me further and further forward, pressing into the small of my back. But now, in this tiny roadside toilet I felt it take hold, a hand propelling me forward, away from the past, from the ever-present ghost of my mother in the corridor, my father in the bedrooms, from the past where I had reeled from room to room. I had dreamed of drowning in an ocean torn apart by storms. I had wanted to drown, to sink beneath the waves into the deeper, silent, solitary wetness. There was a sneaking but persistent inevitability in my dreams. I knew — the way you do in dreams — that I had no alternative but to drown.

I sat on the toilet looking down at the clean white lining in the undies I had pulled down to my knees and felt a slight tension shift inside me. No blood after all, just a small smudge of clear mucus. I pushed a pad into them anyway. My period would come today, maybe tomorrow and I didn't want to be caught in the van with blood seeping into my jeans. The undies were pale blue with tiny fish printed on them. Undies that Emma had bought me, knowing how much I dreamed of the ocean. They were little girls' things, pale and innocuous and cute, although the frilled elastic left red marks across my belly and hips. All of my underwear was like this; decorated with pictures of stars or flowers, little bows tacked into the front. That's the first thing I'll do when we get there, I thought, I'll buy myself real underwear — women's underwear — I'll throw these away.

As I walked back into the diner, past where the waitress had been sitting, I glanced out the window. A flat gravelly yard with two half-eaten cars and a wire fence collapsing across itself. I turned away. My eyes grazed the surface of her table, her magazine and empty coffee cup and the curved white basket sitting on the bench seat. Blankets wrapped like a cocoon around a tiny child. I turned to see if she was looking and leant closer, reaching a hand to tuck the blanket around its little face. But the skin was cold and hard and firm. I pulled my hand away too quickly, catching the blanket on my wristwatch. It spilled the tiny body out of its wrappings and I saw the stiff little arms, the painted curl on its forehead, the glass eyes that tipped back in its head on tiny weights. I turned again, checking to see that the woman was still out of sight, and quickly wrapped the doll back in its blanket and replaced it in the basket. I couldn't help but feel it didn't look right — not how it had been — but I turned away and hurried past the empty tables and out the door.

'I'll be there in a minute,' Jason called, as the door swung shut behind me.

I climbed up into the back of the van and slid the door across, clutching at my stomach. I closed my eyes and tried to think of something else. Something soft and gentle. I tried to remember the way Jason's touch made me feel lit up inside, but that only made me think of the baby nested in its blankets, with its skin so hard and cold and plastic. I thought about my mother, about the sound of her voice. I hummed the lullaby she used to play for me.

'What's the matter with you?' said Callum. 'Where's Jason?'

As he started the engine I saw Jason coming across the car park, his fingers digging beneath the butcher paper for his chips, and behind him I saw the woman watching us from behind the closed door of the restaurant. One of her hands was resting on the chrome rail that served as a handle and the other was in the pocket of her dress. Perhaps she couldn't have children, maybe that was why. Perhaps she was a woman with the mind of a child, trapped in a world where everything was a harmless and inconsequential game. I think about her often. I even went back later, when I was travelling north, but she was gone. She frightened me that day but later I thought I understood. Later I believed there was something comforting about a dead-already child who was never hungry or dirty or wet. A child who never cried.

When Jason jumped into the passenger seat he brought the smell of hot chips with him. When he leant back to kiss me his lips were salted and slippery. As he ran his tongue over my bottom lip I closed my eyes.

'Let's go,' he said. 'No more stops — we'll be there before nine. Then we can get some real sleep. In real beds.'

'Where are we going to stay?'

'My parents' place. It's a bit rundown but what the hell, we could do worse. It's in a good spot, looking out over the harbour, all it needs is a bit of a clean and whatever.'

'What about your parents?'

'They've retired to the coast. The house is mine. They were going to sell it but the market was down so they decided to give it to me instead. A pre-death inheritance.'

'So it's really your place?'

'It's where I grew up.'

I settled back against the seat and looked out the window. It was late afternoon, the light was full, almost green, melting like butter over the highway. I tried to imagine Jason as a young child, a little boy with a room full of toys; balls and baseball cards, model spaceships dangling from his ceiling, dirty clothes crumpled on the floor. Jason as a teenager with a small but loyal gang of boys he ran with, a string of girlfriends he barely differentiated between. Jason with a mother and father who sat at home and stared at each other across a kitchen table, wondering what had become of their little boy.

i think you are a whole city
and yesterday when i first met you
i started moving
thru one of your suburbs
where all the gardens are fresh
with faces of you
flowering up

— Earle Birney

L ong before we reached the city I could hear it humming in the ground, like laying my cheek against a railroad track to hear the train coming, or against the ground to hear the earth beat. When we reached the outer suburbs it was night and they swelled from the ground like a faerie hunt, wild with light. At first nothing — a few houses, some lights — and then the moon, which seemed to dip her head to follow us through the streets, appeared paler. Her glow diminished until I could not see her at all. Instead there were roads that floated over each other, and old brick houses like greeting cards stacked on shelves. Then they grew taller. Two storeys. Three. Clusters of them, like old women huddling together in grey coats. We dived beneath the harbour in a tunnel that was like the inside of a worm; like being inside someone's throat when a dentist shines his torch onto their teeth, moist and secretive, with white tiled walls.

We drove into the city because Jason wanted to see someone about the deal before we went to the house. As we moved through the crowded streets, there were people bunched together on the foot-paths, so many that they seemed like flocks of birds with their wings clipped, moving in formation as the traffic lights blinked: WALK, DON'T WALK, WALK, DON'T WALK. They wheeled around street corners and poured, like sticky molasses, into buses and ferries and subway entrances, swerving around street vendors selling cigarettes and magazines.

As we turned another corner there were still more people; shiny-feathered crows with coats like wings. The buildings were lower, chairs and tables balanced against the traffic beneath neon strips. Long-legged women leaned against telegraph poles smoking cigarettes and watching the traffic watching them. We passed a tattoo parlour where two fat men were playing cards on the kerb, one of them licking his fingers over each one. More neon, twisted like red licorice.

In Oxford Street Jason slowed down, trawling through the crowded streets. When we stopped at a set of lights, a woman leaned in the passenger window of the van. She had long legs and plastic, light-tipped hair, a cigarette between her breasts and a pair of clear plastic wings — like a child's toy — on her back.

Callum smiled at her as she asked him for a light. When the lights turned green Jason pulled over closer to the kerb to let the traffic past. Cal was leaning out the window talking to her as Jason lit himself a cigarette and waited.

'I'll bet you've never been with a woman before, have you, Cal?' said Jason.

'Leave him alone,' the girl drawled.

'You want to talk to this low-life skank,' Jason said, 'get out of the van. I've got better things to do.'

Callum turned quickly to face him, but something changed his mind and instead of protesting he pushed the door open and stepped out onto the footpath. As Jason flicked on the indicator I put my hand on the door handle to follow Cal. The sight of his back and his long legs loping away set off a lurching fear in my gut. I felt suddenly nauseous and alone, worried about when I would see him again. I looked over at Jason, my mouth open to ask him to wait, to chase after Cal, to bring him back to me.

'Don't worry about it,' Jason said. 'We'll get him later.'

'How? He doesn't know where we are, where we're going.'

Jason leaned out the window and called, 'Hey, Cal. I'll get what's left of you in the morning. Meet me at the el Alamein fountain at ten.'

Cal turned back with a questioning look on his face and I reached over to put a hand on Jason's arm. I heard the girl with the plastic wings laughing and saw her take Cal's arm like a debutante. He waved at me and smiled jauntily. 'I'll see you tomorrow,' he called. 'Time to have some fun.'

Cal directed one more odd look at me and then at Jason, like a schoolboy indicating a crush, and turned away. I sat in the van with my sweaty palms pressed against the door handle, ready to jump out and follow him, but what then? What about our money? Our van? A place to sleep? Where would I be following him to? Jason snorted a quiet laugh and when I glanced over I saw him looking at me. When I saw his face, at once familiar and unfamiliar, I felt frightened. Of all the people I had known at that point in my life he was the least well-known, virtually a stranger, but what did that mean? Of all the people in my world my mother was dead, my father was gone and my brother had deserted me. I didn't know where to go from here. I didn't know what choices to make and so I made none. Looking back I wish I had followed Cal — taken him back from her and found some other way, some other story for us — but I didn't do anything. I settled back against my seat and looked out at the street in front of me. As we turned the corner I saw Callum follow the girl across the street and sit leaning on a sticky table while she flicked her plastic wings and folded his money neatly, running her nails along each crease.

He looked like a stranger. How could it be my brother sitting across from a hooker in some bar in an unfamiliar city? How could it be my brother who, after all those years of planning to get away — *together* — left me with a stranger at the first sight of another woman? I closed my eyes and saw the flash of city lights seep through my pink lids, felt the van jolt over uneven streets and heard the roar of cars and buildings and people and trains and the endless frightening strangeness of it all pushing into me. I was tired. I leant my head against the closed window and tried to remember the sound of night falling.

Somewhere in the suburbs Jason pulled the van over to the side of the road. I opened my eyes and looked dazedly out the window. Row after row of houses and ugly blocks of units, bars on the windows, cars parked half on the footpath, the sound of someone's tyres squealing. On the other side of the road I could see a small park.

'Wait here,' he said, 'I just have to see these guys and set it up.' I nodded absently. Too tired to think. Too queasy to want to hear anything other than the relative quiet of the van parked instead of moving. 'I mean it,' he insisted, 'I want you to wait here. These aren't the kind of guys who like surprises.' I looked over at him leaning towards me, watching my face to make sure I understood.

'Okay,' I said, 'I'll stay here. Where would I go anyway?' He didn't nod, but looked at me carefully before leaning forward to kiss me. His kisses were still a gentle shock, so surprisingly tender.

After he'd been gone for ten minutes I started to feel a little better and I propped open the door of the van to feel the night air. It was cool but not cold, fresh despite the undertones of oil and exhaust fumes. I felt claustrophobic. The city leaned in all around me. I wanted to run through it until I found its edge, push out into the flat warm air that ran around me without buildings and cars to poison it. I crossed the road to the park, and pulled off my shoes. The grass felt good beneath my feet, soft and almost wet it was so green. I sat down beneath a tree relieved to feel the earth beneath me again. Looking up through its straggling branches towards the sky, I tried to block out the sound and presence of the city around me. I tried to imagine myself in the middle of a wide space where this was the only tree and I was the only person. After a while I closed my eyes. Too tired to keep my head tipped back, too tired to concentrate on dreaming up the past.

I felt someone beside me and opened my eyes, surprised to feel that they were heavy with sleep. How long had I been sitting here? As I looked up I saw Jason standing silently beside me, his hands clenched at his sides. 'Get up,' he said quietly.

I rubbed my eyes and stretched my arms up. 'Sorry,' I said, 'I just needed to get out of the van for a few minutes.'

'I told you to wait for me.'

I pushed my shoes onto my feet and leant forward, placing one hand against the tree to stand. As I half-stood I felt his hand on my upper arm and I looked up at him, ready to say I didn't need any help, to say I was fine, and then I saw his face caught in the flash and slide of someone's headlights. His jaw was tight and his eyes, looking straight into mine, were furious. I frowned, wondering what could have happened to make him so angry. Did something go wrong with the deal? Was the stuff we had brought not good enough? I reached out my other hand and placed it on his forearm. 'What's wrong?' I said gently.

He spoke slowly and carefully, as if he was speaking to a small child. His voice was contained in tight syllables. 'I told you to wait in the van,' he said. 'What are you doing out here?'

'I just wanted some fresh air. I don't feel so good. A bit carsick or something.'

He reached his arm forward, wrapping it around my shoulders as he turned me back towards the van. I felt his fingers dig into my shoulder, pinching into my skin. I cringed slightly and moved my shoulder, thinking that perhaps he didn't realise, still believing that his anger was not directed at me, but as I moved I felt his grip tighten. His hand slid up over my neck until he reached my ear and he pressed something there, held it, and I fell weak-kneed and bloodless to the ground. He was kneeling over me, his breath on my back, and one hand holding my head as the other pressed into the flesh behind my ear. 'I told you to wait in the fucking van,' he said. 'I made it perfectly fucking clear. If you don't do what I tell you things could go wrong very quickly. Do you understand?'

I gulped and nodded my head, feeling my tears run into his hand. I could barely see and the nausea in my gut had welled up into my throat. I tried to swallow as he leant forward over me, his mouth against my cheek. 'I want to keep you safe,' he said, 'but you have to do what I tell you, okay?' I nodded slightly, although even that tiny movement sent a bolt of pain down from my ear to my shoulder and back. I felt faint but afraid to move. My mouth was dry. I wanted to say *yes*, wanted to say *anything, anything you want*, as long as he would let me go, as long as he would get up and that look in his eyes would disappear and his mouth melt into that other, tender mouth whose kisses were like water. I mumbled a faint *yes* and he moved away, his hand sliding down from my ear to my shoulder. I half sat up and as I did he brought his knee up into my chest, punching it into my breast. I felt the last of my breath explode out of me and fell onto the ground. I heard my blood beating, and the sudden awful stillness of not being able to breathe, and my heart which seemed to stutter, and an odd thud that echoed in my ears and faintly, faint enough that I had to frown to hear it, I heard him tell me to get in the van, that he'd be waiting and we'd go home. I rolled over onto my knees and put my hand against the tree to stand up. Jason strode over towards the van, the keys swinging in his hands. He was whistling, I remember that most clearly of all. It made me feel disconnected and hollow. As if this moment, the pain that still throbbed in my body, was somehow imaginary. I felt my stomach clutch and lurched forward as a stream of vomit spilled from my mouth.

We spent the night sleeping in the van across the street from his parents' house, although I didn't realise that until morning. When I woke up, Jason was leaning against the side of the van smoking a cigarette.

'Welcome home,' he said, nodding at the house. From the street it looked decrepit. It was painted an odd shade of green that was peeling away to reveal underlying layers of pink, white, yellow, and blue. The front porch leaned and most of the original wrought-iron railing had been replaced with unpainted boards. The garden was overgrown although between the stringy weeds there were clumps of mint, thyme and rosemary.

Jason told me to wait, so I watched him cross the road and vault over the front gate which was half-buried in the ground. He cupped his hands around his face and looked in at a window, then leant back to look around the side of the house. He turned the door handle, rattling the door, but it didn't open. The house was locked and dark. It seemed long-deserted. He looked back across the road towards me then glanced up and down the empty street before taking a step backwards and kicking at the door just below the handle. It fell open with a loud crack. He grinned at me as he crossed back towards the van. 'Come on then,' he said. He opened the van door to grab his cigarettes from the dashboard, wound up the window and locked the door.

I was nervous, wondering if anyone had heard or seen him. He put his arm around me as we crossed the street and kissed me on the neck. When we reached the front door he leant against the outside wall and lit a cigarette. 'Go inside and check it out,' he said. 'I'll be in in a minute.'

Inside it was dark and cool. I walked straight through the house into the kitchen, which opened through two French doors onto a deep verandah. Down the back stairs was another garden full of sweet herbs, and broken statues of angels and women. Between the clinging weeds were uneven stone paths, a birdbath which had tipped over and cracked in half, a knot-garden swelling from its neatly jointed brick pathways and a gazebo with a few scraps of white paint still clinging to its turned posts.

I wandered down the path — past the lavender and spent sweet peas, the hollyhocks and dishevelled thyme — to the garden's edge. No gentle slipping, no fence and neighbour, but a sudden unceremonious edge.

There was a small stone table there, at the end of the garden, with a chessboard carved into it, two stone benches. I settled back against one of them. The land slid down from the edge of my feet. It was not quite a cliff, just a steep incline that hesitated before it tipped into the harbour. The grass was cool beneath me, and tickled with a light scratch. The earth's coppery fragrance blew against my thighs and ankles. As I looked out I could see where the sea ended and the sky began. A line like smudged charcoal spread itself out thinly on the horizon. When I squinted I could break the ribbon into pale slices, each thinner than the one before, melting into each other, twisting against each other.

The breeze was picking up, ruffling the harbour's surface into smocked grey linen. I could see the breeze flower as it rose up the steep incline, swelling and budding across the trees and grasses. It stooped and bent around the sagging fence, flickering through the lavender and sea-grass to push its way over the last few feet of garden. My ankles were thick and dark against the green grass; solid and somehow permanent in the giving density of leaf and blade. I smelt the water. The fresh salt air flying up towards me.

I imagined this hour stretching into days, into months and years. I imagined our lives lived in this garden. The long quiet afternoons and gently breaking mornings. The two of us in the garden, Jason reading, me playing the flute, or perhaps both of us lying reading, half-asleep in the summer heat. Lying on my side on an old blanket with a plate of fruit and a bottle of wine as he placed his hand delighted beneath mine and felt her secret kick.

In summer, guests would come early for tea. The garden would be freshly sprinkled with water. The path stones would gleam as if polished in the early morning light, moist and cool beneath bare feet. As they walked through the tangle of lavender and sweet peas, there would be a sense of crossing over, of leaving behind the dust and sadness of the world outside. The gazebo would wait in the shade and a kettle would rest on a slatted cedar table. I would be warm and round, smiling as I scooped powdered tea and water into a bowl and mixed it with a bamboo whisk. We would burn sandalwood and as we settled in to an afternoon with friends he would go out into the garden and I would watch him play with a little child — chasing a red ball through the late afternoon — until they both fell, shining and warm, beside me.

In winter they would come later in the evening. We would be warm and secretive. The path would be scattered with crumbling leaves. Instead of sandalwood there would be cloves and tiny candles and as he leant to kiss me we would hear her coming over the stones in her black patent leather shoes. She would sit between us as we sipped cool white wine from translucent porcelain. The taste of the wine and the sound of the harbour spilling up the mountain would hold us together.

That day it was spring and there were no guests. No children.

I looked up into the clouds as they threaded rain through the sky. I watched it fall through the sudden afternoon. Darting and spitting and flowing through the limitless sky. The rain turned the sea darker and darker — the pure colourless drops and colourless wind. Lightning forks tuned the air, making it hum.

On the harbour below a ferry had settled into a steady rhythm of rise and fall as she turned across the heads. The rush-hour hydrofoil skimmed past on its improbable legs. The ferry tipped. Outside her windows there was first sky, and sky, and sky. And then harbour, grey and puckered, filling the glass frame. And then sky again as sudden and surprised as a child.

From the garden it was easy to see the soft turbulence the ferry left behind; how it curled in on itself in ever-diminishing rushes, how it cut across the softly curling bow-wave of another boat. Broken up. The crushed ribbon of her wake spread out in a long, pale drift from shore to shore.

As I turned to go back to the house I heard an engine start up. By the time I reached the front verandah Jason was pulling out from the kerb. He waved at me from the window, his smile jaunty as he called out, 'I'm gonna go and get the bloody fool.' I stood on the front porch for a long time watching the empty street.

When I turned to go back into the house I saw an old woman standing in the front garden next door. She was holding a small garden fork in her hands. I waved and she smiled and waved back at me. The sight of her friendly face, her easy smile, made me content. I looked forward to living in this city, with its water and cliffs and closeness, becoming a woman in this oddly perched house, living a normal life. As I put my hand on the door I saw her still standing, watching me. I turned and walked over to the fence to say hello. We talked for a few minutes, she told me where the nearest shop was, where to catch the bus. When I asked her where the nearest library was she smiled and said I could borrow books from her if I liked. We talked about what we liked to read and she went inside to collect a small handful of books. 'Here,' she said, 'something to start you off.'

I thanked her and, as I wandered back to our house, I could feel the warmth of a smile spreading through me. I took the books out to the back garden and settled onto an old chair, flicking aimlessly through them all until I was caught by one in particular. It was a warm afternoon and I soon drifted into a dreamy listlessness, imagining myself as the heroine of the book, wandering through cold European rooms with heavy furniture that bruised my ankles when I brushed against it.

That night I fell asleep waiting for the boys to return and awoke the next morning to the sound of Callum and Jason making coffee in the kitchen. Their voices rumbled playfully beneath the chink and clatter of cups and teaspoons. I rolled over beneath my blanket, feeling the contours of the mattress beneath me, the stitches running through each valley of its unsheeted surface. The pillow, too, was faintly yellow in the morning light.

I'd been too tired the night before to make the beds, to start rummaging through unfamiliar cupboards for somebody else's sheets. A couple of blankets had been laid over the lounges, and another over the piano in the dining room. But the room was still cold. The window I'd opened in the evening let in gusts of early morning sea-air. Luscious and rich with the scent of salt and fish, but so cold that the timber floor startled the soles of my feet. I wrapped the blanket around myself and stumbled out to the kitchen, hearing the van start as I poured the last of a pot of coffee into a cup. I could see Callum in the garden, his face caught in a thin spoonful of light, his hair rumpled and a blanket slung around his shoulders like a toga as he held a coffee cup between his hands.

'Hey, Cal.' He turned and smiled. The same early morning smile he had always had, even as a child. His cheeks were round and still flushed with sleep, his eyes half-closed and one side of his face creased up. We sat together on one of the stone benches and watched the morning rise out of the harbour. I looked back towards the house, thinking of the blankets stretched over everything, the dust lying caked on the kitchen benches.

'I suppose we should start cleaning the place up.'

'Let's go into the city,' he said.

I sipped at my coffee and watched the light spread towards us over the harbour. The light was so different there. Empty, almost. It was caught in the water and bounced up in shards, reflecting off the windows of houses, and boats, and green leaves. I leant back against Callum, feeling the tempered warmth of his skin and the muscle beneath it as he shifted to place his arm around me.

Two hours later we got off a train at Wynyard and walked through a tunnel full of tiny shops onto a city street. Callum took my hand like a child and smiled and we stood, looking up the side of a tower whose glass windows reflected the buildings and clouds around it like a mirror or a harbour.

I was once a single, monolithic entity, but now I am broken open, all my walls have been breached

— Susan Johnson, *A Better Woman*

I do not want to feel weak, and for a long time I never did. Even in my father's house I wielded a peculiar and particular kind of power. In fairy tales power, or magic, is a gift given by a fairy — like the gift of seeing or speaking or hearing — but it is just as easily taken away, and it is this that makes it dangerous. You cannot assume it is yours to keep. It is hers to give, and hers to take away, and quite often it is as dangerous as it is useful. I remember a tale in which two sisters go to a well at different times and are approached by a fairy woman in disguise. When the first sister meets her dressed as an old beggar woman the girl draws water for her from the well. In return the fairy grants her a gift; every time she speaks, diamonds and roses spill from her tongue. When the second sister goes to the well she is approached by the fairy disguised as a grand lady. This sister refuses to draw the fairy any water, but is given a gift anyway; when she speaks snakes spill from her mouth. It would be easy to prefer diamonds and roses, but roses are thorny and diamonds hard-edged and sharp. A snake is smooth and slippery and is, after all, a symbol of wisdom. Secretly, I preferred the gift of wisdom to the gift of beauty.

As a child these things seemed simple to me. It is only now I realise that I was wrong, that I should have chosen the roses.

Although I remember being a child, I don't remember being treated as one, and perhaps this is why I didn't know how to become a woman. I didn't know how to be easy with a man. At times Jason was gentle. There were nights when he lay in my arms like a child as I ran my fingers through his hair and told him stories. He fell asleep and I watched his eyes flickering beneath the veined lids. When he woke up I asked him what he had dreamed about and he lied. He said he had no need for dreams. But everyone dreams, even if they don't remember.

I was curious about this man who thought he had no need for dreams. Perhaps it was curiosity rather than love. I wanted to *know* things about him. I wanted to penetrate his secret sleep. The things he was hiding when he turned away, when he wouldn't speak. When I asked him questions he evaded me, or answered as if I had asked him something else entirely. In the middle of conversations he fell asleep or walked out of the room. I didn't follow him; if all my questions had been answered what then? I guess I would have been saved, but from what? I still don't know which of us it was that really needed saving. It's easy to say it was me, that he was to blame for everything that went wrong, and it's true that he seemed to set the tenor of our relationship. But it was also me. He set up barriers between us that I refused to overcome. I loved him in my own confused and contradictory way. I wanted to know everything I could about him, but I also loved him for his secrets, because they were his and not mine. I no longer wanted to be the one who kept secrets.

Sleeping he was as innocent and open as a child. His skin became warmer and more ruddy; tiny beads of sweat gathered on his upper lip. One afternoon he was lying on our bed, a hand resting between his thighs and the other beneath his cheek. His lips moved. I leant closer to him, straining to hear. Once I thought I heard him say my name, once he said *oranges*. He seemed vulnerable, although it is an odd vulnerability that he revealed, as if he knew that I wouldn't disturb him. He was soft and warm like a snake curled in the sun. Ready to strike.

On the day Cal and I went into the city we wandered for hours through the stores. They seemed endless to us; each of them cavernous and brightly lit. We walked through arcades full of hat shops and delicatessens, clothes and shoes and bags and perfume and books. We spent hours ambling through a second-hand bookshop, walking away with a bag each as pleased as if we had discovered gold. We went into a department store and wandered for hours through glittering racks of china and electrical goods. I bought a necklace, or rather two necklaces; two halves of a tiny heart which the man behind the counter engraved with *Jason* and *Germaine*. I hid them in the bottom of my bag of books. I didn't want to see Cal's face cloud over the way it already did when I talked about Jason and me. I wanted that day to be perfect. The next day I went to give the half of the charm with my name on it to Jason. We were standing in the garden, out by the gazebo, and he had been telling me how he used to sit out there as a little boy and throw things as far as he could to try and get them into the harbour. How he had pegged the neighbour's cat out once, its legs desperately clawing at him as he pushed it out into the air. I laughed when he told me about the scratch which the cat had left on his chest, and how he had told his mother it was from falling off his bike. 'And she believed you?'

He laughed, that strange snorting laugh of his: 'Dumb twat,' he said. I looked away, shocked at the way he talked about his parents. I felt young and ridiculously unsophisticated. I wanted to be able to share stories in which my parents were the ridiculous and despised objects of my hatred, but what I felt for them was never like that. In a way I felt that his hatred of his parents was ordinary, and I wanted desperately to be ordinary.

'I bought you something,' I said. When I handed it to him he looked suspicious, but he smiled at me. When he opened the little bag and pulled the charm out onto his palm it glittered and I smiled. Then I heard him laugh again, that same laugh, and the smile fell from me. I felt cold.

He told me he would never wear something like that. Never. Only an idiot would think he would. It was tacky. And cheap. And I don't remember what else. I didn't dare look at him, frightened that I would cry, or laugh, or I don't know what — something that would make him angrier. In the end he threw it over the edge of the garden and when I didn't move, didn't even watch it fall, he grabbed hold of the charm I was wearing and wrenched it off me. I could feel the fine sharp line where it had cut into my neck before it snapped but I was too frightened to lift my hand to see if it were bleeding. I looked up as his arm flung out over the harbour and watched the charm fly through the air, glittering prettily.

*   *

I heard the telephone ring in the hall. By the time I picked it up Jason was standing behind me, scratching at his tousled hair. 'It's Elliot,' I said.

He took the phone from my hand and turned his back to me, leaning his head forward in a gesture of privacy, of intimacy. Almost awake, he was uneasy. Sleep seemed to puddle around his feet as he took on the peculiar angularity of his waking self. I wanted to hold him, but he was so precise, so scientific. When I touched his arm he jerked his body from me and gave me a quick dismissive glare. I walked away. The soft mumble of his voice receded behind me.

As I reached the end of the hall I could just hear his voice. 'Where's Cal?' he called to me. Callum was outside in the garden, sleeping on a blanket in the sun. From the kitchen window I could see him, his long body spread carelessly, his feet and hands protruding from the edge of the blanket into the long, seedy grass.

I heard Jason hang up the phone and come into the kitchen. He stood behind me and rested his hands lightly on my shoulders, kissing the back of my neck. One hand slid down to my waist and rested there. I could feel the heat of him pressing into me. I felt the weight of his mouth like the hot entry point of a slow bullet that burrowed into my gut and swelled. 'You taste good,' he said, and I smiled, tipping my head back as he ran his hand around and cupped my chin, running a fingertip over my mouth. I kissed his finger and reached my hand back to touch his flat muscled belly. 'Do you love me?' he said.

No, I thought to myself. Silent and persistently, but I couldn't say it. Who can stand in the centre of a furnace with a thimbleful of water and say no? Who can remember what it is like to be a child or an old woman — with the whole future or past of a life spread before you — and say no to life? No is irrevocable, permanent, safe and dishonest. Yes is a possibility I was not yet willing to give away. A charm for putting off the burning.

I felt cold. Empty. I pushed my fingers against my closed lids. When I opened my eyes, I saw stars. What would it take to make me weep? I sit in darkened cinemas and touch my cheek where the tears drop. They are safe tears. Dishonest tears. They are the tears of a melodramatic and dishonest soul. My own life did not move me. It was too real. Too empty.

I listened to my heart beat, hearing the swoosh and echo of its chambers, hearing the soft pulse that persists even when I am sleeping. Constant. Immovable. Irrevocable. The tin man walked thousands of miles along a yellow brick road to the grand and illusory city of Oz. In the echoing chambers of the wizard, knees clanging like cymbals, he asked for a heart and was given a clock. Time is not an emotion; although it is as immaterial, unclutchable and inescapable as love. But the thing which measures love is not love. A stethoscope can measure a heart, but it cannot tell me whether I loved him. Lovers measure each other's hearts with an imaginary clock — *I will love you forever, till the end of time. Till death do us part.*

'Forever,' I mumbled and behind me I felt Jason smile, felt his hand cup my shoulder, his mouth rest gently on my shoulder-blade as he ran a fingertip over my arm.

'Have you got something nice to wear?' he said, leaning over my shoulder and taking the biscuit that was resting forgotten in my hand. He absently took a bite and looked out the back window. When he saw Callum he downed the biscuit and headed outside. As he passed through the door his voice floated back to me, 'Get changed. We'll leave in an hour.'

When we arrived at the house there were cars parked everywhere — all the way up the street and in the yard and even in the neighbouring yards. Jason pulled the van up onto the kerb and parked in the front garden of a house two doors away. An old lady came out in a housecoat, yelling at us before we even got out of the van. Jason laughed and put an arm around her thin shoulders. 'Settle down, Grandma. We'll be gone in the morning,' he said, and turned away to pull a carton of beer from the open back of the van.

'Look what you've done. Look. *Look*,' she said, tears running down her cheeks. I didn't dare turn towards her. What would I have said? She got down on her hands and knees and peered in under the van at her crushed flowerbed. As Jason hoisted the carton up onto his shoulder she stood and hit him across the back with a rolled-up magazine. He stopped and turned around, putting the carton down carefully on the grass. He took her by the wrist, pinching her papery skin, and pulled her towards her home. When they reached the door he opened it and shoved her inside. I saw her fall on the floor, her tiny feet sticking out into the hall.

'Let's go,' he said as he swung the carton onto his shoulder and strode through the rest of her ruined garden. I turned back to look at the old lady, who was slowly getting to her feet. When she turned to look out through the closed screen door I smiled at her nervously. I wanted her to see that I was just as powerless in the face of his carelessness as she was. She didn't smile back and when Jason turned to take my hand he saw me watching her. 'By the way,' he called back at the old woman, 'if you call the cops I'll come back and I'll fucking kill you.'

I felt my face turning red with horror and turned away before she could see me properly. *Just keep walking*, I thought. *Just pretend it's nothing. Nothing at all.* Behind me I heard her door slam and the lock turn. I thought about our neighbour — Edna — and how Jason was always careful to be polite to her. She must love him, I thought. He buys her flowers and fixes her fence. What is it that makes him kind to her and not to this woman? At the time I struggled to understand but now I think it may have been a calculated difference. He couldn't afford for Edna not to like him. She might call his parents to say he wasn't looking after the house. She might listen too carefully, look too closely. A stranger on the other side of town was no threat. She didn't know who he was and wouldn't dare to challenge him again, but Edna had known him since he was a child and she wasn't afraid of him. He knew that.

Inside the house there were people everywhere, spread over the floors and furniture, standing in the halls. The smell of beer and pot and barbecue wafted through the throng of bodies as we made our way out into the backyard. There was an old car with its bonnet up and a motor suspended above it on a makeshift tripod. Several men were standing around it. They called out to Jason as he came down the back stairs, raising their beers to him in salute. Callum and I were left standing awkwardly as Jason settled into a conversation with them. I wandered back into the house, finally finding a seat in the lounge room where a group of young women were drinking together. None of them said hello; at first I thought I would introduce myself but somehow their conversation never allowed it to happen. I stared off out the window, watching Callum walk past occasionally, hearing Jason's laughter from the yard grow louder and louder. It was after ten o'clock when Callum came to tell me he was leaving.

'Fuck that boyfriend of yours.'

'He's your friend,' I said. Callum downed the last of his beer and tossed the can into a corner with the rest of the empty cans.

'Yeah, well, you're welcome to him.' I stood up and wrapped my jacket around my shoulders. 'He says you're to wait,' Callum said, watching me, waiting for me to make a choice, a matter of loyalty. I should have gone with Callum; by his silence and his look he was asking me to. There was no one in that house I could talk to, nothing to do other than drink or smoke, alone in a crowd of people I didn't know. I looked away, through the open kitchen door into the yard where Jason was. I could hear his laughter getting louder as he got drunker. In a few hours he would be morose and reckless. There was a woman standing beside him. She placed a hand on his shoulder and tipped her head towards him. He brushed her off and laughed again. I heard him say something that made all the others laugh. I smiled. Beside me I heard Callum swear under his breath as he turned and walked away. I followed him through the house, past the open doors of bedrooms where various groups of people were locked together, sweating and naked. One girl raised a vacant face to watch me as I walked past. She seemed oblivious to the guy banging her from behind. I stared at her, at the look she gave me as the guy behind her moved away and was replaced by another. I turned away only to see another face looking blankly into mine, a girl sitting on the toilet seat across the hallway from the bedroom, a child's pink hair-tie strapped around her upper arm as she slipped a needle into her vein.

By the time I reached the front yard, gulping in the fresh night air, Callum was pulling out into the street. I saw his face in profile as he leant out the window to check the traffic, the hair blowing across his cheek. I waved at him to wait but he didn't see me.

Inside my chair was still empty. I wrapped my jacket tightly around me, curled my feet up and closed my eyes. Somewhere, under the noise of all these people, there was the sound of music playing. Loud and almost tuneless, supported by the throaty wail of an alcoholic voice screaming lyrics that I could not understand, but music never-theless. I held onto it. Listening carefully to each beat until it began to fall against my own pulse. I turned my head into the chair and scrunched down into a ball, wrapping the jacket around my shins, and fell asleep.

Callum did not, as I assumed, go home. When he showed up several days later he told me that he had driven for hours through the streets looking for the girl he'd met in the Cross the first night we were there. Eventually he parked the van and started walking, asking people. He finally found her at four in the morning. She answered the door wearing the plastic wings she'd been wearing when he first saw her. He followed her into the room and sat on the edge of her bed. A neon billboard lit her sheets. Coca-cola red.

She asked him for money and he offered her everything he had in his pockets. They walked to a cafe where she scored from a waiter. On the way back to her room she put a hand on his arm. 'You're real sweet,' she said. Cal blushed and dipped his head and she laughed at him, but in a gentle kind of way. 'If I'd had someone like you I wouldn't have ended up like this. Working the street and all. Guys like you never hook up with girls like me though.'

'I like you,' he said.

'Yeah,' she mused, looking into his soft face, 'maybe we can get something together.'

She burned the spoon and melted coffee-coloured dreams for him. Caramel. Honey. Ran her hand up the inside curve of his arm and placed two fingertips against the lush weed of a vein. Her fingernails were pale blue. Almost shining. She lit him up with a synthetic light that caught and blazed in his skin, in his gut. She began to hum to some strange tune as she rocked over him, her plastic wings flicking, and the light took him and bent him in half like a spoon and all he could see was her wings — beating — and the city outside her window. Wild with light.

In the morning when I woke up, the house was quiet. One guy lay asleep on the floor of the lounge room. Through the back door I could see the litter of empty cans and bottles, a broken chair. I could smell vomit and beer and stale smoke as I walked through the house looking for Jason. Every room had a light scattering of sleeping bodies, many of them half-dressed. Each of the beds held at least three bodies. There were half a dozen used needles in the bathroom sink, more in the shower and one floating in the toilet bowl. In the backyard someone offered me a joint. In the side yard a couple were kissing. In the front yard there was still a car, someone asleep in the back seat. No sign of Jason. I looked up and down the street. I had no idea where I was.

I walked away from the house, hesitating on the lawn of the old lady whose dead flowers were now decorated by a sleeping man. When I looked towards the front door I saw her watching me and I moved towards her. Perhaps she would let me use her phone and call the house; perhaps Jason would be home and I could ask him to come and get me. I had no money for a cab and I didn't know which way to walk, let alone how far I had to go. As I reached the bottom of her stairs I saw her take a step backwards. I reached my hand forward to reassure her. I smiled, but she backed away. 'Dirty slut,' she said, and slammed the door.

In the end I went back to the house and borrowed some change from the guy smoking his joint in the backyard. He offered to drive me home but I assured him it was unnecessary, Jason must be at home and would come as soon as he could. The first phone booth I found was broken — the change box ripped out and the handpiece disconnected. It was almost an hour before I came across another one. I let it ring out. I put the change back in several times, letting it ring over and over again. I walked until I found another phone and did the same thing. I kept walking, trying one phone box after another, ten of them, twenty. It became a ritual. I knew there would be no answer. I knew there was no one there, but I kept moving, following roads that led in the direction I thought I should be going. I imagined myself moving through every phone box in the city, calling and calling. Eventually I saw a street I recognised and turned towards home. When I reached the house it was almost dark again and I was exhausted. The back door was open and as I walked up the stairs I heard Jason's laughter. He was sitting at the kitchen table with one of the guys I saw him talking to the night before. They were both holding beers and as I reached the bottom of the stairs I heard Jason's voice. 'Of course I'm fucking her,' he said, 'that doesn't mean she's my girlfriend.' As I walked into the room they were both laughing. He was still drunk, I realised when I saw him, his eyes were red and his face flushed. I could smell the beer and pot in the room. I tried to stay calm, to think clearly.

'Why didn't you answer the phone?' I asked.

'Why the fuck should I?' he said. His mate laughed again and Jason turned towards him smiling as I moved past them, almost stumbling with exhaustion, towards the bedroom.

Callum called me a few weeks later and I went to meet him in a cafe not far from where we lived. I had missed him. Needed the comfort of his familiar solidness. But when I walked into the cafe and saw him half-slumped over a table, his hands curled around an empty cup, I realised that something had changed irrevocably. His skin was so raw from synthetic love that the inside of his elbow was scratched and red. When I took his arm to cross the street he flinched. He listened for the wind as it tunnelled up the street to meet him, and seemed threatened by it. He was thin, thinner than I remembered him. He picked over a plate of salad, absently scratching himself — his wrists and throat.

When we got back to the house he wandered around, asking me several times where Jason was, and when I said he wasn't there Callum looked puzzled and ambled off, looking into each room carefully. He fell asleep at the kitchen table and I half carried him to a bed. He was small enough to be a child. Light enough that it shocked me. Was this the man I thought would save me? The one who talked about dragons and oceans as if they were mere trifles? He half roused as I pulled the blanket over him. 'I'm in love,' he said.

He wandered in and out of closed doors. He hollowed out the room. His skin was wrapped so tight that I believed I could hear his bones clicking as he walked. His face was thin, I could see the vivid bones beneath his skin. He took my hand in his to read my palm, something she had taught him, but all I could see were the bones of his hand and his dry skin, the ragged claw-marks on his arm as he impatiently pushed up the sleeves of his shirt. He refused to show me his own palm, saying only that he had a short lifeline and anyway was born a Scorpio — a natural victim of obsession. He said, 'Who am I to disappoint fate?' I wanted to erase the fine lines on his palm. I wanted to tell him that his fate wasn't written on his body, any more than my fate was written onto mine, but his washed-clean eyes seemed to desiccate my breath and I could only talk to him about other — ordinary — things.

I wanted to run my hand up the inside of his arm and erase the scars where he had been trying, so hard, to make love to himself. Where she had been making love to him. He talked to me about Selene and I could see him kissed and flushed and smiling while the lights flashed over his skin in her third-floor room and she hummed the same distracted tune and he smiled and said, 'What a beautiful song.'

Every morning he came into my room and looked at the empty space on the other side of the bed, expecting Jason to be there. When he wasn't he mumbled something apologetic and walked away. When I found him later, in the kitchen or the garden, he didn't say anything about it and I never asked. It was as if the morning had two beginnings and one of them refused to acknowledge the other. One of them was secretive and almost not there. Sometimes I forgot. Sometimes it was as if that early morning greeting never happened. We were diligent in our pretence.

Occasionally, at night, he went away. He walked down the street with his shoulders hunched against the night air, even when it was warm. The coldness was inside him, unaffected by his clothes or his skin, which was already fading, the warm redness washing away. He was becoming something other than what he was back home. He was suddenly a man and I was unsure how to speak to him. What to say.

On television I watched a documentary with the sound turned off. It was about adopted children being reunited with their biological mothers. Each of them embraced willingly, desperately, but they often had nothing to say. They discovered finally, despite their hopes, that they were strangers after all. This was the most disturbing thing. They sometimes looked the same; the same hair, the same eyes, sometimes a gesture of hand or hip, but days later the faces of the mother and child were bemused. *It is not what I thought*, they mouthed at the camera, *they are not what I imagined*.

When Callum came home he looked drained and sad. He barely glanced at me as he walked through the lounge room. He stopped halfway out the door to ask me for money and I offered him what I had in my pocket — a hundred dollars and some change. 'It's not enough,' he said, shaking his head.

'I have more. There's some in the bedroom.'

'How much?'

'How much do you need?'

'A thousand.'

I looked at his thin hands resting nervously in his lap. A thousand dollars. We had that much. More than that, but I wasn't sure how much I could take. Jason was careful with the dealing he did. He never used, although he drank regularly, and sometimes smoked pot. He made a lot of money on that first deal, but it wasn't enough. He always wanted more. It made me nervous when he had it in the house, or in the van. I was always more comfortable when it was just money rolled up in neat cylinders in a box. He always said I could take as much as I needed but I was reluctant to test him. Reluctant to take more than I really *needed*. 'What about five hundred?' I offered.

'Maybe,' he said.

It was well past midnight when I found him in the garden talking on the phone. He hadn't heard me coming. 'I don't have it all yet but that doesn't matter,' he said. 'This is me, not some job off the street. You have to see me.' As he listened to the person on the other end of the line — to Selene — he tipped his head back and watched the sky. 'Just this once. Then I'll have more money. I promise.' After a few more seconds of listening he hung up and turned back to the house. At first I thought he hadn't seen me but then I saw his body shift slightly, trying to turn away. 'How long have you been there?'

'Long enough. How much money does she want?'

'It's not like that. She loves me. I know she does.'

'She's a hooker, Callum.'

'She kisses me. She doesn't kiss anyone else. She told me.'

'And you believe her?'

'Why shouldn't I? I trust her. Trust is the basis of any relationship, remember.'

I moved closer to him, close enough to see his face. In the evening light his skin was translucent, the same sickly, pale colour as the moon. 'It's not a relationship. You're a client. A job.'

He turned away from me. His body determined despite its thinness. 'You don't understand. It doesn't matter. She's the most amazing woman I've ever known. She's intelligent and beautiful and sexy and she *knows* stuff. She understands me. She listens to me and I don't have to do anything for her. She never hassles me about anything …'

'Except money.'

He glared at me and I realised I had gone too far. 'What would you know? You let him do whatever he wants. You let him fuck you even when you know it's wrong. You know it.' When he pushed past me I could feel the heat in his body. I opened my mouth to say something but he was walking so fast, striding through the long grass, that by the time I thought of something to say he was so far away I would have had to yell for him to hear me.

He was running away, up the side of the house, with nowhere to go. Where could he have gone? To a temporary lover who held him by the hour? To a plastic-winged stranger whose voice was sibilant and resonant. To a woman who was no woman but a child, dressed up to dream. How could he say he loved her? He didn't even understand what love was. When I thought about love I knew that it should be all-consuming, frightening and irrevocable. Love should be like a disease that gets inside you, burrows into you like a tick. It should know every cavity of your body. Love *knows* you. Love is not an escape from the everyday, from yourself, it is a burrowing inwards. What did she know about love? What could she teach him? This by-the-hour stranger who was familiar, but never personal.

If you will come

I shall put out
new pillows for
you to rest on

— Sappho

One o'clock on a Sunday afternoon and Jason was still sleeping. Several times I had walked into the room. At first I was tentative, stepping carefully around the bed to pick up dirty clothes and towels. Even smiling at him curled around a pillow like a lover. Later I was impatient. The rest of the house was clean. The windows were thrust as wide open as they would go, the scent of lavender oil floated through the dusted and swept hallways. Clean sheets pinned to the line flapped madly in the wind that broke like a wave over the garden. The bathrooms gleamed like new china, the kitchen benches were smooth and dustless beneath my fingertips, clean glasses glittering in the dish-rack. The beds were freshly made. Clean pillowcases and sheets and plump doonas folded neatly at each corner. Except for our bed, of course, where Jason still slept. His hair tufted and ridiculous. His mouth open like a child's and his hands folded beneath his cheek. Pure innocence until I opened the door. Beneath the scent of newly washed floors was the heavier, almost greasy smell of his skin. The sour smell of alcohol in his hair and on his breath and on the sheets.

I threw open the window and the wind pushed the sheer curtains over my head like a veil. I caught them in my arms and tucked them behind the chest of drawers but the wind tugged at them, pulling them easily over the sill. I caught them again and twisted them until they were wound around me like a wet sheet being wrung out.

'What the fuck are you doing?'

I was stunned, stopping still and almost pulling the curtains from their hooks as I lurched uncertainly on my feet.

'Christ, Germaine, I'm trying to sleep.'

'I made you some coffee.'

'I don't want coffee. I want to sleep.'

'Oh, come on. It's after midday. Everybody's up.'

His voice rose slightly as he sat up in bed and ruffled his hair. 'Everybody? There's only you and me here — and Callum — and I'm asleep. At least I was until you came in.'

'Come on, get up. You'll feel better. If you sleep all day, you won't be able to sleep tonight.'

'I don't want to fucking well sleep tonight. I want to sleep now.'

I opened my mouth to speak but no words came. Jason moved across the room towards me, stood right in front of me. He looked strange through the twisted cotton curtain. Like a ghost.

'Get out of there.' I struggled with the curtain, turning slowly and unsurely in its grasp. 'Come on. Hurry up.' He grabbed at my arm beneath the fabric and turned me around, yanking me so sharply that I fell. He grabbed me again and this time I tripped, my torso turning faster than my feet, and banged my head against the bottom edge of the open window. I felt the bruise rise to the skin just beneath my eye, the split skin weeping.

'Hey, settle down. You hurt me.'

'You should have let me sleep.'

'I just wanted to get the house clean. And spend some time with you.' I wriggled out from under the curtain. It twisted away from me and fell easily into place before the wind caught it and pulled it outside. Jason stood watching me, his whole body still, as the wind changed its mind and flung the curtain towards me, like a sheer white bubble. The edges slipped free of the window frame and it flew over my head. The breeze was so fresh as it touched my skin. I longed to be outside in the garden where the wind might catch me. I closed my eyes and tipped back my head, letting the curtain drift over my face, opening my mouth just a little to let a laugh come humming up through my throat.

'Fuck,' he said, and I felt his hand crack against the side of my head, felt my head snap backwards and something in my throat stretch tight, far too tight. Then it bobbed back like some ridiculous toy — like a submerged balloon struggling for the surface. I felt him reach for me as I fell. His arms went around me and his hands held onto my forearms as I slipped onto the floor. I opened my eyes and saw him behind the curtain that had blown between us again. 'I'm sorry. It's just I'm tired, you know. Really tired. I need to sleep. You should have left me alone.'

'That's okay,' I said, marvelling at the texture of my voice. At its strangely weightless quality, as if each word had been caught in a soap bubble and floated out of my mouth in distinct round orbs. 'It's okay. You sleep. I'll go. I have things to do.'

I stood and pushed myself away from him, just gently, feeling the tautness of his gut beneath my fingertips, the firm muscle and tendon of his wrists and hands and arms. *Fine. Fine*, I thought, as I walked beyond the reach of the curtain and felt it drop behind me. I skated across the timber floor, skirting the bed where the night before his hands had rested beneath my head as he rocked me to sleep.

He didn't wake up until late in the afternoon. When I heard him get out of bed I walked away, tracing the path that wound through the garden towards the broken angel. He followed me, putting a hand on my arm and turning me towards him. I felt the clutch in my belly. Love? Is that what it means, the trembling unsurety, needing to see his face and not wanting to? I kept my head lowered, my eyes studying the shape of his bare feet. He placed a knuckle beneath my chin and raised my face to him. I heard him catch his breath and glanced up. He was staring at the swollen bruise and half-closed eye that seemed to cover the whole left side of my face.

'Oh God, I'm so sorry,' he said. He seemed childlike, insecure and frightened. One of his hands cradled my cheek as he kissed my mouth. 'I didn't mean to hurt you.'

I knew he was waiting for something. What did he want me to say, that it was okay? That it was an accident? I looked at his face, the skin suddenly thin and almost translucent with horror as he traced a forefinger over the open wound. I flinched slightly and watched him drop his hands like a guilty schoolboy, fidgeting uncertainly with the hem of his shirt, pushing one hand into his pocket. I could see his eyes shining, almost tearful, and I felt myself moving towards him, ready to take his hand and tell him anything, anything at all, that would make it all just go away.

'It's okay,' I said feebly, aware of him watching me, and when he lifted his gaze to meet mine it was filled with such gratitude that I was sorry I had ever doubted him, ever wanted to hurt him too. I leant my head on his shoulder and he kissed the crown of my head.

'Here,' he said, and I felt his hand pressing a tightly wound tube of money into my palm, 'buy something for yourself.' He kissed me again, long and slowly, his hands pressing into the small of my back.

In a dusty arcade in the city I found a shop full of second-hand instruments in well-worn cases. I stood looking in the window for several minutes, fingering the money in my pocket. When I walked through the door a bell rattled sadly, and a man looked around the doorframe from the back room. His chin dropped as he eyed me over his glasses.

'Can I help you?'

'Do you have any flutes?'

He showed me a row of flutes laid out on blue crushed velvet. I picked them up one by one and tested their weight in my hands, bringing each to my mouth and blowing gently across them, testing their timbre, their fluidity. The third flute I tried was lighter than the others: a silver Muramatsu AD with French cups, a B foot and in-line G. Despite a few minor scratches it was in good condition. I replaced it and moved on, testing each one and watching the man behind the counter.

'This one. Does it have a case?' I said, pointing at the Muramatsu.

'It's a bit battered. It's done the rounds.'

'What about this one?' (A shiny, silver-plated Emerson.)

'That's a beautiful instrument. Just like new.'

'How much?'

'Five hundred.'

I picked it up. The metal was cool against my fingertips. I blew a few notes and put it back down.

'What about this one?' I pointed at the Muramatsu again.

'Well, it's a better flute. I bought it from a man whose wife was a professional flautist.'

'Really? Maybe he just said that to get a better price out of you.'

The man shook his head. 'He said she didn't want it anymore but there's nothing wrong with it. It plays fine. Just fine. She had arthritis, I think he said. Or maybe it was Alzheimer's. No, definitely arthritis. In her hands, her fingers. Said she couldn't play anymore. It just upset her to have it around.'

I pictured them. Lovers who had grown old listening to each other. She to his voice and he to her music. I saw her standing in a glass-walled sunroom full of bright-leafed ferns and palms. The flute was resting in her hands, which were bent strangely, the knuckles swollen, the skin crumpled and papery. She lifted the flute to her mouth and blew but her fingers could not move quickly enough. She faltered. When he came in she was looking out the window with tears in her eyes. She didn't move as he took the flute from her fingers, didn't even glance at him as he rested a hand fleetingly on her shoulder and turned away. Somewhere in the house — on top of the piano — was a photograph taken several years ago. It was a black-and-white print on old, heavy paper. Her face was bent at a slight angle with eyes closed and the flute resting lightly against her chin. Her fingers were caught in the midst of playing a delicate, light-headed solo. Each finger smooth and graceful, each one sure.

'How much?' I said. The sales assistant hesitated before he answered me, looking down at my hands placed flat on the glass cabinet. I felt the weight of his measuring gaze on each finger, tracing their length and suppleness.

'Do you play?'

'A little.'

He asked for a thousand and I pretended to hesitate, frowning slightly, resisting the urge to stroke the instrument. We agreed on eight hundred. Cash. He shrugged slightly and I heard him whistling as he searched the back room for the case.

It took him several minutes to find the case, which was indeed old though not as battered as I had imagined, its wooden exterior scented with beeswax polish, the wine-red velvet interior worn through in places. I took the instrument apart myself, nestling each piece in its place and gently latching the neat brass catches.

'Just hang on and I'll write you a receipt,' he said.

I thought about saying no and just walking outside, swinging the flute case at my side, but the look on his face was suddenly strange. Suddenly suspicious.

It took him several minutes to write out a receipt. Each letter formed carefully, his tongue protruding between his teeth and his brow clenched in concentration. He folded it in half and pressed the crease between his fingertips.

'Thank you,' I said, and then I was gone. Out the swinging door with its cheap signs attached lopsidedly with blu-tac. Down the street with the flute at my side. My flute. The smile on my face ridiculous.

I will teach my child — my daughter — how to play. When she is a newborn baby lying in her cradle, still fresh-skinned and star-fingered, I will play for her. Just as my mother did for me. The notes slipping across the sheets, into her dreams. I will stand at the window of her room — the room which looks out onto the garden at the back of the house — and wait for the wind to raise its song through the trees. Wait for the wind to come rushing over the cliff-face and through the garden. Through the rosemary and the sweet peas and the spike lavender until it bursts through her window — through the wet glass — and the breath in my mouth will be tangled with that of the sea and the garden and the milk-sweet smell of her skin.

The weather was turning colder. Each day the garden seemed somehow crisper. Edna spent less time in her garden, having already trimmed back her roses. Every few days she swept up the leaves that fell in drifts beneath the large tree that shaded her back verandah. She passed me a small bucket of lemons and a book, a biography of Marie Antoinette. I picked her a bunch of lavender and made her a bottle of herb vinegar. We sat together, in her garden or mine, watching the light fall over the harbour. The sweet peas were finished, and the leaves of the rosemary were more silver-grey than green. The light, too, had changed. In the afternoon, the light over the harbour was weighted with water. Even when there was no rain, the water waited all day. It was not the sweaty, warm moisture of the tropics. Not the kind of moisture which makes everything go mouldy; curtains, cushions, even towels in the linen press. Nor was it the kind of sullen humidity that makes you sweat and wallow as if you're in a sauna. This moisture was kinder. This was the water my father dreamt of; rain. Just waiting to fall.

I watched it gather over the harbour as I took the flute — *my* flute — from its case. The clouds stretched out; growing thinner and darker until instead of clusters there was just one mottled sheet of grey spread over the sky. The wind, which had been gentle in the afternoon, began to pick up. Plucking at the surface of the bay beneath us.

'Looks like rain,' Jason said from behind me. I took the pieces of the flute and twisted them together. 'The washing's going to get wet.' I blew a few notes, my fingers settling gently into the cups, testing each note, then a few scales. It had a beautiful sound — soft and resonant.

'I have to do something first.' I took my mother's key from my pocket. It was soft and slippery, warm from the heat of my body. She would never play again. I would never hold her again. She would never hold me. She would not be there when my child was born. She would not come into the room and smile at me holding my child in my arms. She would not be there to teach her how to play. Somehow I would have to learn how to hold my child, how to love her. I would have to understand what it means to be a mother. My mother had had her flute since she was my age. Since she was childless. She had promised it to me, believing it would become something passed eternally from mother to daughter, gathering the threads of our maternal line and giving them weight, a material reminder of the bond between generations of mothers and daughters. This tiny piece was all that was left.

The wind was firm, its long fingers running through the harbour, puckering the surface like a fabric full of pulled threads. I placed the flute in my lap and took it apart, keeping only the end piece in my hands. It took me several minutes of fiddling to remove one of the keys, and several more to ease my mother's key into its place. I put the Muramatsu key in the case, tucking it beneath the lining in the bottom left corner. I was tempted to throw it out altogether — I would never use it — but I didn't. If I ever sold the flute I'd have to switch them again.

This time when I lifted the flute to my lips and rested my fingertips on the keys it felt better. More welcoming. More like my mother's flute. Of course she never let me play her flute. She bought me my own when I was about four and every day we practised together. Sometimes she would listen to me, tipping her head to one side with her eyes closed, or watching my fingers intently, or my mouth. If I got it wrong, she would play it for me herself, then it was my turn again, then hers. Back and forth until I got it right. As I got older it became a game — a competition. She would begin and I would follow. Sometimes we would play the same tune for hours, over and over again, getting faster and faster each time until we fell breathless against each other, laughing.

Then we would play it properly.

There was no one there to play with me anymore and, as I began, I could feel each note pressing into the silence of the afternoon. The notes flew up and found grooves in the fabric of the wind, pleats, and settled in. The wind gathered each note in her apron and cast them, seeding the air over the garden with music. Inside my head I could hear my mother's flute, the reedy quality of her breath like an afterthought beneath my own. With my eyes closed I changed the tone of her playing, bringing it down closer then softer, until it was the wind I was playing with — the breathless impatient wind daring me to play faster, to play recklessly. I found myself rocking against the railing of the gazebo, letting the beat of the timber against my thigh set a tempo. Inside my body I felt my baby turning, the faintest flutter, and I caught my breath. The tune I was playing was cut short in the middle of a note. I swallowed it whole, the last three phrases left unplayed as they tunnelled into me, through the winding skinless snake of my gut, into her.

'You're pretty good at that,' said Jason.

I had to take a breath before I answered him, more from shock than anything else, as if I had closed my eyes in an empty room and opened them to a crowd. I lay the flute in my lap.

'Play something else.'

I looked away from him, at the now-dark harbour. 'There's something I want to talk to you about.' How do you say these things? I wondered what it was that he thought I was going to say, whether what I had to tell him would be better, or worse. Suddenly I wished I could think of something else, anything else, I could tell him. Something less dangerous. Something which I could simply say and he would nod, perhaps ask a question or two, and then we could go inside. He would put on the kettle and I would rinse out the teapot. But this was not like that. This was the type of conversation followed by silences — long ones — or raised voices and broken glasses. Sometimes by smiles, sometimes by doubt, but always by something too big to fit into a conversation. Something too awkward to be said *just like that* and then left behind.

'What? My dog's dead?'

'You don't have a dog.'

'So what is it?' I shook my head and turned away from him, running one hand over the upturned saucer of my belly.

'I'm pregnant,' I said, and here, just as I imagined, he hesitated. I had my back turned so I couldn't see his face, so I would never have to contemplate the first emotion that moved over his skin. Or the second. But I could feel it. Or I believed I could. The raw emotion pushing into the small of my back just like the wind over the harbour. Only warm. A hot flush that pressed into my back, holding me so firmly that I could not turn around. I just couldn't.

When he began to ask me questions my answers were quiet and simple. *Yes. Three months. No.* I wanted to calm him. I wanted him to be as calm as the water beneath us. The water that could be so still it reflected the sky like a mirror. The dark harbour now restless with the storm, its surface grazed and impatient while far beneath it was cold and still. I wanted to smooth over this moment and move forwards — to a child playing in the garden. A honeyed afternoon sweet and thick with light. A peaceful ordinary existence where he would take my hand and we would smile together over her softly shining head. I felt the weight of him behind me — he hadn't moved but I could feel him clenched behind me, the muscles of his fists and shoulders bunched tightly together. The almost-cracked restraint. He asked me questions but each of them was flat and distant. I answered him automatically, quietly, knowing that each question was insignificant, only a longing to fill the awkwardness of our life, of this moment, with some hope of knowing what to do.

Listening to him falter clumsily through to understanding I realised that he didn't know what to do. This man who, for the little time I knew him, always seemed to know what to do — or at least to know what he wanted to do. It frightened him. Despite my feeling that I didn't know enough about what was happening to my body, he knew even less. He had been unprepared for our bodies to betray him. For my body to swallow up the small moments of gentleness he offered and turn them into something solid and real. He had believed he knew what he was getting into, how to make it work to his advantage, but this was something he hadn't been prepared for. He asked me inane questions because he didn't know what else to say, because he was waiting for something to shift, for him to see how he could use this the way he used everything else that happened. He asked simple questions because, for once, he didn't know all the answers.

'You could be wrong,' he said. 'It could be something else.'

What else, I wondered, was there? What was it he imagined *it* could be? Did he mistrust me so much, even then, that he thought I would lie to him? Think I did not know myself enough to realise when somebody else was living in my body? 'I am going to have a baby,' I said as I turned towards him. A breeze supported me as I stood, feeling suddenly sure. I had not known what I would say, but his stubborn stupidity, his weakness, made me sure. At that moment I both hated and loved him. I would have liked to push him over the edge of the cliff, watch him struggle to grasp hold of the air as he fell towards the water. I would have liked to take him in my arms and cradle him like a child. I would have liked to have been held by him and been able to turn away. He stared at me. His eyes were as steady as ever, but I saw in them the same thing I saw that day when he first saw me; curiosity and fascination. He was angry, but it was not his usual kind of anger, not the deep certain kind. He was angry because he was afraid, because he didn't know what to do, what to say. I had been uncertain, silently doubting whether she would ever be born, but at that moment I knew I would have this child.

I waited for him, in the middle of the conversation we were having while I watched the rain begin to puncture the harbour. A hundred thousand needles being driven into its soft grey skin. We both waited, and after a while I realised that at some point I had lost the thread of what it was he had said, of what we were saying to each other. So I stood with my back to him, just waiting, for too long. Finally I heard him stand up and walk across behind me. I could almost feel his hands reach me, touch me. The anticipation a physical thing that jumped in my skin. I felt him move past me down the steps and across the garden. I waited several minutes until I was sure he was gone — until I could no longer hear him or feel him — before I lifted the flute to my lips again and began to play.

It was as if that great rush of anger had washed me clean, emptied me of hope, and, gazing up at the dark sky spangled with its signs and stars, for the first time, the first, I laid my heart open to the benign indifference of the universe.

— Albert Camus, *The Outsider*

Things shifted. My body began to change shape slightly. Although I didn't have morning sickness I felt incredibly tired and I spent a lot of time sleeping, curled up in bed. My body exhausted and unintelligible. I watched the light of day slide into the room and out again, warming the timber and the sheets of the bed. I traced the strange dark line between my belly button and my pubic hair, the linea negra. I grew fat and worm-white in the dark, glowing dimly beneath the sheets. Jason moved further and further out, until he seemed to be teetering on the edge of some strange circle he had drawn around me. As if I were in the middle of a huge china bowl and he was skating around its edges, not quite sure whether to leap off onto the table top or slide down the inside slope of the bowl. He spent more and more time away from home, driving across the continent, making deals he didn't need to make. Taking risks. He drank more often and more heavily, and was increasingly distant when at home. At times, coming across me in the garden or the kitchen, he seemed surprised that I was there at all. He looked at me as if he didn't know who I was, shook his head and turned away. I missed him, or at least I missed the presence of the person I wanted him to be. I craved someone to talk to besides Cal — who was retreating more and more into his own world — or Edna, whom I kept at a safe neighbourly distance. I was uncomfortable with being pregnant and alone. Everywhere I turned, at the clinic, in shopping centres, on television, I saw pregnant women with their partners. Sometimes fighting, but always together. Jason was never there. At first he was gone for just a few hours here and there, then there were whole days, even weeks when I didn't see him.

He'd come home in the middle of the night when I was sleeping. He'd creep into the bedroom to wake me, placing a hand on my pillow and lifting the hair from my cheek to lean in and whisper with his mouth against my skin. He whispered so quietly that when I shifted slightly I would slip back into dreams instead of waking. He'd sit on the edge of the bed, remove his shoes, and slide in beside me. Sometimes placing his hand — curious and careful — on my belly.

On other nights when he came in I was already awake. Already waiting in the dark for him to place a dry mouth against my cheek and whisper urgent, drunken secrets. I'd keep my eyes closed, trying not to scrunch them too tightly, trying not to breathe too lightly, or too deeply. I'd turn over and pretend — again — to be dreaming. I didn't want to be discovered awake. I didn't want to spend hours at the kitchen table, cold and sleepy, desperate to be in bed, while he stumbled around dropping things, banging cupboards and leaving taps running. He was ridiculous. Impossible. Extravagant.

In many ways it was an ordinary life — the everyday shunt and shift of it. It was all I knew, and all there was for me. I know now that I could have walked out the gate, gone to a social security office, a shelter, a neighbour, but all those things seemed extreme and unimaginable. My life, in the moment I was living it, never seemed that bad, and I certainly didn't want anyone else to think it was. I didn't want to be one of those women you see in photographs with bruised and empty eyes, staring out of some strange unknowable life. I didn't think of myself as a prisoner and so I didn't think of escape. Despite his strangeness I needed Jason. When he was away I missed him like all young lovers — desperately, achingly — and when he was around I dreaded the morning I would wake up and find him gone. I loved him. I had already been saved — he had saved me. He was my knight in shining armour.

Callum and I had planned and plotted our escape for years but I don't think either of us had ever really believed it was possible. It took somebody else to show us it could be done. To me, Jason and the things he had led me to, the life I had become a part of, were as inevitable and inescapable as my father's love had seemed. Callum and

I had dreamed and made plans, but they were children's plans, childish things that were complex, fragile and ultimately impossible. We needed Jason. I think Cal knew that. I think it was the thing that haunted him at night, the thing he needed to hide from. I think it was the reason he stopped looking at me. The thing he couldn't live with was the knowledge that he, as much as I, had needed to be rescued. In the isolated kingdom of our childhood he had been the hero — my older brother, my Sir Galahad — but as the years passed and we never managed to get away our dreams soured. When Jason came it was the end of all our imaginings. When Jason came, Cal gave up his dreams of being a hero.

Jason was a difficult man, but he was also clever and loving and exciting. He knew about things I had never thought possible, never dared to dream were real. Things that had seemed exotic and somehow mysterious to me. Ordinary things like going to the movies, or parties, or dinner in a restaurant, but also more mysterious things. How to make money — something even my father had struggled with — how to talk to strange men who seemed frightening and dangerous to me. He wasn't frightened, like I was, of the police or neighbours or strangers. He laughed about my fears and put his arm around me and I felt safe, protected from the world, but also afraid. Mostly I was afraid that it wouldn't be real. That I would have to turn the world inside out again before I could find a place to just live, day to day. A place I would be happy. I felt guilty that I wasn't happy, and reluctant to say anything to him about the nagging discomfort I felt about my life. He had saved me, delivered me to the land of milk and honey. I should have been satisfied. I placed my hand over my gently swollen belly and held back the choking glut in my throat. I had no strength, no ideas, no will to change the world. I didn't want to risk losing what little I had, only to find that the world was even emptier, even thinner, than it already seemed. At times I dreamed of an ordinary life — or what I believed was an ordinary life — a life where I dressed like the women I saw on the streets, where Jason held my hand as we walked along the sidewalk, looking through shop windows. Where we spent our idle hours sipping cappuccino in cafes or laughing with friends.

The one time I said something like this to him we were watching television. A young couple in their apartment somewhere in America — New York perhaps — they were newly married. I looked over at Jason. The screen threw a flicker over his face. When he glanced at me he smiled, reached over and squeezed my hand. *Why aren't we like that?* I thought. *Why don't we live like that?* I gazed at Jason's hand. At his firm knuckles and the worn cuffs which slid over his wrists. *Are we happy?* I wanted to say. Not to know what he thought, really, but because I wanted to be happy, wanted to know what that was like, but I wasn't sure how it was supposed to feel. I needed him to tell me, because I didn't know what was real — this life? The life I had left behind? The lives I watched on television or read about in books and magazines?

Jason always had this air of imperturbable surety. He always knew how he felt, what he believed. If I thought about my life at all, it made me afraid — not of him or my father or anyone else, but of the strange empty space where I should have been. I felt hollowed out at times, but also strangely full of some unknowable creature that could not possibly be me. In some ways I still believed what I had been told as a child; that I was a fairy princess who had been rescued, that this was my happily ever after. The thing I struggled with was that, although I wasn't sure what happily ever after might mean, I doubted this was it.

The couple on the television were talking about having a baby. 'It's time,' she asserted. Her partner nodded and smiled.

'I love you,' he said, and they caught each other in an easy embrace that seemed more friendly than passionate. Beside me, Jason snorted and as I turned to look at him he was shaking his head.

'What?' I said.

'It's just so unrealistic. Look at them,' he thrust his arm towards the television, 'who really talks like that? Nobody. No guy lets his woman just tell him what to do like that. Bloody poofter.'

'I think they're sweet. He listens to her. What's wrong with listening to the woman you love?'

'Nothing. But a man has to keep a family together. You don't know what that's like. A man's responsible for money and all that. A roof over everyone's head. You can't do that and be weak.'

'I could get a job. Make some money.'

Jason shook his head and I felt the ground shifting beneath me, knowing that somehow I had missed the point. I was wary of saying anything else and upsetting the delicate balance of our conversation. Unlike the women we watched on television, I didn't know what to say, or what not to say. I felt lost and stupid and incredibly naive in the face of his uncompromising certainty. 'I'm making enough to take care of us,' he said. 'More than enough, as long as we stay here, where we don't have to fork out for rent. That's not the point. I brought you here. I'm responsible for you, especially now your idiot brother's gone and got himself hooked.'

'Cal's alright.'

'Cal's a moron who thinks some cheap street bitch gives a fuck about him. All she cares about is his money. *Our* money.'

I tried to sound strong and independent but my voice trembled slightly. 'I said I'd get a job if we need more money. I'm not useless.'

Jason shook his head, frustrated with my stupidity. 'For what? To support their habit? What kind of job do you think you could get anyway? You've got no skills, no experience, you're clumsy and not too bright. You couldn't even get a job as a waitress. Look at yourself.' Jason paused and shook his head again, weighed down with the responsibility of my inadequacies. I held my hands tight in my lap, trying to make myself seem as small and weightless a burden as I could. 'Forget it,' he mumbled impatiently.

'What do you want me to do?' I said. Jason looked up at me, his expression a mixture of exhaustion and frustration. Looking into his eyes I felt the coldness of the night spreading out around me. If he had told me to leave where would I have gone? I had no money in my pockets and I wouldn't have dared to ask Jason for any, if he was throwing me out. I had no idea how or where to find Cal. Sitting there, watching him measure me, I had sudden, frightening visions of myself sleeping in a park or an empty railway station, giving birth in the mud beneath a bridge or in a derelict building. Holding a child I had no shelter or food for, leaving her on the steps of a police station and turning away to what? Hunger, cold, loneliness. Why had I come there? What was I doing in that strange city, that strange house, with a strange man? I barely knew him. I didn't know him enough to trust that he would not turn me out onto the street. If I had known that this was love, that this was what escape and happily ever after offered, would I still have left my home? For a moment I hated Cal and his moral certainties. I hated him for his willingness to foster years of dreams of escaping from something that never touched him. Not in any real way. How dare he make choices for me? Decide that I needed to escape? I had been safe at home with my father. Loved. Secure. With Jason I was lost and desperate, knowing I could neither go back nor go forward. I bit my tongue and stared down into my lap, waiting for Jason to speak, my whole life a tiny and inconsequential scrap in his hands.

'Look,' he said, his voice low and tender, 'I'm no monster. I love you, not like those stupid people on tele, or in books. This is real. I know it's not always like you thought it would be, but you have to forget those fantasies. Real life isn't like that. I'm not Prince Charming and you're not Cinderella, but I do love you and I'll never leave you.'

I almost wept with relief as he put a hand on my knee and leaned in to kiss me. He could be gentle when he wanted to, and loving, and it was this — more than anything else — that made me believe in him. He loved me. He told me this all the time. And I believed him. I had no choice.

One night he stumbled up the stairs outside the back door, falling over with his keys jangling. Swearing at himself, at the stairs, and his clothes. In the morning I found him asleep with his head resting on the top step, his shirt on the bottom step and his jeans around his ankles. I stepped over him and walked along the path in the unforgiving daylight to catch the bus to the pre-natal clinic.

I had asked Cal to teach me to drive. We were having lunch at a cafe in the city. One of those tiny little places where all the tables are made of chipboard topped with formica and the chairs are bolted to the floor. An ancient pinball machine sat in the corner and a cluster of teenage boys huddled around it.

'Why don't you get Jason to teach you?' he'd asked. I looked away, watching the boys pushing the machine while the lights flashed and rang. All at once they leaned back from the machine and roared triumphantly.

'Looks like they're winning,' I said.

Cal grabbed my hand. 'You can tell me, you know, I can help you.'

I looked down at his thin hands, blinking to hold back the sudden tears, I shook my head and flicked my hair back over my shoulder, looking him in the face and smiling. 'It's your van, Cal. Will you teach me or not?' I knew, by the way he tried to stop me from looking away, that he wanted me to acknowledge something. He wanted me to confide in him, but I had lost faith in Cal. He was thin and weak and powerless. His skin was thin, his body fragile, I couldn't afford to put my faith in him, even though he needed me to. Finally he had agreed to teach me to drive and that afternoon we picked up a book of road rules for me to study. It was something, at least.

Callum was waiting for me outside the hospital at three in the afternoon. He seemed tired — looking down at my hands, at my feet — anywhere except at me as he helped me up into the driver's seat. When he had clambered into the other seat he leaned forward and looked out at the traffic.

I watched him sitting beside me. He seemed thinner and more morose, more distant. We fought sometimes, I couldn't remember us ever doing that before, not like that, not seriously. It frightened me. He and Jason were all I had and I didn't want him to become a stranger. I didn't want us to be the kind of brother and sister who only saw each other at Christmas, and even then reluctantly. He turned his head to see if there was traffic coming from my side and I smiled gently at him.

'Watch the road,' he said. 'Wait till you're ready then ease out into the traffic. Make sure you indicate first.'

I nodded and watched the endless stream of cars racing past, anxiously waiting for a break in the traffic. When it came I pulled my foot back slowly from the clutch, dreading the sudden jump and stutter which would mean I had stalled.

'How did it go today?' he asked.

'It was only a checkup — just so they can keep an eye on us.'

'You have to change lanes here — make sure you check your blindspot first,' he said. 'I thought something must have been wrong when you didn't call till so late. You said you had to be there at ten o'clock.'

'It takes forever. Mostly just waiting around. One waiting room after another.'

'Turn here. Then move straight over into the other lane so we can turn right. How come it takes so long? What if you had to be somewhere else?'

'I don't think they think of that. If you were important enough to have other things to do you'd be at a private practice.'

'You could if you wanted to, you know.'

I suppose it was true — I could have asked Jason for more money. He would have been happy to present me with money as long as he didn't have to worry about 'women's stuff'. But I didn't want to. Not for the pregnancy anyway. I would rather wait and use the money for the baby when she came; for bassinets and nappies and prams. I didn't mind going to the clinic — a bus ride, a train, a few hours alone in a strange waiting room. As long as I had a book with me it wasn't so bad. I talked to the other mothers, most with at least one toddler hanging off them. They were bored and sleepy. We discussed breast-feeding and nappy brands.

I drove through a small intersection with no lights. Callum frowned. 'Did you see the stop sign? You're supposed to come to a complete stop. If it's a give-way sign you just need to slow right down, but a stop sign means stop.'

I looked over at him. 'How's it going with you and Selene?' I asked.

'Selene went to see her folks today. They're in the city for a few days. Called her last night and asked her to meet them. She wasn't going to but ... ' he shrugged, 'you know, they're her parents. I'm picking her up after and we're going down south to pick up some stuff.'

'More stuff? Don't you have enough?' He looked out the window, rubbing his right wrist over the back of his left hand nervously.

'She thinks they might give her some money — some cash — she says they do sometimes. To help her out.'

We were quiet for a while, Callum watching the cars and absently chewing his nails when we sat at the lights. Going over the bridge the traffic was almost stopped. Luna Park slid up from beside and beneath us — its face grinning at me idiotically as we crawled past.

I had never been to Callum's new home, which he shared with Selene. From what he had told me it was small, and mostly empty. Judging by the way he looked when I saw him there was very little food, or hot water. I pictured their two-room 'home', the piled-up coffee cups with crusted milk in the bottom, the odd chairs and shredded lounge, the dirty sheets and dirty windows. I wasn't sorry I hadn't been inside, although I was curious. They lived in the suburbs on the opposite side of the city from Jason and me. I would have liked to walk into his home and sit at his table — talk with him, watch Selene boiling a kettle and pouring coffee. I would have liked to know who she was — this oddly bloodless, plastic-winged stranger. My brother's lover. If he ever invited me I would go, but for now I was happy not to know everything, to be able to imagine he was, in some way, still mine.

I'd only seen her a few times, and then mostly from a distance; framed in the van window as Callum pulled away from me, leaning against a shopfront in high heels and a plastic-sheened mini, white-skinned elbows leaning on a windowsill smoking a cigarette, or glaring at me as she signalled at Callum through a restaurant window.

She dropped him at our place sometimes, but never came in. Other times he turned up alone, when he intended to stay a little longer. A few days. We spent those days — our days — wandering around the garden. He followed me as I absently dug and turned the soil. Weeding here, planting half-grown cuttings there. He stood over me in his too-big clothes, shoulders hunched and hands in his pockets. Sometimes he held things for me, garden forks and cuttings that seemed to droop from his fingertips. He slept a lot. I fed him. Occasionally we talked, but most of the time he seemed content just to sit and wait for me.

He stayed at our house several nights of every week. Those mornings I would wake to find he had already left the house. I would discover him at the bottom edge of the garden. He'd take that one step across the fallen fence-line and stand with his toes over the rocky edge where the grass wouldn't grow. He was always looking down — not out towards the water or the horizon where my eyes were drawn — but down through the desperately clinging scrub to the scrabble of rocks below. It frightened me. I'd take his arm and lead him back over the fence-line. Back to the chess table or the gazebo where his strong black coffee waited. He looked so light and careless, as if he could take another step and find himself lifted by the wind where it hit the cliff-face and turned towards him. As if he wouldn't fall, but rise up twisting, frail and weightless as a dry leaf.

Sometimes the phone rang in the middle of the night and I would hear him stumble from his blankets to answer it. His voice was deep-throated and hoarse with sleep, mumbling like a child. He would laugh about it later — *The Night of the Long Knives*, he called it once — but most of the time I heard him hang up and pull his boots on, then the van would start up in the street outside. In the morning I'd fold the blankets he left half-crushed on the lounge, plump the cushions and place the folded warmth in the hall closet, wondering when he would sleep beneath them again.

Now I turned and looked at his familiar face, at the lines which tracked down beside his mouth and the way his chin dipped. *He is almost a stranger*, I thought, *how did that happen*? 'I didn't think she needed any money,' I said.

'What's that supposed to mean?' he snapped viciously.

'Nothing, I just thought …'

'You think you're so perfect? You think you're better than her? Why don't you look at yourself for a change.'

'Are you comparing me to her? She's a fucking prostitute, Callum. A street-slut.'

'And what are you? You think Jason is any better?'

'And where else can I go? Home? You know I can't do that.'

'Be by yourself for a while. You don't need him, you don't need anyone.'

I watched the people in the cars around us, smiling and distracted, singing to the radio, fixing their hair. A couple in the car next to us leaned over to kiss as we stopped at a set of lights. I wished it were that simple.

'I love him. We're having a baby.' He looked over at me sharply, his eyes questioning me, pinning me until a blush burnt my skin and I turned away again, watching a car pass so close beside me I could see the cheap little handbag the woman passenger had on her lap.

'You can't avoid it forever. He'll find out, he probably already knows. I just don't understand why you decided to have it at all.'

'She deserves to have a chance.'

'What about what you deserve?'

We drove the rest of the way in silence, Callum occasionally grunting when I did something wrong, but not commenting as I changed lanes suddenly, cutting off another car, or when I raced through a set of lights which turned red before I'd crossed the intersection.

I felt vulnerable without his usual gentle prodding, his quiet advice. I worried about being pulled over after careening through a round-about without using the gears properly, or indicating at all. Callum turned away to stare out the window. He was tense and his hands were fisted by the time I turned into our street. It was shaded and cool there, the traffic thinning out as we climbed the hill and I parked outside the house. I clambered down from my seat and looked at the side of his face; the familiar mouth held stubbornly closed. 'Cal?' I said. He shifted over into the driver's seat. He didn't turn his head around, flicking the indicator down and looking into the rear-view mirror instead.

'I have to go,' he said.

'Why don't you come inside?'

'Selene's waiting for me.' I waited for him to look at me, but he deliberately held his head still, staring out into the street. 'I have to go.'

'But …' I saw him shift, his hands fiercely pulling at the gearstick, and felt the van move away. I opened my mouth to call out to him but what more was there to say? Nothing. I watched the door swing closed as he turned the corner.

I was exhausted. I fumbled with my key in the lock, dumped my purse on the hall table and walked through to the kitchen. I removed my shoes while the kettle boiled and loaded a tray with teapot and cup, a small jug of milk and the book I had been reading in the clinic waiting room. I looked out the kitchen window to the garden, to the light already beginning to shift as the sun sank behind the house. The first few feet of garden beyond the kitchen stairs were already shaded, already so dim that the busy-lizzies seemed even more waterlogged than usual, more succulent. When the kettle boiled I poured the water over the leaves and carried the tray out into the backyard — to the chess table. My bare feet felt so delicious in the cool grass, so gently held. As I passed through the garden I saw Edna walking toward her back door and waved.

'Lovely afternoon,' she said. I nodded and smiled. 'You look tired, love, is everything okay?'

'Just the usual,' I said. 'I didn't know having a baby would be so exhausting.'

Edna smiled, shifting the basket on her hip. 'I'm off to the store,' she said, 'do you want me to get you anything?'

I shook my head and thanked her and as she moved away into her house I smiled, feeling tired but satisfied with the soft afternoon. The simple pleasures of tea, books, a friendly neighbour.

I was just pouring my second cup, turning the page of my book, when I heard Jason's new car pull up out the front. It stuttered and scraped over the kerb and I cringed at the damage I imagined to its underside, the torn muffler. Jason's voice echoed in the street as he swore and slammed the car door. I sipped at my tea, and wedged my book beneath my thigh, hoping he would go inside and fall asleep in front of the television. Instead he came up the side of the house, singing in his cheery, off-key voice, and jingling the keys in his loose hands.

'Hey hey,' he sang out to me, 'here she is — the woman herself. Mother-to-Be.'

I looked out over the cliff, wondering what excuse I could make to go inside — to get away from him. Could I plead tiredness? Cooking responsibilities? Housework? 'Hey,' I said quietly.

He lunged over the path to me, crushing the nasturtiums beneath his heavily booted feet, and planted an eager kiss on my forehead, sliding down to my cheek and ear. His breath reeked of alcohol and impatience. His skin still carried faint traces of perfume. He fumbled with the teapot in an attempt to pour himself a cup of tea, spilling most of the milk onto the grass at his feet. I looked down into my lap, knowing that when he was drunk he liked to pretend he was not, to go through the motions of a normal existence, an afternoon in the garden with tea, and that anything I did to betray that would infuriate him. When I reached towards him, to take the pot from him, he wrenched it away from me, sloshing most of the contents onto the ground. He glared at me, as if I had somehow meant to imply that he needed help.

'How did it go?' he asked.

'No problems,' I said, uncertain as to whether he really wanted to know, or whether he was just fumbling through his drunkenness, trying to set the world straight with simple questions which have simple answers. I wanted to tell him more, to draw him in to what had become my world instead of ours — the shared world I had imagined for us — but I couldn't think of what to say, how to say it. How would he react to tales of queues of overblown women with yellow-capped jars of urine? Or nurses who gossiped over me as if I wasn't really there. Or doctors who felt my ankles and belly as though I were an under-ripe avocado in a fruit shop. Two hours in a waiting room, only to change into an open-backed gown and be ushered into another — smaller — waiting room. I turned my head slightly and saw him out of the corner of my eye. His twitching hands and uncertain profile glazed with sleeplessness and the rugged self-assurance of alcohol. I watched him sip at his tea, dribbling it onto his shirt and smudging it away absently as he glared intently over the cliff.

'How long is it now, anyway, until the baby comes?' he asked.

'About twenty weeks. They can't be too accurate with these things.'

'It's a bit hit and miss, isn't it? But us fathers-to-be we know all about that, don't we? About not knowing the truth.' I glanced sideways at him and found him staring at me. His hard gaze watching the blush that stretched over my face. 'It's easy to see you're going to be a mother, isn't it? Perfectly obvious,' this as he not-so-gently prodded at my swollen belly, 'but us fathers you can't tell. Anyone could be a father and you wouldn't know it. Anyone.'

I sat silently as he watched me. His eyes were a shocking blue. 'Just like anyone could *not* be a father and think they were. You could lie to him or trick him, couldn't you? Any woman could. It's not too hard to fool us men, is it? We're pretty gullible when it comes to this stuff. Sperm-proud.'

I turned away, looking past him, focusing on the leaves behind him, the pattern they made against the sky.

'I don't fuckin' know,' he said. 'Maybe there is something kinda strange going on here. How do I know what went on back there?'

'Nothing *went on*. I hardly ever even left the property. There weren't even any strangers around the last few months — no cattle-hands or anything. We were doing everything ourselves.'

Jason hesitated with his wrist resting on the edge of his knee and his teacup balanced in mid-air. Neither of us looked at the other, but I could still watch him out of the corner of my eye. I saw him drop his eyes to his knees — his hands. I saw him falter, not knowing whether to say what he was thinking, but finally blurting it out.

'Your father.'

I stood up quickly and clumsily poured the dregs of my tea over the grass, my book slipping to the ground behind me. He grabbed my wrist and yanked me closer to him. I fell onto my knees in the almost-damp grass.

'Not this time,' he said. 'This time you stay here. Talk to me. I deserve to know the truth about what the hell was going on back there.' I looked into his eyes, my stomach knotted like tumble-dried sheets, but I couldn't speak. He wrenched at my wrist and I dropped my cup onto the grass, my hand bent back too sharply against the inside of my arm. I clenched my teeth against the pain, against the urge to cry out. 'Tell me,' he hissed.

I closed my eyes and breathed in, trying to breathe through the pain as I had been taught in childbirth classes at the hospital. His hand was so close to my face that I could detect the scent of a woman's sex on his fingers. My eyes flew open and I looked straight at him.

'What, Jason? I don't know what you mean.' I said it defiantly, staring into his eyes, daring him to doubt me, and he glared back. So angry that his clenched lips trembled whitely against his teeth.

'You don't know? You don't fucking know.' He threw my hand away and I toppled backwards, landing sprawled on my back in the grass. He leant over me on all fours so that when he yelled at me tiny droplets of spit sprayed over my face. I shimmied backwards, frightened now, desperate to get away from him, but he clutched my hair in his fist, holding me close. I wrenched my head to the side, feeling some of my hair pulled from the scalp, and looked towards Edna's fence. My eyes desperately scanning to find her. Jason laughed and turned my face back towards him. 'Don't worry,' he said. 'No one's there.'

I looked up at him, stunned at the sudden quiet that hung in his speech, the quick stillness. He leant close to my face — so close that when he began to speak again, biting off each syllable viciously — I was frightened that he might bite the end of my nose and I pushed my head as far back as I could into the soil. 'You little bitch,' he whispered, 'you whoring little daddy's girl bitch.' He pulled my dress up roughly over my hips and tore at my knickers. 'Daddy's bitch,' he said again as he drove his fingers into me, tearing at my skin with his ragged fingernails. I bit my lip and held my body as still and quiet as I could, just waiting for it to be over. I rolled my eyes towards Edna's fenceline, shifting my fear from Jason to her, worrying that she would come home and find us here, locked together. I looked towards the sky as he shunted backwards, one hand on my throat and the other on my hip as he drove his face into my sex, biting viciously until I could smell the coppery scent of my blood. I closed my eyes and waited for the rain to fall.

There's this much of the lily left in me.

— Lesbia Harford

He came home with flowers. Huge bunches of plump, flesh-white lilies. He brought them in from the car and placed them all over the house, kissing me as he walked through the door. The whole house began to smell of lilies. On his final trip he brought a bottle of champagne, which he placed in my arms with a smile.

'I'm sorry,' he said, kissing my shoulder, 'can you forgive me?'

I stood silently, wondering what to say. I felt the itching sting where he had bitten into me. The flush of embarrassment when I rang the hospital to cancel my appointment, ashamed of what the doctor might say if he did an internal. When the nurse on the phone insisted, telling me I was putting my baby at risk, I told her I would be seeing someone else from now on. A specialist. A private obstetrician. 'What's his name?' she said, 'I'll send your history over to him.'

'I'm not sure of his address,' I said, 'I haven't actually been yet. My boyfriend set it up. He wants me to have the best treatment available.'

'I just need his name. We have the details of all the obstetricians in the city. It's very important that he have all the information he can about your pregnancy so far. All the blood tests and the ultrasound.'

'I don't know,' I said, already leaning over to hang up the phone, 'I'll call you when I find out.' I stood in the quiet room and put a hand to my belly, feeling her turn and tumble inside me. Hundreds of women give birth all over the world without having to see doctors every month. I would just wait until I went into labour and turn up at the hospital. Everything would be fine I told myself, I would just have to be extra careful in the last month or so, when it was time to give birth — make sure there wasn't a mark on me.

I kept seeing myself lying on the table, my feet pulled up to my bottom, a pale sheet over my knees, and the doctor standing beside me — frowning at the sight of my scratched and bruised sex. I couldn't face that. Couldn't face some stranger standing beside me while his neatly gloved hand prodded at me and his arrogant uninterested face asked me questions about *how* and *why*. What would I have been able to say, that I fell over? *It was a table, doctor, a doorknob, the stairs.*

When Jason leaned in to kiss my mouth I turned away slightly, determined not to give in. Not this time. A light frown passed over his face, but he seemed determined to be pleasant and quickly smiled again. 'Get dressed,' he said, 'something nice. We'll go out for dinner.'

'I don't know.'

'When the baby comes we won't have much time to ourselves. We should make the most of it, don't you think?'

'I don't have anything to wear.'

He smiled and kissed my mouth, knowing that I would go, knowing that already I was relenting. 'I'll wait for you out the front,' he insisted. I tried not to smile as he kissed me again. Tried not to feel the soft melting that spread from where his mouth touched mine to where his hand was cradling the small of my back, holding me gently.

We drove into the city and walked through the Rocks until we found somewhere to eat. There were people everywhere. The air was warm. We sat outside, watching the harbour water as it glittered beneath the lights of the city. I closed my eyes. It was a perfect night. Jason gently put his hand beneath my elbow as he leant forward to ask me a question, his eyes soft and concerned. I tried to remember why we were here, tried to focus on the sting as I crossed my legs and shifted gingerly in my chair, but it seemed so long ago. A different time. A different man. I watched his face as he scanned the menu, the familiar cheekbones and shining sweep of clean hair that fell over his shoulder. I leaned closer, breathing in the smell of his skin, freshly scented with aftershave and soap. He smiled and took my hand, turning it over to kiss my palm.

We ordered a bottle of wine and drank a toast to the city night. We talked about the weather, the way the air seemed lighter and clearer on nights like those, with the smell of the ocean washing in from the harbour. He reached over to run the pad of his thumb over my lip.

We talked. He asked me how things were going with the baby, how I was feeling. He listened carefully as I told him about my trips to the hospital, the blood tests and boredom and frustration. My fears about the birth. He promised to get me into a private clinic. I told him it didn't matter; we were nearly there. We talked about what to call her when she was born. I remembered the list of names I had written out in the back pages of my journal, trying to recall my favourites. I recalled the delight with which I had bought the blank book and fine-nibbed pen, how I had gazed at the fresh white pages, picturing them filled with stories about how happy we were. Stories about being pregnant, being with Jason. Our whole lives together. One of the first things I had done was turn to the back and press the pages out flat, hearing the slight crack of the book's spine, and rule the two neat columns headed *Boy* and *Girl*. I had filled the column for girl quickly, finding it harder to choose a boy's name that I liked.

I didn't keep a journal anymore, although I still wrote things down. Sometimes I would write pages and pages, but always on scrap paper, on the back of envelopes or receipts, on serviettes and old newspapers which I hid carefully at the bottom of the garbage.

Weeks ago I had come home to find him in the garden. I could smell the smoke before I saw him standing beside the forty-four-gallon drum we used as an incinerator. I came up behind him and put my arms around him, placing a cheek against his shoulder. 'Good afternoon,' he said. Instead of answering I had lifted my head and kissed the side of his neck, gazing vaguely into the flames. I saw a page curl up blackly, the ink growing darker and the page turning first yellow, then orange, then falling away in black flakes. I stood up straight and looked at the back of his head. He didn't move, didn't turn to see why I had moved away from him.

'That's my journal,' I said, keeping my voice as steady as possible, although the last word trembled slightly. Jason half turned his head, his eyebrow lifted as though he were a condescending critic at a grade school production. 'Did you read it?'

'I don't think you should keep a journal,' he said.

I flushed furiously red. Angry that he had ferreted through my things to find it. Angry that he had opened it and read it and, far from being ashamed of invading what little privacy I had, chosen to flaunt it and destroy it. I bit my tongue and struggled to find something to say. Looking at the back of his neck, at his loose shoulders and easy stance I was reluctant to say anything at all. I knew now that with him anything could be a cause for anger, a reason for him to turn on me, and as I stood there I felt my stomach clutch and the baby turn. My distended paunch felt obvious and ridiculous. I closed my eyes and tried to imagine it away. Tried to conceive of a different life. A different kind of freedom. When we left home I had thought everything would be different, and it was, but not like this. I never imagined it like this. I felt immobile, trapped in my own body with this huge, tumbling child inside it. Every time we fought I felt the circumference of our lives — of my life — grow smaller. In the garden I had thought would be the site of our happy lives, he slowly clipped and clipped and clipped away, training my limbs to grow in unnatural ways, cutting back the leaves that protruded. I was trying so hard to be whatever he wanted, just as the trees in those ornamental gardens bend themselves to the forms of their loving keepers, but it was difficult. I did not know which form he wanted me to take and every day I woke and patted the edges of myself, checking that no branch stuck out, no leaves protruded through the wire cage. The difficulty was that I had no idea what shape I was or what shape I had become or what shape I desired to be. I no longer knew where I began and he ended or whether the distinction between us existed. At the same time I felt oddly and unnaturally separate, struggling to fit my gangling and improbable roots inside his neat borders and carefully articulated paths. I always seemed to be too far away or too close, I never understood the rules, but he always knew what needed to be done. And did it.

'Don't ever fucking write about me,' he said, 'you're a shit writer anyway. It's not worth the paper and ink to write down that crap.' He flourished a torn page in front of my face, not turning around but holding it up so that I could see. His voice rose to a nasty effeminate shriek. '*Every time he kisses me I feel like a torch has been lit and I have been chosen as the Olympic torchbearer. I keep running even though I'm exhausted, even when I feel like I just want to lie down and give up, because*

I know it is a glorious and pure thing to be kissed by him.' He laughed and threw the page on the flames, tearing another one from the book in his hand and holding it up in front of him. *'Be careful I tell myself. But who knows what that means? How can you be careful with a broken heart? I ache for him to hold me. Body to body. But when he does I'm terrified. When he does I feel his heart beat and it surprises me that he has a heart at all.'* He threw the page on the fire and pulled out more, ripping them out until he flung what was left of the book into the drum. He turned around and I saw the flames light up his hair from behind like a weird halo. He leant in close to me, took my chin in his hand and looked. There were tears on my face that I was too slow to wipe away. As he leant closer I had to hold myself so tightly not to flinch. Not to pull away. His mouth landed on mine and he kissed me. A long, slow, comforting kiss. By the time he pulled away my body had let go and my eyes had closed. He held his face a bare inch away from mine and smiled, running his fingertip down to the tip of my nose. His voice was low and quiet. 'Don't you ever write anything like that down again. You do and I'll kill you, and no one will know or care.'

He kissed me once more, lightly, on the cheek and walked away. I stood watching the flames, seeing the cover of my journal bend and blacken, feeling the heat that touched my cold face. I stood until I heard the car start out front, until I heard him change gears as he pulled away from me.

I don't remember seeing that last page burn. As I sat in the restaurant watching him smile at me, the glass of wine at his fingertips and his other hand resting lightly on mine, I tried to smile confidently. The way I knew women in love should smile. 'We could call her Marina,' I said, 'because she'll be born near the ocean. Or Brooke.'

'It could be a boy,' he said. I shook my head and he laughed. 'Sometimes you don't get what you want.'

I smiled into my bowl. This was not what I wanted. It was just how it was. I would have a daughter. I would raise her as my mother had raised me. I would teach her all the things my mother had taught me. I would play for her in the garden, or in her bedroom at night as she fell asleep. I would teach her about music, how it lived and breathed inside you. 'She'll be a girl,' I said.

He smiled at me and took my hand across the table. 'Just don't be too disappointed when you're wrong.'

At the table next to us a woman was wearing a short, fluorescent pink veil, topped by a plastic tiara. She and her friends had obviously been drinking for hours. They laughed loudly — drowning out the noise of the boats on the harbour, the people in the street. I heard one of them say, 'A man in the house is like a lawnmower in the kitchen.'

The bride-to-be leant forward earnestly, taking the hand of the woman beside her. 'It's true,' she said, 'ever since Dad retired he's been driving Mum nuts. He just doesn't know what to do with himself. Now he's planning this massive trip around Australia and she's like *no way*, she'd rather masturbate with a pineapple.'

The whole table shrieked with laughter. I felt Jason move closer to me, leaning his head against my shoulder so that I could hear his voice. 'How's Callum doing with that girl?' he asked.

'Selene. Okay, I guess. He seems happy.'

'They don't have what we have though.' Glancing at his face, his intent gaze fixed on me, I was struck by his persistence. I shrugged lightly and turned away. What we had was different to what Cal and Selene had, and I know that in some ways it was better. We were never drug addicts. We weren't sick and deathly pale and hooked inside each other like parasites, eating each other alive. Or at least we didn't seem that way to other people. 'Do you remember when we met?' he said. 'You and Cal on that little old farm, stuck in the last century. You were so quiet. You barely spoke, but I knew — I knew the first moment I saw you that you were special. We're both passionate, driven people and sometimes that means we're difficult, but it also means what we have is special.' I felt his gaze pulling on me, insisting that I turn to him, but I didn't. He reached out and took my hand. 'You are happy, aren't you?'

I looked at the harbour, a boat slipped silently past, coloured lights swaying along her rails. Above us the stars were shining, the moon was almost full. The baby was quiet inside me, finally sleeping. I closed my eyes and tipped back my head, breathing in the sharply salted night air. When I opened my eyes, I smiled at him and took his hand. What else could I do? As he leant forward to kiss me I saw the triumph barely concealed in his eyes, in the way he held his mouth. I closed my eyes when he kissed me. I didn't want to see it. His little victory. I was a long way from home. A long way from anywhere I could have felt safe. I had no choice but to kiss him, to hold him, however cautiously.

As he kissed me, I remembered the story my mother told of the true lover who survived a terrible night, while her beloved changed shape into all manner of horrors in her embrace. With his lips on mine, and his hand at my throat, I could feel him shifting and becoming many things, and I held on because I knew that I had no choice. I held on because no matter what he became I knew him, he would always be Jason. As he pulled away I looked over at the woman in the pink veil. She was watching me quietly as her friends leant forward over some morsel of gossip. She looked sad. One of her friends placed a hand on her shoulder and she turned away, but not before giving me an oddly complicit smile.

After dinner we walked around the harbour. He put his arm around me, his hand resting gently on my hip. The city was beautiful at night; the lights glittering above us were reflected in the water that slapped against the wharves. The ferries and boats shone. A group of people in evening wear passed us, the women laughing delightedly as they skipped by, their arms around each other. We headed towards the Opera House, passing the ferry terminals, and following the walkway as it swept around. A girl struggled past us with a cello in its case. A group of young boys hurtled by in a flurry of sweat. I watched the boats, the lights that traced the arch of the bridge and the eggshell curves of the Opera House.

Ahead of us a man was leaning his forearms against the rail. A bottle dangled from one of his hands. As we got closer he stood upright, hurled the bottle into the water and turned to walk away. I saw him look at Jason, registering him out of the corner of his eye and turning back with a questioning look on his face. Jason took my arm, his fingers pinching slightly, as the man took a few steps forward and stood in front of us.

'Jason, right?'

'David,' said Jason, holding out his hand. The two of them faced each other uneasily. Up close David's face looked familiar and after a few seconds I remembered him from one of the parties we had gone to when we first arrived. He'd passed out on the floor of the lounge room for several hours. Some wit had drawn a moustache on him with a red marker pen, and an ashtray rested on his stomach.

'This must be Elliot,' he said, reaching his hand out towards me, 'Jason's told me quite a bit about you.' He took my hand and gripped it tightly, shaking vigorously as he looked at my face. 'You look kinda different to what I imagined. Darker, you know. I thought you said she was a blonde, mate.'

'This isn't Elliot. This is Germaine.'

David frowned slightly at Jason before turning to me again. 'Sorry darlin'. Innocent mistake. I'm pretty bad with names, you know.'

I nodded at him and smiled awkwardly. After a brief and uncomfortably polite conversation the boys excused themselves and walked away a couple of metres, tipping their heads forward and talking earnestly as I leant on the harbour railing. Jason looked uncomfortable, one hand digging in his pocket as he used the other to punctuate his conversation. I couldn't hear what either of them was saying; only the faintest rumble of their voices that slid up and down. Accusation. Question. Reply. At one point they both turned to look at me, David's face concerned, Jason's wary. He waved at me and smiled. David shook his head and I heard his voice as clear as day, 'I don't know, mate.'

After several minutes they turned back towards me and Jason took my arm. The three of us walked on towards the Opera House, Jason quiet and David talkative — telling jokes he had heard but couldn't quite remember the punch lines for. None of us was laughing.

As we turned to walk back to the car park David excused himself and strode towards The Rocks. Jason became fidgety, taking his hand from around my waist and driving it into his pocket. The gentle concern of a few hours ago was gone, replaced by his usual preoccupied disregard.

'I have to go out later,' he said.

As we drove over the bridge I watched the boats bobbing uncertainly in the harbour, their lights sometimes engulfed by the shadowy water. Far out towards the heads a late-night ferry was making its way towards Manly. I watched the lights go out in a house perched near the edge of the harbour, seeming to sink away into the darkness.

'Are you happy?' he said softly.

'I love you,' I replied.

It was hardly what he had asked but I could not lie. I didn't know what else to say, what else to offer him that would be gentle enough to divert him, but not so distant he'd know I was deliberately avoiding answering him. I hoped that, just this once, I would be faster than him, that just this once our conversation (which was another round in the endless battle we were fighting, the fight I was always losing) would end in a kiss goodnight and a peaceful sleep. I always felt at a disadvantage when he came at me like this, startling me with his gentleness, with questions designed not to find out what I thought, but to measure the extent of my inadequacy. Even when my answers didn't infuriate him he remained grimly unsatisfied, grinding his teeth in frustration. He would breathe through his nose and stalk off.

'You're a liar,' he usually said as he left the room, casting it back at me. It hit me softly but dug deep, burrowing into my gut until I was weak-bellied and ashamed. I struggled to find the truth he wanted to hear. I wanted to find the place inside me he believed I had hidden away. I wanted to break myself open so he would be satisfied and we could be happy.

We drove the rest of the way home in silence and he did not look at me as I clambered out of the car. In the empty house, the lilies had already started to droop, the pale gold and red of their stamens had dusted many of their throats, staining the white flesh a dusky orange colour. In the kitchen, one bunch lay across the bench, its stems in the sink. The flowers crushed beneath a saucepan.

The angels keep their ancient places,
Turn but a stone, and start a wing!
'Tis ye, 'tis your estranged faces,
That miss the many-splendoured thing.

— Francis Thompson

Callum believed in love in a way I never would. He dreamed about Selene. He looked off into the distance when he talked about her, his eyes shining. He told me about the shape of her shoulder blades, how they curved into his hands, how they slid beneath her skin. He told me about the texture of her skin. I looked at my hands, at the calluses beginning to fade from my fingertips. Jason was somewhere in this city, his body slicing through the crowds impatiently, his hands deep in his pockets, his mind following the path beneath him. Did he have friends? People he confided in? People he was close to? Did he talk about me? What did he say? I couldn't imagine him leaning forward so eagerly. I couldn't imagine his voice this dreamy, this soft, as he held forth on my doubtful charms. I wanted to be in love. I wanted him to love me, but I didn't believe he could. I wanted to walk hand in hand and smile secretly at him across a table in a restaurant and have strangers smile at us. I wanted him to put his hand on my belly and smile when she began to turn inside me. I wanted it to be *our* child, *our* angel, *our* precious daughter. I wanted to feel what Callum felt — innocence, hope, love.

'She walks like an angel,' he insisted.

'Angels fly.'

'Her voice is amazing, when she whispers I get goosebumps.'

I turned away, watching the water slap against the poles that supported the wharf beneath us. A few feet from us people were throwing coins into the water where a group of young boys were floating, their naked torsos shining as they dived and bobbed like fish. One boy sat on a strut that crossed diagonally between two of the

155

support pylons, his knees drawn up against his chin, his thin legs laced with small scratches. He caught me watching him and grinned. I fished a coin out of my pocket and threw it up into the air. As it fell I saw him dive, the water distorting the shape of his limbs, his thin arms trembling as he slithered through the water. He came to the surface with my coin in his hand, waving it triumphantly over his head. 'Why can't you just be happy for me?' Callum pleaded.

'She's a hooker, Cal.'

'That's not all she is.'

I looked down at the water. Part of me wanted to hurt him, wanted to be cruel. Why should he be happy when I wasn't? I didn't understand how he could fall in love with this woman who was paid to create the illusion of care, and have her love him. What was it that made him capable of being loved and not me?

I looked over at him. He was frowning down at his reflection in the water. His face pinched with worry. I put my hand on his arm.

'Just give her a chance,' he said, 'you'll like her.'

'Okay, Cal. If that's what you want.'

'I'll call her, maybe we could have lunch together?' He was smiling now, his whole face shining. 'I'll be right back.' He ambled away a few feet. I smiled at him, at the little-boy enthusiasm which I remembered so clearly and which I had seen so rarely in the past few months. I smiled as he turned to give me the thumbs up.

At lunch they sat close together, his hand in her lap and her hand resting lightly in his. Up close she didn't seem so harsh, although she was still oddly plastic. Her thin hands were covered with a light spray of freckles. Her face was bland beneath the make-up she was wearing, but when she looked at Callum and smiled she seemed different. Warmer. Her bare stomach, beneath the tiny midriff she wore, was pale. She picked at the skin of her fingers and when I looked down I saw that they were red and frayed, the nails slightly ragged. She put them back in her lap. She leant back in his arms like a child. We discussed the menu, the weather, the crowds outside. When the waitress came to take our order Selene whispered to Callum, who ordered for her. I hunched lower in my chair, looking out the window at the beautiful people. The perfect city girls with their perfect nails and perfect teeth. I studied the frayed edges of my fingers. The reflection of my unmade-up face in the window. The scratches on my knees. The waitress walked away without taking an order from me.

'Don't you want anything?' Callum asked me.

'The Penne. And coffee.'

Callum got up and walked over to the counter to place my order. I felt awkward alone with her.

'You have nice hands,' she said, 'long fingers.'

'Thank you,' I replied awkwardly, turning my hands over on the tabletop.

'Callum's hands are different. He has real short fingers. They're kinda stubby.'

I nodded uncertainly. Why was she telling me this? Was she just trying to make conversation? I suppose she felt as awkward as I did. She must have been wondering why he brought her there. I thought about what Callum might have told her about me. He could have said anything. I shifted uncomfortably in my seat and glanced over to where he was standing. His hands dangled at his sides, his thumbs almost as long as his fingers.

'His thumbs are kinda long though. It's weird, you know,' Selene continued.

'I suppose he has hands like Father.'

'He wouldn't like that.'

I looked past her, squinting against the afternoon light that blazed over her shoulder. How much would Callum have told her about our father? About home? I placed one hand protectively over my belly.

'We'd like to have kids one day,' she said. I turned to look at her, my head swinging round so fast that the hair flew out from my head. 'Not yet, of course, but some day. Callum really likes kids. So do I. I reckon it must be great to be pregnant. He would be so into it, you know?'

I nodded my head stupidly, trying to imagine them together — really together — her plump belly and his smile, his hand resting on hers, her head on his shoulder. The baby rolled beneath my clothes and I sucked in my breath as she knuckled into my hip.

157

'Is it moving? Can I feel?' Selene slid over closer to me and placed a hand over my belly, just below my navel. The baby kicked vigorously, rolling over beneath her warm hand. She laughed with pleasure and slid her hand over towards the side. 'She's so strong. You can really feel her stretching. Strong-willed. What are you going to call her?'

'I don't know yet.'

'She'll need a good strong name. My sister had a strong son — too strong for her — and she thought it would help to give him a powerless name, you know, but it didn't. Apparently he's a real brat and she yells at him all the time, but he's just confused. It's not his True Name.'

I glanced over at Callum, who was leaning against a street light outside talking on his mobile phone — when did he get one of those? He looked different. More competent than I had imagined. His head was tipped forward slightly against the noise of the traffic and the people who flowed around him. He was frowning and shaking his head.

'Callum has a good name. It's the right name for him. I had my friend do a chart up for us and apparently we're almost a perfect match. Imagine that.' I smiled at her absently. Callum had turned his phone off and was making his way across to us, weaving between tables full of people.

She leant closer to me, her hand once again resting lightly over my belly as the baby turned. Her head was close to mine. I could hear her breathing, smell the acrid scent of her sweat beneath her freshly washed hair and cheap perfume. 'Don't worry,' she muttered under her breath, 'I won't hurt him. I love him.'

As Callum reached the table she moved away from me, her hand sliding down over my belly and squeezing my fingers as she turned towards him. 'Who was on the phone?' she asked.

'Stan. We need to go and get him. Martin didn't show up and he's freaking out.'

'I can go. You stay here with Germaine.'

'I can't let you go on your own.'

She shook her head at him as the waitress brought our meals and placed them before us. As the waitress walked away, Selene leant forward and took Callum's hands between her own. 'I'll be fine,' she said. 'I know Stan. He trusts me.'

Two weeks later I met Callum in Manly and we walked towards the beachfront. It was late afternoon and the crowds were thinning, the well-fed people on the beach leaning against the stone wall, or lazing under umbrellas while their children chased balls and frisbees through the sand. We walked along the promenade, following the concrete path past the surf club.

At the pools I watched the heads of small children in multicoloured rubber caps duck beneath the water as their extended arms pushed at yellow plastic kickboards. A woman sat with her feet dangling outside the pool wall, above the rocks, which were only just beginning to disappear beneath the incoming tide. She was wearing a wide-brimmed straw hat, a red ribbon wrapped firmly around the crown. The edges of her hat-brim were soft with salt-water, drooping over her face and neck.

Callum took my hand as we walked, his palm warm and dry against mine, his fingertips toughened and thick. A group of small boys were huddled over a comic book on the walk. Their heads crowded together as they pointed at particular pictures, read words aloud and laughed together. Callum and I walked around them, raising our hands. We spread a V-shaped shadow over them, dragging it across their sun-warmed bodies. One of the boys looked up at me, his honey-coloured skin glowing with sunburn beneath the towel he had twisted like a turban around his head. One of his friends grabbed at his shoulder and he turned away, but not before gracing me with a huge gap-toothed smile.

We moved further around the bay, the sun sliding up over the cliff-face beside us, warming our footsteps before we walked in them. There were only a few scattered handfuls of people around. One group had been up to the lighthouse, a family of tourists with cameras slung around their necks and towels rolled across the top of their backpacks. The baby turned firmly inside me, reminding me of seals in their fat-lined skins tumbling in the harbour. She knuckled her round head into my ribs, her feet burrowing down into my pelvis.

She should have turned by then. She should have been head down, ready to be born. I had avoided the clinic for months. Waiting out my pregnancy in isolation. Reading from the pile of pregnancy and childbirth books I borrowed from the library or bought from the shops. One night I lay awake feeling my belly clench, sure that I was in early labour and terrified that my daughter would be born prematurely. I called the hospital and hung up three times before taking the keys to the car and driving over there. The midwife was kind. They were just Braxton Hicks, she explained, which could be very strong but were not real labour pains. She was more concerned that the baby was still in a breech position and made me promise to come in weekly. The midwife tried to turn her. I lay on the narrow table, white-faced with pain, as the baby tumbled wilfully back into the breech position. The midwife shook her head. 'Baby will have to turn on her own soon,' she said, 'else you'll be having a Caesar. They won't let you go on your own, especially seeing as it's your first.'

I leant against the warm cliff and Callum placed his square-fingered hands over my belly. He turned his head to the side as if he were listening. Like the midwife who settled the trumpet-shaped tube against my belly and leant over me to listen to the baby's heartbeat, her eyes far away. What did he think he would hear?

The baby pushed at his hand, stretching against him, and he pulled away as though someone had pinched him. His face open and smooth like a saucer. Then he laughed. Sudden laughter that bounced over my head. One hand was resting on the stone wall over my shoulder as he tipped forward, his forehead touching mine.

When we reached the small curve of Fairy Bower there were hardly any people. A jogger in a tight tracksuit bent and stretched before moving off up the hill behind us. There was a small restaurant. A handwritten sign hung from a nail in the glass-panelled door: *Closed*. A fenced area beside the restaurant had a few thick-timbered outdoor tables, bolted into the cement, and in front of them was a small kiosk where a young boy sat listening to his headset. His glazed eyes were bored and indifferent. We bought two ice-creams — he didn't remove his headset or say a word — and walked barefoot off the warmed concrete path onto the beach.

Sitting on the sand that sculpted easily and warmly to our bodies we looked back towards Manly and the promenade. From here the people were just small spots of colour. Strangely abstract. The brightly coloured children darting along the beach like dropped pins scattering on a polished floor. Callum pointed out a small flock of surfers floating in the sheet-flat water.

It was getting cold. I pulled my cardigan around me and nestled in to Callum's shoulder, feeling the warmth of his body settle over my skin. But my belly was cool, swelling out between us as round and soft-firm as an avocado. A breeze swept around from the harbour, raising goosebumps on my legs and arms, on my throat and thighs. She couldn't feel it. She was not affected by the vagaries of the weather — of clouds and breezes, sunlight and salt-spray. For her I was the air she breathed, the food she ate. Soon she would be born and then … Then the wind would chill her, the sun burn. She would be hungry and lonely, helpless and dependent. How would I know what to do? How to hold her? What would I do when my body no longer served her so automatically, so easily? I felt the fear clutch at me. A soft contraction — the gentle warm-up of Braxton Hicks — pulled at me. I did not want her to be born. I wanted, somehow, to keep her inside me forever. To keep her safe.

'What's wrong?'

'Nothing. I just … I'm scared. I don't know anymore. I don't think I can do this.'

'You didn't have to do this, Germaine. You didn't have to have this baby.'

'It's a bit late for that now, isn't it?'

I strode away from him, pulling my cardigan firmly over my swollen breasts, over my distended gut. Driving my bare feet against the concrete path until I felt it grazing my reddened soles. The concrete so cold now that my toes were almost numb. The pads on the base of my feet felt thin. In some places the path was wet. I wondered whether it ever closed over, whether you could be stuck out here unable to get back to the lights slowly coming up on the beach-front.

'Wait,' I heard him call from behind me. 'Germaine. Wait!'

I did not turn around, but waited for him to catch me; the breeze pushed at my crisp and pointed face. I felt him come up behind me and put his arm around me. The warmth in his skin fleshing out the thinness of my cardigan, warming my skin. I turned towards him. 'It's okay,' he said.

We walked slowly back around the harbour. Callum on the water-side, and me carried along between him and the cliff-face. When we reached the surf club there was a small group of young men rolling up ropes and carrying their boats into the storage shed.

'Coffee?'

'Can we get something to eat?'

I sat at a small metal-topped table sprouting like a thin mushroom from the pavement. The chairs were cool and uncomfortable, the arms digging into my side. Callum came out, digging into the butcher's paper he was carrying, licking his fingers and blowing on them. He sat down opposite me and unwrapped the fish and chips, which steamed and sweated on their wrinkled paper dish. The waitress came up behind Callum, placing the coffee clumsily before us, spilling half of mine into its saucer.

'You're so big. When's your baby due?' she asked.

'Soon,' I said.

'Is it your first?' she said to Callum.

I smiled into my coffee cup, listening to his serious voice, 'Yes. We're pretty excited.'

'Wow. I don't think I could ever do that, you know. It must be pretty scary.'

'Well, you're young yet.'

She glanced over at me, trying to assess how old I might be. 'Yeah. I guess so. You never know what might happen, but I don't think so. It would interfere with my weekends too much.'

'It's not going to interfere with mine at all,' he said, and I couldn't help but laugh. His face, too, rose in that teasing little boy's smile. The waitress smiled uncertainly at us and turned away, the tray banging at her shins.

I looked down the Corso towards the harbour where the rush-hour ferry had unloaded its cargo. Swarms of people were moving across the road and past the supermarket. Some went into the hotel, others into cabs and buses, a few strode off down the street, dissipating like clouds before a cold wind, until finally there were only thin streams of them weaving about in the distance.

I asked him about Selene — about how their relationship was going. Selene was little more than a stranger to me, although when I thought about her I remembered the feel of her bony fingers on my belly. I looked over at Callum. His hands had fallen open around his coffee cup. He was staring into it, and the racket of the boys who clattered past on their skateboards only hollowed out his awkward silence.

'I don't know,' he said. 'She hasn't been home.'

I almost laughed. 'We sure are a pair, aren't we? And so are they. God, they could be off partying together.'

'You remember when she went to pick Stan up after lunch the other week? Well, she called me when she got there to say she was staying for a few days — he's down the coast somewhere — and we had a fight. I said some stuff I shouldn't have. I haven't spoken to her since.'

'She'll be back.'

Callum stared at me, his face closed and stubborn. 'How do you know? I saw her a few days later. She was across the road — six lanes of traffic. I couldn't reach her. I called out but she can't have heard me. She was facing the other way, looking in the shop windows at clothes and stuff. Some guy came up and started talking to her and they walked away together. I couldn't see who he was, but I think I might have met him before. He was kind of familiar.'

'So she's mad at you. It's the first time you've had a full-on fight so she's giving it to you — punishing you. She'll be back and you'll be so glad to have her back you'll forget to be mad at her. You'll forget everything.'

'I'm not like you. I can't just forget things. I can't just pretend bad stuff never happens.' We sat in awkward silence as I fiddled with the edge of the tablecloth, with the change in my pocket. 'I never should have come here,' he muttered.

I wondered what he meant by *here*; a continuous, inward-turning spiral of places he shouldn't have been. The house, the table, dinner, the city, the beach, the promenade … an endless spool of possibilities that spun backwards into the inescapable and irretrievable past.

'Why don't you come home with me? You can stay for a few days. I could use the company.'

'I don't know. I should be there. In case she shows.'

'We could go to your place first. Leave a note telling her where you are. Come on. We'll get some movies from the video shop, some junk food. We'll see if you can finally beat me at Scrabble.'

'Ha!' He looked up at me, his darkly worried face turning lighter — only just — with a studied laughter. 'As if you can beat me! Last I remember the score was five up in my favour.'

'I don't think so!'

We finished our coffee and carried our light-hearted argument down the Corso to the car park behind the Manly Hotel. I needed his help to clamber up, my ungainly body stiffening in the cool night air. As I drove out of the car park I asked him which way and he gestured vaguely. As I turned up the hill I realised we weren't going back to his place, that he wasn't going to leave a message for her, penned in his childish handwriting on a notepad or the back of an envelope. Instead we drove through the quietly busy suburbs, through streets full of the to-and-fro traffic of workers travelling home and Friday evening revellers going out again.

Never be happy out loud
And I'll keep the secret

— Emma Bull, *The Stepsisters Story*

Callum had been at our place for a week before Jason came home. We'd been sitting at the kitchen table, the Scrabble board set up between us and freshly made mugs of tea at our elbows. It was Callum's turn. He was arguing — laughingly — over the spelling of the word *fugue*. I lunged across the table for the dictionary and he put his hand over the top of mine, stopping me from opening the book.

'What? Scared to know the truth?'

'No. I wrote that dictionary. I know every word in it, and fugue is definitely spelt f-u-g-e.'

'No way! That would be Fuge — like Mt Fuji without the "ee" on the end.'

'How dare you insult my spelling,' he said, laughing. With his other hand he picked up the teaspoon lying beside him and held it with the rounded end in his palm. 'I will have satisfaction,' he called out in his garbled Spanish-Mexican movie voice. 'I challenge you to a duel!'

'Very well, you despicable fool, have it your way. Spoons at sunset, it shall be.' I ran for the kitchen counter and grabbed a wooden spoon from the jar near the stove. I stood facing him in the closest thing I could manage to a fencer's pose. 'En garde!'

'Dark and devious woman, have at thee!'

Callum lunged across the room, waving his tiny teaspoon in the air. I collapsed into helpless giggles at the sight of his serious face, the brows drawn together over his eyes, his mouth in a thin line, trying desperately not to laugh as he feinted and turned. Behind him I saw Jason come into the room.

He was slightly drunk, but home early — only ten o'clock. I dropped my spoon hand to my side.

'What?' said Callum, 'do you surrender so easily?'

I hesitated, watching Jason lean against the doorway. When I didn't answer him Callum wavered, lowering his spoon and turning to see Jason behind him.

Jason raised an eyebrow at him and slowly smiled. I watched the two of them slap each other's backs like long-lost friends. The boys sat at the table and Jason studied the board. We were near the end of the game, and I was fifty points in front. 'We could start again. Do you want to play?'

'Only if you promise not to slay me.'

'Ah well. That depends on whether you are an honourable speller.'

Jason laughed at me, his face softening as I smiled back at him. Callum tipped the pieces off the board into the box and began to turn them face down. Jason turned over a page on the scorepad and wrote each of our names at the top, underlining each one. I made him a cup of coffee — white with two sugars — and we began to play.

'So, how long are you staying this time?' Jason asked.

Callum looked over at me questioningly. It was his call. He could stay as long as he wanted, I wasn't going to ask him to leave. 'Well,' he said, 'I'm not sure.'

'Not that it matters. I'm sure Germaine likes to have you here. She certainly worries too much when you're not here, and you can keep her company while I'm busy.'

'Are you working?'

I looked over at Jason, wondering what he would say. Whether he would tell Callum what he refused to tell me, where he went, what he did with himself during the long hours he wasn't here, with me.

'I have people to see. You know how it is.'

We settled into the game. By midnight Callum was winning and the last few pieces were left resting in the base of the box. I pleaded tiredness and tipped my remaining letters into the box. As I got up to leave the table Callum and Jason both stood, and I was struck by how odd this seemed, how quaintly romantic and old-fashioned.

Callum kissed me goodnight and Jason — not to be outdone by my brother — came around the table to put his arm around me.

'I'll tuck you in,' he said, and turned me towards the hallway.

In the bedroom he sat on the edge of the bed watching me undress. I brushed and plaited my hair, feeling awkward with his eyes on me. The baby turned beneath my skin.

'God,' he said, 'that's really weird.'

'Huh?'

'The baby. You can see it moving.'

I pulled a shirt over my head but it only covered half of my rounded stomach. He came up behind me and put an arm around me, resting one hand flat on my belly. We waited in the quiet, both our heads bent over her. When she moved he looked up at me, his face perturbed, took his hand away and shook it.

'That's weird. It feels revolting.'

'It's not revolting! That's our daughter.'

He shifted his arm around me a little tighter. Had I gone too far? His hand slid down to circle my wrist, holding tight enough that the bones felt crushed together. I held my breath. 'Are you going to bed or not?' he said as he stood up and I moved past him, pulling back the covers and sliding in beneath them. The sheets were cool, but the weight of the blankets as he pulled them up over me was reassuring. 'Good night,' he said.

'See you in the morning.'

He leant down to kiss me and I closed my eyes. His mouth landed uncertainly on my cheek before gliding around to my mouth. He slid one hand beneath the sheets and cupped my breast. I moved towards him, running one hand up to his shoulder. He pinched my nipple between his fingers, firmly at first and then too hard. It hurt. I pulled away.

He looked at me oddly, as if examining an exotic specimen in a jar of formaldehyde and finding it suddenly turning beneath his hands. 'That hurts,' I said.

He shrugged and leaned in closer, pulling the sheet down to reveal my breasts. He bit at my right nipple. His hand in my hair held my head against the pillow and I struggled against crying out. My fists were small stones beneath the sheets.

My jaw was tense. I listened carefully to the sound of Jason making his way back out to the kitchen, joking about something with Cal. I thought about getting up, striding out into the kitchen and screaming at him. I thought about pulling a jumper over my head and walking out the front door, taking the few steps down the path to the gate, and then what? The long, empty street. The neighbours peering from their windows to see me in my shirt, undies and bare feet. I blinked steadily and uncurled my lightly throbbing fingers, laying my hands flat against the sheets. *This is my life*, I thought. *This is my bed. I have made it and now I must lie in it.* I thought of the morning, when I had seen Edna weeding her garden, how we had talked of simple things — the weather, the fine crop of tomatoes weighing down her plants. We had chatted aimlessly. Meaninglessly. And all the time I was rotting inside. Frightened to fall asleep. Frightened of what each new day brought. When the slight cramps of false contractions pulled at my stomach I waited with my breath held, not wanting her to be born yet. Inside me she was safe. Inside me she couldn't be hurt, couldn't cry, couldn't bleed. I had gone too far, swimming out from the frail shore until the water, which flowed around me, turned from easy comfort to a grasping creature. I was too far out at sea, waving and smiling at the people on the beach. How could I cry out? How could I let them know how completely I had failed? Cal gave up everything to save me and I brought him here. To this. I could have run, but to where? In the city I saw homeless people all the time, mumbling bag ladies and dirty-faced children who were thin and empty-eyed. They frightened me. I cringed when they held out their hands for my money. Going to a shelter meant revelation, confessions. The price of safety, of another escape, was a humiliation I didn't have the strength to face.

At the hospital a nurse once sat and placed her white hand on my arm. She was wearing a gold ring and pale pink nail polish. She smelt faintly of expensive perfume. She asked me if I needed help, if there was anything she could do, and I couldn't say a word. I wanted her to like me, to admire me. The last thing I wanted was her pity or, worse still, for her to see through it all and realise it was all me. All of it. That it *was* my life and that, although Jason was not perfect, it was me who did it. Disaster after disaster and at the core of it all not somebody else — not Jason or my father — but me. I could have said something to that nurse — confessed the awful sordidness of my life — but I wanted her to respect me and I knew that if I told her the truth she wouldn't. I wanted her to like me but I knew I was unlikeable. I wanted to get away but I knew that, whatever it was, the poison that was destroying my life was mine. Inside me, barely hidden beneath my skin, was the rotting ugliness that taunted Jason.

I wanted to be pure and clean. Empty. I played my flute every day partly because, when I did, I could feel myself being emptied out. I could feel my lungs expanding and my blood thinning. I closed my eyes and concentrated on the pure, almost empty, sound of the notes, and when, hours later, I lay the flute in my lap, I felt light-headed. Hollowed out. I sat, as still as I could, barely breathing. Holding on to that clear, beautiful emptiness. Trying not to think, not to beat, not to breathe. Trying to listen. Trying to find something inside me that was not rotten. Somewhere, buried in me, I knew there had to be something — some tiny cell — that remained unpolluted. If I could only find it and crack it open, it would burst like a nuclear cloud and burn away everything else. I would be incandescent.

I sat like that, paused and waiting, until the world intruded. My body ached, the weather turned, the noise of the traffic or the ocean intervened and it all came crashing back and I felt defeated as I looked down at my heavy, ugly body and tried not to cry.

Jason didn't come to bed that night. When I woke in the morning I walked tentatively through the house in my bare feet, looking into each room in case he was there. Callum was sleeping in the spare room, and in the kitchen the coffee cups and ashtrays were dirty but there was no sign of Jason. I made myself a cup of tea and went back to bed, my feet firm and confident against the polished timber floors.

I read for a while before falling asleep; the book open on my lap and the tea half-finished on the table beside me. When I woke again the sun was fingering its way through the curtains. Callum was out of bed; his sheets pulled up beneath the pillow. In the kitchen I rinsed out my cup and made a fresh pot of tea. I could see him standing at the end of the garden, his shirt hanging loosely from his bony frame.

I stood on the verandah, searching the garden. Somewhere in the tangle of green foliage Jason could be walking. Waiting for me to come outside. I glanced over at Edna's house, relieved to see her garden empty, the windows and curtains still closed. I felt vulnerable in my bare feet as I stepped down onto the grass; the fresh dew and tiny sparks of grass pricking my soles. I thought about the tale of the little mermaid who willingly gave up her tail for legs but whose every step after that was agony, as if a thousand tiny swords pierced her soles at each step. She could not cry, could not speak, but she danced like an angel for the man she loved. I walked slowly, listening to the cups chatter together on the tray. I placed it on the rickety table we had set up in the gazebo and wrapped my arms around myself, my hands in my armpits. I walked past where Callum and I had spent yesterday afternoon pulling the last of the weeds from the knot garden and trimming the rosemary hedge that surrounded the angel statue. One of her wings was damaged, the long wing cracked off. We found the broken pieces half-buried in the ground beneath her. Soft moss had grown over them. Callum had offered to carry them out to the rubbish bin but I said no, I liked them there. I liked the pieces of her wing half-buried in the soil beneath her.

He didn't seem to hear me as I walked up behind him. He was standing on the other side of the fence. Balanced so tenuously on the edge that when he shifted his toes a handful of tiny stones stirred and dribbled over the edge.

The harbour below was still. One of those mornings when the water seemed transparent, reflecting the cloudless sheet of sky above it. I stepped over the fence, wishing for a rail to hold onto. I considered taking his arm, but worried he might pull away, unbalancing me so I fell like a stone at his feet. If I looked over the rim the ground below disappeared — it was only through my feet that I knew it was still there. Callum glanced sideways at me and smiled. His eyes closing in a scrunch of flesh. He tipped his head back to feel the warmth of the morning sun, letting the weight of the light pull the sleepy folds smooth.

Below us the land skidded away into a tangle of rock and scrub. A few trees pointing at the sky, their trunks at improbably acute angles to the sloping ground in which they were rooted. Far below us the harbour lay still, the morning air resonating with her salty breath. When I looked down I could see my belly protruding. If I moved my head slightly she hung over the edge — a large grey-cotton balloon suspended above a sheer drop. If my daughter were born here I could stand on the edge and she would fall weightlessly into the harbour below, a bird forced from its nest by the strange, muscular force of its mother. A sky birth. I smiled at her floating on her balloon-string umbilical cord, tumbling gently in the fingers of wind that tugged at my hair.

I bent my right knee and extended my foot in front of me until it was stretched out over the cliff edge. The breeze rose up to meet it — the force of it quite shocking — like a hand cupped beneath me. I reached my hands out and floated them against the wind, feeling it rise against the soft white flesh of my wrists. I felt brave suddenly. And weightless. As if I could step out and the air would hold me gently, like a child cradled in its mother's arms.

Callum put a hand on my arm. 'Hey,' he said, 'let's drink that tea before it gets cold.'

I turned to look at him, pulling my arms down and placing my foot firmly on the ground. I felt heavy again. Awkward. My daughter squirmed inside me, pulling at my skin which was already stretched too tightly. I turned to step over the tangled fence-line — pivoting on the ball of my right foot. I felt the ground give way. The gravel beneath me shifted and slid away. I found myself unbalanced. The toes of my left foot curled in an attempt to hold onto the ground as my right foot dangled over the edge. The breezes held their breath. Teasing me. I could feel the terrible drop beneath me. The grazes and scratches and snapping bones that clutched at me. Callum turned, grabbing at my arm and pulling me forward. I landed on my knees, scraping them like a schoolgirl. My hands too, as I tipped forward, scraped on the ground. The grazes stung. The blood and bruises rose quickly to my palms and knees. I worried that they wouldn't heal quickly enough. That during the labour I would have scabbed knees and hands. I already felt like a child before all the confident, middle-aged women in the waiting room. I saw the way they looked at me, a child having a child, a teenage mother. All the stories they imagined, all the terrible things they had heard about people like me. They smiled at me, but not the way they smiled at each other, not out of comradeship, but out of a kind of awkward pity. Perhaps it made them feel better about themselves, the way donating money to a charity made them feel better. They assuaged their consciences with a tiny smile but never asked me to join them for coffee, never offered to call me. I was always conscious of the fact that I was not, definitely not, one of them. And now here I was, on my hands and knees in the dirt, my hands as dirty and bloody as a child who has fallen off her bicycle. I watched the blood well in tiny beads and felt the throbbing ache spread across my palms. I would be giving birth soon. I would clutch at the rails of the hospital bed and my scabbed hands would crack and bleed. I knew now, suddenly and almost startlingly, that when I became a mother and reached out to hold my daughter it would be with these child's hands.

In the middle of the night the house was quiet. I heard a bird calling me. He was perched on a fence, his twig-like claws gripping the top rail. As I walked towards him he flew off and the fence disappeared. I ran to follow him and realised I had run over the edge of the garden, into nowhere. One of my wings was broken and I felt the muscles in my shoulder pull uselessly against the sky. Like a boat with one oar I spiralled through the air. The bird flew in front of me, its beak large in my face as it squealed, its worm-like tongue poking out at me. Its cry grew louder and louder, piercing my skin as I tumbled helplessly. It was laughing. Screaming. Laughing.

I woke to the realisation that the telephone was ringing in the hall and sat up quickly, the blankets falling away from me. I heard Callum roll over in his sleep and I stood up, bumping against the doorframe as I walked out into the hall. I saw Callum's door open further up the hall, and then Callum himself was stumbling up the hall towards me. With one eye open he grinned at me, rubbing at the side of his face. 'I'll get it. Go back to bed.'

I stood in the bedroom door, watching him flounder towards the still-ringing phone. He picked it up and slid down the wall, sitting with his knees drawn against his chest as he mumbled into the phone. I turned away and went back to bed.

Inside my room I closed the window and drew the curtains across. Pulled the blankets more evenly over the bed and fumbled a pair of socks onto my chilled toes. I was soon warm again. Callum's deep, night-time voice settled easily beneath the sound of the wind rocking the house. I pulled the bedclothes around my shoulders and curled around the pillows, drawing my knees up beneath me.

I was almost asleep again when I heard Callum come into the room and say my name.

'Yeah. I'm awake.'

'I have to go.'

'See you soon.'

'Can you come with me?'

I turned over beneath the blankets and looked up at him. He was standing in the doorway, his hand resting against the door frame. 'What time is it?'

'Please,' he begged.

I sat up, pulling the blankets with me. A pillow slid off the bed onto the floor. 'Can't it wait till morning? You go. I'll come over later.'

Callum lingered in the doorway, looking towards the front door. His fingers drummed on the timber walls, his feet fidgeted beneath him. His eyes watched the hall as if a train was about to leave. The last train. He came to sit beside me on the bed. 'You have to come,' he said. 'I need you to come with me. That was Stan. He hasn't seen her either. Nobody has. It was him that was with her on the street that day — when I saw her, you remember? He's pretty pissed. He broke into our place — that's how he got this number. I have to find her before he does.'

'Why?'

'She owes him money, lots of money, and he's not exactly patient. He'll hurt her if he finds her.'

I looked at his hands. They were lying open in his lap, catching his words as they spilled into the dark room. 'Okay, I'll come with you. Is there anyone you can call first? Friends? To see if they've seen her?'

'A couple of people, maybe.'

'Do you have their numbers?'

'Sure.'

'You call them while I get dressed. Then we'll go.'

By the time we reached Callum's place the morning light was just beginning to stretch over the building. The apartment faced the street, so the only light came from a streetlamp just outside the laundry window. It was a small building, with walls the colour of pale coffee. As Callum opened the door to the unit the first thing I saw was the tumbled look of the room. At first I thought this must have been how it always was — much as I had imagined it — but then I realised it was because someone had been here. Someone had turned the furniture over and ripped the doors from the kitchen cabinets. Callum's and Selene's clothes were strewn over the bedroom floor and spilled out into the hall. The pockets were all turned inside out. The bed had been stripped. Callum reached for the light switch and flicked it several times before he gave up. He pulled the floor lamp up and looked beneath its shade, but the globe had been shattered.

I followed him as he walked through their few rooms, kitchen, laundry, bathroom, bedroom. A small sunroom that must once have been a verandah but had been closed in with sliding glass windows. Two chairs sat together in the corner. A rug lay scrunched and curled against the wall. A smashed vase of soft brown flowers lay on the floor. 'God,' he said beneath his breath, over and over again, each time we walked into another room. The wallpaper on the bedroom wall was mouldy in one corner. Someone had been shredding it, pulling it off in long streaks to reveal mist green paint and the flocked underside of the paper. As Callum picked up a pillow from the floor half a dozen eggs rolled out of it and smashed at his feet. He got down on his knees and started sweeping his hands over the worn-thin carpet, pulling the gluey threads together. 'Oh God, oh God. What a mess. I can't believe this. It's such a mess.'

I knelt beside him, placing one hand between his peaked shoulder blades. What could I say? What was there to say in the face of this? Callum wiped his hands down the sides of his pants and shook his head. He looked away, over the piles of bedclothes and the mattress pulled halfway off the base.

'I'll get some stuff to clean up with,' I said.

'And a torch. Some light bulbs.'

'Have you got any?'

'Downstairs in the storage space.' Callum fumbled with his keys, finally singling out the one he wanted and handing it to me. 'The space is the same number as the apartment, it's to the left. There are light bulbs in one of the boxes.'

'I'll be back in a minute.'

I left the apartment door open behind me as I walked into the hallway. At the far end was a door with an Exit sign over the top of it. It was a heavy door. I had to pull back hard to get it open a few inches, but then it gave easily, swinging back against me. The concrete stairwell was cold and echoed harshly, each footstep loud in the funnelled space. The fluorescent light was raw. As I looked down at my hand on the rail I saw each pore, each tiny hair. I was glad I couldn't see my face. My five a.m. face.

Upstairs Callum would be kneeling on his bedroom floor. Everything he owned was stretched around him in a tangled mess. How strange it was to walk into his apartment — to see his ordinary life in a strange home. Some things I had recognised; his taste in books, his clothes, his handwriting on scraps of paper. Other things were oddly unfamiliar. Pot plants. I'd never imagined him as someone with huge palms in his lounge room, or someone who ate Irish Stew from a can. The prints on the bedroom wall, too — of women tied and tangled, crouching naked in high heels or lying prostrate over a red car — seemed at odds with his quietness, his deference.

Other things were obviously hers. The thick towels, the pastel printed sheets. The splay-backed, gold-lettered novels spilling from over the bricked-in fireplace. The bent teaspoons collected on the mantelpiece like silver-plated flowers. In the kitchen there were smashed glasses, bottles of cheap wine and scotch. I wondered what their life was like. Whether they sat huddled up together on the lounge. There was a quilt on the lounge room floor. Did they lie together beneath it? Eating chocolates from each other's hands and sipping at cheap wine or scotch from washed out Vegemite jars. Watching soap operas or quiz shows. Late night infomercials.

How did they live the ordinariness of bent teaspoons and needle exchanges? Did they do it in the ad breaks? In the lounge room or bedroom? Did they do it together? For each other? I remembered the frightened little boy Callum had been at each of his immunisations. The tears on his face as he turned towards me at the sight of the needle, at its swift stab into the flesh of his thigh.

At fourteen he needed a tetanus injection. Even then he was horrified. Father walked out of the room and stood on the verandah looking out to the sheds as he listened to Callum screaming. His voice bounced off the timber floors. Emma held his hand tightly in hers. Callum squeezed so hard that her fingers were pale and bloodless afterwards. I stood, helpless, on the other side of the room watching his terrified face. He was like one of the cows after the calves have been sent away, standing at the gate for days, their eyes wide with terror, bawling in the direction of the departed trucks. They were stubborn, having to be driven forcibly back to the paddocks. They would return over and over again, refusing food and water, starving themselves to death.

Callum too refused. In the end the nurse jabbed blindly at him, the needle scratching across his thigh before it dived into the skin. She drove the plunger swiftly, her grim face set. When she left the house, walking past Father, she was shaking her head.

'Chicken shit, isn't he?' Father said.

She turned to look at him. Surprised to find him there in the cool shadows, not looking at her, but at something far off in the distance. 'I've never seen a child so terrified,' she said.

When I reached the bottom of the stairwell there was another door. Newer this time, and easier to swing open beneath its strip of neon light. The undercover car park smelt of spilt oil and petrol, of damp old shoes and musty stored things. It was dark; the lights mostly broken. At the far end one light was on its way out, flickering half-heartedly from white to grey.

Each car space was numbered, the white numbers painted by hand onto the concrete floor. To the side of the stairwell was number six, then seven and eight leading up to the left. Callum's place was sixteen. I crossed to the other side — twenty-two, twenty-one — and walked swiftly down the row until I reached their space. The storage ran along the walls so that, if you were parked in your space, the nose of your car nudged up against the handle. Most of them were like baseball cages; floor to ceiling areas of diamond-patterned wire and a door with a chain and padlock. A few were closed in with cheap strips of timber panelling. Callum and Selene's storage area was of the wire type, but someone had pegged a curtain of sheets to the inside of the cage, navy blue with a tiny pattern of cream diamonds.

At this end of the car park there was a strange smell, a kind of fetid warmth. It was a bit like the smell of a burst sewerage pipe. I wondered whether the pipes were leaking down there, or if there was one of those filthy cupboard toilets tucked into one of the dark corners. There wasn't much light as I fumbled with the padlock, finally getting the key into the lock and disentangling the chain. The door swung open, pulled by the weight of the chain that was still threaded through its handle. I bent forward slightly to look inside but it was darker in there. So dark it was hard to see anything at all, but the smell was stronger. So strong that I gagged and had to take a step backwards. When I looked up at the back wall I saw a pale string swinging slightly from the ceiling — a light switch. I pulled it and the bulb hanging from the ceiling lit up, the naked globe swinging alarmingly as I let go of the string.

On the floor, amid the jumble of boxes of old shoes and clothes, of crockery and chipped glasses, cheap curtains and electrical cords and aerial lead, was a cleared space. Big enough for one or two people to sit together if they hunched up their knees. This was where the stench came from. On the cold concrete floor lay Selene — her wide-open eyes staring startled at the swinging globe, at the brutal light striping the walls of boxes and garbage bags and cheap chipboard shelving. Her mouth was open and her perfect, orthodontically enhanced teeth seemed too large for her small face.

I reeled back, pulling at the string to turn out the light and missing. I felt my stomach heave and knelt on the cold concrete as a stream of vomit spilled from my mouth. My stomach clutched sharply and I placed a hand over it as I retched again, feeling something warm and wet slip down my thigh. When I reached my hand in under my dress my fingertips came away wet. I held my hand in front of my face and looked at my dark fingers. I couldn't think what it meant. *Blood*, I remember thinking, *is the baby coming? Now?*

When I got back upstairs Callum had been carefully folding her clothes and putting them back in their drawers. He'd placed her books next to his in the righted bookcase. Sweeping up the remains of her shattered vase he'd pictured the new one he would buy her — a fluted glass vase of pure translucent blue. The colour of the wings she had been wearing the night he met her.

As I walked into the apartment he was in the middle of the lounge room holding a garbage bag, carefully placing handfuls of torn pages inside it. He turned towards me when I said his name, looking at my empty hands. It was only then I remembered the torch and light-bulbs, wondering whether I should turn around and go back. 'Where's the stuff?' he asked.

'Callum.' It was all I could say. My voice caught in the same deep groove as her stillness. Caught in the cup of her upturned palm with the fingers half-curled around nothing. Caught in the sight of her crushed body melting against the cold concrete floor. The sight of her eyes staring straight up as the light swung by overhead. I stood in front of him with my empty hands, my empty mouth open but nothing escaping. Barely even breathing. I felt the baby turn and another slight gush of blood spilled down my leg, the sudden indecency of life twisting inside me. Life so rough and red-rich with colour. I saw, but did not see, Callum come to stand in front of me.

'What is it? Is it the baby? Is something wrong?'

Once again she twisted inside me, her fists or feet caught in my pelvis, pushing her head up into my lungs. I moved my hand up to touch the roof of my belly, to tell her somehow, *Be calm, be still*. I looked at Callum, his familiar face bent down to mine, the sun-pleated skin drawn in concern. I spoke to him but he couldn't hear me. The words barely reaching beyond my teeth, words exhaled rather than spoken. I reached out to take his hand, clutching instead at his forearm, at the warm flesh. I pulled him forward until his hair tickled the end of my nose, his curls turning into the corners of my mouth. When I spoke they got stuck between my lips, wet and secret. 'She's dead,' I whispered.

As the words came from my mouth I felt my belly clutch again and another gush of fluid. I reached my hand down to my crutch and felt the warmth spreading on my fingertips. I looked down and saw it run over my foot, thin and faintly pink at first, then suddenly a deep red thread that widened into a ribbon that covered my ankle. I felt oddly calm. I gave in to the blood streaming out of me, to the unanswerable and irrevocable demands of my body. I would go to the hospital. I would lie beneath clean sheets and listen to the nurses and doctors mumble reassuringly. I would nod calmly and think about nothing. Nothing except my body clutching and pushing, stretching open to deliver my daughter. The sight of that swelling blood on my shins took away everything. I didn't have to think, didn't have to go back down there and deal with her body, her death, Cal's grief. 'I'm bleeding,' I said, and smiled. I heard Callum swear and felt him take hold of me as I began to slide away.

The kitchen knife was not full of spangle-light
And this is not how I meant to share with you

Light-headed I rode away,
My arms around a prince's waist,
Blood welling from your shoe
To stain the white horse flank.

— Emma Bull, *The Stepsisters Story*

It was warm. I trailed a fingernail down the vein in my arm, tracing the pale lines that ran like rivers beneath my skin. I was imagining her — my child — silent and long-fingered inside me. She twisted and I caught my breath. Stunned by fear. She was huge. I couldn't imagine her small and squalling. She was something firm, silent, and wide-eyed. Something alien. I wanted her to be born.

I did not want her to be born.

Who would teach me how to hold her? How to feed her? I watched a woman in the park with her child turned into her chest. She smiled at me as she shifted the child from her left to her right side. Her firm, high breasts were pale, her nipples dark and puckered. Her child suckled confidently, his hand fisted at her hip. She was smiling. She turned and flicked her hair and the smile on her face was so easy it hurt me. She knew already my ineptitude, even though I had yet to live it. I was mirrored in that easy smile. An imperfect reflection. Was the mirror flawed or was I?

I lifted the sweat-heavy hair from the nape of my neck. Callum and I walked across the car park towards the square, blank-faced hospital. Outside Emergency people lingered in exasperated silence. Their smiles were grim. I wondered how long they had been waiting, and for what. One woman was grey-faced and determined. The cigarette in her hand burning away unnoticed. A taxi driver leant on the hood of his car, studying the black crescents of his fingernails. There were people everywhere. Sick people. Needy people. In the elevator I felt huge. People crammed in. Squeezed beside me. An old man leaned into my belly and my daughter moved indignantly beneath my skin, the watery blood gushing out of me. At the third floor I spilled out of the lift and took a deep breath.

Callum left me in the waiting room for the antenatal clinic to go and make a phone call. His face was pale. Selene was dead, her body cold and comfortless in the basement of their building. How long could she have been there before we found her? It had been two weeks since I last saw her. Almost that since Cal had spoken to her on the phone. Her skin was thick and white, all the blood had pooled in her back, her hand was bent to hold the needle still protruding from her arm. Her eyes were open. Watching me. Accusing me. Her skull threatening to crack through the bloodless skin.

I heard Callum's voice rising as he yelled into the phone, but I couldn't hear what he was saying. My head was full of the echo of the basement. The cold, empty cages. The blinking fluorescent light. The tick tick tick of the light cord as it swung above her, its plastic knob hitting the walls.

Callum came back and stood in front of me. His eyes didn't meet mine. His hands were buried deep in his pockets. 'He says he's not coming. He has to be somewhere this afternoon. He'll come tomorrow if you're still here.'

'What?' I said. My voice echoing across the plastic floors and walls and chairs, coming at me from the other side of the room.

'I have to go.'

Three hours alone in a waiting room full of women's magazines. Pages and pages of scandal and fashion and sequins and splashy headlines: *Is he unfaithful? How to tell.* A roomful of women, shifting on weighted thighs and sighing over the 'slight discomfort' of their ungainly bodies. A handful of small children played listlessly with the broken toys left to amuse them. A nurse walked past every half hour or so, checking for new arrivals, ticking names off lists, taking each woman's yellow-lidded urine sample away on a tray like a waitress. I did not hear my name until it was called a third time and when I stood up my right foot had gone to sleep. I stumbled when I tried to walk, the pins and needles stabbing into my toes.

The doctor didn't look at me when he came into the cubicle. He was reading my chart and standing half-in, half-out of the curtained space. His serious face was young. He walked into the room once, hesitated over something on the paper in front of him, then went out again without even looking at me. I clenched my toes against the sole of my shoe. Selene's toes were pale, the nails painted Barbie-doll pink. When the doctor came in again he raised his face to me and smiled in the blank non-committal way they all seem to smile, before looking back down at the file in his hands.

'You don't have an appointment until next week,' he said.

I nodded, even though he wasn't looking at me. I watched him run his manicured fingernail down a page, clenching my sleeping toes.

'Is there something wrong?'

'I'm bleeding,' I said, feeling childish and stupid.

He looked at me, his wide eyes startled but also suddenly interested. Soon there was a nurse standing beside me as he did an internal, gathering some of the blood to send to a lab. He rested a long cotton stick in the fluid, watching it intently. He frowned at the swab, comparing it to a thin piece of card in his other hand. 'The amniotic sac is still intact but you'll have to have a Caesarean as soon as possible.'

I sat watching his round head bobbing like an overstuffed seedpod on its stem. It took me several seconds to realise he was talking about me — to me. I opened my mouth to say something. He glanced up from the chart, which he was busy writing in. 'Yes?'

My hands were twisted in my lap, the knuckles bent against each other. A question ricocheted inside my skull — *Why Why Why Why* — but I couldn't speak. I wanted Callum to be there. I wanted Selene to still be alive. I wanted Jason to be gentle, to be rushing to the hospital, arriving flushed with concern to hold my hand and kiss me gently. I wanted him to hold me. A tear of self-pity slid over my face. Once she was born there would be no more possibilities. She would be real. She would be mine but she would not be his.

'It's the best thing for the baby, that's what we all want, isn't it?' said the doctor. I looked at his soft boy's face. At the way his head was tipped to one side, asking but not asking. It was one of those questions people asked of me a lot when I was pregnant. Questions that implied that if I didn't agree I would be negligent somehow, careless with my own health and that of my child. *We*, they said all the time, and there was no answer for that, of course *we* wanted what was best for the baby. He said *we* knowing I couldn't disagree, that only a fool would disagree, would insist on the *I* of an unemployed, underage pregnant child against someone like him. What did I know of the mysteries of the body? How blood moves, how the skin stretches? Selene's body was empty. Mine was leaking — uncontrolled, unbidden. What did I know of my internal horrors, of the danger I was to myself, to my child? Death was cold. Emptiness. Nothing. A frighteningly still body in a small concrete room. I knew nothing. I knew I should be grateful. Relieved. Trusting. I knew if I started to cry in earnest he would call a nurse, and she would call a counsellor who would sit on the edge of the plastic-mattressed hospital bed and reassure me it was okay, hundreds of women have Caesareans every day. It was a safe way to be born. The baby would be safe and normal. Everything would be okay. It wouldn't hurt. I wouldn't feel a thing. I wouldn't even be conscious when she was pulled headfirst from my gaping wound. No one would be there to greet her except the competent nurses and efficient surgeon. I wouldn't be able to say anything. Nothing at all.

He placed a cool hand over my own. 'We'll get you moved up to a ward as soon as there's a bed available. They'll monitor you during the night in case there are any problems. Surgery will be tomorrow morning. The nurses on the ward will help you with anything else you need.' He turned on his heel and left the room, the hospital blue of his coat slapping against the door as he passed.

I spent the whole night awake. My feet sticky with sweat. My skin suddenly perishable and unsound. Suddenly permeable. I pictured the knife slicing my skin, peeling me like an orange. The young doctor, pressing his manicured hands into me. I watched the nurses as they frowned at charts. I watched the women, the patients, quiet and docile in their beds. Complacent and trusting. I wanted to run.

Run, I whispered to myself, *run*. I willed the pains to come. I walked to the bathroom clenching my belly in a vain, desperate effort to control my own body. *Now. Come now before they betray me. Before I am forced to betray my own child. It is not safe here.* In the toilet, I locked the door and crouched against the wall, running my hands over my belly, over my daughter. Feeling her foot as she flexed against me. I looked at my watch — 2 a.m. Somewhere on the ward a baby was crying. I slipped my knickers down to my ankles and readjusted my crouch, resting my back against the wall. I slipped my fingers into myself, pushing in as far as I could go, scratching at the swollen fleshiness of my cervix, the slippery thickness that was stretched over my baby's head. I clenched my belly and pushed down as hard as I could, feeling my cervix pulse, hoping to push the water down, scratching at myself with the tip of a nail, feeling the warm blood slip over my fingertips. If I could only break the skin of her bubbled world, perhaps she would be born; perhaps she would slip out quickly and quietly onto these tiles. There would be no need for doctors and anaesthetists and scalpels. I would be quiet so no one could hear. There would be breathing and pushing and a small head, which would look, at first, like a wrinkled nutshell but when pushed out into the half-light and turned would be a small face. She would be caught. Born. I took a deep breath and pushed again, as hard as I could, pushing my index finger into my cervix as far as it would go.

At 10 a.m. I had not slept and the smiling nurse was calm and sympathetic. 'It's hard to sleep, isn't it? You must be so excited.' I was silent as they wheeled me through the halls of the hospital. From the ward to Ultrasound with its dark green curtains and quiet monitors humming. In the lift again with the wardsman smiling vaguely and tapping at the thick file at my feet. In a room with white tiled walls, like an empty bathroom, 'Don't worry, everything will be fine,' a nurse whispered. Her voice hummed like the machine strapped over my belly to measure the baby's heartbeats. I watched the monitor. My daughter's pulse seemed fast to me, the little red heart blinking rapidly, but the nurses smiled reassuringly and walked quickly out of the room. 'Would you like us to call someone?' asked the last sister. 'Anyone at all?' I shook my head. Who would have come, who should have been there? Callum's lover was dead and he had gone to face her empty body. Jason seemed disconnected from that moment. I couldn't imagine him there. Anyone else was too far away. I longed for my mother. I closed my eyes and tried to imagine her standing beside me, her hand curled around mine, or standing at the window with a flute raised to her lips. I turned away with tears in my eyes.

Who was there to call — now or later? It was too late. I would have to do this alone.

I was looking out the window as the anaesthetist slipped a plastic-sheathed needle into the canula already embedded in my vein and told me to count backwards from ten. 'Everything is going to be just fine,' a nurse whispered. 'When you wake up, you'll be a mother.'

It was too late. The white rabbit had disappeared down the rabbit hole. My mother was dead. My daughter was here, almost here, almost born, and I knew nothing. I did not know how to be a mother, how to hold her. How to keep her safe. She was not yet born and already I had failed her.

The summer I began to bleed, Emma told me I had *become a woman* and taught me to store the bloody pads in a secret, sealed bin under my bed until I had a chance to sneak away and bury them near the riverbank, far from the house. She told me to be careful, never to let my father or brother know that I was bleeding. She insisted it was women's business, secret and shameful, and that they should never have to be confronted with the detritus of my womanhood. She never looked at me when she taught me these things. It was something she refused to acknowledge as part of her own body's history, something I felt only my own body was unclean enough to do. She was furtive about getting me pads, secreting them in a drawer in my room rather than handing them to me with whatever else she had bought for me. I asked her once whether she wanted me to take her own and bury them as well and her face grew thin and sharp. She stared at me and shook her head. 'No,' she said. 'I don't bleed.'

It took me at least half an hour to cross through the paddocks where the long stalks of grass whispered to each other. It was hot and dusty and the red soil stained the soles of my feet. Emma warned me to stay on the tracks and roads, to stay out of the paddocks, to stay out of the scrub. She knew there were snakes there, hiding in the scrubby stringy grass that scratched my shins. She knew their poisonous tongues flickered over their lips as I passed.

I knew that I too was poisonous. I knew that my secret mouth had begun to speak in silent, bloody tones and what it spoke of was something more terrible, more *pure* and terrible, than anything ever would be again. I knew my body was a dangerous secret to be kept from feeble minds. I knew if I confronted them with the secret of my poisonousness that they, not I, would turn away, would find their skin firm and hot with fever. They would shiver and tremble and fall on the sand that would run like dry rivers away from them.

Emma taught me how people once believed that witches used their menstrual blood to perform all kinds of magic. Some said that if you buried your menstrual blood in the ground it would become snakes, wise and dangerous creatures, who came at your call and did what you asked of them.

I used to bury myself in the hot sand of the riverbank. I would find a tree and crawl under its leafless branches where the polished holes of snakes opened themselves. I would dig a trench and lie in it, burying myself from my toes to my armpits in the humming sand, and lie with my eyes closed. Slowly the sand would warm and I would feel it sliding against my ribs, against the soles of my feet. I would feel this second desiccated skin shifting around me like a snake, curving against the warm poisons beating inside me, and relish it.

There was a nurse on the ward with neat, black shoes. The square-heeled kind with a buckle at the front. She wore thin white stockings and a flat navy bow in her hair. She had a ladder in her stocking, a dark stripe against her firm, confident shin. Her staccato heels clicked on the linoleum, legs swinging sharply across the metronomic tick tick tick that measured my dreams. I lay and stared out the window, drifting in and out of sleep. I woke in a tacky sweat, the drip tangled around my fingers. Blood, sweat and thin milk collected on the sheets, on the plastic-coated mattress. I was damp and knotted with confusion. The nurse was clean and crisp. The screaming of birds in a tree across the road scaled the concrete building, slipped in through the windows and scoured her smile. The bells of the nearby school chapel curdled the humidity.

I pictured neat rows of private school girls in dark uniforms and little wide-brimmed hats. They melted like ice cream in the heat, their sticky serge sliding off shining white teeth, off perfect cream skin. The schoolgirl grins sliding over teeth chattering *Hail Mary. Hail Mary, full of grace.* The prayers clicked like rosary beads in their hollow mouths.

If things had been different I could have been one of them. Neat and safe and unafraid, measuring my life by bells and classes. I could have giggled over pictures of TV stars. My biggest problem could have been getting good grades. I pictured them clustered in the schoolyard and waiting in the street for the bell to ring, sneaking cigarettes out of their pockets and telling each other scandalous lies. How this one was secretly in love with that one's boyfriend. How that one had cheated on her geography exam. I was never going to be one of them.

The plastic crib was clean beside me, my fingernails ticking against it like a child at the aquarium. *Wake up, wake up little fish.* The birds were screaming, the girls were melting. I watched her sleeping, her rounded scalp furred like a peach. Her perfect skull that I did not crush. She had been saved from the brutality of my body. My dangerous cunt. What a weapon my body had become. My vicious skin. The muscles that would have torn and stretched and twisted her. I would have hurt her. My body, which had been her only home — her safe place — would have turned on her, become suddenly dangerous and bloody. Did they turn away — the nurses and doctors — did they see my marvellous horrors and recoil? What did they see on the vague ultrasound screen that made them so concerned, whispering behind a hospital-green curtain that I could not do this alone? The doctor had leaned over the bed, his warm hands pressing gently on my belly. Could he feel the snake curved and ready to strike? The swollen pomegranate of my womb pushing out of its pelvic cave. My cunt still virginally taut. The demure lips still pressed together. Still silent. Was I rotten?

I was concealed again inside my skin, the rupture stitched. The seams complete. I remembered the rolled hems and French seams I painstakingly produced under Emma's instruction. I saw the surgeon with his head tipped to one side, like Emma, whose neat, thimbled fingers pleated and pressed, while the tip of her tongue protruded between her teeth and the glasses rode low on her nose. The candlelight flickered at his cheek as he bent the cloth — the flesh — between his prim fingers. He was humming and muttering to himself, impatient to be done. Did he bite the end of the thread to break it?

Did he bury the knot beneath the surface? Are his stitches even, like a quilters, ten to an inch? Fifteen?

My daughter's face was round and small. Her cheeks flushed. When she stirred, her head turned into the sheet. When she began to cry her mouth was wet and red and suddenly I was terrified.

Who would teach me how to hold her?

I took her out of her plastic crib and held her tentatively in my arms. She was so light, so frail. Standing up, I felt the clench of the wound in my gut, felt the stitches that held my body closed, gripping the flesh, pulling at the tissue and muscle and skin, holding me together. My body began to tremble slightly and a rush of blood flowed out of me. I glanced at the drip trolley beside the bed, at the child in my arms. I stood terrified. Afraid to take a step in case I fell. Afraid to put her down in case my arms failed me and I dropped her on the floor. I looked at the other mothers sleeping in their beds, their babies beside them. No nurse was in sight and I could not call out, my mouth stopped up with fear, my tongue huge and dry. I began to cry. Each sob wrenching my body. Each gulp of air a painful stretch of freshly stitched tissue. I felt the wound begin to seep. Blood was pooling beneath the bandages, weeping into my hospital gown. I felt the tears fall down my cheeks onto my daughter, onto her soft, new skin. Her perfect face, I was going to fall. It was the only thing I knew. The only thing I could do. I was going to fall and there would be no one to catch her.

She feeds as firmly
as the heart mills blood

— Jennifer Maiden, *The Winter Baby*

In the middle of the night the house was quiet. So quiet that her cries, kitten-soft as they were, echoed up the hallways. I got out of bed and stood over her cradle, pulling back the white net to reveal her cocoon-wrapped body. She had managed to free one small fist and was trying — eyes scrunched tight and head turning, — to get it into her mouth. Her soft gums and wet lips slipped in her tiny face. Already I could feel the milk swelling in my too-heavy breasts. The prick and dampness.

I picked her up and lumbered awkwardly back to bed, pulling my nightshirt open and laying her beside me. I placed a pillow between her and my stitched stomach, which was still tender. She fumbled for my nipple, sucking instead at the round lumpiness of flesh. Without the milk flowing into her mouth she soon pulled away, her tiny fists pummelling at me. I settled the nipple in her mouth and she began to suck in earnest. Her protests still coming between each suck, as if she meant to tell me she was hungry, to tell me I had taken too long.

I fell asleep with her still attached to my breast and woke in the early morning to find her rolling against me. When I pulled her up above the blankets her face was crumpled with sleep, new enough to be easily moulded and stained by the slightest pressure. Her ears were flattened against her scalp, but her head was round, perfectly round. In the ward at the hospital there were five other women, each with newborns whose heads were egg-shaped, a couple of them peppered with rosy 'stork' marks from the pressures of their births. My daughter's head, however, was round and perfect, her pale flesh unmarked.

It seemed oddly unnatural, as if she had somehow appeared, perfectly formed, from nowhere.

I changed her nappy and rewrapped her blankets, tucking her into the crook of my arm as I shambled down the hallway to the kitchen. Last night's dishes still sat in the sink. Coffee cups and beer glasses stacked against the tiles. With one hand I filled the kettle and set it to boil. Callum was already outside, winding his way slowly through the garden. He never trod over the fence-line anymore. Never watched the slide of rock and scrub into the harbour.

The first few days after we found Selene he was stunned and quiet. It was nearly a week before the police asked him to come and identify her body. They had spent a few days trying to contact her parents who, in the end, refused to come into the hospital to see her. The cop who spoke to Cal said he wasn't surprised, that families like hers often didn't want to know, didn't want to see what had become of their precious daughter's body.

When we arrived a young man came out to get him from the waiting room. Cal was holding the baby at the time and stood up to follow him. It wasn't until the man looked down into her face and frowned that Callum turned back and handed her to me. I sat in the waiting room, amid the rented pot-plants and worn-out magazines. Only one other person was there, an old man who was muttering into his fists, a drip trolley at his elbow. He was wearing a pair of pyjamas with a large red stamp that identified them as belonging to the hospital. Eventually a nurse came in and smiled at him, 'Edward,' she said, 'I've been looking everywhere for you. It's time for afternoon tea.' She took his arm, his other hand gripping the drip trolley that rattled along beside him, and led him out of the room.

The pale walls and anonymous prints of waterfalls and babies seemed somehow ridiculous. I had imagined the walls bereft of illustration — white perhaps, or soft grey — but they were a pale shade of mint like every other place in the hospital. I had expected this room to be different. In the wards people were still alive, there was still hope, and the soft-sell comfort of waterfalls and babies seemed okay, but here it was almost insulting. Who would ever smile at the plump baby posed in a flowerpot? Who would be comforted by the pallid pretence at cheerfulness? Even the plump palm sprouting in the corner was mildly offensive. It felt strange to be in the same hospital, in what looked like the same waiting room as the antenatal clinic. As if birth and life and death all take place amid the same smells, on the same polished plastic floors. Callum wasn't gone for long. He walked back into the waiting room as if nothing had happened — as if he had been to see the doctor about a mild cold. I asked him if he was okay and he nodded absently, digging in his pocket for the keys to the van.

'Might as well go home,' he said. 'Unless there's anything else you need to do?'

I shook my head. How ordinary it all was, just another chore; pick up some bread and milk, pay the phone bill, identify the dead. Driving home he didn't say much. His sentences were still jumpy and dislocated. His eyes scanned the traffic and road signs nervously; a photograph would have revealed him as calm but perhaps a little lonely, a little distant. His arms were healing but his body still clung to the nervous tics of an addict. He was mumbling to himself as people do when driving alone, thinking of other things and other places, of work to be done or things left undone; the unwashed dishes and open windows. He spoke as if he was reminding himself, over and over again, of something he needed to remember but was certain he would forget.

'They cut off her wings. As if she were cut in half, lengthwise. Her back was gangrenous. Does that mean it was green? I don't know how. Two weeks. Two weeks for her wings to be clipped. How can she fly if her wings are cut away? She looked so damn *thin* without them. Just her shoulder blades — the raw cream bone. Slimy and almost-green. They said it wasn't so bad. Because it had been cold. The ground was cold beneath her. Like a cellar. Like fruit in the cellar. Or wine. But they still had to cut off her wings. Slice them away. Muscle and sinew and skin and feathers. Nothing left. Like paper dolls. The kind we always had at Christmas. Their wings made of folded cardboard or paper doilies. Insert tab A in slot B. Sometimes we would lose them. They would fall off, do you remember? And we would look everywhere but never find them.

'*Probably just an overdose*, that man said to me. Looked at me as if it were my fault. All my fault. As if I loaded the needle and slapped up

199

the vein. As if she didn't know how to do it to herself. All alone in that room. So cold. Perhaps it was me after all.'

His conversation slid past me as if it was water and I was stone.

The police called again a few days later, to say that the cause of death had been determined as an overdose. Case closed. Callum nodded at me when I told him. There was no inquiry. To them it was simple, she was a junkie, her death was unremarkable. To Callum it was astonishing, frightening. To Callum it was so many things he didn't know how to think through them all, how to comprehend them, let alone say them.

So now he walked around the garden in circles, around the paths and the one-winged angel, muttering to himself and shaking his head.

At the cemetery he began at the gate, the low-slung chains which mark out the territory of the dead. He walked up and down each aisle, stopping at each grave as if it were a shelf in the supermarket, scrutinising the labels, reading them aloud. Occasionally he would read one out to me, his voice flat and passionless.

It took an hour of wandering around the cemetery to find Selene's grave. The turf at the foot of her headstone had not yet settled its roots into the soil and looked more like carpet tiles than grass. Inviting us to bend down and lift up a corner and discover the worms turning beneath, the polished lid of her box, or her sneering indelicate face glaring back. At the same time it seemed impossible that it could be her beneath the small marble plate laid in the ground. Callum's lover. Someone he had made love to. Someone he had fought with. Unlike my mother, she was someone my own age, someone real — faulty and damaged and unlikable, but real.

Someone had placed a bunch of flowers in a vase — orange and red and yellow gerberas held upright with florist's wire. Callum knelt to read the inscription on the gravestone with a perplexed frown. It had only her name, date of birth and death. Like many of the newer stones it had nothing to say about what had happened in between. So many children are born each second, and so many people die; their names become insignificant. We leave only enough information for avid genealogists — enough to pencil into a sketched family tree. Selene had no children, no marriage and so she must be a child, a *beloved daughter*. What else could she be? Beloved wife, beloved mother? What else was there? Anything at all seemed trite or ridiculous. I couldn't think of anything that would have said something about who she was. If it had been me lying in the freshly turned soil the inscription would have said '*Mother*'. That too would have been a lie.

The baby shifted in my arms. The shape of her limbs beneath the knitted blanket reminding me of how it felt to have her beneath my skin. I poured the boiling water into the pot and went onto the verandah to call Callum before I sat down. He looked up at me and I waved him over, settling into one of the soft old cane chairs outside the kitchen door.

We sat quietly together; the baby nuzzling into my breast as Callum poured the tea and pushed it across the table towards me. I saw him watching her curiously. Distractedly. I wondered what it was like for him, to see his sister with a baby at her breast. To be living in his sister's house while his sister's lover was elsewhere and his lover was dead.

He sat holding the baby in his large, frail hands while I showered. We ate together, played games that he wandered away from in the middle of a turn. He waited patiently for me when I was feeding or changing the baby. He drove me where I needed to go, his pale face intent on the road in front of him. Driving carefully and slowly, as if he had almost forgotten how to drive at all. He snuck quietly around the house when I was sleeping. I would find him sitting blank-faced at the table, or on the floor in the middle of the lounge room, his face as lost and unsure as a child's.

He took the baby for a walk. Late one afternoon, when the trees were dark shadows, I woke to the sound of him lifting the pram onto the verandah, his keys rattling in the lock. The baby was asleep, curled like a leaf in her pram. Her face was red and puckered from crying and I felt my gravid breasts throb with the weight of the milk she hadn't drained. I had slept for hours, gratefully and greedily. Rather than wake her, he lifted the pram up the stairs and wheeled her into the lounge room, placing her beneath the window where, when she woke, she could see the stars pinprick the sky.

We called her *the baby* or *pumpkin*. Callum called her *peaches*. I was frightened of naming her, although Edna, when I told her this, laughed at my superstitiousness. When my daughter lived inside me she didn't need a name. She was just the dark seedling of a person, but giving her a name would make her a part of this other world, the daylight world. Names are powerful things — the gateways to a kind of magic which can protect or harm. In fairy tales knowing someone's True Name can give you the power of life or death over them. I had to be careful. She would have to have two names — the private and the public. Her name and her True Name. Her name was something to be given, but a True Name must be discovered; it was something only she, and a handful of others, could know. She needed a name everyone could know her by. It had to sound okay not only when she was a baby, but also when she was a girl, a teenager, or a woman. It had to sound right whether called out across a crowded street or a schoolroom, or whispered against the sheets by a lover. It had to be a name she would learn to write easily, that would also lend itself to an elegant signature years later. A name fit for any sort of woman, but not one that conjured up sadness or hopelessness. A name to fall in love with over and over again. I asked Jason about it but he evaded me.

I sat at the table, his hand on my thigh, the newspaper spread out before us. As we finished each page he lay his thumb and finger on the corner and looked at me with a vague and polite question. I shook my head slightly and he got up to put the kettle on. When I finished reading I looked up. He was standing with his back to the sink, his ankles crossed, watching me. The morning light broke through the window behind him and held him cupped in its warm hands.

'Are you happy?' he said. I felt the warmth settle in me as I brushed my palm over the newspaper and looked at my hands. My fingertips were bruised with black ink. I fidgeted uncertainly.

I opened my mouth to speak. My tongue confused. Tied. He took the one stride he needed to reach me and kicked my chair out from beneath me. As I fell I heard his voice, jumbling and clattered between that of the chair and the floor and the shushing sound of the newspaper falling around me.

'Say fucking something,' he said.

I cast around in my Sunday morning mind for something to say, thinking of the book I had been reading, the film I saw on television in the hospital, the daily soaps with their endless falling in and out of love as if it's as easy as that. Those long-legged, perfectly made-up women who wander in and out of their bedrooms with hooded eyes always knowing what their lovers want to hear.

I glanced up at him crouching beside me. He looked so sad. So disappointed. His hands fell weightlessly on my own as he helped me up.

'I don't know,' I said. 'I don't know.'

In the end I called her Sara. Small and simple and elegant.

I told Jason what I'd decided before I wrote it on the birth registration forms, hoping somehow that he would approve or disapprove. That he might be enthusiastic or so horrified he'd protest. I was sitting at the table with the papers spread out before me, sorting through all the forms the nurse had given me when I left the hospital.

'What's this one?' he said.

I glanced over and shook my head. 'That's for single women,' I said.

He put it down in front of me, on top of the birth registration form. 'Fill it out,' he said. 'I'll drive you down and you can start paying for this brat yourself.' I looked up at him, confused and shaking inside. Suddenly frightened that he meant I would have to leave, have to find somewhere, some way, to live without him. I closed my eyes against the thought of having to manage on my own and wondered what to say, how to understand what he meant. I looked up at him, blinking back tears. 'Bloody hell,' he said, rolling his eyes, 'just fill out the form. You'll get money from them.'

It took me several hours to fill out the long and rather complicated form and still there were things I left blank, not knowing what to put in the white spaces. He walked through the room occasionally to check, looking over my shoulder, correcting me when he thought I'd written something wrong. When he came in and saw it finished it was after lunch but he insisted we should take the form in straight away. I told him we couldn't, that we still needed two people to verify that I was a single mother. Jason took the form from me and stood reading through the section I showed him. Finally he filled in one section using Selene's name, dating it several weeks ago. Then he stood tapping the pen against the thick paper. 'What about that woman next door? Edna?'

I swallowed hard. As horrid as it was to see Selene's name on the paper it was better than having to draw Edna into this lie. I tried to think of a reason she couldn't or wouldn't do it, something Jason would believe, but in the end I took the form and nodded.

What was I going to tell Edna? What would I tell *them* if they rang and questioned me about Jason — who had refused to allow me to put his name on any of Sara's forms, even her birth certificate? Who would I tell them was her father? What would I do if some officious bureaucrat insisted I name someone — anyone. Would I have to tell them I didn't know? What would they think of me then? Would they stamp a large red letter on my file? Would I be the joke of the department, the source of endless hours of gossip? *You know that teenage girl, she doesn't even know who the father is.* I could just imagine them, secure in their perfect lives, behind their perfect desks, with the screen turned away so I couldn't see the bright flashing words that came up when my name was entered. Slut, slut, slut, the screen would flash, and the woman with the name-tag would smirk and tell me to take a seat. While she photocopied my driver's licence and electricity bills she'd point me out to her workmates and they'd laugh or shake their heads. *How does she live with herself?* they'd say.

When Edna opened the door I looked up at her and tears fell over the milk-stained buttons of my blouse. She stepped outside and put her arms around me. I put my head against her shoulder and she pulled me against her. I could smell her skin and the faint perfume of fabric softener on her dress, feel the frailty of the skin on her throat, the dampness of her hair. Most of all I could feel her arms around me, clasped together over my back, holding me more firmly than anyone had for years. No tentativeness, no apologies or doubt or remonstrances. She just held me.

When we went inside she didn't ask me any questions, just filled out the form and handed it to me. She offered to watch Sara while I went down to the office to lodge it, but I said I would take her with me since she was due for a feed again soon. 'Well,' she said, 'another time,' and I nodded. I wanted to stay sitting at her table, listening to the music that drifted in from another room. There were photographs all through the house, hundreds of them leaning in frames on every surface. In one of them a young man stood leaning against a new car. He was dressed in an army uniform. He was smiling and squinting at the photographer, holding his hand up above him to block out some of the glare.

'That's my son,' Edna said. 'He loved that car. He bought it just a few weeks before he was sent over. When we got the telegram saying he'd died I went out there and sat in it for hours. It still smelled like him, even then. One of his jumpers was on the back seat, and a half-empty packet of cigarettes. It sat in the garage for months, but then one of his mates came back and asked could he take it off my hands. I was happy to see it go to someone who had known Dennis.

'You're such a lovely young woman,' she said. 'I know it's hard now but it's true what they say, time heals all wounds.'

When I got home Jason bundled me into the van. I fed Sara as he darted through the traffic, grumbling about how long it had taken me. 'What did you talk about anyway?' he asked. 'Don't bother. I don't want to know.'

In the social security office I waited in line for forty minutes only to be told to wait again. Jason became impatient and left. By the time I had filled out another two forms and spoken to a man so flustered and tired that he barely even glanced at me, the office was closing. I was grateful for the five dollar note I found in my pocket, almost praying with relief as I caught a bus home. Sara was grizzling and unhappy the whole way; her nappy was wet, but I'd left her bag of things in the car and didn't have anything clean to put on her. The wetness of her nappy soaked into my jeans. At home the house was quiet. I found Cal asleep in front of the television, a bowl of cereal congealing on the floor beside him.

Jason didn't come home for nearly three weeks, and when he did he spent two days sleeping. Dozing on and off. I'd find him in my bed, on the lounge, in the garden. One afternoon I was standing at the end of the garden with Sara in my arms when I heard him cough behind me. I turned sharply, almost dropping her in fright or surprise, to see him curled on the timber floor of the gazebo. A blanket tucked beneath his cheek.

He opened his eyes to stare at me before standing and walking over to stand behind me. I could feel my body tensed against the air before me, against the arm he wrapped around my stomach. He lifted his hand to Sara's cheek and gently traced the line of her jaw. 'She's so soft,' he said. As I turned back towards the house he put out his arms and asked if he could carry her. I looked into his face, bent down over hers, and felt my belly clutch. Not with fear but with a sudden unrestrained jealousy. After all these months of feeling that he didn't want her, didn't love her, how dare he suddenly intrude on this. On us. He had made it clear that he didn't want anything to do with her, why should that suddenly change? Why should I have to share her? I had a letter from Social Security saying I would be receiving a sole parent pension this week. That I was, in effect, a single mother. That was what he had wanted. He had, in fact, insisted on declaring to the world that Sara had nothing to do with him. I shook my head and pushed past him. A day later he was gone again and I was shocked to find myself relieved. Everything was easier without him.

At three months she was rounder than she had been at birth. Her skin was flushed and firm, her wide eyes dark. She watched me when I fed her. One fist arched over my breast and the other wrapped beneath my arm. At night I nursed her in the kitchen, especially early morning feeds. If I turned the light on over the stove there was enough of a glow to see by without it being too harsh. I tried at first to sit in the lounge and watch television, but the light of the television flickered, and there was nothing to watch at that hour — or else I would get caught up and spend the whole night watching re-runs of old sitcoms.

In the kitchen it was quiet, the only sound that of the garden and the harbour. Trees scratched against the walls of the house, or the wind beat their ragged sticks together. I watched her eyes watching me. At first they were a warning, as if the nipple wouldn't slip from her mouth if she could hold me with her gaze. Other times I thought she was studying me, wondering what kind of woman I was. What kind of mother. Although she was so young I imagined her thoughts formed in sentences, the thoughts of a woman much older and wiser than I was, measuring the weight of my womanhood. At times I heard her voice in my head — a voice without sound, fossicking through the basket of my thoughts. *Not this one*, she would say, her tiny head shaking from side to side. Her dark eyes were still on me. They were not the eyes of a child.

There was no clock in the kitchen, so I couldn't tell what time it was. I didn't think to look before I got out of bed. It didn't really matter. It was still dark enough to be night — not the almost morning light of five or six a.m. She let go of my nipple and tipped her head back, resting it in the crook of my arm as she peered at me, her tiny features drawn together in the middle of her round face. I heard someone at the front door, fumbling with keys.

When Jason got the lock open he pushed the door roughly. I heard it bang against the wall and bounce closed. He swore and tried again, closing it behind him this time. As he came up the hall I shifted Sara around to the other side, buttoning up the front of my pyjamas with one hand as I did so. She looked at me indignantly before turning her face away. I heard him go into the bedroom, shuffling around in the dark as he took off his boots and kicked them across the floor. I waited quietly, listening to him moving around the room, turning back the sheets. When I heard him lie down — the sheets rustling against his skin — I sank back in my chair. Sara was beginning to squirm. Not satisfied yet. Not ready to sleep. She fidgeted beneath her rugs and got one hand free, clutching at the front of my shirt with it. Her mouth was round and half-open, already sucking at nothing.

As I began to unbutton my shirt again I heard him rolling over in the bed and pushing back the blankets. Setting his bare feet on the floor. I turned her towards my chest so she could catch the nipple in her mouth, and listened to him come up the hall to stand behind me. She butted her head at my breast, her open mouth missing the nipple over and over again. She looked ridiculous and desperate. She was beginning to cry. Her eyes were screwed up in frustration. She got a mouthful of white flesh from below my nipple into her mouth and sucked madly, gulping at nothing. She used her fists to push the breast away. I pinched my nipple between my thumb and fingers and rolled it slightly until the milk welled up before slipping it into her mouth. She sucked greedily. Her mouth and cheeks moved rhythmically as she scratched at the skin of my breast.

I took a deep breath to ride over the pain of her first hard sucks, over the jolt as she bit the blister just beneath the nipple, until I felt the delicious sexual kick as the milk let down and felt her pause, gulping noisily at the sudden rush. She pulled away and a thin stream of bluish milk sprayed over her cheek. As she turned back to catch my nipple between her gums again I heard Jason snort behind me.

I half turned, catching sight of him leaning against the doorframe in an old t-shirt and thin cotton jersey shorts. 'Christ. I thought it was going to get better.'

I looked down at the top of her head, at the roughly triangular softness of her fontanelle beating to the same pulse as the milk in my breast.

'It was bad enough before — you were so *big*. But this!'

I looked down at Sara. Her eyes were drooping. Her hand had fallen away from my breast. I tucked it into her rug and leant back in my chair slightly to see if she would give up the breast but she nuzzled in to me, not yet ready to let go. 'I read that men sometimes worry that women get too turned on having a child at the breast.' I turned to face him as she fell away, a small trickle of milk in the corner of her mouth. She sucked at nothing in her sleep. 'Maybe you're just jealous,' I said.

Jason shook his head and walked away, back into the dark of the hallway. I sat smiling at the table, suddenly conscious of his tentativeness. Of the way he leaned in doorways, or at the edge of rooms. He avoided touching me, looking at me. He threw challenges at me but no longer pressed his face into mine with each syllable. He was frightened, cautious. The solid bulk of my pregnant body had repulsed and fascinated him, but this was something else. Now I had become two women. Two bodies. A split and shifting entity that leaked and bled and was — for him — oddly incontestable.

I met a lady in the meads,
　　Full beautiful — a fairy's child,
Her hair was long, her foot was light,
　　And her eyes were wild.

—Keats, *La Belle Dame sans Merci*

I saw a woman pull up outside the house in a yellow car. She sat for several minutes after turning off the engine, checking her lipstick in the pull-down mirror, brushing her shining blonde hair which she then shook out in a loose cloud around her almost-bare shoulders. When she leant over to pick up something from the passenger's seat I saw her profile, smooth and beautiful. I pulled back from the window, my back resting against the wall. My heart was hammering against my breastbone. What would I do if she came to the door? I thought about all the things in our life that might bring someone to the door; the lies to Social Security and the birth registry, Selene's death, the drugs that Jason still kept hidden in boxes beneath the house, amid old cutlery and cast-off furniture. There was no one else in the house. Callum was outside in the yard somewhere. Jason had gone to the corner shop to get the paper and milk.

I watched her get out of the car and check the number of Edna's house. She stood looking at our house, her level gaze measuring each window frame, the shape of the door, the angle of the roofline against the sky. As she walked through the gate I watched her skirt slide around her ankles, the way her hair floated in a blunt-cut wave. I didn't answer when she knocked at the door, pulling further back into the hallway so she couldn't see me but I could still see her. Would she hear me? I held my breath. Held on as long as I could, until my lungs were almost cracking with the strain of it. She would feel me watching her. The weight of my curiosity and fear, but I could not close my eyes. Even when she frowned slightly, her brows drawn down together in concentration as she pulled a piece of paper from her pocket to check the address, she was beautiful.

Over her shoulder I saw Jason coming up the street, the paper rolled under his arm. The milk swinging in his hand. When he saw her car he hesitated, registering its familiarity, before turning to see her standing on the front porch.

'Elliot,' he called out. Her face as she heard him call her was suddenly luminous. She walked towards him and he took her in his arms, the cold milk resting in the small of her back as their mouths met.

Elliot, I thought. It was the name his friend had used for me, that night on the harbour. It was the name I had refused to consider ever since. A slip of the tongue. A mistake. I had deliberately tried not to remember the way the man's face looked when Jason corrected him. He had been so sure. He even wanted to disagree. *No*, he seemed to insist, leaning towards Jason, *I'm sure you said her name was Elliot*.

I turned away from the window as he leaned to kiss her mouth again, one hand rising to rest behind her head, to fossick in her hair.

My lover's lover.

I could not watch them, my alien lover whose mouth used to hover on mine, used to hesitate with gentleness, with imprecision, with desperation. His lover whose back arched slightly beneath his hand. Whose pale hair was ruffled by a breeze and intimately lashed against his cheek. I wondered how his mouth formed with hers. Was it soft and pliable, the wet skin splitting open like ripe fruit. Did his tongue twist with hers? His hand lifted the hot hair from the back of her neck and cradled it like a baby, like *our* baby. Was his mouth hard on hers? Did he press into her like a knife-edged spoon, and scoop her out and bite until the blood, the sweat, the lust ran? Did he swallow her? Or was she more tentative fruit?

My lover's lover had been secret. An unknown root burrowing between our skins. The stranger against his ribs. Her heart beating in his flesh, in mine. Flesh to flesh to flesh. And there she was. Leaning into him, her head tipped back to receive his mouth. Light glittering on her shoulders and in her hair and along the curve of her cheekbone. She seemed made of light; built of it, cell by lustrous cell.

He watched her car round the corner as she drove off and stood there for a moment, his body still turned away, before turning to study the house, his eyes scanning the windows with a worried frown. I pulled further back into the shadow, my back pressed against the wall. I listened to the insect hum that pressed into the silent air. *Please, let him not see me*, I thought. I waited a few seconds before edging away, sneaking out into the garden, settling quickly into the grass, pressing my arms and legs into the long itchy green to make it seem as if I had been lying there for a while. When I heard him come out onto the back verandah I held my breath, waiting for one of us to know what to do.

'I'm going out for a couple of hours,' he said.

I sat up and ran my hands through my hair, trying to look as if I had been asleep. I squinted up at him through the foliage and nodded, waving vaguely. It felt false and ridiculous, my arm jutting out awkwardly into the air and swaying above me. Is this how people feel caught out in a rip, far from shore, their arms flailing at the sky in a gesture of hope and hopelessness? I wanted to say something, to scream accusations and scratch his mouth where her lips had been, but at the same time I wanted him to just nod and turn and keep going. Didn't want the uneasy peace between us to be shattered. I turned away from him and tipped my head forward, scanning the page in front of me without comprehending anything.

Late at night I heard a car outside in the road. The tyres half-melted in the heat, loose stones pressing into the bitumen and crunching, like toffee in my teeth. The sound echoed against the windows, against our silent house, our silent room, our silent bed.

Our silent sex.

In our silent house Jason was fucking me and the skin fell away from his face. The shape of his bones was revealed. I could taste her lingering there. Holding on. Her breath rocking between his teeth. I scaled his bones. Opened out the seed of him, the root of him, the bent branches stripped of skin under my teeth. I was tempted to tear back the woody flesh and seek her out. I would ringbark him. Was she there? I would reveal her touch, the burnt-in rings of her around his heart. Was she here, in his pocket, in his sleeve, in his shoe? Was it her hand that printed a message in the dusty window of the car, surrounded by a child-like heart?

I would hunt her out. His temptress. His other lover.

He leant across the sheet in sleep and sighed and his skin burned me. His belly rested against my fists and suddenly he was a stranger. Opening and closing like a fish brought up on the sand. He rolled over and his skin whispered secrets against the sheets — secrets about her, about him, about the sweaty silky fish of that other sex, *their* sex, and I closed my eyes and the sheets burned. They burned like aluminium, like cedar, like flesh. They burned bright and hard and white and they reeked. Their scent was hard-edged and satisfying and they wrapped around me, those burning sheets, they held me like a lover. Like a mother.

Sleeping he was open like a letter, like a book divided along its spine. Was this the page? Was this where she had traced her finger over him? Over me? I would slide across the sheets, across the timber. I would tip him out of his bed. I would singe the hair from his skull and trace the knots of his scalp. Was she here, traced like a map beneath the veins that travel from wrist to armpit to groin? I would hunt her out. I would scent her out like a dog. Like a bitch. My hand in his pocket, in the crease behind his knee. I would find her out.

His mouth lay open and I studied his teeth. Did her tongue light here? Run across the broken stack of his eye tooth? His mouth was wet and secret. *My* secret that he had given away. Mine. I was burning. Wetly burning and smoking like forest timber. I longed for dryness. For the desert untouched and unswept. Without sweat.

Two weeks later there was a photograph of her in his pocket as I generously — calmly — cleaned out his shirts before washing them. My fingers almost pulling out the seams. It had been taken in one of those automatic booths. An address and phone number were scribbled on the other side — somewhere up the coast, not quite an hour's drive from our home. Hers, it must be her hand that scribbled across that slippery paper while leaning on something not flat, not steady. I dialled the number seven times. No answer. Was he there now? Was he lying with his hand beneath her breast listening to the phone ring in another room and whispering, 'Don't get up, lie still, lie here. I'll talk to you.'

I lay all night in our tangled room with the clean sheets. His shirts hung around the memory of him. I pulled his jacket from the hook behind the door and crushed it under my cheek and lay with the phone at my fingertips, not even listening any more as I pressed the re-dial button. Again and again.

'Hello … hello … It must be her, Jason, you should go home.'

Then it was his voice I heard. His voice so loud in this empty room, muffled by her sheets and his hand across the phone. 'No …'

The phone was ringing and ringing and ringing and nobody answered. Nobody was home.

The next morning I was in the garden with Sara. She was lying on two layers of blanket while I weeded the garden beside her. She had a rattle in her hand shaped like a tiny red and yellow plastic barbell, which she was busily sucking. Occasionally she would hold it out in front of her and shake it at the sky. Slowly we moved around until I was weeding the beds near the end of the garden and she waved the rattle at me, laughing to herself. I turned to see her looking not at me, but at the sky out past the edge of the cliff. I called her but she didn't turn to look at me. Instead she thrust her tiny fist at the cliff edge again. She was frowning; the features of her face drawn together in concentration as she shook her toy at the cliff. I knew she was trying to tell me something; that she wanted to see past the edge of the garden. So I picked her up and stepped over the fence with her in my arms and we stood on the edge. I closed my eyes and tipped back my head as the wind rushed up towards me. It was a beautiful, clear day. Each leaf on each struggling bush and tree seemed sharply defined, drawn with a finely pointed pencil on the blue air. The harbour below us lay as still as ice. The boats on its surface barely moving. She struggled in my arms, freeing the fist with the rattle and shaking it out in front of us. Then she let it go. Or rather she didn't let it go, she threw it. It flew out of her hand and fell at least twenty feet before it hit the rock-face and began to bounce and roll towards the harbour below us. Sara started to cry. I tried to turn her towards me, to comfort her. She squirmed in my arms, twisting to see behind her and beginning to make a garbled, screaming noise. I closed my eyes. Feeling the grit of tiredness scratch across them. I don't know that I was thinking about anything except how calm the harbour seemed. How gloriously quiet. I realised she wanted to see where the rattle had gone so I grasped her around the waist and held her out over the cliff.

She spread her arms and legs like a starfish. She looked as if she were flying. If it hadn't been for my hands at her waist she would have been. Flying. I imagined letting go and seeing her slide through the air like a diver, chasing her rattle. She laughed and kicked one of her legs, clapping her fat hands together. I held her there as long as I could, feeling the strain in my shoulders and wrists as she kicked and turned. She was heavy. She was always heavy. Her tiny hands and dimpled legs wrapped tightly around me, or pushed at me, bruising my chest and arms. I was always holding on, holding on for what? Her face was drawn together in a dark frown, her eyes angry as she squirmed against me, against the ache in my arms, in my fingers twisted into her clothes. I ached all over from the strain of it, from the sheer effort of keeping her here, where she had never wanted to be. She was always looking away, always longing — as I had — for something else. Something clean and new and pure. The air rushing up into your face as you fell. The unweighted freedom of falling which, although it was all about weight, would also feel like not being held. Not holding on, but letting go, finally. Finally just letting it all go and not having to think, not having to hold your breath or think or be careful but just to fall. Effortlessly. Calmly. I wanted to let her go, to see her fly. It was what we both wanted.

When I fed her I wanted to tear her from my nipple and throw her across the room. *Leave me alone*, I wanted to scream. *This is my body, not yours.* She gazed up at me with her level, calculating gaze and I was so terrified by my desire to be rid of her that my mouth was dry. I left her crying in her crib while I walked out into the garden, but the sound of her bellowing followed me. I was crying helplessly when I heard Edna calling to me over the fence that perhaps it would be okay to give her a bottle, to give up this one little thing. When she offered to watch Sara while I went to the chemist I wanted to clutch her to me and hold her. I was so relieved, so grateful that someone else had taken things into their hands, and I did not have to feel it was just me struggling to understand this tiny, squalling creature who clutched at me and made my nipples crack and bleed, made my womb clutch and throb every time she sucked.

I left her sleeping with Edna while I went to the chemist and bought bottles, formula, teats — all the paraphernalia of the bottle-fed baby. I couldn't do it anymore, not after that. I couldn't let her get inside my head the way she had been in my body. Sucking away every ounce of breath and blood and life I had. My body was tired.

I should have felt guilty, but when I sat down that afternoon and watched Edna slip the bottle into her mouth all I felt was relief. A great rushing flood of relief that threatened to sweep me away. I had to leave the room. I didn't want Edna to see how grateful I was to be free of my child. At first I had wanted to breastfeed her. I had been convinced it was the right thing to do, and somehow it had become the one thing I was holding onto to make me feel that I was — in some small way — being a good mother. A good enough mother. It had become the centre of my sense of myself as a mother that I could do this, and not only that I could do it, but that anyone watching had to believe it was easy. Natural. That both Sara and I loved this time together. The specialness of it. The bond it created between us. The strain of pretending — every minute of every day — that I didn't resent her clutching, hungry mouth latched onto my throbbing nipples had exhausted me. I went in to my room and lay down on the bed. Alone. The tiny, joyous miracle of being alone. I closed my eyes and fell asleep.

The next day I left Sara with Edna while I went to the shops and bought extra formula, nappies, sterilising solution and wipes. I told Cal I was going away for the weekend to think about stuff. It wasn't exactly a lie; I needed to think. I needed to find Elliot and watch her and think about her. I didn't know — at the time — what I wanted to do when I found her, but as I pushed the trolley around the supermarket all I could see was Elliot in Jason's arms, with the milk leaving its damp impression in her dress. The way he held his hand beneath her elbow as if she might drift away if he weren't careful. Had he ever held me that way? I wanted to punish her. I wanted to question her. I wanted to cry in her arms. I wanted to know what it was that he felt when he kissed her. When he held her. I wanted to know what she tasted of, how she smelt. I wanted her forgiveness, her beauty, her purity, her love. I wanted to kill her.

As I stood in the kitchen showing Cal how to make up sterilising solution for the bottles and teats, how to level off the scoops of formula and mix them with boiled water, how to test the temperature before feeding Sara, I thought about her. About going to her house and knocking on her door and saying ... what? Over and over again I played it out in my head, never getting past the moment when she opened the door and I looked up into her shining face.

The last train from the city to Gosford on a weeknight left before midnight. It sat at Central Station for half an hour before doing so, as cleaners walked along the aisles picking up cigarette packets and food wrappers and newspapers. A handful of people waited on the platform; most sat on the moulded plastic seats outside the ticket gates. Only two of the small shopfronts were open — a newsagent and a takeaway food joint. The restaurants and showers were closed. Suspended over the central ticket-holders entrance was a bank of screens showing departure times. The station was mostly deserted. According to the blinking green screens the next train to Gosford left at eleven-forty p.m.

This part of the station was old. The vestibule with its glass-domed ceiling was faintly Victorian. If you took out the plastic seats and the vending machines you could have, instead, long wooden benches and potted palms. The place could be filled with ladies in long bustle-backed gowns and piles of luggage. Men in frock coats. It could almost be a ballroom even, filled with bobbing jellyfish gowns and the same thin bearded men. The band would be at the far end, near the restaurant and souvenir shop. Travellers would come in through the huge arch at the other end where the taxis stop, but of course there would have been carriages instead of cars, and quiet young boys in brass-buttoned uniforms would hold out their hands to help the ladies down from their carriages. But it wasn't so grand anymore. Central Station was dusty and worn. The only hope was offered by the trains on the other side of the ticket gates. The trains that left from this part of the station were those that travelled outside the limits of the suburbs. They were not the rattling commuter trains; the nine-to-five jump-in-jump-out kind.

I settled down on the lower level of a two-tier carriage, a few cars down from the end. With twenty minutes left before the train was due to depart there were only two other people in the carriage; a middle-aged woman reading a shiny new sex-and-shopping novel, and a young man in jeans and a blue collared t-shirt staring out the window. He turned to look further down the platform and caught me watching his reflection. From my seat on the lower level of the train I could see people's shoes as they wandered past. I settled my coffee between my knees and leant across the seat to dig my book and headset out of my bag. The battery on my headset was almost dead, so I didn't turn it on.

The trip to Gosford took about an hour. The train raced quietly along the northern suburbs line without stopping until it reached Hornsby. From there it moved out of the suburbs, through the quiet, outlying areas of the Hawkesbury, through mountains and along the edge of still waterways spotted only occasionally with the lights of houses. At home they would be asleep. Callum and Sara. Jason — who wasn't there when I left the house — probably wouldn't be home all weekend, and why should that matter? This was not about him. It was about a few hours, perhaps even a few days by myself. No baby or brother or lover. No one to follow me through the house with questions or doubts. No one to clutch at my breast each time she woke. No one to follow me from room to room, a presence as tangible as a rock inside my lungs. Nobody and nothing to worry about just for a night. For one day. To let it all go in one simple gesture. To walk away leaving the dishes in the sink and the washing piled in the laundry and the garden path unswept. I could still feel the exquisite joy of walking out into the street and catching a bus to the station with empty arms that swung weightless at my sides.

219

I opened my book and flicked the pages till I found my place, but I didn't start reading. I hadn't been able to concentrate on reading for a while now. There always seemed to be something else pulling my attention away. Something else that needed to be done. At times it was just knowing that Sara would wake soon, or the washing almost-dry on the line with a storm threatening, or a meal not yet eaten. Other times it was nothing really. The smallest thing could distract me.

I was sitting in the carriage of a train heading out of the city. Just for a little while. A stolen moment of solitude, of self, in what had become a life full of playing at being someone else's daughter, sister, lover, mother. I was riding in a soft-backed chair at almost-midnight by myself and part of me wanted not to get off the train at all. Part of me wanted to keep going until the train ran out of wide-gauge rails somewhere near the Queensland border. I would let go of everything in one fell swoop. I would be one of those faces people photocopy and staple to telegraph poles. *Missing*. Only who would do the photocopying? Who would walk the streets for me, stapling my picture to telegraph poles?

I looked up and down the carriage. Again the guy in the blue shirt caught me looking and smiled. He tipped his head to the side and made a face at me and I smiled back. I turned the page of my book and started to read the first sentence of Chapter Two: 'They had been married, and childless, for sixteen years.' I had read this one sentence — this single-sentenced paragraph — at least ten times. I knew it off by heart. I was not convinced, although I knew it was probably true, or at least it had once been true. I found it difficult to concentrate on somebody else's life. The intricate details of kitchens, bedrooms and bathrooms laid out between two thin, cardboard covers. Unless, of course, I became trapped there as well. Then I could spend hours poring over each paragraph, each sentence. Weighing each word to find where each character's heart lay. To find what it was that made them turn and smile, or weep, or not turn at all. Perhaps if I knew what someone else would do I'd know what I should do. It was a strange and ridiculous kind of magic — of fortune telling; turn the page and find a life.

We passed through a station; the sudden rush of light and concrete pressing close to the windows just at the edges of my vision startled me. I pulled back from the glass and laughed quickly and uncertainly at the ridiculousness of being frightened by a train station. The stranger smiled at me again. I went back to my book.

At Gosford station he followed me up to the doors and stood behind me. 'Hi,' he said, and I turned to look at him, smiling uncertainly. Although I felt fine about smiling at him across an empty train carriage, I was not sure about talking to him when he was standing so close. I could smell him. I could hear him breathing. I glanced around the carriage, wondering in a kind of vague, paranoid way whether Jason had followed me. Perhaps he was sitting slumped in a chair nearby, just out of sight, watching me. Waiting for me to smile at this man again. Waiting for me to talk to him or take his hand or indicate, in some half-conscious gesture, that I was flirting with him. Maybe Jason had set me up, maybe this guy was a friend of his, someone he knew, someone who had agreed to test me. I felt the panic taking hold as the doors finally started to open. A small rush of air, the faint wheeze as they rolled back on their rails. I pressed my chin against my chest and bolted from the carriage, striding across the platform to the stairs.

I caught a cab to the hotel. The driver talked non-stop all the way, asking me questions about my life. The life I was trying to escape, if only for a little while. I lied to him, as convincingly as I could. I was a writer, I said, here to gather information for my next book. I wrote romance novels. My publisher loved me. I wanted it to be true. I wanted to have an apartment somewhere, full of plush furniture and clean surfaces, where I entertained beautiful people and drank expensive wine. When we got to the hotel I bolted from the car as quickly as I could. The clerk gave me an odd look as I leant over the desk to grab the key from her hand and stumbled out of the reception area. 'Wait,' she called after me, 'don't you want to know about the breakfast service?'

When I reached my room I walked straight into the bathroom and turned on the shower, throwing my clothes on the floor. In the shower I hand-expressed some milk and let it flow down my stomach onto the tiles. I could see Sara's tiny face frowning at me as it slipped down the plughole.

The next day I caught a bus to The Entrance, where Elliot lived. I walked along the street aimlessly, still toying with the idea of going to her home. Knocking on her door. When I saw her it was a shock. Sudden and violent. The awful familiarity of her face — the face I saw at every corner, imagined seeing every night in my bed — suddenly real. Plump and fleshy. Her hand folding a lick of hair back behind an ear as she leant over and looked in a shop window. I watched her profile; her perfect mouth was slightly open, her eyes distracted, her brows drawn down into a small vee. I imagined us as friends, pictured her leaning towards me over a cup of coffee and lazily, incidentally, putting her hand over mine, kissing my cheek when we met and when we parted. I pictured her with Sara on her lap, feeding her small crumbs of cake from her own plate. I saw her in his arms in our kitchen, and me at the window with the rain like clear silk sheets between us. Her head turned towards me, laughing, as I ran down the stairs and out into the garden. I imagined the two of them walking together with our child on her hip. Hand in hand. Laughing. Her shins were the colour of warm toffee.

A breeze sidled into the street and washed around her, lifting her hem like a tentative lover. I pictured Jason's hand brushing up behind her knee. I walked along the street and stood behind her, looking in at the same window, watching her reflection washed and perfected in the glass. I reached out my hand to the back of her sun-stained head. I was as dark as a stain behind her. I wondered if this was how he saw us — his lover and his other lover — light and shadow, bright and dark. Should I speak to her? What would I say? *Does his breath burn you?* Or something ordinary. Something women say to each other when they meet in the street. But my mouth was dry and empty. I didn't know what one woman should say to another when they had different lovers, or none at all. What did women say when they shared a lover?

I wanted to hear her voice, and never to hear it. To touch and not to touch. To burn her skin with words and see her turn away from the window towards me. I wanted to see her eyes shocked, or apologetic, or something — anything — damaged. Like mine. I looked off down the street. I could keep walking, past the delicatessen that was only two doors away, or the chemist. But she was alone and I might never see her again. Never have the chance to cut her down in the street. Perhaps I could just follow her for a little while. See what happens. Perhaps she would recognise me. Perhaps I could strike up an ordinary conversation with her. We could have coffee and shop for cheap jewellery, or books. We could have the kind of conversations people have when they are strangers who meet each other once and never again. Even people like the vaguely familiar women of the antenatal clinic with whom I had gossiped and laughed, sharing a short-lived and particular kind of intimacy.

When she walked into the shop I stood on the footpath for several minutes. *Just walk away. You can do it. Leave him to her, her to him.* Inside, the sullen shop assistant was filing her nails. She glanced up disinterestedly as I came in, smiling distractedly at me before going back to her nail. I looked through a bin full of odd pieces — ten dollars or under. Elliot flicked through a rack of white linen, then pale pink cotton. As I moved to stand next to her she was fingering a deep blue silk dress, almost black. 'It's beautiful. It would suit you,' I said.

'It's kind of dark, don't you think?'

'Why don't you try it on anyway? What harm can it do?' I felt like Snow White's wicked stepmother — just one bite, it can't hurt you. I can't hurt you.

'You'll tell me if it looks shocking?' She tipped her head towards the sales assistant. '*She* certainly won't.'

We laughed together and the shop assistant looked at us suspiciously. The faded curtain of the change room didn't close properly. I watched Elliot bend to pull her shirt off over her head. Her fine, long-fingered hands rising as she slipped the dress down. The silk whispering against her skin. I watched her feet as she switched from side to side, looking in the mirror.

'Tell me the truth,' she said, 'what does it look like?' She pulled the curtain aside and looked straight into my face. Not smiling or laughing, but somehow shining. Her hair fell like a spoonful of light over her shoulder. In the mirror I could see her back; the smooth sculpted bend of her spine. I pictured her arching to meet his hand. His half-open mouth, his breath on her skin. His hands cupping her breasts like fruit. I caught my breath as she half-turned and smoothed the fabric down her thigh.

'It looks good,' I said, and through closed eyes I watched her smile.

Ten minutes later we walked out into the street together, laughing. The saleswoman was carefully refolding, rehanging. Her face full of the nothingness of working girls stuck behind shop windows. Elliot drifted towards me as someone walked past us. I felt the warmth of her body turn into mine and found myself suddenly — shockingly — wet-lipped. I smiled. All innocence. Glittering like a fresh-skinned snake.

Late in the afternoon we were settled on her verandah, the sun slipping behind the hilltops and the sweet-rot smell of bananas clotting the air. Another pot of tea. She smiled and pulled a cigarette from her packet, holding it gracefully between two fingers as she brushed the hair from her face. She was, when you looked carefully (and I was being careful), quite plump. Her heavy arms and dimpled elbows more round than the angular precision of catwalk girls. Her hair flew across her face in even the slightest breeze. Her temples shone with sweat. She was richly scented, like a fox. Sharp. Somewhere in the room behind us music was playing. We had fallen into silence and I watched her close her eyes to listen to the music as it washed out to us.

'I think I may well be in love,' she said, 'although I don't think it will work out.' She hesitated and I held my breath, not knowing what to say to make her stop, or whether I wanted her to. 'I've been seeing someone, but he's already with someone. They even have a child, although he says that neither of them really wanted to have her. It just happened.'

'Have you ever seen her?'

'His daughter?'

I hesitated, wondering if she knew and was testing me. Wondering if the intentness of her gaze meant she was waiting for me to slip up so that she could pounce. 'The other woman.'

'Who she is doesn't matter. I like to fantasise about her, though. It feels very incestuous, very dangerous.'

I was thinking about what it would be like to kiss her, just lean over across the arm of her chair and kiss her cheek. She would move away. I would be a fool. I wanted to say, *What would you do if she kissed you?*

I said, 'Do you want him to leave her?'

'I think the only way I can love a man is if he already belongs to someone else. Sometimes when we're lying together I breathe in and it's her I want. It's her I dream about.'

'Does she dream about you?'

'She knows about me,' she opened her eyes and shifted closer, looking at me carefully, 'but he doesn't think so. Our little secret. Hers and mine. The conspiracies of lovers.' She smiled. 'Would you like some more tea? Something else? A glass of wine?'

When she leaned over me to stub out her cigarette I could feel the weight of her breast on my thigh, her hand on my calf. She kissed me, lightly, on the mouth and I felt suddenly lost and childish. I wanted to be in her arms, to have her in mine. All night. Swallow her whole like a plum, but I couldn't do anything. I was motionless. Flash-flooded. Drowning. I had to wait, bide my time. There were other ways to make her mine, to make her *not* his.

We stood in the kitchen. I was rinsing glasses as she pulled a bottle from the cupboard. 'Red or white?'

'Whatever you prefer.'

'What about something to eat?' I turned to face her as she leant across me to pull a corkscrew from the bench behind me. *I should go home*, I thought. *Jason is at home; he'll be waiting for me. He'll want to leave in a few hours, to go out drinking or to see his lover.* I almost laughed out loud but instead tilted my head forward and found my face suddenly caught in the spill of her hair. I breathed in her fragrance and goose bumps rose over my skin. Was she in love with him? He with her? Did she know what she was doing, what I was doing in her house? Did I? I turned away.

'I guess we could go out but I don't really feel like it,' she said.

She opened the fridge door and knelt in front of it, pulling things from the bottom shelves, 'Some salad, fresh bread, some cheese?'

'Perfect.'

I was in the kitchen of my lover's lover, slicing tomatoes, washing lettuce. We were laughing and drinking. The timber benches were laced with wine, with fresh lemon juice, with tomato pulp. As I took a sip of wine the phone began to ring.

'That'll be him,' she said. I watched her thinking about it. She put her hand on my arm and I closed my eyes, leant forward.

I remembered his mouth as she took me in her arms. The promise of her breath. I watched the thin slide of her eye beneath its skin. Those eyes that had seen him slippery and wide-eyed with sex. My hand moved along her shoulder blade. Her skin, bruised with light, brushed against my fingertips, against my mouth. The spider in my mouth spinning, drowning, swallowing. Spinning. Her hands were here and here and here and I felt her breath slide between my heavy breasts, along the curve of a rib, rushing hot and warm to my nipple where the milk beat. My lover's lover inside my skin. Biting, sucking, breathing. I pulled her up and kissed her mouth, her milk-wine kiss.

I sank into her skin of sand. My poisonous tongue promising emptiness, promising rooms with polished timber floors and a frail blue light that was not cool or wet but was nevertheless tidal. My libellous tongue slippery with promises, wet with the shine of her skin, her sweat. My lover — my lover's lover — was shining wet in my hand, on the tip of my tongue. Hooked inside her, inside each other's bodies, as we came to the edge. I watched her face as she moved above me, her mouth open and her hair falling into mine. She reached down and threaded her fingers into my hair, pulled my mouth towards hers as her fingers moved inside me. I turned away, resting my head on her shoulder as I felt my body clench around hers. Felt that moment of pure joy stretch through her into me. I closed my eyes and let my body fall open. Felt the sudden rush as the clouds that pounded inside me burst open. We came like starved children. Parched and hungry. Greedy for a pure and selfish bliss. Like children melting with heat, sparking with it, until the rains come and they run out into the fields and turn their faces up, mouths open to receive the sky as it washes over them.

Somewhere in the milk-sweat-shine of that night I saw her watching me, alert and delicate as a cat. I saw her startled mouth as she leant against my throat and whispered: 'It is you. I knew it was you.'

★　　★

I spent the weekend at Elliot's house. In her bed. I learned the weight and curve of each part of her body, each syllable of her skin. I called the hotel and told them I'd decided to go home early. I engineered a disappearance. Nobody could have found me, I had gone away, disappeared into what he thought was his own secret country.

I colonised her body voraciously, selfishly sucking up the fluids that spilled from her like water. Tracing the faint lines of her veins, the blind beat of those I couldn't see. I catalogued her. Silently and obsessively. When she slept I prowled through the house, memorising the titles of her books, her magazines, her taste in music. The fresh flowers she placed in improbably skewed hand-made pots around the house. I fossicked in her secret spaces, in the cabinets where she kept tubes of make-up and lotions, perfumes and cleansers and other half-magical concoctions.

Her kitchen cupboards were stacked with delicacies and exotic spices but bare of essentials. She fed me chocolate at midnight. In the morning she brought me a peach. It was so ripe it seemed to burst through the skin when she pierced it with her fingernail, the juice dripping onto her naked thigh. I laughed and bent to suck it from her skin, the tastes mingling together. She twisted the fruit open and fed it to me from the tips of her fingers, twisting them on my tongue, tracing the tops of my teeth and leaning in to taste the flesh and fluid that quivered on my lips.

She lay all afternoon in the garden with a book, glasses resting precariously on the end of her nose. She never seemed to wear clothes. Her nakedness was almost too much for me. I could have taken all day to travel the length of her palm, to find each road and lose it again. I wore a gown that became looser each hour, finally slipping from my shoulders beneath the fig tree that stooped to give me fruit from its branches. She read me passages of poetry — both good and bad — laughing at the bad and relishing the good, rolling the syllables over on her tongue.

Late in the afternoon she read to me from her journal, passages she wrote before she met me. Passages she wrote that morning when she came to my house:

I sense someone watching me but I cannot be sure. Is there someone in the house? Is it her? Could he be so stupid as to ask me to come knowing she will be here? Does he suspect me? Perhaps he has noticed that I move closer when he reeks of her, that dark and musky odour which almost overpowers his own. I am eager to scent her out. She is delicious, as rancid and feral as a wild cat. Perhaps this is part of his game, to tease us each with the other, to make us complicit in his strange life. I long to see her, to touch her skin and bite gently at her lip. Somehow I wished that she had been there and not him. His hands were still cold from the milk he had been carrying when he ran his palm over my thigh. Her hands would be warm. She would be capable of holding me.

At two in the morning I woke. The house was quiet. I went into the garden and stood beneath the fig tree, fruit rotting sweetly on the ground, and looked up through the branches into the sky. The moon was almost round. I'd forgotten to measure the days. My body had not yet started to bleed again since Sara was born and I felt cut off from the calendar. This seemed proper to me. The timeless, watery existence of a newborn child and its mother did not belong in the same calendar as those who woke and slept in twenty-four-hour rhythms; day and night, dark and light. Instead we loped from one feed to another, one stumbling inexact moment to the next. Catching sleep in batches or notes, rushing at it and grabbing it in selfish handfuls or lying awake and sleepless all through the night, even when Sara was sleeping. I had tried to measure time against clocks or calendars, against some concrete thing outside myself, but somehow they were always wrong. Days and nights simply slipped away into nothing or piled up at the bottom of the garden, unseen until I stumbled on them in my rush to be somewhere else, somewhen else. I had replaced the calendar of my body's blood with the rhythms of milk. The suck and swell of my mother-self. I cupped each of my breasts in my hands and weighed them. They were still heavy with milk, but lighter than they should have been, especially when she was not here to empty them. I rolled a nipple between my fingers, teasing the milk ducts until the milk came down in a thin blue rush. I remembered what it felt like to have my daughter at my breast, to have her hand resting on my skin. My breasts yearned for her gulping, indelicate suck. They felt thin and light, as purposeless as a basket full of holes.

Sunday afternoon Elliot fell asleep in the garden, curled around a book and a small basket of fruit she'd been picking. 'I have to go home,' I said. 'I have to see my daughter.'

She sat up and looked at me, her sleepy eyes flickering over my face in confusion. 'I don't understand,' she said.

'Sara needs me.'

'Are you going to bring her here?'

'Is that what you want?'

She smiled at me, seeming relieved, and leant forward to catch my bottom lip between her teeth. 'Silly you,' she said, 'of course you can come. Stay as long as you like.' I watched her stretch as my stomach fell. Open and empty. *As long as I liked*, meaning *not forever.* I opened my mouth to speak, to protest, to beg, but I couldn't find the words. Didn't have the heart, the strength, the will. When she finished stretching she looked at me and saw my expression, my terrified face. 'What's wrong?'

'I'm not sure,' I said. 'I thought we had something. I thought you loved me.'

'I do,' she purred, 'oh honey, I do, but I want children too, you know. Someday.'

'We could do that. There are ways.'

She shook her head and I felt the coldness of the afternoon spreading through me. The cool grass chilling my palms. I wanted to shake her. I wanted to make her understand how perfect this was — us — but she wasn't thinking about us. She was thinking, already, about another life where she was married to a beautiful man and they had perfect children and he loved her and she loved him and it was all so perfect, so easy, and I didn't belong there.

'I don't understand,' I said, shaking my head, but I was lying. I understood that I didn't belong there any more, that I never had. I had wanted something real that I could hold onto. I had wanted the whole deal. The Romantics Package, including *Forever* and *I Love You* and *I'll Always Love You.* The white picket fence.

'You'll still come back?' she said. 'I don't want this to be over yet.'

I rested my palm on her shoulder, tracing the dip and curve of her waist and hip. I shook my head, already feeling myself turning away.

229

Already heading home. I bent down to kiss her. She didn't stir. Didn't move to stop me, to hold me.

I went to the house to collect the handful of things I had brought with me. I heard the first few drops of afternoon rain begin to fall. As I walked into the lounge room I saw her standing on the verandah, watching me through the sliding glass door. She placed her small hands, flat-palmed, against the glass. I could see every crack, each line between the pink-white expanses of skin. The rain pooled in the spaces between each finger and spilled in rivulets from the heel of her palm. Such small hands. Too small to hold me.

I watched her slip her hands down to her pockets. I saw her shift uncertainly on her bare feet. She looked smaller than I ever thought she was before, like a child. The rain soaked through her thin dress. Her skin was wet. If I had kissed her again she would have tasted like rain.

I do not know
who I was when I did those things
or who I said I was
or whether I willed to feel
what I had read about
or who in fact was there with me
or whether I knew, even then
that there was doubt about these things

— Adrienne Rich, *Dialogue*

When I arrived at the house it was quiet. I walked down the side, through the high gate near the laundry door and straight out into the yard, past the windows of each room. No lights were on. In the backyard a pale block of light spilled from the kitchen door into the shadows of the verandah but I couldn't hear anything. I sat on the bottom step to take off my boots and placed them neatly — heel to heel and toe to toe — beneath the railing. As I stood up and walked over to the kitchen door I could see Callum sitting at the table. He had Sara in his arms and was feeding her from a bottle. They both looked content. She had her hand wrapped around one of his fingers and was watching him. Every now and then she stopped sucking to smile around the teat in her mouth.

I heard someone else in the house. Someone in sock feet walking down the hall towards the kitchen. Jason walked across behind Callum towards the kitchen window. I took a careful step backwards and held my breath as he filled the kettle in the sink.

'Do you want one?' he said, and I almost answered before I heard Callum and realised that he wasn't speaking to me, that he hadn't seen me.

'She's nearly finished this and then I'll put her back to bed.'

'What time is it?'

Callum looked over her round body to his watch, 'About eleven. I don't think she'll wake up again before seven.'

'I'll make up another one and then if she does wake up, I'll feed her.'

Jason made two cups of coffee and a bottle of formula. He sat down opposite Callum at the table and watched Sara. She had let go of the bottle and was smiling across the table at Jason. The two of them were making baby faces at her. Jason leant across the table and tickled the bottom of her foot, which she pulled up towards her belly in delight. I heard her laugh, the soft, almost garbled sound of it, mixing with the scent of the garden at night, wet with dew. It looked odd, somehow, to see two men at a table with a baby. At the same time I didn't move inside to join them. I couldn't break up the rhythm of their conversation, or their play. I stood in the dark of the verandah wondering what time the next train left to go back to the coast. How long Elliot would let me stay with her. I wanted to go back. To run away. My daughter didn't need me. Looking through the window I could see Jason holding out his finger for her to wrap her hand around, and it seemed so natural. He seemed happy, something I couldn't ever remember seeing in him before. He had been content, at times, or faintly victorious. Proud. But this was something else. I barely recognised him. I didn't want to walk in and break it — that moment. Cal's face was round and warm again, almost healthy. They seemed so prime time, so supernaturally adept and confident with Sara. I wanted to break into the room and take her in my arms and run, and keep running as far and as fast as I could. But she would cry. She would wail. She would batter her fists against me and I would be bruised again. Black and blue. I wouldn't know — as suddenly and mysteriously as they did — how to comfort her. How to make her smile. I hated them — both of them — for the warm light that spilled through the window. For their easy smiles and the clean kitchen and the row of bottles sitting rinsed on the sink. I hated them for making her smile. It was obvious they didn't need me. She didn't need me.

I turned away from the window. As I stepped onto the ground I heard a stair creak behind me. I stood still and held my breath, wondering how loud the sound had been, whether it had carried from here to the kitchen. It didn't seem to have, so I bent forward and pulled my boots out from under the stairs. I was in the process of pulling my boot up over my sock when I heard the back door open.

'So you finally decided to come home,' he said. I stood quietly, still facing away from him into the garden, as I turned this idea over in my head. *Home. Finally.* I wondered whether it would be possible to say something about his absences, his lover, his home. Was it possible to say to him, *finally*, when he had been, just seconds ago, calm and fatherly and gentle? I felt him come down the stairs and place his hand on my shoulder, the fingers gripped so firmly that the tips were turned in under the bone. I heard Callum call out to him from the kitchen, but he didn't answer or turn around. Instead he leaned closer, his face pressing into mine.

How long had I been away? This question gained weight. Each syllable was so important that I needed to take them one by one and turn them over in the palm of my hand. Had I been away long enough to shift from being a woman he could no longer approach to someone he could? Long enough that Sara's flesh was no longer a part of mine? Long enough that the time she spent inside my body had grown hazy with distance? I put my hand over my belly, trying to remember what it felt like to feel her tumbling beneath my skin, how it felt to be one body, to have the borders between us seem as fluctuating and uncertain as a shoreline. I saw her in Callum's arms with the bottle tipped to her mouth. Her plump pink cheeks resting against him, her body curled in to the warmth of his chest, the beat of his heart, the dust-dry smell of his skin. I had stayed away too long. She had become someone separate from me — someone other than the child whose body turned darkly inside my own. We were no longer two women. I couldn't hold her to my breast anymore. The milk was almost gone, dried up. She sucked willingly at the bottle, content to let the synthetic stuff slip into her. She would not turn automatically when my nipple grazed her cheek. She would not cry to be in my arms, wanting to be near the smell of milk that was already fading from my skin. She would not turn to me in bed and nuzzle against my sleep-warmed skin. And he knew this. She had become something I had hoped she would never be; the kind of daughter I once was. A child who draws comfort in a father's arms.

'Aren't you going to say anything?'

'Like what?'

'Like where you've been, for a start.'

'You know where I've been. Callum knows.'

'Don't play games with me.'

'You're the one who plays games.'

'Well, that makes two of us, doesn't it?'

We were both standing now, him on the top step and me on the ground. His mouth was clenched. I saw Callum come out the door behind him with Sara sleeping in his arms. 'Hey,' he said, 'it's late, Sara's just gone to sleep.'

'What the fuck does she care about what Sara needs. She ran off without even a word.'

'Callum knew what was going on. Everyone knew except you. You weren't here. You're never here.'

'I don't have to be here. I won't change my life because of what you want.' I could feel my body bristling with anger at him. At Sara for sleeping so peacefully, for not needing me anymore. I was angry at all of them for being so closed off from me. None of them needed me. Not even Elliot with her soft mouth. Even she wanted him instead of me, and watching him — his self-assured, self-righteous face — I felt everything build into a huge hot ball in my stomach. How could she want him? How could she stand to have him touch her? What could he possibly do or say to her that made her feel anything at all? He was so arrogant and cruel. He felt nothing. Everything he did, even in his sleep, was part of some monstrous calculated strategy he had for keeping control. He didn't know what it was to be loving or caring. It was all some perverted performance. How had any of us ever believed he cared about us? Cal and Sara and Elliot and I were just pawns in his little power games. He didn't need me and I wanted to be rid of him.

I felt the heat, the sweat, rise in my hands. I remembered the phone ringing in Elliot's kitchen and not answering it. I could feel all the words pushing at my teeth, tumbling over each other until my tongue stumbled. The noises scratched at my throat as they rushed past. I wanted to leave, but I couldn't stand the thought of leaving her with him and I couldn't imagine taking her with me, she was so content. She seemed so safe. Had I seemed safe and content? Had I been a happy child — or at least one who others saw as well cared for?

Jason's face in front of mine was close — so close I could see each pore of skin, each follicle of eyebrow hair. The exact shape of his cheekbones and mouth. Even this close and this angry he seemed oddly perfect. His skin was clear and fine-pored, his chin smooth, his hair freshly washed. He even smelt clean. I stumbled away from him and he came after me, his body so firm I saw his footprints press into the earth. His eyes were sparking and the tiniest drop of spittle moved over his lip as he talked. Each word growing on the last. We were standing in the garden, our bodies braced against the air between us. I didn't know anymore what I was saying, or what he was saying, only that my voice was stretching over his. I saw it like a flood of water spilling into his face, rising above his mouth and nose. I saw him gasping for air, drowning in it. Clear ice-blue water, as cold as the harbour at night. My throat was raw with the effort; I felt my body held tight, each cell as firm and fragile as glass, trembling in the pure rush of words.

It wasn't until he placed his hand on my arm that I noticed Callum had come down the stairs and was standing beside me. 'She's asleep,' he said, his voice soft and astonished.

I looked down at the child in his arms, wondering what he meant by this. Did he want me to see her and wonder at the odd beauty of her sleeping face, or to remember the hormonal rush of love a child deserves, or just to tell me *shush, not now*? I stared at her, suddenly silenced. All three of us stood looking at her, sleeping peacefully in his arms in the middle of the night in the garden. And then I began to see it, as if the idea slowly congealed out of the black air. Something not quite what I had seen before. Her little face turned up towards the stars was as still and calm as an empty room. Her mouth was slightly open, a tiny bead of sweat on her upper lip.

She was asleep, I realised. She was sleeping in the middle of a storm of noise. I clapped my hands above her face and Jason grabbed at my wrists, saying, 'You'll wake her.' And then he stopped still and looked at her. She hadn't stirred. She hadn't even frowned or turned away in her sleep. I leant down close to her, my hair spilling over her pale yellow blanket, and screamed into her face.

I ran into the house, the two men standing looking after me. I pulled my flute from under the bed and raced up the hallway, piecing it together as I went. When I reached the bottom of the stairs I was already playing. I blew each note carefully. I piled them up against each other in long knotted strings, a confused mass of arpeggios and

237

melodies and anything else, everything I could think of, everything I could remember. I thought of my mother, leaning over the cradle to play for me, her long-fingered hands settling gently over each key. I remembered myself lying beneath her, caught up in the winding spell of each note threaded onto an invisible string, following as she strung them up like Christmas stars around my room. I remembered reaching for them, wanting to hold each precious cell of sound in my warm hands, wanting to swallow them, wanting to feel each note beat in my gut. And here was my daughter, as still and silent as the grave.

My heart beats at around seventy-eight beats per minute. It was the first thing my mother taught me to hear. She held me against her breast and placed a fingertip on my knee and tapped out the beat of her own body on mine. When I had mastered this, and could tap out the beat of her heart without too much trouble, she said it was time to listen to my own heart. She came into my room early in the morning, before I had woken up, and just as I was about to open my eyes she placed her hands over them. Lie still, she said, it is the quietest time of the day. If you are careful and if you lie as still as you can you will be able to hear your own heart. She said this was the first, the one true rhythm and if I could learn it thoroughly everything else would follow.

When Sara was diagnosed as profoundly, quite possibly congenitally, deaf, I went to the library. I looked at medical books, found tracings of the heart beat, recordings which the keen student could listen to in order to discover the rhythms of the unhealthy heart. Arrhythmia and palpitations had been recorded and placed in small brown boxes on the library shelves, complete with commentary and notes.

Though I searched for hours, afraid to ask the librarians, I could not find the other diseases of the heart. No budding expert had gone into the field and recorded the frightened heart, with its desperate and loud banging, or the heart which had cast off its moorings and discovered the mouth. There were no greedy, lustful hearts, no cold hearts. I found no recordings listed under *despair* or *fecklessness* or *hard-hearted*. A search for a wooden heart turned up a treatise on the properties of heartwood, and whether or not it could be made to form the shape of a bowl.

There are no recordings of a broken heart.

I went back to the little pile of cassettes I had pulled from the shelves, to the earphones that plugged into the wall, and listened to a recording of a heart with a hole in it. There was no name attached to the recording other than that of the gentleman who had made it. I do not know if the heart belonged to a man, a woman or a child, whether the person whose heart was so sadly lacking was happy, whether they had ever managed to fall in love, but as I listened to that limping and uncertain beat I knew that it was possible; that even those whose hearts have been breached can beat.

She was six, maybe seven, months old the day I watched her rolling on the floor, trying to catch dust motes in her hands. Was it possible she heard something? Anything? When I placed my hands over my ears I could still hear, if only faintly. If I pressed as hard as I could there was still a faint swoosh swoosh. They say if you hold a seashell up to your ear you can hear the ocean, but what is it that you really hear? I heard a man on the radio who insisted that what you heard was really just yourself, echoing back through your own eardrums, that what you hear when you hold a shell to your ear is the beat of your own body. I looked at Sara, lying with her cheek against the floor, her face drawn in concentration. Could she hear herself? I stamped my feet on the floor and she looked up at me, startled. The floor in the hallway was timber, long boards of the stuff whose polish had long since worn away. I sat on the floor and drummed my heels against it and she copied me, laughing. It made me think of an old film I had seen where a room full of madwomen drummed their heels against the baths they were locked into. I got Sara to lie down beside me and did it again, holding my hand over her left ear as I pressed her other ear to the floor. Her plump cheeks trembled slightly and she smiled, bringing her hands up in front of her face and making one of the signs I had managed to teach her. *Mummy*, she insisted.

I moved my hand from her tiny ear, cupping her soft cheek in my palm and smiling. *Who am I kidding?* I thought. What point was there in teaching her to hear me drumming my heels against the floor until the skin was worn away and the timber cracked. Would I spend my whole life beating out rhythms for her on these old floors? Would I become like the girl in the red shoes, endlessly keeping the beat until I fell down dead of exhaustion, or wore my feet to bloody stumps?

It was quiet. Only Sara and I were in the house, I lay listening to the afternoon settle. I saw the dust motes and watched Sara's tiny hands held out to catch them. Her fingers were long and agile. She held up a fingertip and pointed at the dusty air. *Snow*, she said, her fingers rippling in the air. *Star.*

speak — my tongue is broken;
a thin flame runs under
my skin; seeing nothing

— Sappho

It's not that long ago I was my father's daughter. Although I never truly felt it at the time, looking back I see myself as having been somehow more whole, more complete, than I became. Uncontaminated. I remembered myself as an inviolable, monolithic creature but my daughter had penetrated to the very core of me and ruptured every organ. Now I was vulnerable, despoiled. A great wound had been opened in me, just below the sternum, that revealed my heart. Each time she cried I felt it wrench. The blood, which had only just begun to settle, to clot, would be torn away, rushing towards her in a blind and desperate *beat beat beat*. I had thought her birth would tear me open, but that the wound would heal. I looked at the still-livid scar, which remained tight-lipped, dark and sour. I couldn't see the other wounds, but I could feel them. My heart and gut were pulled to the surface, forever raw, forever vulnerable. When I stood up I felt my bones crack. I could hear them. I was wounded, wide open. She had her fingers buried in me, her tiny teeth tore at me. When she was sleeping the wounds settled sometimes, grew thin scabs, but then she would cry and I was newly splintered, ready to bleed.

Despite my father's intrusions there was always some other, more secret, impenetrable core he could not reach. I could close my eyes and will the tears away, will the pain away. I could draw myself — what I thought of as myself — back into some small corner that he could never discover. It was that inviolate territory that he sought out night after night. The same thing Jason wanted. Despite everything, despite almost drowning in fear every day, this one small thing held me up. I saw the desire for it in Jason's eyes and hands. The way he could not be still when he was near me. His eyes flicked over me, his hands clutched and loosened the unravelling air. He grew daily more like my father. The way he tried to dig deeper into me each time, scrutinising every inch of me, burrowing deeper beneath the skin, trying to hunt out and colonise every last cell and sinew of my body. I held my secret chamber close. Well-hidden. I was as careful and as secretive as a witch in hiding from the Inquisitor. He would not find me out. I would be as close-mouthed as they who, stretched on the rack or laced into boots that broke their feet, never relented. Buried deep inside them was a secret root no one could uncover. It sustained them, even in the flames. Jason would fail as my father had failed, growing steadily weaker. Finally unable to insist, falling flaccid and defeated against me. I waited for him patiently, ticking off the bruised hours.

Sara, too, was self-contained. Although no longer joined we seemed to share the same internal solitude. She learned to walk with quiet determination. Her silence made her appear more alert, more digni-fied than other children. At times she still frightened me; when she fixed me with her dark, measuring stare. Other times she stood at my side, not clinging but complicit, watching Jason warily. Or she lay in her cot, staring wide-eyed at the ceiling, seeming to concentrate on something. When I walked into the room she ignored me, intent as she was, and I found myself turning to look where she was looking, almost expecting the air to be coloured by her stare.

She was less than two feet tall but she extended the measure of my soul by miles, stretching me to my limits. Jason was unnerved by her, retreating into jocular cruelty or dry laughter at her strange silence, her half-formed gestures. He walked away, unable to meet her gaze or touch her cool skin.

She sat on my lap like a doll, curiously upright and straight-backed. Although she was soft and plump she didn't want to be held close, to be nursed in my arms. She struggled upright and stared straight ahead. She reminded me of those paintings of the Madonna and child where they both strike such awkwardly formal poses — their eyes fixed over the viewer's shoulder, negating their presence in a wilful appeal to that other, less knowable audience.

Jason took on a job with a transport company, driving trucks from

Sydney to Adelaide and Perth. He was gone for days, sometimes weeks at a time, and returned exhausted, his face grey. He grew weaker, his flesh pale except for his right arm, which was sunburnt and warm to the touch. He developed a sense of tired purposefulness that I had never seen in him before, and arrogance — revelling in telling me stories of the hapless bicyclists and learner drivers he had forced off the road.

The house seemed emptied of everyone's presence except my own and Sara's. Edna came over sometimes, but mostly I would go to her house, more and more ashamed of the state of my own. Our house was neat and clean, but I grew more certain that our life — the secret, silent viciousness of our love — revealed itself in the way our house breathed, in the timber floors and bare surfaces. The tables devoid of flowers or cloths. The empty rooms. The heavy, waiting silence that crouched between us when he was away. I worried that Jason would come home unexpectedly and find her here. I didn't want him to know we still talked. I didn't want him to know I confided in her, although I would never tell her the truth. Not the things he was afraid she already knew. Sometimes she looked at me sadly and I wondered if she did know. She put her hand on mine and kissed my forehead and I felt comforted, but also awkward and ashamed. I smiled and turned away. I returned her books and borrowed more, but only one at a time, since I had to hide them. I avoided mentioning the books I had never returned, the ones Jason tore up and threw away, insisting they were drivel and I was never to bring junk like that into his home again. Now I hid them, one at a time, at the back of my drawer, or between the mattress and the bed. I was careful to push them in as far as I could but still worried he would find them.

Cal grew more silent every day, more removed from the realities of my life that was filled with the milky desperation of mothering. I caught him watching me sometimes, leaning in a doorway with his thumbs hitched into the belt-loops of his jeans, his face still and sad. I would look up at him and smile; offer to let him hold her, play with her. She sat awkwardly on his lap. Despite their physical proximity they were as far removed from each other as the harbour is from the desert. He held her dutifully, not looking into her face, ignoring her simple attempts to speak to him with her hands.

The nurse at the child health centre gave me a number to call, and a woman from a deaf help association came over. Her job was to help people understand what their deaf child needs, how to cope. I made tea and we went out into the garden. Sara played on a blanket beside us as we talked. Carla was kind and friendly and I began to relax and enjoy her company. Our conversation wandered from Sara to other things, to books we'd both read. I made another pot of tea, and another. We laughed together. By the time Jason came home I felt relaxed and newly confident. Happy that her willingness to stay and talk was more than a professional duty. I felt as if I'd made a friend. When Jason walked into the garden I stood and kissed his cheek and introduced him. Those first seconds I could feel my body tight and raw, waiting for the sudden jar, but he was warm and loose, his smile easy. I couldn't see the pulse that beat in his temple on bad days. I was proud of how he looked that day; tall and strong and golden. He smiled and reached out a hand to shake hers, chatted to her briefly about his work and our Sara. *Yes*, he agreed, *she is a beautiful little girl.* He smiled and I let the tension that had flared in my neck flow away. He placed his hand on my arm and with an apologetic smile at Carla asked me to come inside for a minute. Carla said she'd watch Sara. When I looked back Carla had crouched down on the blanket beside Sara and was playing with her.

I walked up the back stairs and into the kitchen, turning to see Jason standing beside me. He yanked me into the house, pulling me into his arms until I had to tilt my head back to look into his face. I felt my warm, relaxed body weak with disappointment and an odd kind of relief. Lately, when he turned, I felt a sense of release, an end to the constant waiting, always wondering when it would come. The waiting was the worst part. My body ached at night from the constant pressure of holding myself in, pressing myself down inside my skin. When he lashed out I let go, felt it all slide away, the wound coil of my body flicking out towards him, unravelling into his fists. He pushed his face into mine, pulling me closer to him with his arms, his fist in the small of my back hot and resolute.

'Get that stuck-up bitch out of my house,' he said. 'If I ever see one of those freaks in my house again I'll kill you.'

I frowned slightly, unsure what he meant. What did he see in her that I didn't? What defect that shone through her clean face and neat hair and manicured nails? I heard something outside and glanced at the door, suddenly terrified that she would walk in and see us together. What would he do? Would he smile and hold my arm firmly behind my back, twisting to make sure I didn't say anything he disapproved of. Terrified to speak because I no longer knew what he wanted me to say. My back ached, low down where the pressure held me upright. I didn't want her to walk into that room, wasn't ready to see her face shift, her pity flash towards me and weaken me, make me small. I closed my eyes and held my breath and willed her to be gone. I couldn't bear to be laid open in front of her, have her see the horrors inside me that spilled out and poisoned the air whenever I dared to breathe. To speak.

There was no one there. I couldn't see out the window but as I closed my eyes I heard them faintly, I heard Sara's laughter. 'What will I tell her?'

'I don't give a fuck what you tell her just get her out of here and make sure she never comes back. I don't want you being influenced by people like that, people who don't know anything about us.'

Us. I nodded. Anxious to go. Ready to walk out into the garden and make excuses and pick up the baby and stroll into the house and lock the doors and never ever leave again. Don't open the door. Don't turn the key. Crawl under the bed and feel the floorboards cool and firm against my cheek. The familiar quiet. The careful emptiness.

There is only us here. Nobody else.

In a dry country, where the birds sing only once in their lives — and that once the day their hearts are broken — a woman came to live. She brought with her only a small suitcase with a broken handle. Inside the suitcase were her journal, her telescope and the handful of clothes she owned. She had come from a cold, wet country to marry a man she had never met. She was quite an adventurous woman. The man in question had been married before, although never successfully. His wives had all turned out to be a little too womanly, *which was a matter of great distress to him. Unfortunately for both the man and his former wives he lived in a time when his preference for male creatures like himself was both common and criminal.*

247

At any rate, the woman came with her small suitcase, and the two were married with as little to-do as possible, both being of a practical rather than a sentimental nature. They dined on cheese and dates and some rather ordinary wine and the man showed his new wife to her room. Although adventurous, she was relieved to find she was not yet to share his bed. When he left her alone she unpacked her telescope and her journal and placed them on a table she dragged to a position beneath the window. It was a bright still night and she spent many hours stargazing, noting the position of the stars in the unfamiliar sky.

The next morning, at breakfast, the man informed his wife that he would be flying out that afternoon on business. They talked briefly about the practical considerations of his departure — the time his flight was to leave, the date and time of his return. What little there was of their relationship could certainly wait until his return. He handed her the keys to the house, a great clanking ring with a key for each room. She thought it rather odd to have a house where each room required a key and, being not at all timid, she said so.

'It's an old house,' he said, 'with many secrets it wishes to keep.'

The woman laughed at his rather melancholy dramatics. 'We shall see about that,' she replied.

Her husband, quite startled, froze with his fork halfway between his plate and his palate. 'Wife,' he exclaimed, 'the secrets of an unfamiliar house are inscrutable. Perhaps it would be best if I took some of the keys with me?'

The woman looked at the keys that lay on the table between them, her curiosity aroused. 'You may leave them,' she said, 'and I shall undertake not to intrude on the secrets of your antique house.'

The man nodded, relieved, and pressed his fork into his mouth. The two discussed which keys she was free to use and which one in particular she was to leave unused. It was a small and rusty key.

Some of this story you will already know, so we can skip over the details of her curiosity growing and her wandering through the house, peeking into each room. It is perhaps enough to say that although the man's house was beautiful and large it had nothing in it of particular interest to his new wife. Eventually she found herself before the rather ordinary door of the room she was not to enter. Here again we can skip over her indecision and simply say that, of course, she opened the door and, of course, she stepped inside.

What did she find there? What do you think? She found the secrets of her husband's heart, all bound up together, and her own heart broke open and bled upon the key. For all our curiosity about love there is some part of it that is, oddly enough, destroyed by a complete knowing. Think of faith. Do you think that priests and mystics and such would give up their lives for love, in a quest to unravel the Lord, if they did not believe it was impossible? Think also of the Holy Grail, and the knights who quested in vain after the unattainable and unknowable thing. Love is all about, in some odd way, the struggle to understand a mystery, and yet its very mysteriousness enthrals us, holds us in its spell.

If you stand outside the room and are given the key and someone whispers to you, Open it, you will know everything there is to know about your lover, about love, *you should wait. Think carefully. If you know everything about the body, how it beats and moves and grows and decays, will you love it more? If you know everything about a poem or a story — if you pull it apart and it lies in tatters bleeding at your feet — what have you gained? Remember why you came here. Remember what it means to love carelessly, generously, eagerly, hungrily; a gourmet rather than a dietitian, a traveller rather than a mapmaker, a lover rather than an anatomist, a storyteller rather than a linguist.*

One morning I was standing in the kitchen looking out into the garden as I rinsed bottles in the sink. Sara was sleeping. She had been awake half the night. I was tired but I knew better than to fall asleep. I wanted to treasure this time alone, while the house was quiet, unfilled by her presence. I thought, *The house is empty.* I thought, *I am alone with my own thoughts at last.* I walked through the empty rooms of the house, my unfilled hands restlessly fidgeting with the seams of my dress. I thought to myself, *He has gone away.* I considered inviting Edna over for a pot of tea, Sara would wake soon and the dishes hadn't been done for days. There was a month's worth of newspapers piled up in a corner. The table was caked with Sara's breakfast cereal. A line of ants made its way across the counter, through a puddle of spilt honey and some sugar, to a crack in the tiles. No visitors, I didn't have the energy to clean it all up just for a few minutes' company.

In Callum's room I found little evidence of him. A small scattering of change. A lost sock beneath the bed. His smell only faint. He hadn't slept here for a long time. Perhaps days, perhaps weeks. He'd been so distant I hadn't even noticed when he slipped away. On the bedside table was a folded piece of paper with my name on it, covered by a fine film of dust. The keys to the van sat next to it.

I'm sorry. I guess things with Selene made me see finally that I wasn't capable of saving you. I know you think you didn't need to be saved, that you don't need to be saved now, either. But I'm your brother and I know you better than anyone else. I worried for a long time about whether I should just go. I tried to talk to you but you don't listen. You need to leave, Germaine. If I thought you would come with me I would ask you again, but I think that would be another mistake. I know that you have spent the whole time since we left home ignoring what happened, trying to just put it out of your head, but you can't. Some things can never be forgotten. They can only be survived. I thought it would be enough to leave, but it's not. I don't know what else to say except that I love you. I'm going home for a while. I have things to settle there, too. Perhaps one day when we are old we will shake our heads and tell Sara how foolish we were when we were young.

Cal

P.S. I've left you the van and caught the train home. Em says I can use the ute when I get there.

I folded the scrap of paper into my pocket, collected my flute from my room and walked out into the empty garden where the last of the mint straggled over the soil. The flute was cool and heavy in my hands. As I reached the end of the garden I looked out over the quiet harbour. Barely a breath of wind. No boats slicing across her impeccable surface. No ferries or hydrofoils or shoals of fish to disturb its inscrutable silence. I lifted the flute to my lips and closed my eyes, breathing in the scent of the harbour far below, the fresh salty tang of its body as it swelled and bellied into each cove. Breaking open on the rocks and sand of the shoreline. My mouth was dry, the notes mournful. I heard a gull croak far over to my left and raised a note to meet its cry. Behind me the empty house waited, and my silent child — the long days of silence and awkwardly fingered words that I was only beginning to be able to form. She would never listen to me play and I would never hear her speak. The gulf between us grew wider every day. She retreated into her silence, turned her back on me or closed her eyes when she did not want to listen. I had no stories to tell her, could not sign fast enough or agilely enough. Already her fingers were impatient with mine. At times she grabbed my hands and shook them, or placed them in my lap, as frustrated with my inarticulateness as I was with hers. I did not have anything to teach her that was not made of sound. Stories. Music. I felt each note somehow whittled in the air, sent to whom? Who was there to listen anymore? Each note was weighted with fear, with loneliness, with a soft but desperate *need* to be heard. My fingers were tight with anxiety, flexing against the awful silence that built around me. I wanted to speak. I wanted to be heard. If no one could hear me, if no one was willing to hear me, then what point was there in speaking, in playing? I may as well fall silent, too. Become as wilfully, terribly silent as my daughter.

These orange silences
(sunlight and hidden smile)
make me want to
wrench you into saying;
now I'd crack your skull
like a walnut, split it like a pumpkin
to make you talk, or get
a look inside

— Margaret Atwood, *Against Still Life*

We walked across the park scented with beach salt and barbecues and the sandpit desperation of other people's children: 'But I was here first, it's my swing, it's my turn, it's my bucket, it's mine, mine, mine, mine.' Families moved like flocking birds, separating around trees, around tables, and meeting seamlessly at the other end, stalking territory like frontiersmen. Spreading checked cloths and blankets and paper plates and eskies. The sharp-edged flowerbeds taut with light; no dead leaves, no drooping heads. The dangerous dunes, thick with dropped branches, were carefully barricaded behind wire fences. The ibis glared, their feathers torn and grimy, as Sara picked red seed-heads from the grass and filled her pockets. They tore the sand-spiced sandwich from her hands, her wet red face was startled and indignant. Later she was bored and sullen. The other children turned away from her mouth, her curious tongue that protruded between her lips. The hands that flickered at them. She sat beneath the yellow plastic slide with her hands flat on its underbelly. Laughing at their tumbling, rattling descents, their vibrations trembling at her fingertips. One child pushed her out from under the slide.

'Out out out,' he yelled.

She screamed at him, her tongue twisted and confused. He was astounded and repulsed by her noises and yelled at her with his hands fisted at his sides. She smiled. He pushed her and she slipped over. Tears slid down her red cheeks, sand-crusted snot congealing on her upper lip. At the bus stop she sat on my knee like a doll, her flat hair dry and pointed, her tap-washed face still filmed with grime and sand. Her fists patiently twisted in her lap. Trees whipped the bus-shelter

255

like rain or heat. They snapped on the corrugated tin roof that wanted, like me, to melt. Wanted to slide over onto the pavement, onto the fat old lady who peered down the road. The fat old lady whose varicose veins disappeared into her nylon thighs, who was desperate and late, whose watch did not keep the same time as bus-drivers and traffic lights. The sickle-spined palm whipped the perspex roof — snap, snap. The fat old lady. My daughter's twisted fist in my lap.

I imagined standing up, hitching the baby high on my hip, her plump thighs straddling me, her complacent hand on my breast. I imagined walking over to the kerb, stepping down onto the blacker black. Taking three steps, four, out into the traffic and bending down. Laying her down. The back of her thighs dimpling against the sticky bitumen. I pictured her sun-hat blowing away. Gone.

I imagined getting on the bus; no bag, no stroller, no bottle and dropped cap and one hand to count the change and not enough of it and scrabbling in the dried wipes and spilt milk and anxious rattles in the bottom of my bag and the fat old lady sighing and the bus driver's eyes rolling and the stroller folding like a tangle of coat hangers, only heavy and pinching as I lurch up the aisle, and the easing between knees that do not shift and the muttered 'sorry' and the sympathetic smiles of unsympathetic strangers and the banging of seats and dropping bottles and the ticket in her hand, in her mouth, and the ticket man looking out the window and fiddling with his badge and waiting for the ink on her mouth to dry and the person beside me who shifts and sighs and half-smiles as if to say *Useless young mother* as if to say *In my day* … only they never — hardly ever — say anything while they rustle their plastic bags full of clean new shopping and at the other end the health care nurse waits with her chart and her red pen and her starched white dress and her ladderless stockings and her flat-heeled sensible shoes and her ticks and crosses and patience and support and the crushed ticket and bits of biscuit pleated into the pages of the book which she picks out with her manicured fingernails before she smooths the page flat as best she can even though the pen won't work on the milk-stained food-stained sand-stained page and weighs the baby and measures the baby and smiles comfortingly at the numbers but not at my unironed shirt and the unwashed jeans and the lost shoe and when the baby starts to cry and

I just sit there waiting for her just for one second for one fucking second to shut up so I can breathe so I just take a breath while the strange sound unsettles the other mothers with their well-dressed disposable nappy babies with their clean bibs who cry like babies while she wails like a demented seal and the nurse says *Shush now* to the back of her rocking head that pushes at the bruised pit of my arm and I pull away and the nurse frowns and she just cries and cries and pushes her head into my skin, into my bones which snap in her tiny fists.

But when the bus pulled into the kerb I stood and hitched her up against my hip, gathered two shopping bags in each hand, change for the bus, the folded stroller held awkwardly under my arm. I could hardly breathe as I paid the bus driver two dollars and we took a seat. I wondered if he could tell. Could he tell? I watched his eyes in the rear-vision mirror as he pulled out into the road and I quickly looked away when he caught my eye. She was asleep. Silent. The sweat beading like pearls on her upper lip.

There is no charm against loving a child. At least none that I know of. But loving a child is a dangerous and frightening thing. Women have always known this. You see it in the shock of women who have just fallen in love with their child for the first time. Not necessarily the day they are born, or even a week later. Sometimes months pass, even years, and you think you are safe and then suddenly you feel it, buried inside you as surely as the worm that eats out the heart of an apple. You see it in their eyes as they huddle together at parties and playgroups, gathering comfort from gossip about their children's first teeth, first words, first smile. But it's there. Buried beneath all the easy sentimentality.

I remember my breast growing warm in the sun when I would sit outside to feed my daughter. It was a delicious warmth that spread from my smug bones. It was not the quick heat of lust but something else, a guilty, unnatural passion. Sitting there, feeling my womb clench as she sucked, feeling the blood gush out of my body in heavy clots as the milk let down (a rush unlike anything else I've ever known), I fell in love.

Like other mothers I have wrapped my daughter and myself in pastels, hoping to hide what I really felt. I wanted to be a Johnson & Johnson mum. I wanted to be soft and complacent and bovine and *safe*. I thought motherhood would be a retreat from the chaos of loving violently. But motherlove is nothing if not violent. How could it be anything else? All that pain and screaming and blood and sweat as your body heaves and cracks itself open to bring a child into the world. And that moment when you're lying there and you know, you just know, that this is what it's like to die, only you don't. Only you're alive and so is your child, but it's still there. That death. That fear. But also the acceptance of it, the giving in to it in order to pass through it. And your body is cracked open and you leak. The blood keeps flowing out of you for weeks afterwards, heavy, dark blood. And the milk flows down your still-distended belly in the shower, and you get the three-day blues, or worse, and the sobs rack you and the child whose hand and mouth clutch at you. And you look at her, really look at her, and breathe in that heady, heavy, earthy scent of her skin that still reeks of you, of the inside of your body. And you see her fists — her whole body — clenched against the outside world, against light and openness and the terrifying unfoldedness of her body. All that air. And you hold her tight and your body throbs as she sucks sucks sucks.

It is an awe-ful thing.

Late in the afternoon I was sitting at the table in the back garden with a cup of tea and a book; watching the garden shift in the late breeze, listening to the careful silence of our house while Sara slept. I heard the truck shift down through the gears and pull onto the side of the road, Jason's dark boots on the path, his body pushing at the silence like a pin. I stood up. Walked up the back stairs and filled the kettle.

I watched him through the kitchen window as he sat at the old chess table. His hair was stiff with dirt, his jeans black, his knuckles coated with grease. He was soft and pale with exhaustion, his eyes dark hollows in his face.

I lined the tray with a white linen cloth and put it on the bench near the fruit bowl. I scooped three measures of tea into the dented silver pot and placed it on the tray with cups and spoons and a small saucer of biscuits. I poured the boiling water over the leaves and fit the lid into its perfect groove. He looked up as the screen door clicked closed behind me, but his body stayed slack in its seat. I turned the pot three times before pouring. Two sugars for him, and a dash of milk in the frail china cup. He wrapped his huge hands around the cup awkwardly and sat staring into it.

I bathed Sara, washing each of her plump limbs carefully, tipping her head back to wipe the dirt from beneath her chin. She pushed at my hands as I washed her hair, gesturing angrily at me to stop. We played hide and seek with the face washers. I pushed her toys beneath the water and released them so that they popped up out of the water. She laughed and tried to catch them.

After the bath I sat her on the kitchen floor with a handful of toys while I peeled potatoes, the dirt making my hands a deep brown. I rinsed them under the tap and looked out at him, still sitting in the same place. His rough hands still curled around the cup. The day had slipped beneath its cool sheets. The morning glories closed up their blue umbrellas. I chopped vegetables and filled a stainless steel pot with water. Sara sat in her high chair watching me and chewing on a rusk. The faded linoleum thickened and set beneath my feet. Jason sat in the garden like one of the stunted shrubs that cling to the cliff-face.

I took the warmed plates out of the oven and set them on the table. I mashed a handful of vegetables for Sara and set them to cool on the windowsill in her red plastic bowl. While I served dinner he stood bleached and stolid in the shower. Sitting at the table he was thin and watery, his clean hair brushed back from a pale forehead. The pulse in his throat threatened to dislodge his silence, to whisper some beating indiscretion. We discussed the ordinary pieces of our lives, Sara's new tooth, the crack in the path where the weeds were flourishing.

'How was the drive?' I said. He looked at me, his fork resting on the edge of his plate.

'Okay, I guess.' His mouth curled and pursed around the fork, his teeth pushed into the soft meat. Sara forced a plump fist into her bowl and mashed potato against her mouth, sliding her hand up into her hair. A stalk of hair grew pumpkin-orange above her ear. 'Why can't she at least eat properly? She should be able to by now. I ate with a spoon at her age.'

'She's not you. The nurse said she might be slower at some things. She might just take a while, that's all.'

'That's bullshit.' He traced a smooth spiral on his plate with a piece of bread and pushed it into his mouth gently and precisely, his fingers were pinched together. He placed his knife and fork on the plate. 'She's a freak.'

I walked around to pick up his plate and he took hold of my wrist. Firmly. He pulled me down until our faces were level. His mouth was firm and dry and hollow and my back ached, my head ached. He pushed his mouth against mine and bit at my lip until a tiny slip of blood clung to my teeth. He leaned past me to stare into Sara's face. 'Freak,' he said, 'fucking stupid little freak.'

'Don't do that,' I said sharply.

'Why the fuck not?' He leant close to her again, his voice rising in a clear bell-like song, 'Freaky little deaf girl, mama's little door-post. Stupid little fuckwit.' She smiled at him, holding out her fist full of food to him and laughing as he took her whole hand in his mouth. His pale eyes were keen and insistent. 'Speak,' he said. He looked so intently at her, as if he meant to make her wet slippery mouth suddenly form clear English syllables. She burbled pumpkin-laced nothings. I rinsed and stacked the dishes in the sink. He sat waiting. 'Where's the fruit?' he said. He liked to eat an orange after dinner. He used to say it cleansed his palate and aided digestion.

'There isn't any.'

'Isn't today your little shopping expedition?' His mouth was thin against his teeth as he pushed a fingernail between them. 'I gave you the money, Germaine.'

'There wasn't any fruit.'

'No fruit? No oranges?' His mouth hesitated, slipped. The words formed sharp angles against his tongue.

I watched the dishes slip into the soapy water.

'I told you to buy oranges. I rang you especially to tell you I'd be home and to buy a few things. I gave you five fucking hundred dollars before I left. I told you exactly what to do. Weren't you listening?' His hand was clenched beside the plate. Sara's fat fists were pistoning into her red plastic bowl.

'There weren't any in the trolley.' I waited as his silence pushed at the small of my back like period pain. Even when he was quiet, and I turned my back to him, I felt the weight of him; felt the heaviness of his presence in this room, this house, this street. He didn't move but I sensed the threat that was barely contained in him. He was coiled tight and tense, ready to flash out and strike at me in less time than it takes to blink. If I said the wrong thing, if I used the wrong inflection, the wrong word, he would be close. He would spring from his chair and have me in his arms, in his hands. I closed my eyes and breathed carefully.

He spoke slowly, as if I did not speak the same language as him. 'What do you mean there weren't any in the trolley? Why didn't you put them in there?'

I shook my head slightly as I pulled Sara from her high chair, mopping at her mess roughly with a cloth and carrying her up the hallway to her bedroom. Sara's fat dimpled hands pushed at mine as I changed her clothes; wrapped her in a warm nappy fresh from the drier, a clean white singlet, and a soft yellow bunny-suit with little pop-buttons all the way from her feet to her chin. I licked my lip clean and dabbed at it with the edge of the singlet I had taken off her. I kissed her good night, turned out the light and left the door ajar.

Jason was standing in the garden, smoking a cigarette. It was the only thing I could see of him from inside, just a vague shadow with a tiny point of light that glowed bright and then dull. I cleared the table and wiped it clean. I could see his cigarette moving in the dark, the tiny spark of it threatening me. I could feel him waiting for me, knew that the longer I stayed inside, the longer I resisted his silence, the more precarious my position became. He would wait until I came to him, until I willingly submitted to his questions, his interrogation. I dug my hands into my pockets as I walked outside.

'She's gone to sleep?' he said as I came to stand beside him. I nodded absently at him, looking out over the garden's edge at the lights of a ferry crossing the heads. It was moving through the spangled wake of the moon. As he turned towards me I saw his face bruised by the darkness. I tried to frame what happened in my mind. Tried to make it perfect. Tried to remember how to speak, how to string together words into sentences, sentences into paragraphs. I opened my mouth and felt my tongue swell uncomfortably. One wrong word and his hand would lash out. I felt the heat in my cheek, the hard hot flash. His hands were ready, balanced at the end of his wrists in expectation.

'There just … There weren't any oranges in the trolley.' He rolled his eyes at me and drew on his cigarette, looked out over the cliff. I saw his body shift and flinch. I spoke quickly, as quickly as I could, trying to hold off the moment. 'I did go shopping. I took the list. I had Sara in the front of the trolley and we were just going up and down each aisle. She was wriggling around a lot, though — you know how she hates to sit still in those things. She kept standing up and trying to jump out into my arms and then trying to get things off the shelves or out of other people's trolleys. Anything at all. Salt and paper plates and dish liquid and fabric softener and cartons of sour cream and … well, anything at all. It was a bit confusing. I kept having to put things back on the shelves and putting things in the trolley at the same time — the things you said. Sometimes she would take off into the next aisle, because she got down out of the trolley. Once she crawled under the shelves and I had to practically lie down on the floor to get to her and I was calling her name, but of course that didn't do any good, so I was banging on the floor. Must have looked a real idiot. Anyway, we made it to the checkout and I wasn't really paying much attention to what I was doing because I was trying to stop her from getting everything off the rack near the checkout. You know how they put all those lollies and stuff right there, where she can reach. But I was stacking it all up on that little moving thing and I realised it was all wrong, everything was wrong. It was the wrong trolley. We were both tired, so I thought it didn't matter that much — most of the stuff we needed was there — and there were some nice things, unusual things. Things we've never tried before.'

I looked over at Jason. He took a drag on his cigarette and then flicked it over the cliff-edge. I watched it tumble down through the trees like a firefly suddenly falling out of the sky. I felt him move beside me, just slightly, and the tension rose in my shoulder blades.

From the corner of my eye I saw him raise his arm behind me and I held myself still, determined not to flinch. But his hand fell on my shoulder softly — as gently as a lover — and I felt his body shaking beside me, trembling slightly. Then I heard it, the soft tumbling air coming up through his chest, rattling on his lips until it spilled over. He leant his head on mine and I felt the laughter spill from him.

'What is that noise now? What is the wind doing?'
                        Nothing again nothing.
                                'Do
You know nothing? Do you see nothing? Do you remember
Nothing?'

— T. S. Eliot, *The Wasteland*

Outside the house the street was quiet. The afternoon hush seemed to spread from the sulk of flowerbeds and dry bottle-brush trees along the kerb. Every now and then a car passed — the noise of it muted by the closed windows and drawn shades of the room. Sara was sleeping, her long bones warming in the afternoon sun. Her cheeks were flushed with dreams. I saw an old man turn into the street on the opposite side of the road. He held his body like a prayer, like something thin. I remembered the well-thumbed hymnals in the church pews on Christmas Day. Their pages so thin they were almost translucent. The many fingers that had held and turned them, the mumbling prayers whispered into them. He seemed lost, his head casting about to peer at the numbers on drooping letterboxes and dusty kerbs. He looked up at the road, checking for traffic before he crossed to our side of the street. The way his arms were held away from his body made my breath catch. The way he walked so low. The way his hands were held just so. His face was worn and familiar. I remembered the crease where I used to run my fingertips along the skin from brow to chin. My father.

I leant back from the window, letting the curtain fall like a bridal veil across my face. I watched him bend and peer at the letterbox next door, and then at ours. He unfolded a piece of paper from his pocket, a folded and re-folded scrap of blue, and compared it to the house, holding it up like a painter's brush and squinting against the sun. He stood at the gate carefully folding the paper and easing it into his pocket before swinging the gate open. It stuck halfway. He edged through and walked up the path. I moved back from the window, sliding along the wall as he bent and put his hand to the glass, looking in beneath the arch of his palm. He stood in front of the door and placed the palm of his hand against the warm wood. *Is this the house?* he seemed to be asking, *is this the place?* and I could not reply.

He knocked lightly, his head tipped to one side, listening to the wind beginning to rise to him. After several minutes he stepped back and I let slip the threads of the house's silence. He took a step away from the door, his hands absently resting on his hips, just as he used to when he was watching the cattle come loping through the paddock towards him. Distracted and thoughtful at once. He turned to walk back down the path — back out into the street and the soft lazy day. I imagined him walking from here to the main road, the road that slips quietly down towards the harbour, and then further. Walking and walking until the path beneath his feet crumbled and disappeared into soft red soil. But he didn't. He stopped at the edge of the verandah and looked off to the side of the house. I saw him hesitate and then he turned to the left. As he moved around the house I followed him. Past the windows of the empty front bedroom where nobody slept because the noise of the street couldn't be kept out, past the bathroom with its cracked and mottled glass, past the bedroom and the kitchen windows until he was standing in our tangled garden. I stood at the kitchen door watching him. I remembered the night I had watched him from our house. The night I saw him dancing; how his feet had raised the soil until it danced around him, touching his pale skin. The red ghost of my mother.

Quietly I padded barefoot back through the house and picked my flute up from where it was lying in the front room. I ran my hand over it, settling on my mother's key. I moved back through the house and stood again in the kitchen, to watch him through the screen door. At first I couldn't see him. I thought he must have given up after all, must have slipped away, but then I saw a movement at the far edge of the garden and I realised he was sitting on the stone benches of the chess table. I let myself out the back door; careful not to let it slam behind me, easing it gently closed. I placed the flute at the edge of my lip and began to play.

So careful, so quiet were the notes. The soft strains of a lullaby, a child's tune. The first thing I remember my mother playing for me, the first thing she taught me to play. I walked slowly through the yard, skirting the knot garden and our fallen angel, the hidden nest of spent mint and basil, the flourishing tangle of citronella. As I moved beneath the jacaranda I saw his shoulders move higher but he didn't turn around. I played gently, easing the sound into the garden, between the shadows of shifting leaves and falling flowers, my bare feet like cats amongst the purple fall of blossoms. He turned his head to the side and I moved out, carefully sidestepping the bite of the bougainvillea so that I could see his face. This was what I wanted, right then, to see him first. To see his face complete.

As I reached him he turned towards me and my breath stuttered, the notes falling helplessly into each other, like children in a chain that stumbles. He was so old. His skin so creased and soft, so paper-thin. His hair was thinning, the soft curve of his forehead more pale and mottled than I remembered. I clutched at words, at anger and resentment, but I couldn't feel them. Those things were for my father; they were for Jack, not for this man who was him and not-him.

We stayed just so, neither of us certain how to end or to prolong this moment. How to extend and finish it. Something I began as a game — hide and seek, blind man's bluff — seemed now ridiculous and childish. I did not want to make myself a child again, especially not then, especially not with him. I wanted so much for him to see me as a woman. I wished that Sara would wake — that I could have brought her out to the garden and put her to my breast. To be calm and beautiful, to *be* somehow my mother — to make him see that in me — but I could not. Instead I prayed for her, for both of us, that she would sleep through this moment. I hoped fervently that she would not wake while he was there.

I made tea and we sat at the table, a fresh white cloth spread over it, each of us uncertain. He sat carefully, as if he had to be careful how he held himself now, conscious of each bone, each filament of flesh placed just so. I poured the tea and watched his mouth as he tipped the cup towards himself. Even his mouth was softer, the edges blurring into the once-burnt flesh around it. Here, in this green garden balancing over the harbour, he seemed too dry. He was dust-like and uncertain — his power suddenly distant.

As he began to speak I noticed the softness in his voice. I had to lean in to hear him. The voice that used to belly out across paddocks — calling lost horses and dogs to return, startling the flocks of black-winged birds from trees — was barely audible over the rush of the wind and the harbour and the unheard breath of my baby sleeping. I leaned my elbows on the table and took my cup between my two hands, listening to him tell me about his home.

'Cal said you might come back if you knew about Emma,' he said. 'She'd not been well, not well at all. The rain did us in. It came too late. That's always the way. The soil came in the window. Once there was one breach the house gave up and the mud came in at every opportunity. Nearly an inch thick in places. Everything turned red. I found Emma eating the soil in the yard. Handfuls of it. It was wet in her mouth like blood. She lay down one afternoon and never got up again. Half the cattle are gone. I found an old bull stuck in the mud and had to shoot him dead. When I went back he was gone, sunk beneath the soil. The whole place's gone under. She died on the Thursday. She was thin and pale when I found her. Thin as a line. They took her away. Cal's there now, doing what he can to keep the place going.'

All of it gone. Not the physical kind of loss but something worse, something he couldn't survive. He had tried to imprint himself more permanently in the reality of his body and the earth, inhaling flesh with every breath of air and dust, layering himself in thick, soft folds. But he'd been betrayed by the soil, great clouds of it gusting through him. The land he thought belonged to him had become the only thing he remembered, or that remembered him.

His conversation was stilted. He forgot, halfway through a sentence, what it was he wanted to say. His voice died off in the middle of a thought, the thread lost or forgotten. He talked to me of yesterday, today, tomorrow, last week and ten years ago all in the same breath, as if they were all the same moment. His hands flickered uncertainly, grasping at things and letting them go. He clutched the teaspoon, left pale stains on the tablecloth. He spoke to me about the colour of the soil, the way it seemed to breathe, the way it folded around him during a storm, as if she was holding him again. He left off halfway through a sentence, lost in contemplating the shape of his hand laid flat on the table. He reached over and placed his palm face up in front of me. He said, 'See, your mother has deserted me. You have to come home.'

I shook my head. 'I'm never coming back. She's gone. The only thing left is to remember she always loved you.'

'Not at the end.' He shook his head, laid his hands flat on the table. 'She couldn't love either of us in the end.'

'That's not true. She loved us. She loved *me*. She always loved me.'

He looked up at me. His blue eyes the only thing still clear in his washed face. 'You don't remember, do you?'

I leaned back in my chair and turned my head so that I did not have to see him watching me. 'I don't know what you mean.'

'She didn't just die, Germaine. She killed herself. Because of us. Because she found us together that day.'

I shook my head. It couldn't be true. I remembered the first time with him. I remembered the day she died. The nurse. My mother's thin white body beneath the sheet. I looked down at his hands that trembled as he reached towards me. I pulled away. I knew he was wrong. I knew it as surely as I knew anything. He was old and his mind had grown as frail as his bones. I looked out over the clear blue harbour, watching the boats dipping into its wet skin. It was all so long ago. So far away. I was not that little girl anymore. I had become a woman of water. A mother, like her. Somewhere in the long moment between her death and this moment she had shifted, had become someone he did not recognise. And so had I.

I knew I should have felt something. But I couldn't. I took his hands in mine and rubbed the edge of my thumb over his palm, tracing the deep lines of his heart and head. His hands were soft and clean. They were not the horned and thickened palms of my father, his red-stained hands with dust built up beneath the fingernails. This close to him I barely recognised this man. We walked out into the garden. I wanted to shake him, to rattle him between my hands and demand that he reveal himself, as if he were a magician wrapped in a cloak of old age, of fragility. I showed him the harbour far below us. He stood a foot in front of me and I placed a hand between his shoulder blades, feeling him breathe beneath my fingertips. His breath was weak and inconstant. For a moment I thought I could push him and watch him fall. He was so light he would break up as he fell;

271

pieces of him as light and flat as paper would flutter on the air as they drifted down to the rock and the harbour. Confetti. Ashes. He half-turned his face towards me and I saw his forehead, with the grey hair receding behind it. His brow spotted with age, his eyes sunk in darkly wrinkled sockets. I dropped my hand to my side and turned away. Back to the house.

'Where are you going?' he asked me.

I turned around and looked at him standing there. 'It's time for you to leave,' I said. 'We don't have anything more to say to each other.'

'I'm your father,' he said.

I shook my head and looked past him. 'No,' I said.

As I turned away he called out to me again but this time I didn't turn around, although I stood with my back to him to hear what he was saying. 'Where am I supposed to go?' he asked, and I shrugged my shoulders and walked up the back stairs into the house, locking the door behind me.

A man lived in a stolen country. He was lonely and frightened. His body had begun to wither and his cattle to wander. At night he walked through the endless rooms of his home in bare feet, running his hands over the cold stone walls. In the morning he found his three daughters sunbathing in the garden. They lay with magazines over their faces. He sat down among them and turned down their stereo. The three girls peered out from their Cleo *and* Cosmopolitan *and* Vanity Fair. *He looked at their curious faces and began to weep.*

One of his daughters placed a hand on his shoulder and made the same noises his wife made for her when she was a tiny baby. One of his daughters placed an arm around his waist, as his wife was wont to do when they were courting. Her eyes were closed as she stroked his back with her sun-warmed palm. One of his daughters collected his tears in glass jars and placed them in a row by his side. 'What is troubling you?' she said.

'I am old,' he replied, 'and my wife is dead. My body is breaking. It is time for me to leave. I cannot help but remember how it was when she left. I had loved her all my life, but I didn't know how much until she died.'

The daughter nodded her head as her sisters crooned and stroked. 'Go on,' she said.

'I want to know how to measure love,' he said. 'I want to know how much I have been loved before I die.' The three daughters looked at their father. Their dead-already, grieving-already father whose love for them could only, by implication, be measured by their deaths. With their arms around him and their heads inclined they wondered what kind of disease love is that it must be measured by absence.

He gave them a week to decide how much they loved him and he agreed that he would give up the thing, whatever it might be, that each of his daughters loved as much as him.

The first daughter came to him (I do not mean his first-born daughter, she was only his first in the sense that she made up her mind more swiftly than the others, as was her wont, and came to him before her siblings). She believed she knew about love; she had read the magazines she draped over her face to prevent freckles, she had done all the quizzes they contained and passed with flying colours. He was sitting in his favourite chair reading Hemingway. When he looked up his face was wet. She knelt beside his chair and took his hand in her own. 'Father,' she said, 'I love you as much as the ocean.' Her father nodded and vowed never to go down to the ocean again. Never to even touch the sand. Never to go out in his boat to fish and dream. Never to stand and look out to the sun as it rose out of the ocean's smooth surface in the morning.

The second daughter came to him. She believed she knew about love; she had fallen for the boy at the local video store. She had watched all the movies he recommended to her and wept for the lovers they contained. He was sitting in his chair reading Chekhov. When he looked up his face was wet. She knelt beside his chair and took his hand in her own. 'Father,' she said, 'I love you as much as the stars in the sky.' Her father nodded and vowed never to look at the stars again. Never to even go out at night. Never to wander in his garden and stargaze and dream. Never to stand and watch the stars as they faded out of sight in the morning.

The third daughter came to him. She believed she knew nothing about love, doubting whether it even existed. He was sitting in his favourite chair reading Kafka. When he looked up his face was wet. She knelt before him and took both his hands in her own. 'Father,' she said, 'I love you as much as salt.' Her father stared at her, wondering what to make of this. He had never been a great lover of salt.

What became of him? The man who gave up oceans and stars and salt? He missed the ocean and the stars but found other things to distract him. He studied the earth, grew flowers, played chess and restored old clocks. As for the salt thing. Well, his food was bland but at first it did not bother him. Then he went blind from a lack of salt. His body stumbled and his hands shook. He sat in his favourite chair, when he could find it in the cruel maze which had once been a familiar home, mumbling endless recitations that he remembered only imperfectly.

He wept, but his tears were oddly clear and hung on his cheeks like queer jewels. They did nothing to wash away his fears. He dreamt of the great salt lakes shining beneath the sky and died knowing, finally, the measure of his daughters' love.

This is the room I have never been in.
This is the room I could never breathe in.

— Sylvia Plath, *Wintering*

It was late in the evening when Jason arrived home. The air was still. I could hear him well before he entered the garden, before he moved through the gate or down the side of the house. Before he even entered the street I knew he was coming. I felt it.

I was in the gazebo, Sara was lying in a mass of blankets and pillows at my feet, almost asleep. Although she couldn't hear me I was playing for her. Her eyes followed my fingers as they tripped over the keys. Her head was slowly tipping to the side, swaddled in hand-washed blankets. I was playing Debussy. My mother used to play Debussy for me, to soothe me to sleep. *Le Petit Berger* or *Arabesque No 1*. I tipped my head towards Sara; I saw the leaves and branches of a tree move, the ripple and glissando of thin gum leaves. The playful clumsiness of the fig. Quietly now, she was almost asleep. Her eyes more closed than open. I saw the light come on in the kitchen, and then his shadow moving through the garden towards us. I thought suddenly that I should hide her. Perhaps I could cast her out in her basket. Over the cliff and out to sea like Moses in his basket of rushes. Or like Winken, Blinken and Nod — who set sail among the stars — sailing along the Milky Way until morning faded the moon away and they found themselves safely asleep in their beds.

'What are you doing out here?' he called to me from halfway through the garden. His voice was loud and boisterous in the almost quiet, almost asleep night garden. I stopped playing and lay the flute across my lap. A ferry moved across the harbour; a tiny paper boat strung with fireflies. He stumbled up the stairs towards me and planted a clumsy kiss against my throat. He smelled of sleeplessness and rushing home and alcohol. And *her*.

I turned away, towards the ferry beginning to tip as she moved across the heads, her lights almost disappearing in the waves that rushed in from the harbour. I couldn't really see the waves — the water seemed flat and calm — but I could see the shape of the water's shadow as it swallowed the lights and pulled back again, drawing away. The boat leaned into the waves, tilting madly.

'I said, what are you doing?' He fumbled a cigarette from his shirt pocket. 'Well, aren't you going to answer me, you fuckin' whore?' I looked at the flute in my lap. Its comforting silver length glowing like mercury in the half-light of evening. It looked so slippery and light, as if it would bend in my fingers, as if it was watery and pliable. As if my hand, when reaching for it, would slip straight through and catch instead the stiff threads of my breath inside. 'She doesn't want to see me any more,' he said, 'does that make you happy? She's *in love* with someone else. Fucking dyke.' He laughed as he leant against the rail and looked at me, out to the ferry in the harbour and then down at his hands. I thought of my father's hands, grown so soft and clean. Of my mother's hands like those of a magical creature — long and seemingly boneless. Of Callum's hands that even when full, were always waiting to be filled. Of Sara's hands which snapped and twisted at me in rage or regret. Her fingers that flicked and turned in her eagerness, the digits agitated and surreal. Her hands that were her tongue and throat, glottis and epiglottis. Her fisted silences.

Jason thrust his hands towards me but they fell helplessly at his sides. He stared at them as though they were unruly children. His hands that could not stay still, which were forever pulling at the threads of the world, unravelling everything. Picking at the carefully stitched hems and seams of his life until we all fell in pieces at his feet.

'Look at me, why don't you? You got what you wanted. I'm yours.' He twisted around and threw out his arms, drunkenly melodramatic and ridiculous, almost toppling over the rail in his eagerness to be martyred. Should I have reached for him or let him fall? He staggered and tripped, landing sprawled on the ground beside Sara.

Her sleeping face was undisturbed. He wiped a strand of hair from her face and I could almost feel the softness that drew his fingertips, the smooth plumpness warm to his touch. She turned away from him, wrinkling her nose at the intrusion of his touch. 'She doesn't like me,' he said, leaning back against the railing. 'Why doesn't she like me? You're in it together. I see it. I see the two of you watching me, plotting against me.' I smiled to myself and he saw it, leaned forward eagerly. 'That's it, isn't it? That's why I can't get at you. I can't pick her up without her screaming. It's always you and her. Well, it won't always be that way. Little girls grow up, you know.' He looked up into my face, his smile small and vicious. 'All little girls are daddy's little girl eventually.'

He picked up her sleeping body, bundling the blankets into his lap. She stirred in her sleep and opened first one gluey eye and then the other. She was quiet and startled, looking up into his face. His large hands seemed soft in this light; he moved one of them to cradle the back of her head, the hair curving up between his palm and her skin. He ran one hand down the side of her cheek and throat, along the curve of her shoulder — the warm skin flushed with sleep. He ran his thumb along her collarbone and traced the edge of her shirt against her skin. The night air was still. I could hear the ferry below, slipping between the waves, lights swallowed by the dark water that swelled around it. Not a breath of wind. 'You're beautiful, you know,' he whispered in her tiny ear, 'just like your mother.'

I tipped forward in my chair and slid onto the floor. The flute slipped from my lap and clattered on the timber, one piece rolling away from the still-jointed whole. I could barely hear him. I could barely hear his voice as it scratched at the timber. 'Beautiful,' he said, 'beautiful.'

I lunged across the floor towards them, grabbed her clumsily and dragged her into my arms. I was hurting her, pinching her arms in my hands like an eagle with its prey. Her cry was loud and awkward. The not-quite-right howl of a strange creature in the dark — of someone who cannot hear themselves when they cry out. *Beautiful.* I stumbled through the garden, falling several times, dropping blankets that tangled at my feet and tripped me up as I ran. I fell beneath the jacaranda and the angel, among the lavender and across the stairs. I fell into my room and locked the door against his laughter, which came raucous and extravagant along the hall. I fell across the rug and into the quiet space beneath my bed. *Beautiful beautiful beautiful child.* I clutched her to me, pushing my hand over her mouth to keep her quiet. We pressed into the corner; my back huddled against the timber slats, dust clambering in my throat. I pulled her to me and held her head against my chest. I felt her heart beating hard and fast against my own.

He was lumbering through the garden. His feet flattening the ground beneath him. He was on the stairs, in the hall, outside the door. I heard his hands, trembling and furious, banging at the door. I heard his voice so quiet and still it barely moved. I held her tighter and tighter, feeling the tiny bones fidget beneath the skin. 'Come out here,' he said. I heard the scratch scratch of my flute being run along the walls, like a schoolboy rattling fences with a stick. I pushed further into the corner. I heard him blow into my flute, the sound thin and fluttery. I heard him whip the timber walls with it and knock something over — a picture, a vase — and smash it on the floor. I heard his huge hands and flat feet and in between it all the soft metallic whistle and click of my flute being beaten against the walls. Laughter rose in his throat, *Come out come out wherever you are.*

He fell quiet. Several minutes of just the sound of her breathing. Perhaps he was gone. Perhaps he was waiting outside the door in the hall, in the kitchen, in the garden, under the house. I closed my eyes and saw his hands swelling, growing hard-edged and firm like timber. Huge hands that could rip open the doors of the house, tearing back the walls like frail cloth. He was hunched over the house like a child — only huge — his hands reaching out and tearing back the roof to reveal us tiny tiny inside the house beneath his huge huge hands which tipped us out and made us run. I closed my eyes and held her close closer so close that I could feel her heart beat and her breath stumble and she was breathing so loud so loud he was sure to hear he would hear her and take the bed between two fingertips and pull it up and tumble us out. He would pick up the whole house like a shoe box and shake us out over the cliff edge.

I heard him beneath the house. His hands beating at the floor beneath me. The floorboards shuddered. Her fingers softly flicked at my breast like moths. *Shhh. Shhh, quiet now we must be quiet now. Quiet as mice. Still as stones.*

He was tipping over boxes. I heard everything falling, timber cracking and huddled dusty piles of metal things or china falling and clattering and smashing on the soft damp earth beneath the house. I heard the length of my flute as he used it to swipe at a wooden crate, at a box full of glasses that fell and broke, long shards burrowing desperately into the quiet soil.

He was moving beneath the house. His hands pounding against each pylon as he passed them. One hand still holding the flute that clattered against the timber posts, the other holding something heavier and more solid that thudded. I could feel the rhythm of him coming, thud and clatter, thud and clatter. He was coming out from under the house, scrambling up the stairs. Sara was still quiet, her round eyes startled beneath me, glittering like wet glass in the dark. He was in the kitchen again, in the hall, outside the door. *I'm coming, my beautiful girls. I'm coming for my daughter, Germaine.*

I heard a sudden crash as he pounded down on the china doorknob of the room. It fell on the floor and the door gave way, gave us away. It slammed open against the wall behind him and I pulled her tighter. Tighter and tighter, so tight we could barely breathe. There was no room for breathing. No sound no wind not a breath not a word. *Ha!* He said, his steps falling slowly now. So slowly so carefully. Each footfall weighted and measured. *Come out come out.* He yanked at the bed and one of the cold iron legs pushed at the back of my head as he pulled it away from the wall. Sara cried out. Her strangled voice panicked. I placed my hand over her mouth; the other arm still wrapped tightly around her stomach. *So there you are, you goddamn bitch. Come out.* He lunged onto the bed. The rust-laced springs bending towards my head, catching in my hair. I huddled lower, tighter, as he swung the flute between the wall and the bed, striking at me clumsily. I curled around her, her tiny body caught and awkwardly folded into the curves of my own. He struck at me. He struck again and again, angrily and awkwardly. Bruising my thighs and shins and arms. *Hold on hold on.* He struck her plump arm and she cried out again. I placed my hand over the soft revealed skin and felt the wet warmth of blood. I cradled her head against my chest. He

281

struck the back of my hand and I felt my own warm blood flow onto the floor. *Shhh shhh.* I held her tight, so tight I felt the bones shift inside her. *Quiet now,* I whispered, *we must be quiet now.* But she was wriggling against me. Her small hands clawed at my heart where my shirt was twisted open, the buttons undone. Her tiny nails scratched as she began to kick in my arms. He tumbled over the bed, back onto the floor. I rolled over and bundled her tighter, gripping her tiny body tight so tight. I squeezed my eyes and held my breath and kissed the crown of her head. He knelt down beside the bed and peered into the shadows. *I'll fuckin' teach you,* he said.

Carefully he placed my flute on the floor beside the bed. I saw it shining, almost glittering in the light that fell into the room from the hallway. It was bent but not broken, a few scratches, a couple of dents. He knelt beside it and I saw his other hand, holding an old hammer with a heavy head. He placed one boot on the flute. I clutched Sara tighter and tighter; her hands weakly flickering now, almost quiet now, as I held my breath, held on as tight as I could, and watched him draw the hammer higher. I reached out one hand to grab my flute but couldn't reach it. I would have had to let go of Sara. I would have had to push her out of the way and crawl slide rock forwards. Then he would have had her. He would have had us both. *Lie still. Lie quiet.*

He brought the hammer down on my flute. The shiny metal bent and the floorboards shuddered as he beat at it. Sara flinched weakly and I pulled her closer to me, moving my hand up to protect her face as a key flew off from the whole. She was so quiet now. So weakly silent. Her hands bent in to my skin; her soft head was warm and milky against my chest and clung to my skin.

Her last breath was warm and damp with sweat.

We lay together, skin to skin, as he pounded the hammer down on its silvery length. As it twisted and bent beneath him, as it fell flat and heavy and broke into flat dull pieces, as her rhythms shifted apart. We lay together in each other's arms as he left the room, left the house, left the street. We lay quiet and calm in each other's arms. Quiet as mice. Still as stones.

These words are yours,
though you never said them,
you never heard them, history
breeds death, but if you kill
it you kill yourself

— Margaret Atwood, *Two-Headed Poems*

Once she was inside me. The muscles, cells and cavities of her body folded inside mine. We were like Russian dolls nested one inside the other. She was folded inside me and inside her were the intricacies of cells and blood and marrow, the slippery snake of her gut, the fig-shaped fruit of her tiny womb. The unbudded breasts and pin-thin veins traced so close to the surface of her skin that you could see her beating. My blood pulsed in hers, the flaked and dead cells of her flowed out through me. Her air and light and blood were mine. And then they cut her away.

Beneath green sheets and sterile sleep she was sliced away like a burrowing malignant growth. A threat. I would gladly have died with her inside me if that had been what was required. I would have pulsed and cramped with her birth and my death in the same moment. The rhythms of each moment present in the other. Beating inside each other's skins. But I was cut open. The flesh not thick and leathery, the dermis and epidermis slicing easily like a thin-skinned fruit to reveal the womb beneath, stretched and warm, and her inside, nested and curled. The surgeon's cold, plastic-wrapped hands reached in and cut her out. No four a.m. cramping or sudden rush of water, no slow, slow building of pain and the puff puff pant puff puff pant of motherhood. We were both unnatural. Unborn.

Like me she lay beneath the sheets that were meant to save us. Like me she pulled away from the hands that lifted her out into the world. Our skin suddenly rippled with the touch of cold air and hands too large and ungentle to fit our bodies. We cried at the touch of his hands on our skin. Inside our skin, our most secret

285

spaces. His alien blunt-fingered hands red with soil and blood. Rough with it.

We lay beneath the sheets, beneath the bed. Our bruised skin growing cold against the timber floors. My skin was cool but hers was cooler, the bruises settling. The blood guttered in her side, settling in to the weight of the world. She did not breathe. Did not speak. I could feel her body soft and firm, the skin growing more tissued and fragile with each hour that passed. The fat congealing beneath the skin. The blood settling and clotting in her veins.

She was still. So still her skin and muscle settled together, the sinew grew stiff and the bones hardened. Her tiny fingers were stiff inside my shirt, the tips curling against my breast. I kissed her cheek and felt the flesh stick against my lips. The taste of her skin shifting from warmth and milky plumpness to something flat and thick. I closed her startled eyes, their glassy stare cold in the shadowy warmth of our room.

I traced the curve of her shoulder, the soft dimples in her cheek and the light dusting of freckles over her shoulder blade. I knew her skin. Each centimetre mapped beneath my hands. She was knitted up from the cell and sinew of my body. And now she lay beneath me so quiet and still that I did not know her. She was a stranger already turning away. The shape of her face shifting, the quick smile and sudden frown and the simpler, stranger shifts of her presence folded or torn away. The lift and fold of *her* inside her body was gone. She was hollow.

I dreamt I still lay in the curve of her arm, beneath her cotton skin, twisted around her. Her feet were flat, then long, and then they dug into the earth. Her toes were like the brown snakes we shot at in summer. They broke the cracked surface of the globe. They slithered between clods of soil. Now she was firm. Her skin was tepid and peeling. Her blood lay still beneath it. No longer beating. Her arms, her branches reached through the roof, through the clouds that separated like steam around her. Through the dim curve that isolated the earth from everything else, through the endless, shapeless, nameless cold. She sprouted fruit that shone like stars. I lay in her arms. I curved around her. I twisted in my skin and followed her glittering silence till it hummed. I dreamed I was her protector, her lover and her child. I clung to her with a desperateness I recognised as hers, as mine.

I woke in the quiet room with her cheek against my own. Across the floor my flute lay. Each piece trampled and cracked. The old tubes flattened and the keys bent. She could not sing, could not breathe. She lay in pieces in my arms. Separate and pure and damaged and undone. I lifted her up. Carried her gently. I walked through the house. The floors carpeted in broken glass that cut at my bare feet. Her body was heavy, heavier than it had been with her in it. Her hands started to curl inward, the tips of her fingers arcing toward her palms. Her empty body was a lie. Its sullenness. Its stillness. She was never still. Her body spoke. It sang. Somewhere inside her was a secret, a breath, a word. Something other than this cool skin. She lay on the kitchen table while I fossicked through the drawers for instruments to slice her open. I peeled back the shining skin and cracked open the cavity beneath it that held her breath. Emptied out the slippery worm, the flat dead cells, and false heart.

I would find and hold and purify her, each cell and syllable.

I am not courageous. I lay with the sheets and blankets wrapped around my thighs. Tangled. I left the light on in the hall. The pale light falling across the doorway. I sweated and breathed like a strangled fish. I dreamed quickly, sharply. I woke with my hands fisted in my belly. I turned off my phone and locked the windows and doors.

Edna came to the door and stood uncertainly, knocking lightly. She left a small basket of vegetables from her garden on the doorstep. 'Are you there, dear?' she whispered. Her voice was quiet and careful. She seemed hesitant. I longed to open the door to her and share a simple conversation. I wanted to go back to some uncomplicated moment where we were neighbours who shared books and garden cuttings and ambling, pointless conversations. The wilting vegetables were still there. Perhaps she thought we had all gone away, left as suddenly as we arrived, although the van was still parked across the road. Waiting.

I watched. I saw a woman standing on the doorstep. She looked off down the street, tilted back on her heels and peered through the windows. I held my breath as still as hers. I lay on the floor and, through the slim opening beneath the door, watched her shoes leaving; their scuffed heels and worn leathers, their thin socks and pressed hems. She sat in her car for an hour before driving off, while I lay watching, feeling her watching the house. The weight and scent of Sara's bones lying flensed on the kitchen table filled the house until she threatened to spill from the windows, to leak out into the street and touch the stranger. Time grew round and polished while we waited, each of us for the other. The day must have made the car hot, must have filled it with the smell of oil and age and cracked leather upholstery slick with her sweat. I imagined her thighs round and sticky against each other. The heavy bones beneath her flesh, the layers of fat and muscle that would have to be peeled away only to reveal bones too solid to remember. The thick wall of air that must have rested on her chest. I could smell the dark semi-circles that spread beneath her jacket. Her hair grew flat and dark. Her restless hands worried her hair, her skin, her collar and hem.

I watched dust motes fall across a shaft of light. They fell silently, without a sense of touch at all. The flakes of dust as dead as the outer layer of my skin. I couldn't see them land. I stirred the air with my hand and the dust-motes swirled like stars dancing a million light years away. I imagined myself as the stuff of space, the swollen empty sky that swallows stars. When the woman drove away the street was silent, the air cooler. Her business card gleamed like a lost bone on the timber.

I crawled through the hall. The tiny shards of picture-frame glass digging into my shins and palms. The edge of the hall runner fraying against the curled linoleum of the kitchen. My feet and knees stuck and separated with a satisfying sound — a neat ticking. I angled in under the sink and laid my cheek against the dusty pipes. What divinities closet themselves in wasted spaces, behind the fluted, clumped debacle of my insinkerator? The rotting vegetables which root and tangle in her throat. Her alchemy, her perfect beauties, cluster and hide in my mouth, in my crawlspaces, between the bleak and empty coffee jars that whisper glass secrets to the pipes.

I breathed quietly. My body inflated. My folded bones shouldered into less likely compositions of space and something else, something solid. I spilled onto the kitchen floor and made decisions over the dark stains that spread on the lino. I looked up to her tiny hand that lay thrust out over the edge of the table; the fingers curled, the skin mottled. I hesitated over her thighs, my finger in my mouth. Her feet cool against my thigh. Pushing. I peeled the frail skin from her indelicate toes. The bones within like tiny white beads held in the striped muscle. Each one so frail and tiny they threatened to be squashed or snap in my fingertips as I cut the flesh away.

I lay on the floor beneath her and ploughed the floor with my forehead at the memory of her ridiculous fingers as oddly angled and quick-moving as fish. I scoured the cavities within her bones and heated and burned and sanded them until they were as smooth and firm and dry as polished stones. I bored and sanded the holes, measuring the intervals as nearly as I could by memory and instinct. I twisted the pieces together. I polished the egg-shaped end and settled my mother's silver key against it.

I held her in my arms again and closed my eyes to feel her breathe.

I stood at the edge of the garden watching the ocean slip between the heads. I could smell the salt air that drifted against the cliff-face. The afternoon boats were gold with light, shining with delight like children's toys. Their sails were wet with it, their hulls dipping like spoons in the ocean. The clean scent of the sea scratched at my skin. I could almost feel it, almost know what it was to be washed-clean and drifting. To be pure. But I was too far away and the water had too much salt in it. It was not sugared water to sip from a glass, or cloud-bred rain that falls from the sky. Ocean water leaves your skin stinging where it has been sliced open, crusted with salt when it dries, the hair stiff and the flesh tasting of salt. You cannot be washed clean in it. You cannot water a seed with it. The ocean will take hold of you and drag you into its arms. It will hold you close and whisper to you as it draws you deeper, as it sucks you into its eddies and swells. You will be wrapped and dreaming in its silk embrace as it swallows your breath and pulls you down into its seaweed depths. The ocean cannot wash away the red soil that lives and breathes in you. It is too far away, too much, too full of salt.

Your silence
Isn't enough for me
Now, no matter with what
Contentment you fold
Your hands together; I want
Anything you can say
In the sunlight

— Margaret Atwood, *Against Still Life*

I wandered through the house and gathered what little there was of mine. I packed my clothes into the van, a handful of books, a small journal, a sprig of lavender from the garden. I burned everything of Sara's in the forty-four-gallon drum in the garden, breaking her cot and high chair into small pieces with an axe I found under the house. I cleaned everything, swept up the broken glass and china from the floors, washed all the sheets, scrubbed the floors and benches, packed away the china and threw dustsheets over the furniture. I pulled the curtains together to keep out the light. I locked all the windows and bolted all the doors. I wandered through the garden, gathering a handful of stones. I stood at the edge and looked at the ocean so far away.

As I stepped up into the van — alone this time — I turned and looked at the house with its empty windows and falling down fences. It was as hollow as it was the first day we arrived. It had no promises to keep, no secrets to reveal, no stories to tell. It was just a house — a series of empty rooms. I looked at the houses next door and across the street. The same dull anonymity, the same carefully cultivated roses and drawn shades. Who knew what secrets they had to tell? Nobody knew. Nobody spoke. I wound up the windows of the van against the cloying stench of silence that stretched out into the street.

An old woman walked through her gate a few houses down and turned towards me. Her eyes were washed flat, her skin puckered and dust-pale. She was thin and bent over, her black vinyl handbag pressed close to her body as if she feared it would be snatched away at any moment. I had seen her before, walking past on her way to the store or post office, watering her garden in the afternoon. Her hair was thin and white, worn in a softly knotted bun at the base of her neck. As she got closer she looked up at me. She stood still as she caught my eye and I waited for her to smile or nod in the non-committal manner of almost-perfect strangers. She watched me. I sat on the warm seat with the sun stretching in through the window of the van and felt my face caught, not knowing what to do, how to look. I felt a vague nervous prickle in my bladder and labia. She watched through the dusty glass and I felt exposed. I felt my hand touch the glass and the cracked dashboard as she continued walking past me, her handbag clutched to her side. I watched her back in the rear-vision mirror. She shunted unevenly, her shoulders bent forward beneath her thin cardigan. What was she carrying that she held onto so tightly? Were there photographs of children and lovers long gone? Were there mementos? Locks of hair, baby teeth, letters from the war office, brooches or cards? Perhaps she had her own secrets, as unspoken as mine. As she turned into another street and ambled out of sight I started the engine and pulled away from the kerb. I drove through the suburbs, past clutches of old brick houses and apartment buildings, cement-rendered shopping centres surrounded by multi-storey parking and neon, past carefully planted and tended parks and gardens devoid of people, and railway stations where they stood pressed together.

Street signs made me nauseous. They spurted from the ground at ill-considered moments like skinny-legged primary school bullies. I watched a blue car skirt the roundabout. A red-haired girl driving with hands resting, just resting, on the crown of the wheel. Her head tilted. Her mouth pressed closed. A man whose wife sat beside him looking vacantly out the window as he talked and gestured angrily at no one.

At first I drove aimlessly. Just to be moving, to be swaying in the motion of the van. Cocooned and safe in the nowhere of movement. I drove along highways where the long trees stretched beside service stations where everything was greasy and lustred and served in plastic. The air-conditioned smell. Air-conditioned skin. Days of driving, creases thickening in the thighs of my jeans so that even when I pressed my flat palms full of stale sweat across them I was still folded, still pleated. The lolly wrappers stuck to the carpet, between the twigs and leaves and crushed plastic cups and crinkling empty cans that rustled and whispered when I opened the door and unfolded my folded self into air thin with dust, thin with steel and bitumen.

The long coast road slid past me. Nights where the only other traffic on the road was long trucks whose passing rattled the windows of the van. Their lights swayed past me and left the quiet of forested highways in their wake where the moon was crosshatched in thin black leaves. The radio buzzed and hissed and faded out. I drove in silence. Watching for quiet places, for empty spaces at the side of the road, or isolated car parks looking over the ocean, where I could stop for a while. Where I slept and sipped at tepid cups of coffee before driving away. My wheels crunching in the gravelled soil.

Further north the towns were smaller. Villages of timber buildings where the petrol station was tacked on the front of someone's home. A pump sitting awkward and upright in someone's front garden, among the roses and azaleas. The road looped in great round arcs beside a river. Edged with water and huge fields of sugar cane. The soil disappearing beneath lush waves of the grassy crop. Some fields were burnt. Occasionally a field would be aflame, the smoke rising thick with the smell of molasses, a heavy smoke that seemed to cling to the sky. The smell hovering in my skin and hair for hours afterwards.

Then the roadside towns dwindled, fading further and further from the highway. Sometimes I glimpsed one miles away to the east or west. The sun flashing off a cluster of tin roofs. Beside the highway were thin towns full of take-away food shops and pubs. Then slowly the buildings seemed to rise up on their haunches and grow taller. At first just two storeys, then three and four. Then great skyscrapers that sprang surprised from the ground. Entrepreneurs and real estate agents stood on the dunes in their dark suits and contemplated building sandcastles that would huddle over the coast shoulder to shoulder. Late in the day the elongated shadows carved the beach into blocks of gray and yellow. Cool sand and burning sand striped the beach like a tiger.

I walked the streets in flat-soled sandals and a sarong. I felt my hair swish across my shoulder blades as I turned my head, as I watched the city. The warm brick tiles of the mall grew sandy, gritty, dusted.

The air smelt of salt and wet skin, sweat and the desperate incense of cars. Lying on the beach I watched the tourists burn. I listened to them stutter over brochures, hesitate at crossings, and spill into air-conditioned shopping centres. The highway slithered beneath my wheels as I drove past glittering shops whose air-conditioned salesgirls gleamed. Restaurants hunched on the side of the road. Buses lurched across unmarked lanes. The heated breeze pushed at my chest. My knees and thighs sweated on the car seat. I parked beside a river, in the shade. Small children and their mothers paddled in the river water. My lips were dry and cracked. I sat on the step of the van's door and breathed. In the warm and heavy breeze I felt her hands rushing at me. Her fingers still cold and swarming at my throat.

The afternoon was flat and shiftless. The bottles of mineral water on my dashboard misted with sweat. Buildings seemed to give up, shift slightly on their concrete roots and tip across the shore. Their shadows lengthened, swallowing the light, drawing it up to their neon crowns. Sunburnt children dripped ice cream as they catapulted through the mall. Screaming.

I left the coast and drove through more familiar landscapes. Long roads of nothing. Flat landscapes studded with trees only occasionally and even then they were thin and bent, their arms scratching the sky. Clouds caught in their skinny arms like cotton balls. The red soil gathered thinly on the windscreen — a fine film that coloured my landscape with the warm tones of my childhood.

I found quiet places in fields or beside dry dams where the cracked soil welcomed my bare feet. I got into a rhythm of driving and resting. A week or so on the road followed by a few days spent sitting quietly in the almost familiar landscape. Like breathing — the driving a deeply inhaled breath held against the teeth until my lungs began to burn, memories spinning faster and faster, speeding up to the rhythmic hum of the wheels turning and the motor running until my mind was filled and my teeth chattered. My head heavy and humming, my skin tight with recollection.

And then stopping.

Three days in a field, a long cool exhalation. The only sound that of my breathing, or the night air moving against my skin.

I don't know if this is a happy ending but here we are cut loose in open fields.

— Jeanette Winterson, *Written on the Body*

The sun disappeared hours ago behind the hills, dropped like a marble into the sand. The moon is still low — a silver horn slung carelessly against the hip of the sky. There are so many stars. The openness of the fields and the lack of streetlights or houses makes them seem closer and brighter. I have the flute in my hands, against my lip, the sounds coming softly.

I see headlights, like a ferry in the harbour I have left behind, disappearing behind a wave of rock-crested earth only to rise again. At this time of night — with the stillness and quiet — the sound of the engine is loud and intrusive. As the car swoops towards me its lights beam across the landscape like a searchlight.

I play a simple Rondo — it seems to suit the rhythm of the evening; a low, slow undercurrent tugged along by those dipping and rising lights.

The car pulls up beside me and I see the man inside it, a small man in his early forties maybe. He sits behind the wheel for a few minutes before removing his seat belt. I still have the flute resting against my chin. The notes drop like stones into the still night as I watch him walk towards me. I pick up the glass of wine at my heels and take a sip. 'Would you like one?' I ask reluctantly.

He shakes his head and looks around the campsite. 'I heard there was someone out here,' he says. 'Just thought I'd come and make sure everything was okay.' I finger the flute in my hands, running my thumb down her slippery underside. 'I'm Des Harrop, by the way. I run the police station in town.'

I smile and nod and as he stands there we exchange a few mild pleasantries. He asks me how long I'm staying and where I'm going, where I've come from. I answer politely but briefly until we both fall silent, watching the night sky.

'That's an unusual flute, isn't it?' he says.

'It's ivory,' I say.

'Can I see it?'

If I say no what will he say? I take the flute in my hands and roll it into the groove of my palms, testing its weight and softness. In the night air she seems to be cooler and damper, as if she needs to be wiped over with a dry cloth. As if she can still sweat.

I lift the flute a little higher — offering and not offering it to him. He is easily a metre away and takes a couple of steps towards me to take it from my hands. I open my mouth to say something. Like a nervous and protective first-time mother seeing her child in the hands of a clumsy stranger.

'Ivory,' he says, raising his eyes to look at me. 'That's elephant tusk, isn't it?' I don't answer him straight away and he looks down to the instrument lying in his hands. He lifts her gently, like a sword that has been laid across his palms, and examines her. Rolling her over in his hands, running the tip of his index finger over the holes and around the thin bulb of the end. He lifts it to his face, not too close, and gently breathes in. He looks up at me again. His face surprised and suddenly far more intelligent and inquisitive than I imagined it to be.

'It's not elephant tusk,' I say. 'Ivory can be all kinds of bone. Mostly they use elephant tusk because of its qualities — it carves well.' I look at my flute, and then up at him standing before me. He is watching me carefully. 'But this is not elephant tusk.'

I hold those memories in my mind like a rock, like polished river-stones. Now the memory is like hundred-year-old cotton sheets worn thin with sex and sleep and indecision. The years fold up like paper in my pocket and when I tumble them out on the table they are worn through, the letters faded, the notes forgotten, the melodies unsung. I remember the sound of ordinary days. The sound of slow weekdays full of washing and reading and cups of tea. The sound of the stretched thin days when Jason was off driving miles and miles across the country, his heavy hands resting on the wheel — heaving the road into place beneath him. They were days full of waiting. I walked and read and played the flute and sipped at cups of tea with my head tilted to one side, waiting for the sound of his heavy boots on the step, his hand on the door, the deliberate unpacking of his smile.

This is the sound of his body on the mattress, his hand skimming my waist as he bends to kiss my cheek.

This is the sound of my room, of myself sitting on the floor in the middle of my locked room. The flute at my chin, head tilted to hear the notes rise as I play — and I did play — but all I could hear was his hands knocking at the door. *Knock knock*. His hands running flat-palmed down the walls outside my room. His hands cupped around his mouth to whisper between the crack. *Come out, come out, wherever you are.* His hands clutched around my arms, or curled around a teacup.

I remember, although I have tried to forget, the sound of being crouched low on the polished boards under my bed. Hearing him in the hall, at the door, kneeling down beside the bed. I remember my father's face lit up by the reflected shine of the blue window, how he seemed oddly thin and magical when he crept in beside me. Mostly I remember his hands. The long fingers squared off at the end and the palms thick and reddened. I remember how they felt on my shoulders, in my hair and against my skin. I remember the feel of his blunt-fingered hands as they cupped themselves over my breasts and forced their way into my body. His voice muffled against my sheets. The desperate sound of his breath as he muttered into my skin, *so beautiful, your mother, so beautiful.*

We ran away like naughty children with the child already growing in my belly. Her father's daughter, that's all Jason ever said. Leaning over her crib in the hospital, with Callum waiting in the next room. *Her father's daughter.* And we both knew, and didn't know, what that meant. His hands could not hold her even when she started to grow, just as they could never hold me. Like some second-rate horror movie where the women seem only floating scraps of chiffon in his hands. Too light and frail.

But I wanted things to be different for her. I wanted her to take comfort in her father's arms. To sleep with the door open and unlocked and never find herself crouched on the bare boards beneath her bed.

But he said she was beautiful and his hands reached out to touch her. Too close to the bone. So close that the flesh was carved away in a single movement. Falling like a heavily draped curtain till it crumpled on the floor and all that was left was the ripe yellowness of her bones. Everything else whittled away — the locked room, the pretty skin, the hands that would have held on too tight — so tight that the bones shifted beneath the skin — all of it was cut away.

This is the sound of Sara's bones as I dried and fired them, making them strong and pale — not quite white yet, but they will be with age, before they turn yellow again. The sound of hours spent finely measuring and sanding and boring the holes and hollowing out the marrow that clung darkly to her tunnelled secret spaces. Some of the bones were too small, some too thick or knuckled or soft. Some cracked in the process of being cured and bleached. In the end I only just had enough pieces to make a complete flute. I could never have made a modern flute, all those complicated bars of keys and holes. But the old flutes were simpler — before they had factories for churning out cut and punched and moulded sheets of metal. The old flutes were made by hand, crafted by men with long soft-tipped fingers like my own.

So now I can lift her up again and hold her with my fingertips — delicately balanced. I know the length and breadth of her, each cell, each syllable and breath that moves through her. As I take her in my hands I close my eyes. *One more time*, I think, *I will play for her.*

I do not blow, do not breathe, but I hear her. I feel the notes stutter and fall, then cluster together, tripping in their eagerness to tell what cannot be told or remembered or forgotten. She sings like an angel — like a bird whose hollow, wind-whittled bones lift her up and suspend her on the breath of a thousand, a hundred thousand, unspoken conversations. Her tune is simple, although my knuckles crack with the strain of it, with the pure wet weight of her song.